Who Killed Big Dick?

WHO KILLED BIG DICK?

PAUL TOMLINSON

Copyright © 2017 by Paul Tomlinson

All rights reserved. This book may not be reproduced or transmitted, in whole or in part, or used in any manner whatsoever, without the express permission of the copyright owner, except for the use of brief quotations in the context of a book review.

Who Killed Big Dick? is a work of fiction. Names, characters, places, and incidents are products of the author's imagination. Any resemblance to actual persons, living or dead, to actual organisations, or to actual events, is purely coincidental.

Rated R: Contains moderate violence and adult language (in three languages). And images of a fat guy in a black lace thong.

For country of manufacture, please see final page.

ISBN: 978-1542-93066-6

First published February 2017
Publisher: Paul Tomlinson

www.paultomlinson.org

Cover image and design © 2017 by Paul Tomlinson

For Susan Zappala,
who got me an 'I ♥ Bulwell'
shopping bag

Chapter One

The second-worst thing about being on a stakeout is that your butt goes numb after a couple of hours. I'd been sitting outside *Big Dick's Floors 'n' Beds* since lunchtime. The car park had emptied as afternoon turned to evening, and now there was just me. Trying to look inconspicuous in a rusty lemon with no hubcaps. The agency's stakeout car was a yellow 1975 Honda Civic.

I say that as if we have more than one car. We don't. And I say 'we' as if there is a whole team of detectives working at Donoghue Investigations, but technically the only detective there is Fat Duncan. Have you ever heard of Nero Wolfe? He was a fat guy who sat at home all day and was a genius at solving crimes. Duncan Donoghue's not like that. Apart from the being fat and sitting around all day parts. He's an ex-policeman and thinks he's Mycroft Holmes, Sherlock's smarter brother. I think he's a lump of lard that couldn't spot a clue if a naked girl was pointing a neon arrow at it and blowing a trumpet. Or a trombonist. The reason I'm better at this than him is that I can move around outside. Get through doors. Little things like that. Qualities an investigator needs. I once helped Fat Duncan solve a case he was working on. I've been solving cases for him ever since. He exploits me.

The ideal stakeout car is inconspicuous on the outside and comfortable on the inside. The Honda Civic was neither. The heater didn't work and it smelled like an old running shoe stuffed with fish 'n' chip wrappers. And it wasn't much bigger than a running shoe inside. Fat Duncan used to drive the Honda Civic, back when he could still squeeze behind the wheel. It was his weight that knackered the suspension. Hit a pothole and your head smacks against the roof. That's why I wear the knitted hat. That and the fact that Wee Patsy said I was starting to get a bald spot. Going bald at thirty; why is life so cruel? Wee Patsy is Fat Duncan's girlfriend. You know those seaside postcards with the fat woman and the little skinny bloke? Patsy and Duncan would look like that. If they both got sex changes.

As an investigator, I'm pretty good at understanding people, but I've never figured out what Wee Patsy sees in Duncan. And the fact that he has a girlfriend and I don't? Another mystery I've never solved. It's not like there's anything wrong with me. Except that I seem to talk to myself a lot.

I sound bitter. I know I shouldn't. It's not like I *have* to do this. I could get a real job. Have a proper social life. But the thing is, I *like* doing this. I may not be Sam Spade, but I do get to do genuine detective work. I've always thought that 'Joseph A. Lucke: Private Investigator' would look good painted on an office door. If we had an office. The 'A' stands for Arthur, after my Grandad, but people don't need to know that. It's not exactly like the movies. Not many *femmes fatale* in Mansfield. But I did once see a guy who looked exactly like Joel Cairo. I couldn't resist it: I went up to him and asked if he knew where the 'black bird' was. He said: 'I think she's just gone in for a kebab.'

The *worst* thing about stakeouts is having to piss in a McDonald's paper cup and then get the lid back on. If you ever have to do this, my advice would be not to put the straw back in the lid. It's too easy to put the cup down and forget. And the next thing you know, you've picked it up and put the straw in your mouth and, well, I'm just saying it's nothing like a thick shake. Especially if it's still warm. And wear dark jeans, 'cos it doesn't matter how good your aim is, there's going to be splashback.

Ideally on a stakeout there'd be two of you, then one could nip off for a slash while the other one kept watch. But Fat Duncan has never found another me. And he'd be too tight to pay up even if I did have an equally gullible twin. Oh, and don't ever get out and piss up against the car. There's always some old dear gets all hot and flustered and runs away screaming as soon as you get Little Joe out. Worse than that are the ones that come in for a closer look: 'Ooh, I haven't seen one of those since before the war!' Like one of *Monty Python's* Hell's Grannies.

This particular stakeout was taking place outside the discount carpet place up on the old retail park. Not the one by the railway station, the one on the other side where the big DIY place used to be, before they went bust. According to Wee Patsy, it was called *Big Dick's Floors 'n' Beds* because that's where Dick Gorse liked to spend most of his time. Dick's old lady, Charmaine, had obviously heard the same thing, because she wanted us to find out who Big Dick was sharing his floors and beds with. And she wanted photographic evidence to use against him.

I'm not one to judge people, obviously, but I didn't reckon Big Dick was much of a looker. He was one of those big skin-head blokes with no neck. From the back it looked like his head was sitting on a pile of pink tyres for a kid's bike. He wore slim-fit shirts that curved in where he curved out, so that your attention was drawn to the straining buttons. And the sweat stains. His trousers had that baggy, shiny-arse quality that you used to see in bus conductors' uniforms. And he had a tattoo of the Cookie Monster on the back of his hand. Or maybe it was the Virgin Mary. It looked like he'd done it himself. Despite all of this, there was no shortage of Mansfield women who wanted to roll around with him on the pocket springs or the shag-pile. What did they see in him? Maybe it was something you couldn't see.

> *There was a fat bloke called Dick Gorse,*
> *Whose manners were really quite coarse,*
> *But he'd girls by the score*
> *And they came back for more,*
> *He must have been hung like a horse*

Not that I'm jealous, you understand. I once heard Wee Patsy telling someone that I was one of those skinny blokes with a big dick. At least I think that's what she said. Not that I can remember her ever seeing Not-So-Little Joe. Unless she'd seen me pissing against the car one time.

"*Oi*, what you doing here, you lanky bastard?"

From nowhere, Horse-knob Dick was suddenly standing beside the car, slamming his palm against the side window. I jammed my thumb on the door-lock button and shouted the first thing that came into my head.

"Fuck off!"

"Has my missus got you watching me?" he shouted.

His teeth were yellow and his face was getting redder. He looked like a boil about to burst. His shirt was untucked and there was a smudge of lipstick near the hem. That probably meant he'd got lipstick round his knob as well. Lucky bastard.

I turned the key in the ignition and the Honda lurched and stalled. I slipped it out of gear and tried again.

The engine caught, and the usual poisonous blue cloud rolled out from the exhaust. The wind whipped it round and Dick caught a lungful, staggered back coughing. I threw the gear lever into first and let off the handbrake. The front wheels squealed as they spun on the tarmac. They do that when they're bald. I got a last glimpse of Dick, eyes streaming, shaking his fist at me. It was definitely the Cookie Monster. With a halo.

As I pulled out of the parking lot, I glanced in the rear-view mirror and saw Kelly Kenway totter out of the carpet store on drag queen heels. I should have gone back around and snapped a couple of photos with my phone, but I didn't want to risk getting a punch in the mouth. Kelly had been done for aggravated assault at least once to my knowledge, and Dick would have egged her on. Shame, it would have been a lovely bit of evidence: her red lipstick was smudged and she looked like she would have a sore throat in the morning. Or maybe I imagined that bit.

Chapter Two

My flat was above a discount store. The store was basically a pound shop, but they charged more than a pound for some stuff. A door with peeling blue paint next to the shop opened onto a steep, narrow staircase. I pushed the door open, expecting to wade through the heap of free newspapers, takeaway menus and bills that usually lay on the mat inside. There was nothing. I should have taken more notice of this warning sign. The carpet on the stairs was worn through to the hessian backing; at the very edges of the steps you could see that it had once been red. They'd probably put it down to celebrate the founding of the Labour Party. At the top of the stairs was another blue door, its paint slightly less weathered.

I'd moved into the flat when I left school. It was the cheapest place I could find, and at the time I'd told myself that it was only temporary. I've been telling myself the same thing ever since. My key, for once, turned smoothly in the Yale lock of the upstairs door, and I pushed it open. There was a faint spicy smell inside, probably seeping up from the shop below. It didn't completely mask the usual damp smell, but it did make it more bearable. It was better than the bog spray Shelly used to blast around the place: that used to make my eyes run. 'Summer Meadow' my arse. But Shelly's stay had been brief – five-and-a-half weeks, if anyone was counting – and she'd been gone almost six months now. I had the place all to myself again. Except tonight I didn't.

I spotted the neat stack of junk mail on the hall table and the open living room door at the same moment. I always close the doors when I go out. To stop the spread of fire. Or mice. Or whatever. The living room was dark, but I sensed someone was in there. That spicy smell had been aftershave.

There were knives in the kitchen and a baseball bat under the bed, but I would have to go through the living room to get to either of them. The only other door off the hallway was the bathroom. No weapons in there except shampoo and a plastic loo brush. Not even a bog spray. I was giving the loo brush serious consideration, but figured the only threat it offered was a dose of cryptosporidium, and I'd be at as much risk as the intruder.

"Who's there?" I called.

"I am." A deep voice. Male. Familiar.

"Shit!" I whispered.

"Been waiting so long I fell asleep," the voice said.

I walked towards the living room door, reached in and snapped on the lights. The weak yellowish light shone on my uninvited guest. He was sitting in my favourite armchair, making it look like a child's seat. He seemed even bigger than when I'd last seen him. Wide shoulders, broad chest, and thick arms. He stayed in the chair looking up at me, and I still felt small. He had curly black hair that was glossy with oil, big black eyebrows that almost met in the middle, and the kind of brown eyes that women call 'melted chocolate' and I call 'shifty.' His pencil-line moustache arched over thick lips and joined up with a little beard that was pointed like the Devil's. He claimed that his name was Santiago Rodrigo Zambrano Hernandez de Salamanca. It looked terrible on my sister's marriage certificate. It looked better on the decree absolute. His friends called him Tiago Zambrano or 'Tee.' I didn't count myself as one of his friends. To me he was 'Zorro' or 'Sandy.' Or, if I was in a bad mood, 'That Spanish Twat My Sister Married.' His biceps were huge and there were tattoos on both of them: a burning skull with a rose in its teeth on one; a crucified Christ on the other. When a kid gets his first tattoo, it usually says 'Mum.' What mother could object to such a permanent display of affection? Though in Catholic families, the first tattoo is just as likely to be Christ or the Virgin Mary. Again, what mother could object? Tiago wore a tight blue tee-shirt, the little square pocket stretched across the curve of his pectoral, and the sleeves rolled to better display the muscles and the tattoos on them. The images were crisp and the colours vivid: no home-inked Muppets for El Zorro.

"You look pale," I said.

"Prison does that to a man."

I nodded. Was that why he was here? I had provided some of the evidence that helped put him behind bars. Tiago knew this. His voice was deep, like one of those old stage actors. Or Barry White. His Spanish accent was more pronounced when he was speaking to 'the ladies.' They thought it made him sound sexy. Or he must have thought they thought that. It made him sound like he had a short tongue.

"You got out early," I said.

"The priest put in a good word with the parole board."

"You have to suck his cock for that?"

"No!" He seemed genuinely shocked. Then: "I let him suck mine!"

He laughed out loud, a big joyful sound. I couldn't help but smile. I quickly smothered it.

"What are you doing here?" I asked.

I wanted to get this over with: get to A & E before it got crowded with Friday night drunks with pint glasses embedded in their faces.

Tiago tilted his head, looking up at me. I couldn't read his expression: his eyes were dead, like a shark's. I noticed, not for the first time, that one of the brown eyes had a very slight squint in it.

"Are you afraid of me, Joseph?" he asked.

"Am I meant to be?" It would have sounded better if my voice hadn't cracked.

He raised one of his big black eyebrows.

"I know what you did," he said.

"And you know why I did it," I said.

I wasn't about to apologise, and I don't think he expected me to.

"I would have done the same for my sister," he said.

I felt like my big brother was telling me I'd done something right for once, and it felt good. I had to remind myself that I didn't have a big brother. That I shouldn't allow myself to warm to this creep.

"Elise's better off without you," I said.

"How's my boy?"

"Jack's doing fine."

"He's seven now," Tiago said: to himself more than to me.

"We told him you died in a plane crash," I said.

This wasn't true: we'd never tell him that.

Tiago's brow creased, and I wondered if I'd pushed too far.

"Jack's better off without me," he said. "I would be a lousy father."

When he said it, it sounded like 'louse-ee.'

"Is this just a social call, Tiago?"

"You got somewhere to be?" he asked.

I had no answer to that. I was still standing there, waiting for him to get up out of the armchair and hit me.

"When I went away," he said, "the police didn't recover all of my cash. But it is gone."

"I took it," I said. He still didn't move. "It's in a trust fund – for Jack's education."

"That will buy some education," he said.

"Jack's a smart boy," I said.

I was still watching Tiago closely, anticipating his first move. He seemed to be considering what I had said. Finally, there was the slightest nod.

"It is the right thing. The money is his."

I let go of a breath I didn't realise I was holding.

"This puts me in a difficult situation," he said. "I have nothing left. And I may end up owing money to people. Dangerous people."

"You shouldn't gamble unless you can afford to lose," I said.

Tiago nodded slowly.

"You are correct. Though not in the way that you think. Perhaps there is a way for you to help me..."

"I've got nothing to give you," I said.

Tiago looked around my flat and nodded some more. He could see I wasn't lying.

"But perhaps you can do a favour for me. Will you do that? For old times?"

There was a line that was approaching rapidly, and I had to decide whether I was going to cross it. The smart thing would be to say 'No,' and to say it now.

"Depends what it is," I said.

Tiago smiled, thinking he had already snared me. His teeth were large and unnaturally white against his dark skin.

"It is nothing dangerous," he said. "I was taking care of something for someone. I lost it. I need you to find it for me."

He spread his open hands before him and shrugged: in the half-light, his palms looked pale. He looked up at me with his big doe eyes and his hands dropped back into his lap. He hadn't stood up since I had come in. He wasn't trying to dominate. He was almost pleading for my help. Whether this was genuine, or carefully play-acted, I didn't know.

"This 'something' that you lost," I said, "is it an illegal something?"

He raised a hand, palm down, and waggled it by way of answer.

"Not drugs?" I asked.

"Not drugs. Not for me anymore," he said.

I knew that someone else had moved into his territory while he was away: drugs were no longer an option for him.

"It is just something that fell off the back of a lorry," Tiago said.

"How big is this thing?" I asked.

"If the Rathbanians find it before I do, they will kill me."

"I meant the thing you want me to find."

"Oh. You know how big a shipping container is, for a truck?"

I nodded.

"That big," Tiago said.

"That's pretty big. What is it?"

"It is a container off a truck," he said.

"This thing that fell off the back of a lorry...?"

"... is the trailer off the back of a lorry!" He flashed his white grin at me again.

"How do you lose something that big?" I asked.

"Is not easy," he said. He was frowning again. "I was to take the trailer from place A to place B. Someone else was to collect it from place B. But when they arrived..." He spread his white palms in front of him again and shrugged.

"Someone stole your container full of stolen goods?"

He nodded solemnly.

"I know. What is the world coming to?"

"No respect," I found myself saying. "Fat Duncan will never agree to help you."

"I am not asking Fat Duncan."

"I don't do jobs on the side."

"I'm not offering to pay you."

"Because I took all of your cash?" I said.

"Because you would not take my money even if I offered it to you."

Apparently Tiago had more faith in my code of honour than I did.

"I am asking for a favour," he said, "as a family friend."

"We are not friends."

"No, we are closer than that. Aren't we?"

"And if I say 'no'?"

"If I do not have the container back before Monday, then I am a dead man."

"The Rathbanians?"

Tiago nodded. The Rathbanians had taken over the local drug franchise that he used to run. They had also taken over a lot of other things. Including the corner shop that used to belong to Mr. Patel.

"I can't be involved in this," I said.

"I wouldn't ask if I had anyone else to go to, Joseph."

He took out his phone and poked a finger at the screen, giving me time to think over the consequences of turning him away. On the one hand he was the Spanish twat who knocked-up my sister. On the other he was my nephew's father.

"This container," I said, "do I get to know what's in it?"

"Do you want to?"

I thought about that for a moment. Maybe Tiago knew my code of honour better than me.

"No," I said. "As long as it's not drugs or people."

"It is neither, I give you my word of honour." He placed a hand over his heart, as if this was something I ought to take seriously.

I pretended that I did. "If Fat Duncan finds out about this, he'll turn us both in to the police," I said.

"That is a risk we will both have to take, eh?" He looked up at me. Again with the doe eyes.

"I will need some details about the missing container," I said. "Colour, markings, where it disappeared from..."

My phone beeped loudly in my pocket and I jumped. Tiago laughed. I was worried the text was from Fat Duncan, demanding to know what I was doing conspiring with a known criminal. I pulled the phone out of my pocket.

"It is from Natasha in Russia," Tiago said. "She wants to be friends, and perhaps more. There is a link to her social media page: she has some photographs for you to look at. Outdoor shots, very sexy."

I'm not sure what struck me as more odd: that he had given the missing container a name, or that he had a social media account as 'Natasha.'

"I don't promise anything," I said, "but I'll look around."

"That is all I ask."

"How do I get in touch with you?"

"Send Natasha a private message – she'd like that."

Tiago reached down beside the chair and then stood up. He was holding a litre bottle of rioja.

"Only from Tesco," he said, "but we beggars cannot be choosers, eh? I was going to ask you to have a drink with me, but..." He shrugged and held out the bottle towards me. "For you and your lady to enjoy."

"Sit down, I'll find some glasses," I said. "Shelly moved out."

"Forgive me, I had not heard this."

I glanced at him, but his concern seemed genuine.

"Tumblers okay?" I held up two Coca-Cola glasses.

"But of course, we are men."

"Screw top?" I asked.

"Eh?"

"The bottle."

"Oh. No, it is a proper cork."

"Fuck," I said.

I wasn't sure I even owned a corkscrew. Then I remembered that Shelly had left a Swiss Army knife in the hall drawer. I looked down at the penknife in my hand and wondered if I might not end up in A & E after all. I was relieved when Tiago took it from me and opened the wine.

Chapter Three

If you're shadowing someone and they spot your car, you use a different vehicle the next time you go out. This makes perfect sense. But it assumes that you have access to more than one car. The only other vehicle I had access to was a push-bike with no front wheel. Compared to that, the banana-yellow Honda Civic is an ideal stakeout vehicle. I had decided to park it in the supermarket car park across the road from *Big Dick's Floors 'n' Beds*. I'd reversed the car up to the barrier overlooking the road, and was now kneeling on the back seat, peering out of the rear window through a pair of mini binoculars that Fat Duncan had probably stolen from the back of a theatre seat.

As far as I knew, Dick had kept his fly zipped since I'd spotted him with Kelly Kenway. This meant that, according to his usual schedule, he was three leg-overs down on the week. He had to be blue-balled and fit to burst by now. I felt sure that today I would see some action. So to speak. I'd charged up my phone and it was primed and ready to run the 'catching a cheating spouse' app. I'd bought lunch from the drive-thru McDonald's, having agonised over the choice of cup size for my Coke. A 'large' offered greater storage capacity, but that much cola meant greater likelihood of needing to use it before I'd even finished the drink. I'd stuck with a 'medium,' a large fries, and a quarter pounder with cheese. I'd been tempted by an apple pie, but Fat Duncan always insisted that 'dessert' wasn't claimable on expenses. Nor was going large. Tight bastard.

Lunch was a lingering whiff of grease and I was just thinking of peeing over the remaining ice in my cup, when I spotted movement at the side of the carpet store across the road. One of the red Transit vans was backing out and, as it turned, I could see that Dick was behind the wheel. He was obviously heading off for an away-game. I wondered what exotic location he'd selected for his afternoon's nookie. I scrambled out of the back of the Honda and slid into the driver's seat. The car coughed into life at the second attempt and blew out a cloud of smoke like a flatulent dragon. I drove the wrong way around the supermarket car park and out past a No Exit sign, cutting into the queue of traffic that had just started to move as the lights changed. I saw Dick's dark red van disappearing northwards past the church, and set off after him.

I stayed as far back as I dared, half-a-dozen cars between me and the Transit, not wanting Dick to catch a glimpse of the yellow car in his mirror. He turned left at the Superbowl and headed up the hill. At the junction by the Sir John Cockle he was in the right-turn lane, and I thought he might be meeting Kelly for a pub lunch beforehand. But no, he kept going. He was in too much of a hurry for wining and dining. He headed north, and then took a left before he got as far as Chesterfield Road.

We drove along a road I didn't recognise, past quiet little cul-de-sacs of big new-build houses with tiny gardens, and then we were out of suburbia and had fields and trees on either side of us. And still Dick kept going. Perhaps he was trying to make sure he wasn't being followed to his illicit rendezvous. If so, he was doing a crap job of it. I kept a knackered Citroen people-carrier and a parcel truck between us, and he never knew I was there.

He turned off right onto a little winding road with tall hedges on either side, and I turned in after him. I hung back: there were no other vehicles here to hide behind.

We were out in the wilderness now. Or as close to it as Mansfield could manage. We were driving past an old colliery site that the council and its waste contractors had wanted to turn into a landfill site, and that the local people wanted to turn into a nature reserve. Or at least somewhere they could take their dogs where they wouldn't have to pick up the poo. For all I knew, the legal battles were still going on. One day, all of this could be covered in bin-bags. Or dog shit. For now, Nature was reclaiming what she could, and the only visible signs of human occupation were some faded yellow notices nailed to a low wooden fence that said things like 'Not on My Doorstep!' and 'F**k Off BinCo!' or whatever the waste contractors had been called.

This was our district's green and pleasant land, and Dick Gorse was out in search of the wildlife. He turned off onto an unpaved road that was just two tracks of mud and flattened rubble with grass growing between them. The hedges on either side were overgrown and scratched the sides of the van is it made its way deeper into the jungle. I watched it disappear, and decided not to risk the little Honda on the track. I drove on to the next corner and pulled up onto the grass verge. I would follow the van on foot: he couldn't be going far along that track: we can't have been far from the edge of the world at that point.

If I had known I would be hiking through the Amazon, I wouldn't have worn my good trousers and my best trainers. But a professional shamus had to deal with the unexpected on a daily basis, and so did I. I made sure my phone was zipped safely in my inside jacket pocket, in case I suddenly had to run from a pack of wolves, or a big rat, and set off after the departed carpet van.

As an experienced investigator, I knew I'd have no problem following the smears of black oil on the grass down the middle of the track. I'd catch up with the van, snap a few pictures of Dick and Kelly rolling around among the tussocks (or was it hassocks?), and then head home for an early tea. Or so I thought. I stopped to take a pee up against a coconut tree, or whatever it was, and was reminded of some advice my nephew had given me when he was three years old: Uncle Joe, when you have a wee up against a tree, you mustn't touch it with your willy or you might get splinters in it. Jack was a smart kid even then. I wish he'd also said: Don't stand too close, or it will splash back onto your good trousers. But as I walked further along the track, the damp spots soon dried in the dappled sunshine.

The oil smears on the grass had disappeared and there was no sign of the carpet van. I stopped, wondering if I'd missed a turn-off somewhere back along the track. I listened, but all I could hear was the twittering of birds and something making a loud *ack-ack-ack* sound. I half-expected to see a velociraptor break through the hedge further along the track. But all I saw was a black and white flash of something that might have been a magpie, but could equally have been a dodo.

I looked backwards and forwards along the track, trying to decide whether to go on or turn back. I'd got as far as "...if he squeals, let him go," when I saw a movement up ahead. Someone walked across the track and disappeared into the hedge. It was like a scene out of *Alice in Wonderland*. If Alice had been a big girl in black Lycra leggings, a baggy white shirt, and high-heels. Whoever it was, was also wearing a headscarf and huge dark glasses, like mutant bug eyes.

I say 'whoever it was,' but it was obviously Kelly Kenway. A word to the wise, a headscarf and dark glasses does not constitute a disguise; instead they say 'Look at me!'

I hurried along the track to where Kelly had disappeared, and found a footpath crossing the track at right-angles. I turned in the direction Kelly had gone: she was already out of sight around the next curve in the hedge-lined path. I hurried along, not wanting to get so far behind that I lost her too. Then I heard her voice up ahead.

"You are out of your fucking gourd!"

Then she started laughing. It was a smoker's laugh, ending in a coughing fit. I scurried towards the sound, keeping down below the level of the hedge, and peered around the corner.

The red van was pulled up in a gateway, the back doors wide open. Dick had obviously just unveiled it like a cheap conjuror opening his magic cabinet. From his expression, he was disappointed with Kelly's reaction. She was still bent over, gasping for breath.

"The back of a van?" She wheezed. "Seriously?"

The floor of the van appeared to have been covered with off-cuts of carpet. Cheapskate Dick hadn't even thrown a mattress in there. I pulled out my phone and snapped a couple of pictures of them standing there. This might be as far as their tryst went today.

Kelly took another look at Dick's crestfallen expression, and started laughing again, shaking her head. Dick was a bloke, with a capital 'B,' and so totally incapable of seeing this from Kelly's point of view. Another bloke would have looked at his improvised shag-mobile and judged it 'Genius!' – so why was Kelly laughing herself hoarse? She must have seen the brick-red colour slowly rising in his face as his anger boiled, because she said: "Oh, what the fuck?" and crawled into the back of the van. With her bum in there, I wasn't sure there was room for Dick as well, but he managed to clamber in after her. I took a picture of him pulling the doors shut, as Kelly pulled off her shirt behind him. Not quite all the evidence I needed, but we were getting there.

Not for the first time, I wondered how Dick managed it: winning them over despite a total absence of charm of any kind. Maybe he was wearing lucky trousers. Or one of those pheromone sprays off the internet. If he wasn't, then you could bottle whatever he had and make a fortune. I'd even be tempted to try it myself.

I poked at my phone, making sure that the automatic flash was enabled. I didn't think Dick could lock the van doors from the inside, and he wouldn't even have thought it a necessary precaution. I planned to wait until the van started rocking, then pull open the back door and snap some pictures. And then leg it. I knew I could outrun Dick. Especially if he had his trousers round his ankles. At school, running away was one of the few things I was good at.

As the van began to creak on its suspension, I crept towards the back doors. Phone poised, I reached for the door handle. Deep breath. Trying to keep my hands steady. And steeling myself to face what I knew I would glimpse inside. Just the thought of it had the burger rising in the back of my throat. I turned the handle slowly, and the door mechanism gave a heavy metallic click.

Kelly's voice: "What was that?"

I yanked open the back door and thrust the camera inside, my thumb stabbing the on-screen button to capture as many images as possible. I averted my eyes, not wanting to see the conjoined mounds of flesh within.

"Who's that?" Kelly screeched.

"It's that lanky cunt again!" Dick roared.

The van lurched as Dick shifted inside. I took this as my cue to leave. I ran away from the van, then stopped and turned to snap off a couple of shots of Dick emerging from the van. He appeared to be wearing only a tiny black lace g-string. Behind him, Kelly had her arms wrapped across her breasts, looking like a startled hippo.

"You bastard!" Dick ran towards me, barefoot and almost bare-arsed.

I ducked through a gate and ran across a field littered with bits of rusty ironwork. I thought the waist-high thistles would deter Dick from following, but he blundered after me, bellowing like a bull. If bulls bellowed curse words. I risked a glance over my shoulder: Dick was ploughing straight towards me, a thundering mass of red, sweaty flesh. I put on an extra spurt of speed: there was no way I wanted to come into contact with any part of that lump of nakedness.

I broke through another hedge on to a path that ran along the top of a hill that had once been a pit tip. Down at the bottom of the hill I could see an expanse of water that glistened in an oily rainbow sort of way in the afternoon sunlight. I vaguely remembered a news story about two kids drowning there. I ran along the hilltop path. I was still confident I could outpace Dick: I had longer legs, and had less weight to heave around. Still gripping my phone, I lengthened my stride, imagining I was a long-distance runner. Then I was hit from behind by a train. Or that's what it felt like. I fell forwards, the locomotive on top of me.

"Give me that phone, you bastard!"

Dick's voice in my ear, his breath rasping in and out like a steam engine. I held the phone as far away from me as I could, out of his reach.

"Give it here!"

He rolled me over on to my back and sat on my legs. Then he grabbed the sleeve of my jacket, trying to pull the phone towards him. I jerked my arm free and, in an attempt to protect it, shoved the phone down the front of my y-fronts. Dick leaned back and considered the situation for a moment, then reached forward and grabbed the fabric of my trousers with both hands and pulled, tearing the front open over my crotch. He thrust his hand into the ragged hole and began rummaging around for the phone.

"Give it to me!" He yelled. "Give it to me, you skinny fucker!"

At which moment, a little white-haired woman in a yellow anorak appeared on the path beside us, with her poodle on a red tartan leash. She picked up the poodle, covering its eyes.

"Don't look, Trixie," she said. "Oh, my goodness! I've never seen anyone dogging before."

"What are you gawping at, you old bat?" Dick yelled up at her, his fingers still trying to find their way inside my underpants.

"Isn't someone *supposed* to watch?" the old woman asked. "I thought that's why you young people did it in the open."

"We are not having sex!" I gasped.

"You're not? Oh."

She wandered away, looking quite disappointed. She would have been one of those coming in for a closer look when you peed up against your car, I felt sure.

"Got it!" Dick said, triumphantly.

"That's not my phone!" I squeaked.

"Have you got a hard-on, you dirty bastard?" Dick pulled his hand away like he's been scalded.

"I've never been groped before," I said.

Then I heard Kelly's voice: "I'm looking for two men. One of them's wearing a g-string."

"Up that way," the old woman said. "But they've decided not to have sex after all."

"What?" Kelly asked, incredulous.

"I know: all mouth and no action," the old woman muttered.

I relaxed under Dick as he looked over his shoulder towards Kelly, then I suddenly heaved my whole body to the left, hoping to throw him off. As we started to roll over, Dick turned back and wrapped his arms around my body. Our combined momentum took us over, and I felt us drop as we tumbled over the edge of the path and began rolling down the hill, Dick still clinging to me. He was on top, then I was, then he was, over and over as we rolled down. I got glimpses of grass and sky, grass and sky. And all the time, Dick's bared yellow teeth close to my nose. Then I saw what we were rolling towards: a lake of rust coloured water in the bottom of a stony crater that had once been part of the colliery.

"Look out!" I screamed.

Dick looked round, seeing what I had seen. He pushed himself away from me, our clinch broken. We rolled to a stop, a few yards from each other, and only a stone's throw from the edge of the chemical lake. We were surrounded by a lunar landscape of broken rocks and lumps of concrete. Dick sat up, a triumphant look on his face. He was holding my phone. It could have been worse, I suppose: he could have been clutching a piece of my anatomy.

"Not my phone, please," I said. "I'll give you the PIN, you can delete the photos."

Dick wasn't in the mood for an acceptable compromise. He picked up a lump of concrete the size of his head. Placing my phone on the ground, he hit it with the lump of concrete. He did it again and again.

"No!" I wailed. I was still eighteen months away from being able to get a new phone on my contract.

Dick picked up the smashed phone and hurled it into the middle of the lake of rust-coloured water. Then he turned his attention to me, the lump of concrete still clutched in his hand. I scrambled to my feet. I had a brief mental image of police divers trying to find my body in the Irn-Bru lake. I needn't have worried: Kelly Kenway came to my rescue. Sort of.

"What is your fucking problem?" she yelled into my face.

"I was only..."

She shut me up by punching me in the mouth. Blood ran down from my busted lip and dripped off my chin. Kelly swung another punch at my head, knocking me back down onto the ground. I could feel my eye beginning to swell as I tried to scramble backwards away from her.

Dick dropped the lump of concrete and reached for Kelly's arm. She turned on him, and for a moment I thought she was going to punch him. From the look on Dick's face, he did too. Then the red cloud must have lifted: Kelly stepped back, her hands relaxing out of their bare-knuckle boxer form.

"Come on, Kel," Dick said. "Let's get out of here."

"You look a right twat in my underwear," she said.

"You want me to take it off?" Dick waggled his eyebrows like Groucho Marx.

Please, god, no! I thought.

"If you think we're playing hide the helmet after this, you're dumber than you look." Kelly turned and stomped away. She'd worn all-terrain heels for the occasion: they were only four-inches at most.

"Kelly!" Dick looked from her to me to the lump of concrete, the picture of a man with a dilemma. In the end, luckily for me, libido won out and he hurried after Kelly. The image of his jiggling buttocks still haunts my nightmares.

If I'd had a phone, I'd have called Wee Patsy to come and help me. As it was, I had to drag myself to my feet; adjust my torn flies as best I could, and stagger off in the direction I thought my car lay. Stumbling along, dirty, clothes torn, face caked with blood, I must have looked like an extra from a zombie movie.

It was an hour before I dragged myself behind the wheel of the yellow Honda, but it seemed longer. Never had I been more pleased to see the little car. I managed to drive home; though having one eye swollen shut made judging distances a bit tricky. But the only thing I hit was the kerb when I parked the car near my flat.

As I trudged my way painfully up the stairs, I looked back on my day and tried to figure out where it had started to go wrong. Philip Marlowe never got punched by a woman. And he never got his dangly bits pawed by a man in a g-string.

Chapter Four

I woke up with my head pounding and blind in one eye. What had I been drinking last night? Then I remembered that I hadn't been drinking. I was lying across the bed, still wearing my blood-stained clothes and my trainers. My gentleman-parts felt swollen, and not in a good way. I sat on the edge of the bed and pulled off my clothes. I was overwhelmed by an urge to crawl under the covers and go back to sleep. But I had promised to go over to Elise's and fix the overflow on her toilet. Not that I knew anything about plumbing, but it's the sort of thing brothers are supposed to have a go at. Maybe I'd get lucky and stumble on a solution and impress the hell out of her. I'd take my only-for-emergencies credit card with me in case we ended up needing an emergency plumber.

I got to my feet and groped my way through the flat to the bathroom. I sat on the loo and let the shower run until the room filled with steam, then stepped under the water in the hope that it would wash away my pain. The shower was the only good thing in the flat: the water was always scalding hot and the pressure was really good. The way a shower should be. I think I may have fallen asleep on my feet as the hot water wrapped itself around my aching body. I turned off the tap and braced myself, preparing to look at the face in the mirror. I'd carefully avoided it before, not wanting to see it until the blood had been washed away.

Shit, it looked worse than it felt.

I thought about 'phoning Elise and telling her I was ill. But I wasn't going to be able to avoid her for the week or more that the black eye would take to fade. Better to face the music now. I found some 'concealer' in the bathroom cupboard. It had never concealed Shelly's zits, so I didn't hold much hope of it covering a black eye.

"There's something different about you," Elise said, "did you get a haircut?"

"Don't make me laugh, it hurts," I said.

This wasn't the first time Elise had ever seen me with a black eye and a fat lip, though admittedly the last time had been while we were still at school.

"I warned you about trying to pinch Fat Duncan's custard creams, but would you listen?" she said.

A great thing about my sister was that she never made a big deal about things like this. No matter how concerned her expression showed her to be.

Technically, Elise was my half-sister, but we never made that distinction. Neither of our fathers had stuck around very long, so it had always been just Elise and me and mum. When we were younger, people didn't believe we were brother and sister. I was blond and paler than a corpse, and she had black crinkly hair and flawless caramel-coloured skin. And a dazzling smile. I never smiled much. But look close enough and you can see that we both have the same light dusting of freckles, and the same eyes – green, flecked with hazel, or so Elise says. Her son Jack has them too, and he already knows how to use them.

Elise and Jack live in a three-bedroom detached house in a cul-de-sac off Chesterfield Road, up towards the Pleasley end. It had been part of her 'settlement' from Tiago. I'd helped her redecorate when she moved in. Every time I visit, my eye picks out the uneven lines and brush-slips around the woodwork and the slight overlap on one bit of the ceiling paper in the living room. But Elise and Jack have always been happy there. For Elise I think it must symbolise freedom and being a grown-up in her own right. I've never had to be a grown-up, but I'm not a single-mother with a seven-year-old boy.

"Uncle Joe! What happened to your *face?*"

"I got into a fight," I said.

"Did you *win?*"

"Yes, Jack, this is what winners look like."

My nephew was too young to recognise irony.

"You look like Rocky!" He said, with far too much enthusiasm. At least he wasn't freaked out by someone who looked like the Elephant Man's younger brother.

"You let him watch *Rocky?*" I asked Elise.

"I didn't let him: he watched it at Nathan's."

Nathan had an older brother who was teaching the younger boys how to swear and drink milk and then snort it out of their nostrils.

"What have we said about fighting, Jack?" Elise asked him.

"Get the first punch in, and make it a good one," Jack said.

"I did *not* tell you that," his mother said.

"Grandpa Max told him that," I said.

The old man was Elise's and my grandfather: we shared him with Jack, who didn't have one of his own.

"How do you know it was him?" Jack said.

"Because he told me the same thing," I said. "I should have listened to him."

"No, you shouldn't," Elise said. "In this family we don't fight."

"No, we just get our faces pounded into dog-meat," I muttered.

"Joe! Jack, your uncle and I need to talk: go through and watch the television until tea's ready."

"But *muu-uum*..."

"Now, please Jack."

Dragging his feet, Jack made his way through to the living room. He put the television on and turned it up loud. I hated to think what he was going to be like when he was a teenager.

"We should get Jack into some self-defence classes," I said.

"He doesn't need self-defence classes. He's *popular* at school." Elise saw the expression on my face. "I'm sorry, Joe. But you know what I mean. He's not you. I don't want him fighting with other boys."

"*I* never wanted to fight with other boys. I didn't want to fight yesterday: this still happened."

"If I ever think Jack is being bullied, we'll find something suitable for him," she said, "but until then..."

She gave me that look that said: That is my final word. She learned it from mum. I nodded: it seemed an acceptable compromise. Acceptable compromises were preferable to fighting.

"I need to give you my new phone number," I said. "It's a temporary one, until I get my new SIM card."

I pulled the little plastic phone out of my pocket to look up the number. The phone had cost me almost a tenner in Argos.

"What happened to your other phone?" Elise asked, as she put the number into her phone.

I was tempted to tell her that I'd lost it. It wouldn't be the first time I'd lost one. And it wasn't *technically* a lie.

"A big boy took it and ran away," I said.

"Oh, Joe..."

Jack appeared in the kitchen doorway, saving me from further sympathy. "Mum, can I go over to Nathan's after tea?"

"Okay. But I don't want you playing violent video games," Elise said.

"Nate's mum says we can only play the ones that are rated 12 or less." Jack sounded like he thought Nate's mum was the biggest killjoy ever.

"But you're only *seven*," Elise protested.

"But I'm *mature* for a seven-year-old," Jack said, deadpan.

I bit my lip. Elise doesn't like it when I laugh and 'encourage him' because I 'undermine her authority.' She saw what I was doing and glared at me. Mums never miss a thing.

"All right, but nothing stronger than a 12," she said.

I wasn't sure if that was an acceptable compromise, or Jack winning by a knockout. Elise glared at me some more.

"Your lip's bleeding again," she said.

"Fuck!" I said.

"*Uncle Joe!* We're not allowed to say fuck. Or shit. Or bollocks. Mum says."

"Jack!" Elise said.

"I was only *telling* him," Jack said.

"Thank you for letting me know, Jack," I said. "We'd both better not use those words ever again."

"Damn right," Elise said. She winked at me over Jack's head. 'Damn' had been the only curse word our mother ever used, and that only under extreme provocation.

"I should take a look at that toilet cistern," I said. I hoped it might win me an invitation to stay for tea. I'd spent my last cash on a new phone and a £10 call credit.

"Oh, no need," Elise said quickly. Not looking at me, she said: "We fixed it."

"We?" I asked.

I looked at Jack, but he just shrugged: he hadn't fixed it.

"Are you staying for tea?" Elise asked, still not looking at me.

"Does it involve green vegetables?" I asked.

Jack and I both pulled faces, thinking Elise couldn't see us.

"Pizza and chips," she said.

"Pepperoni?" I asked.

"Of course," she said.

"Oven chips or hand-cut?" I asked.

"Do you want your tea here or not?" Elise asked.

"Uncle Joe's right: oven chips aren't as nice."

"Whose side are you on?" His mother asked.

"My own."

I tried to grin at Elise, but it made my lip hurt. She threw another of mum's looks at me – this one was called 'that serves you right' – and pulled a bag of potatoes from under the sink.

"Go upstairs and wash your hands, please Jack," Elise said, "and wash both sides this time, or I'll send you back to do them again."

Elise set about peeling the potatoes. She could do that thing that only mums can do: taking all the peel off a spud in one long streamer.

"A little bird tells me you agreed to help Tiago," she said.

"We all make mistakes," I said.

"Thank you."

"It doesn't mean I *like* him."

"I know."

"And he's still a crook."

"I know that too. But he's family."

"He's not my..."

"Tiago is *Jack's* family," she said, perhaps a little too firmly.

"Does Jack know he's out?" I asked.

"I haven't told him yet."

"Are you going to let Tiago see him?"

"I'm not sure. I never knew my father," she said. She stared out of the kitchen window.

"Me either," I said, "and I also didn't know my father."

"And look how we turned out," she said.

Elise hadn't looked at me once while we were talking about her ex-husband. You didn't need to be Sherlock Holmes to figure out who the 'we' had been that had fixed the toilet overflow.

"I hope you practised safe sex," I said.

"Bastard!" She said, looking at me and grinning.

"I heard that," Jack said, re-entering the kitchen, his hands not quite dry. He pointed to the still frosty box on the countertop. "Isn't that pizza supposed to be in the oven?"

"Bollocks!" Elise said, reaching for the box.

"*Mum!*"

* * *

It was after nine when I parked the car across the road from the flat. There was a light on up there that hadn't been on when I left. I thought perhaps Tiago had come over with another bottle of cheap rioja. I was going to have to lie to him about how hard I'd been looking for his missing container.

When I got upstairs, I was surprised to find Shelly going through my desk in the living room. She looked like she'd done something different with her hair. Washed it, maybe.

"What have you done to your face," she asked, "walked into a lamp-post again?"

"That only happened once, because I was stoned," I said.

"You can't get stoned on second-hand smoke, you knob."

"I got beaten up while I was out on a case," I said.

"You've got a black eye and a split lip. That's hardly 'beaten up.' That's just Friday night in Mansfield."

"Thank you for your sympathy."

"If you want a sympathy card, drop dead. Otherwise, stop whining." She slammed the desk drawer shut. "You've got nothing worth flogging on eBay. What happened to your laptop?"

"Spilt lager on it," I said, "Gaz's fixing it for me."

Actually it was fixed, but I owed him twenty quid for doing it, and I didn't have twenty quid. I didn't tell Shelly that.

"How can you do your job without the internet?" she asked.

"I have my phone," I said.

She didn't need to know that my smartphone was at the bottom of a lake, or that the little plastic brick in my pocket had a screen smaller than a matchbook and lacked the oomph to handle animated emoji, never mind the internet. "Do you want a drink?"

"You've run out of beer," Shelly said.

"There's three bottles in the fridge."

Shelly belched loudly.

"You've run out of beer." As she came out from behind the desk, her foot knocked the empties on the floor.

"What are you doing here, Shelly?" I asked.

"I fancied a shag."

"Really?"

Perhaps my sister wouldn't be the only one doing the dirty with an ex.

"Yeah, but you've put me right off. Look at the state of you. You're pathetic. It's just going to be me and Captain Dildo again tonight."

"Well, thanks for dropping by," I said. "Don't let me keep you from a lovely romantic evening."

Shelly didn't seem in any hurry to leave.

"Janey Pierce said you had a bloke up here the other night," she said.

"Having a drink with my brother-in-law," I said.

"The cute Spanish guy? Does he swing both ways then?"

"We shared a bottle of wine, nothing else."

"I thought you'd finally come out."

"I'm not gay," I said. "You and I used to have sex, remember?"

"Whatever," she said. "It wasn't that memorable."

"Was there something else you wanted, Shelly?"

She looked me up and down, then shook her head. She headed towards the door.

"Pathetic," she said.

"I wasn't in the mood anyway," I muttered, after the door had slammed shut behind her.

I pulled the crocheted blanket off the sofa and wrapped it around me. I stared down at the cracked brown vinyl of the sofa: Shelly and I had sex on it once. I'd nearly dislocated my knee. I shivered, and it wasn't because I was cold. Something was bothering me about Shelly's visit. Perhaps the fact that I was desperate enough to have said 'yes' if she had said 'let's go to bed.' I needed to get myself some of that self-esteem I'd heard so much about.

Chapter Five

I had decided that I would get up early and go out and look for Tiago's missing container. At ten o'clock I was still in bed, wrapped up like a mummy in the covers and the crocheted blanket, and I would probably have stayed there all day if someone hadn't tried to break down the street door to the flat. At least that's what it sounded like. I tried to ignore it, but then whoever it was decided to put their thumb on the door bell, and leave it there. I untangled myself from the bedclothes and went down to hurl abuse at the visitor.

"If it isn't Mansfield's answer to Cagney and Lacey," I said, squinting out into the daylight.

"We're nothing like them," the first one said, "they were women."

"You're right. They were great detectives," I said, "you're nothing like them. What do you want?"

I shall refer to them as Detective Dennis Dockgreen and Detective Bob Keystone. Protecting their identities doesn't really come into it, I just have to uphold the private eye tradition of ridiculing the police. And because it will piss off Fat Duncan if he ever reads this.

The last time I'd seen Bob, he'd got pink eyes and had to give up wearing contact lenses. Even with the infection gone, he was still wearing the black-rimmed glasses. He probably thought they made him look intelligent. I couldn't work out if they made him look more like Woody Allen or Eric Morecambe.

Dennis looked more like a vicar than a detective: he had a round, cherubic face and pouty pink lips. He scowled when he remembered to, but even then he looked like he should be presenting children's TV with a sock puppet. He had to make do with Bob as his stooge. I'd met the pair of them when they were first seconded to Nottinghamshire's Serious Crime & Homicide Investigation Team, or whatever they were calling themselves this week. To me they will always be the Men from S.C.H.I.T.

"Go and put some clothes on, Joe," Dennis said, "you look like a whippet in y-fronts."

I left the door open and they followed me upstairs into the flat. Strays will do that. Bob went straight into the kitchen and put the kettle on.

"There's no milk," I shouted, as I went into the bedroom and pulled on jeans and a sweater.

"There never is," Bob called back, "we brought our own."

"Why are you here?" I asked, as I went back through into the living room. "Run out of crimes to investigate?"

Standing in the kitchen doorway, Bob glanced at Dennis, who was looking around the living room while trying to seem disinterested. The two of them had worked together for so long that they didn't even need to speak to each other. I'd seen them exchange this look before, it said: We know something he doesn't know.

"Cleaner's day off is it?" Dennis said, sweeping an empty cereal box and a juice carton off the sofa onto the floor. He made himself as comfortable as he could on the cracked vinyl. Without the crocheted blanket, it made hilarious farting noises when he moved on it.

"You look different," Bob said, coming through with a tray holding three mugs of tea. "Have you changed your hair?"

"At least I have hair, Kojak," I said.

"Did somebody get out of bed on the wrong side?" Dennis asked.

"Yeah, some moron kept me awake, banging on the door."

"He just called you a moron," Bob said.

"Who did that to your face, Joe?" Dennis asked.

"I'm not allowed to say. It's the first rule of fight club."

"I've never really seen you as the bare-knuckle fighting type," Bob said.

"Who said anything about fighting? I was selling popcorn," I said.

"Who was paying you to follow Dick Gorse?" Dennis threw the question in without warning, hoping to surprise me into giving them information. It was their variation on good-cop-bad-cop: bright-cop-thick-cop. It's part of the double act. But maybe they're not acting.

"Who?" I said.

"We came here for answers, not owl impressions."

I think Bob watches too many bad cop shows. That's why he tries to hang his badge over his belt, like the American detectives. But it keeps falling inside his trousers, leaving an awkward bulge.

"There's CCTV footage from the supermarket showing you sitting in your car watching the carpet store. I'd say you were there long enough to fill two paper cups," Dennis said.

"I was just sitting there," I said. "It's warmer in the car than it is in this flat."

I was curious to know why they had been watching the CCTV footage. But if I showed any kind of interest, they'd clam up and taunt me with 'we know something you don't know' looks.

"So you were there?" Dennis said.

"You just said I was. Yellow 1975 Honda Civic, not many of them around. It's a classic," I said.

"If you say so. We just got one of the new Volvos, didn't we, Den? Two litre. Blue lights behind the radiator grill. Unmarked, of course."

"Nice," I said. "What colour is it?"

"Blue," Dennis said.

"Grey," Bob said, at the same time.

"It's sort of a bluey-grey," Dennis said. "Metallic. Powerful, but not too flash."

If you ever need to spot an unmarked police car, look out for an extra aerial on the back, and a second rear-view mirror on the passenger side windscreen. And scratches down the side; most of them get keyed regularly: kids round here don't have a great deal of respect for the police.

"Whose turn is it to drive?" I asked.

"Mine," Bob said, "I tossed him for it this morning."

"I hope you washed your hands afterwards," I said. It was wasted on him. "Where's your badge, Bob?"

"What? Oh, damn!" He shoved his hand down the front of his trousers to fish it out, and he looked like he was standing there groping himself. I could see the bulge of his badge in his jacket pocket.

"You not going to tell us who you were working for?" Dennis asked.

"Data protection," I said. "It is unlawful for me to give out a client's personal information. Unless you have a warrant?"

"We'll get one, if we think we need one. Just thought you might help us out. As a fellow professional investigator," Dennis said.

"You're investigating something, are you?" I asked.

"Yes, we are," Bob said. "Something pretty big, as a matter of fact."

"That's nice," I said. "Any tea left in the pot?"

"I topped it up with hot water," Bob said. "Had to use three teabags: those supermarket ones aren't a patch on Typhoo."

"Welcome to austerity Britain," I said.

I went through to the kitchen and refilled my mug. I would have looked for something for breakfast, but I knew my cupboards were like Old Mother Hubbard's. I'd eaten the last of the cereal for supper. Without milk.

"While you were sitting warming yourself opposite Dick Gorse's place the other day, you didn't happen to see who it was he was knocking off, did you?" Dennis asked, as I came back through to the living room.

I looked at him over the rim of my mug and raised my eyebrow in an 'I know something you don't know' sort of way. Just for the fun of it.

"That wouldn't be confidential client information, would it?" Dennis asked.

"Who says Dick was knocking someone off?" I said.

"Dick was always knocking someone off," Dennis said.

"Was he?" I sipped more tea.

"Just tell him," Bob said. "It'll be on the news at lunchtime anyway."

Dennis looked from Bob to me and then sighed.

"Dick Gorse was killed last night. The bin men found him in a skip first thing this morning."

"They only found him because of the blood dripping out of the bottom of the skip. He'd been stabbed in the groin," Bob said, with just a little too much relish.

Dennis glared at him to shut up; he was revealing details that wouldn't be released to the media.

"Femoral artery," I said.

Dennis nodded.

"Stabbed with a short-bladed weapon."

"The kind of knife they use to cut carpet," I said.

Dennis nodded again.

"Found at the scene. No fingerprints."

"We don't get many murders in Mansfield," Bob said. "The Chief's quite made up about it. He went out and bought a packet of biscuits. He hasn't opened them yet, but they're there."

"Big day on Great Central Road," I said.

"Long day," Dennis said. "We've been at it since dawn. Who was she Joe? We've seen the CCTV from inside the store. Dick had her up against the wall behind the lino display. Dark hair, big thighs. We'll identify her eventually, but you could save us valuable time."

I finished my tea and put the mug down on the coffee table.

"The only person I saw was Kelly Kenway," I said. "She fits your description. You'll probably find that it was her lipstick on his – shirt."

"Kelly Kenway?" Bob was incredulous.

"Dick never was fussy," Dennis said.

"But she's Psycho-Pete's missus," Bob said. "He got chucked out of the army for being too violent."

"Psycho-Pete," Dennis mused. "What's he up to these days?"

"Works part-time laying carpet for Dick Gorse," I said.

I knew as I was saying this that I was effectively accusing Pete Kenway of Dick's murder. But these two were detectives, and they would have figured it out for themselves. Eventually.

"Means *and* motive," Dennis said. "I think we have a suspect."

"Who knows, the chief might even open those biscuits today," I said.

"Thanks, Joe," Dennis said, getting to his feet amid loud farting noises from the sofa.

"Next time the tea's on us," Bob said.

"Oh, and a word to the wise, Joseph," Dennis said. "Don't go poking your nose into this. Leave the investigating to the professionals."

"Oh, I will," I said, nodding. "When will they arrive?"

They both directed their best scowls at me and then scurried out as quickly as their little legs could carry them. And they took the rest of their milk with them. Skinflints.

The landline telephone in the flat rang just after the downstairs door had banged shut. It was fat Duncan.

"Why aren't you answering your mobile?" he asked.

I hadn't given him my new number, and I hadn't told him what had happened to my phone.

"Long story," I said.

"Never mind, I have news," he sounded excited. It was making him wheezier than usual. "Dick Gorse was found dead this morning."

He paused for dramatic effect. Or to allow room for dramatic chords to be added to the soundtrack.

"Really? But that is terrible. I am shocked and astounded," I said. "How ever did you find out? It hasn't been on the news yet."

"I still have my sources in The Force," Duncan said.

He always said it like that, 'The Force,' so you could hear the capital letters.

"Do they know who stabbed him?" I asked.

"A weapon was found at the scene, but there were no fingerprints on it," he said.

This was a perfect demonstration of Fat Duncan's ability to spot clues. He had told me that Dick had been found dead. He hadn't told me that Dick had been murdered. And he hadn't told me that the cause of death was stabbing. I had as good as told him that I already knew all about Dick's murder, and he hadn't batted an eyelid.

I'm sure he's never read a single Poirot novel. Mycroft Holmes my arse. And as for his secret police source...

"Did Dennis say what time the murder took place?" I asked.

"Around 2am, as near as they can say at the moment, based on body temperature. They will have a better idea after the full medical examination."

Obviously Dennis and Bob had phoned Duncan before they came to see me. He'd told them nothing, and so I had received the mid-morning wake-up call.

"Dennis and Bob will be coming to speak to you," Duncan said. "Tell them nothing."

"There's nothing to tell them, is there?" I asked. "They'll know I was there from the CCTV footage; and they will know about Kelly Kenway as well. The only other thing they'll want to know is the name of our client, and I would never give them that."

"Quite right," Duncan said.

"When Dennis and Bob finally get here, is there anything else I shouldn't tell them?" I asked.

"Don't mention anything about the money we got from the late Mrs. Ableman's estate," he said.

"You mean the cash I found buried in her garden?"

"We don't know that it belonged to her. It was treasure trove. I don't see that the Chancellor contributed anything to the investigation, so why should he expect a share of it?" Duncan said.

"Isn't that morally dubious?" I asked.

I knew for a fact that what he was suggesting wasn't just immoral, it was unlawful. But it is always good to have leverage when it comes to your relationship with your employer.

"If it bothers your conscience, you can pay income tax on your ten percent of it, if you wish," Duncan said.

I hadn't even applied force to the lever and I was already a thousand quid better off.

"I don't earn enough to pay income tax," I said.

"You don't?"

"I reported you for not paying the minimum wage, remember?"

"That was you?" Duncan asked.

"How many employees do you have, Duncan?"

"Well, there's you, and – and Wee Patsy..."

"Wee Patsy does your books one day a week, and you don't pay her, on the grounds that you and she are – cohabiting."

"I can't believe you reported me for not paying the minimum wage." Fat Duncan sounded hurt.

If he was trying to make me feel guilty, he was wasting his breath. This was a man who regularly ate his own weight in all-butter shortbread. Between meals. While I had to have my breakfast without milk. Or cereal.

"I think Cagney and Lacey have just arrived," I said.

I wanted to end the call so I could go and find breakfast. Before I got cranky.

"Who?" Duncan said.

"Dennis and Bob," I said. "Looks like they've got a new car."

"Remember, don't tell them *anything,*" Duncan said.

"I won't."

"After you've spoken to them, you should probably go and speak to Dick Gorse's widow," he said.

"Why?"

"Because she's our *client.*" He said it as if *I* was the idiot.

"*Ex*-client," I said. "I can't very well follow her husband anymore, can I?"

"She might ask us to carry out a private investigation into her husband's murder," Duncan said.

"That makes us sound like ambulance-chasers."

"We've already missed the ambulance," he said, pointedly. "Let's just hope you can catch the hearse before the real detectives do."

That comment about 'real detectives' needled me, as I'm sure it was meant to. What kind of *real* detective would work for minimum wage anyway?

"Right, I'd better go and talk to the real detectives then," I said.

"Yes, you go off and earn your six-pounds-seventy an hour," he said.

"It's gone up," I said.

"Has it? Again?"

"Happens every year," I said.

"We'll have to cut back elsewhere," Duncan said.

Somehow I don't think he had shortbread in mind when he said it.

Chapter Six

I took my credit card out of the kitchen drawer. I don't carry it around in my wallet because I might be tempted to use it, and most of the time I wouldn't have enough cash to cover even the minimum monthly payment. The card is for emergencies only. Normally I don't class having no food as an emergency, unless it's been over a week since my last meal. But Fat Duncan had promised me a thousand quid 'finder's fee,' so hopefully that would be paid into my bank account with my next month's salary. We refer to them as 'monthly' payments, but generally I only get paid when Wee Patsy puts the thumbscrews on Duncan. Or I threaten to set up a squat in his fridge. I judged that the odds of being paid this month were high enough that I could risk getting a fifty-quid cash advance out on my credit card. I could have stood the hunger pangs for a few days more, but I also needed cash to pay Gaz for repairing my laptop. And I needed the laptop back if I was going to look for Tiago's missing container: I had to get the photographs from the foxy Natasha's social media page.

In Aldi I filled a basket with tinned stuff, dried pasta, cereal, and bread, and then added a bag of apples in an attempt to ward off scurvy. I'd tried sucking limes once, but they were so sour they turned my face inside out. The queue for the checkout went along the booze aisle, so I had to pick up a six-pack of own-brand German lager. If Duncan did actually pay me, I could open one to celebrate.

I got home with the food and my laptop a little after midday. I heated some soup in the microwave while I waited for the laptop to boot-up. The smell of the Mulligatawny made my stomach rumble like thunder. It was so loud people in the street below glanced at the sky and reached for their umbrellas. Probably.

The laptop still had that pissy stale lager smell, but at least the keys no longer stuck down when I pressed them. I logged into my e-mail. There was the usual selection of offers of v.i.a.g.r.a from online Canadian pharmacies and Russian girls who were looking for a man just like me. I could have turned the spam filter back on, but then my inbox would be empty every day. There was also an exclusive opportunity to 'enlarge your manhood and provide your lady with the experience she craves.' I could try it free for thirty days without obligation. I wasn't sure what happened at the end of thirty days if I decided not to continue: did they come round and repossess my enlarged manhood? Or perhaps there was a built-in 'auto-destruct' and my knob would just drop off. I deleted the e-mail: better not to risk it. And it wasn't the size of my manhood that concerned me: I was just afraid it would wither away from lack of use. I should probably have taken up Gaz's offer to put some 'decent porn' on my laptop, though I was pretty sure the indecent kind was better.

I ate the soup well away from the computer, not wanting to risk new spill-damage so soon after getting it fixed. I wiped the bowl with a slice of bread avoid both wasting food, and the need to wash the dish. The bread was the white kind that balls up in your mouth if you put a whole slice in, so I ended up opening one of the bottles of lager to wash it down. I drank it in the kitchen, not wanting it even in the same room as the laptop. My after-lunch belches didn't score quite as highly on the

Richter scale as my tummy rumbles had, but I did the best I could.

I dug out the cable to connect the laptop to the printer. They were supposed to communicate wirelessly, but for some reason they weren't on speaking terms. I'd bought the same model printer that Fat Duncan had; that way Wee Patsy could slip me a new ink cartridge now and then. I only ever used it for work anyway. Well, that and to print out a couple of pictures of Jessica Rabbit that I had framed and put on the wall to hide a stain where Shelly had thrown a teapot at me. Luckily I'd ducked in time, so only sustained a couple of minor burns from the scalding tea.

I selected a couple of images from Natasha's web page that most clearly showed the markings on the container, and printed them out at 'finest' quality. Then I printed them again on the glossy side of the paper: I could never remember which way up to load it. I munched on an apple while the photographs dried, and tried to figure out what to do next. If I ever began to enjoy fresh fruit, I'd take it as a sign that I'd reached middle age. I should have bought some of Aldi's fake Mars Bars. If Duncan paid up, I would have a chocolate binge. It's not just for PMT, as I once said to Shelly. That might have been when she threw the teapot.

Having no other ideas whatsoever, I decided to drive out to where Tiago had left the shipping container when it was stolen. Going to the exact spot might trigger something in my brain that would give me my next move. And at least it would take my mind off chocolate. I grabbed another apple on my way out and tried to pretend that I was feeling virtuous rather than disappointed. And failed miserably.

The drop-off point for the container was a scruffy-looking lay-by at the crossroads near the golf course.

There was a pile of grey stone chips by the hedge, left over from some re-surfacing work done on the A-road two years ago, and not much else. I sat there in the car, not even bothering to get out and look around. Vehicles stopped in the lay-by all the time, or used it for u-turns because there was a stupid no-right-turn rule at the traffic lights if you came north from Kirkby. Even if there had been tyre tracks or a half-smoked cigarette from the night of the theft, they would have been bugger-all use to me anyway.

Whoever had taken the container could have gone in any one of four directions: north towards Mansfield; westwards to Sutton; south for Kirkby or Hucknall, or even the M1; and eastwards towards the A60 and Nottingham or just about anywhere. There weren't any buildings in the immediate vicinity; even the snack bar that sometimes occupied the lay-by on the other side of the crossroads was gone.

I pulled out and drove east, past the entrance to the golf club. The closest houses were on this road, but they were in what my mum used to call 'millionaire's row,' and were set back from the road behind tall hedges. People there wouldn't have seen anything on the night in question. And even if they had, it would only have been another truck driving past. There were dozens of businesses locally that received deliveries by lorry: factories and warehouses down by the railway crossing, and the business parks off towards Mansfield. Add to that the derelict sites and building sites nearby, and there were any number of places that you could stash a container without it looking out of place. Shipping containers were such a common site that no one would notice one at all, unless it was parked directly across their path.

Cars and vans sped by in the opposite direction as I drove along the narrow road. I passed the dome of the little observatory on my right. Down the hill was another crossroads, and across from that a mini roundabout at the T-junction at the end of Hermitage Lane. Traffic at the roundabout was held up for a moment as a truck the size of a small house reversed into the loading bay at the back of a factory that made pine furniture. Other drivers were probably annoyed by the delay, but I couldn't help admiring the skill of the driver as he backed the huge trailer through the narrow gateway. I struggled to parallel-park the little Honda unless I could find a space that was twice as long as the car.

As the traffic began moving again, it occurred to me that Tiago must have an HGV licence if he'd been hired to move the container. You need experience to manoeuvre something that size. Whoever had stolen the trailer would also have needed a driver. And there was every chance the driver would need to be someone who could provide the truck to pull the trailer, or maybe a farm tractor that was big enough to do the job. The list of potential drivers locally must be shorter than the list of potential hiding places for the container, so I decided to concentrate my efforts on that. I had a source who would be able to give me a list of names from which I would probably be able to identify the other driver. Eventually.

Uncle Benny wasn't my uncle. And his name probably wasn't Benny. The name had been on the shop when he bought it, so he'd acquired the name along with the inventory. If someone wanted to create a stereotype second-hand bookshop for a movie, they'd make it look like *Uncle Benny's Books*. The shop stood in the shadow of the railway viaduct that cut through this side of town. Outside, the paintwork was a cracked greeny-blue with a sort of white bloom on it like you see on grapes. On the pavement out front were two folding tables with boxes of cheap yellowing paperback; bestsellers from years past, five for a pound. The main window curved round towards the door, and had a big spider-web crack in it. There was an old neon sign hanging on chains inside the window, lit up to say when the shop was 'Open.' Beneath it was a display of 'collectable editions' on a faded piece of cloth with frayed edges. The side street window was almost completely bricked shut on the inside with piles of old books.

The door had one of those old-fashioned bells that ding-dinged as you went in. I also knew that the shop had a couple of hidden CCTV cameras, and that they weren't there to protect the book stock. The air was filled with a mildewed carpet and damp paper smell, and it always seemed cool inside, no matter what the temperature outside. Here it was forever twilight, and every available space was filled with piles and shelves and glass cases of books and more books.

"Joseph, my boy, I haven't seen you in ages!"

Uncle Benny scuttled out of the shadows like a fat little spider. He looked like he was coming forward to give me a hug and a kiss on the cheek. He might have, if I'd let him. I took an involuntary step back, and he slowed his advance. He was a short, round man in wrinkled trousers, a hand-knitted sweater, and brown tweed jacket. There was an old red velvet bow-tie at his throat, and his shirt collar was the colour of old bone and had a bubbled, diseased look about it. He was mostly bald, and his remaining hair was plastered to the sides of his skull: it was that red-brown colour that older men seem convinced doesn't look like it comes out of a bottle. The smell of Old Spice hung around him like a damp cloud. He peered at me through round glasses with tortoiseshell rims, and smiled as if he was imagining what I might taste like in a casserole. It was more likely that he was imagining something much worse than that: he had made his tastes very clear to me soon after I first met him. I will say only that I had seen proof that he wasn't Jewish, and that among his other revelations had been his confession of a fondness for pale, thin men, and a preference for being the 'master' in bondage scenarios. Everyone has a creepy uncle who makes them feel uncomfortable. And if they don't, they can always visit *Uncle Benny's Books*.

"Whatever happened to your face?" Uncle Benny asked.

My lip had scabbed over nicely, and the bruise under my eye now had hints of yellow and green around the outside.

"Bumped into a *Please Mind Your Head* sign," I said.

Uncle Benny nodded, looking like he didn't quite believe me.

'Uncle Benny' hadn't always been a bookseller, though I suspected he had always been creepy. He told me that in the sixties and seventies he had been a 'peterman.' I thought that was a euphemism for 'cocksucker,' but apparently it was criminal slang for someone who broke into safes. Later in his career he had become the bookkeeper for a successful criminal gang, and after that he had been a sort of 'producer,' bringing together the people, equipment, and plans to carry out successful criminal raids. As far as I knew, he had been to prison twice. After the second stint, he had gone into semi-retirement, becoming Uncle Benny. He still maintained contacts in the 'underworld,' as he liked to call it, and the bookshop was just a front so that he appeared to have a legitimate source of income.

I think that Uncle Benny had been one of Fat Duncan's informants when Duncan was working for 'The Force.' I couldn't think of any other reason for him to have taken on a kinky, only semi-retired criminal as a client. Uncle Benny asked for Duncan's help when two teenage boys were trying to blackmail him. One of them was under-age, and was claiming to have been locked up, against his will, and 'punished' in Uncle Benny's dungeon over the course of a Bank Holiday weekend. He had photographs of his own alleged torture and injuries, and some low-resolution images of Uncle Benny wearing only a studded leather harness and a smile: the teenager was threatening to take these to the police unless Uncle Benny paid up. He did pay up. But the demands continued. And the price for silence kept increasing. That's how blackmail works. Eventually, in desperation, Uncle Benny had gone to Fat Duncan. Who gave me the task of silencing the blackmailers for good.

I hadn't been convinced of Uncle Benny's innocence myself; particularly not when he had tried to lure me into his home-made dungeon. But having seen this set-up, and the quality of his DIY skills, I could see that the blackmailers' photographs had been taken in a more professional setting. In the end, I discovered that the two teenagers had a dungeon of their own, where they made bondage videos that they sold to a couple of dubious websites. I made Duncan buy an online membership, there was no way I was doing it with my credit card, and we downloaded the evidence we needed to confront the boys and persuade them to leave Uncle Benny alone. I never found out where the teenagers got the naked pictures of Uncle Benny, but I think that if I'd looked hard enough, I could have found them as self-submissions on someone's male-on-male bondage blog.

All of which, in roundabout fashion, explains how Uncle Benny is indebted to me, and has become one of my sources of 'underworld' gossip. It also explains why I have a lifetime supply of yellowing paperbacks, and an open invitation to sample the delights of Uncle Benny's dungeon, should I ever feel so inclined. Every time I go into the shop, Uncle Benny has this look of excited expectation: maybe this time I have decided to take him up on his offer. And every time I get to see his face fall as I try to keep the counter or one of the book displays between him and me. Ours is always a constant spider-and-fly ballet among the mouldering books.

"What can I do for you today?" he asked, moistening his lips and panting a little. Or perhaps I imagined that part.

"I'm looking for a truck driver," I said.

"Oh, Joseph! You've finally come out! I'm so proud of you!" He gushed like a broken lavatory.

"I'm not gay!" I almost shouted it.

"Still in denial." He visibly wilted. "Then why...?"

"I'm looking for information," I said. "If I was a local crook and I wanted to hire someone with an HGV licence, and possibly his own truck, who would you recommend?"

"Oh, I know quite a few truck drivers. And they're all terribly butch. But that's sometimes a front, you know. You'd be surprised how submissive..."

"Enough!"

I didn't know whether to put my hands up to stop him or to stick my fingers in my ears.

Uncle Benny scurried behind the counter on quick little feet, and picked up an old biro and a reporter's notebook. He began to scribble down details. He stopped and stared into the middle distance, and then added a few more lines. He tore off the page and handed it to me. There were six names on it, with a few additional details about each that would enable me to locate them. There were also some odd-looking symbols, but I didn't want to ask what they meant.

"They are just the ones with known connections," Uncle Benny said. "There are loads of freelancers who are prepared to do jobs with no questions asked, but they come and go like one-night stands."

"Thanks," I said, backing towards the door.

"If I think of anyone else, I'll let you know. Leave me your number and I'll send you a text."

"I'll be in touch," I said.

There was no way I was handing my phone number to someone who was likely to send me selfies of his shaved and oiled genitalia.

"Don't be a stranger!" He called as I closed the door behind me.

Standing in the sunlight wasn't enough to get the smell of damp books out of my hair, so I decided to go home and take a shower. Though really, it wasn't the smell of the books that I wanted to wash off.

Chapter Seven

"Fat Duncan asked me to pass on his condolences," I said.

He hadn't, he'd asked me to pass on the bill for the surveillance of her husband. Instead I awkwardly held out the flowers: they were standard supermarket blooms, not quite enough of them to constitute a bouquet. I'd kept the receipt to put in with my expenses, but I didn't hold much hope of being reimbursed. If I was lucky, he'd give me a quid and say, 'The flowers were from you as well.' That's how 'entrepreneurs' make their money: by shitting on the little people.

Charmaine Gorse invited me in and mumbled, 'Thank you for coming.' There were more flowers in her living room than there had been on the racks in Tesco. There was also a stern-looking woman sitting in a dining chair in the bay window. She clutched a medieval-looking handbag and was wearing a dark cloth coat and what looked like a green bowler hat with a handful of wax fruit on the side.

"My mother," Charmaine said. "Come to support me. She's not stopping."

I think this was said more in hope than in anticipation. The old woman gave no indication that she was aware of my presence.

"Is she...?"

"She's not senile," Charmaine said. "Just miserable and fucking rude," she added under her breath.

"I'm not *deaf!*" Her mother squawked.

Charmaine had gone to the same primary school as me. I didn't remember anything about her, except for one gloomy afternoon when a couple of her friends had stood on either side of her chanting 'Charmaine is a pig's name' over and over. It's funny what you remember. Her surname had been – what? One of the Monopoly board names, I was sure.

"Hello, Mrs. Trafalgar," I said.

"Fenchurch," she corrected me. "As was."

"Would you like some tea?" Charmaine asked.

"Don't put yourself out," her mother snapped.

"I wasn't asking you, I was asking Joe," Charmaine said. "You said you weren't staying."

"I came because family are supposed to support each other in times of grief. Not that I get any support since your father died."

"He died *ten* years ago," Charmaine said.

"There's no time limit on grief," the former Mrs. Fenchurch said.

"You remarried," Charmaine said. "Two years after dad died."

"I needed someone to fetch the coal in. But it's not the same with the second one. At that age they're too set in their ways. You can't retrain them."

I nodded, accepting this observation as truth. It was like sitting with the ghost of Nora Batty. The old woman began unbuttoning her coat.

"I'd best stay, I suppose. Can't leave you alone in the house with another man. Not with your husband not yet in the ground. People would talk."

"Not about him they wouldn't," Charmaine said, nodding towards me.

"Seeing as I'm staying, I will have that cup of tea," Mrs. Fenchurch said, shrugging off her coat without standing up. "I'll have mine in a china cup. Tea's not the same out of a mug with an advert on it."

"If you really came round to help me, you could go and put the bloody kettle on," Charmaine said.

"I'll do it, shall I?" I said. "Kitchen through here?"

"You can't do it, you're a guest," Charmaine said.

"And what am I, the cat's mother?"

"You're *family,* remember? Here to provide support during my time of grief."

The old woman heaved herself slowly to her feet and hobbled slowly across the carpet towards the kitchen. She glared at me as she passed, as if all of this was my fault.

"Will she be all right?" I asked, when she was gone.

"There's nothing wrong with her. She's fitter than I am. She just can't stand it when she's not the centre of attention. Please have a seat."

The banging of cupboards and the crashing of crockery came from the kitchen. Charmaine shook her head.

"I'll offer her a lift home when I go," I said, "if you want rid of her."

Charmaine looked at me as if I was wielding a bolt gun and offering to drive her mother to the abattoir.

"I need her here," she said. "The undertaker said he'd be here sometime after twelve."

Mrs. Fenchurch's head appeared round the kitchen door.

"Do you have sugar, young man?"

"No, thank you."

"Good job. There isn't any. Only *sweeteners.*" She gave a theatrical shudder and disappeared.

"Dick was trying to cut down," Charmaine said. "Lose a few pounds. He'd had to buy a larger size jeans. They're upstairs with the labels still on them."

Her eyes filled with tears. It had only been two days since Big Dick's murder: she was handling it much better than I would have done.

"What did you do to your face?" Charmaine asked, wiping her eyes with the sleeve of her sweater.

Did she really think I'd done it to myself? If I closed the eye now, it looked like I was wearing a tie-dye eyepatch.

"When someone yells *Duck!* you should put your head down," I said, "not yell back *Yes, duck?*"

"Tea!" The old woman crashed through the door with a tea tray. "I've brought biscuits. You look like a stray cat that no one's feeding."

"Mother!"

"Thank you," I said. The tea in my mug was dark and oily-looking. The old woman stood over me, looking down. I helped myself to a jammy dodger.

"They were Dick's favourite." Charmaine sniffed.

I stopped, the biscuit half-way between the plate and my mouth. I couldn't put it back on the plate. What to do? Fuck it.

"Mine too," I said, and shoved it whole into my mouth. I took a swig of scalding tea to wash it down.

Charmaine had that horrified look on her face again.

Mrs. Fenchurch picked up the flowers I'd brought.

"I'll put these in some water, shall I?"

"No mother, I thought I'd open a tin of beans and put them in that."

"There's no need to be snippy. I'm your mother. And you're not too old for a clip round the ear."

"My mother always used to say that too," I said.

"Did she?" Mrs. Fenchurch looked confused.

"Yes."

Mrs. Fenchurch scowled and then disappeared into the kitchen with the flowers.

The silence that followed quickly became awkward. I wanted to leave. Had I been here long enough to pay my respects to the grieving widow? I'd finish my tea and then make my move.

Charmaine's mother came back with a vase of flowers in one hand and a plate in the other. She thrust the plate towards me.

"Ham sandwich," she said. "You need feeding up. Do you want mustard?"

"Er, no, thank you."

"Good job. There isn't any." She put the flowers on the sideboard and disappeared back into the kitchen.

"I wouldn't eat it," Charmaine whispered. "I'm not sure how long that ham's been open. Mum doesn't take much notice of sell-by dates."

I lifted the top slice of bread and sniffed – just as the old woman came back through the door.

"Not Jewish, are you?"

"Er, no."

She nodded approval at this, and stood over me again. I had a flashback to school dinners. I took a large bite out of the sandwich and chewed, tried to smile at the same time. It must have looked like a grimace.

"It would have been better with mustard," Mrs. Fenchurch said. "Are you sleeping here tonight, or in our spare room?"

I thought for a minute she meant me, but she was looking at her daughter. Charmaine thought about this before answering.

"I want to stay here. But I think I'll sleep in the single bed in the back bedroom."

Mrs. Fenchurch thought about the advisability of this, then nodded her head. I could understand why Charmaine wouldn't want to stay another night at her mother's.

"I'll go up and air the bed," the old woman said, "while you finish your discussion with your detective friend."

We listened to her footsteps as she made her way upstairs.

"How did she know you were a detective?" Charmaine asked.

I was tempted to say 'witchcraft,' but didn't.

"It isn't a secret round here," I said.

"Do you think everyone knows I had you spying on my husband?"

"No. I only sat outside his store a couple of afternoons. I don't think anyone saw me."

Apart from Kelly Kenway, I thought.

"You don't think that's why he was killed, do you? Because I had you follow him?" Charmaine asked.

"You and I didn't have anything to do with his death," I said. At least, I was sure I didn't. "Neither of us had any reason to kill him, did we?"

"No, you didn't," she said. She knew I knew she hadn't answered my question. "I hired you to follow him. But I already knew. About the women."

She had deliberately used the plural.

"But you weren't jealous?" I asked.

"I should have been, I suppose. Dick just liked sex so much. When we were first married it was fun. I expected it to, you know, taper off after a while. But with him it was every day. After a while, I just wanted a quiet evening curled up with *I'm a Celebrity* and a bar of chocolate. I couldn't keep pace with him. When he became – less demanding, I knew he was shagging someone else. And I just felt *relieved*. Is that a terrible thing?"

"Some couples have open relationships," I said. "If both partners are comfortable with that, then it's not a bad thing."

"You must think I'm very unsophisticated, but I don't have as much experience with sexual relationships as you do. I bet you've seen things that would make my toes curl."

Oh, how little she knew of how little I knew. Though there had been that encounter in Uncle Benny's dungeon.

"You see a lot of things in my line of work," I said.

"It's a bit sordid, isn't it? What you do. Following people and taking pictures of them doing things they shouldn't be doing. It must make it quite difficult for you to trust anyone."

"I'm lucky. I have people close to me that I know I can trust," I said.

"Do you?"

I nodded.

"You said you already knew what Dick was up to," I said. "Why did you pay me to follow him?"

"I wanted some real evidence. So I could threaten to divorce him."

"I see."

"I'd never have left him. I did love him."

"But you wanted an insurance policy, just in case."

"I wanted a labradoodle."

"Eh?"

"A puppy. I asked Dick if we could get a puppy. But he said no. Said they were worse than children. I thought that wasn't right. If he could have a mistress, I ought to be able to have a puppy. To keep me company. That sounds fair, doesn't it?"

I could only nod.

"You were supposed to bring me a photograph of whoever he was sticking it into this week, and I'd put it in front of him and say: If you can have her, I can have a labradoodle. If he argued, I'd mention divorce and taking half his assets, and eventually he'd see sense and I'd have something warm and cuddly lying next to me on the sofa. I wasn't asking for a lot. And I never meant for anything to happen to him."

She was crying again. I slid the box of tissues across the coffee table towards her. They overshot and dropped off the end.

"Sorry," I said. "It's not your fault that Dick was killed."

"But what if it is?" She asked.

"How could it have been?"

"I might have been able to prevent it," she said.

"You couldn't have known what was going to happen," I said.

"I heard him arguing with someone," she said, "the night before he was killed. I was upstairs in bed, reading *Fifty Shades*. I've read it before, so I was just reading the good bits. And I heard raised voices downstairs. I was afraid it might be the husband of one of Dick's women, so I didn't go down."

"It probably wasn't connected to his death," I said.

"But it might have been. If I'd seen who it was, I'd have something that could help the police," Charmaine said. "And if they knew I'd seen them, they might not have gone on to kill him."

She'd obviously spent some time thinking all this through.

"In all likelihood, Dick was arguing with someone about a bet on a football game, or about the wrinkles in their new carpet," I said. "Murderers don't usually pop round for a visit the night before a killing."

"You're probably right. I just keep wracking my brains, trying to think who could possibly have wanted him dead," she said.

I didn't want to say that there could have been a whole queue of husbands and boyfriends ready to stick the knife in; partners of his various conquests. To mention this now would feel too close to speaking ill of the dead.

"The police will find out who did it," I said.

"Will they?"

"I'm sure of it. They have a whole team working on it. They've already spoken to me about what I saw."

"What did you see?" Charmaine asked. "Did you see who he was with?"

"I – I didn't see anyone," I said. "He may not have been with anyone that last week."

She looked at me gratefully, and I felt like a shit. She was right: sometimes what I do is sordid. I looked up and saw the old woman standing silently in the doorway. She'd heard the last part of our conversation. She looked at me and nodded: I think she approved of what I'd done. But it didn't make me feel any better about it.

"The undertaker's just pulled up," Mrs. Fenchurch said.

I got to my feet.

"Thank you for the tea and sandwiches."

"Will you come to the funeral?" Charmaine asked. I hesitated. Charmaine carried on quickly, trying to persuade me. "I'd like there to be someone there – I don't want it to be just us and, you know, *the women.*"

"I'll be there," I said.

I didn't ask when it would be: they wouldn't have a date until the police released Dick's body.

"Thank you for stopping by," Mrs. Fenchurch said.

She let me out of the front door. I passed the undertaker on the front path. He nodded solemnly. I nodded back. Then I shivered and hurried away, as though he'd been Death himself.

When I got to the little Honda, I discovered that I was still clutching the ham sandwich with one bite out of it. I binned it, not wanting to risk another encounter with the Grim Reaper.

Chapter Eight

I was stuck in a queue of traffic heading north on Chesterfield Road. Someone on the opposite carriageway leaned heavily on their horn and I looked across. It was an old Jeep Cherokee with fat tyres and a big rumbly engine, sitting at the traffic lights. It had dusty green paint and tinted windows.

"Oi, scarecrow, I want a word with you!" A gruff voice bellowed.

I glanced across again. The driver of the Cherokee had rolled down the window and was leaning out. It was Kelly Kenway. She stabbed an angry finger towards me, and I had to force myself not to duck. She was on the opposite side of the road; there was a raised central reservation with a steel crash-barrier running along it, so there was no way she could get to me without driving down to the fire station and doing a u-turn.

The bus in front of me pulled off again, sending a thick black cloud of particulates into the air. The Honda looked like a Prius in comparison. I heard the honking of more car horns behind me and glanced in the rear-view mirror. Kelly Kenway had come to a gap in the crash-barrier and was driving the Cherokee over the concrete kerb, bouncing down onto the same carriageway I was on, and cutting in front of a little Fiat 500 in the process. I hated bullies in 4x4s. Especially when they were coming after me. As the bus pulled up again, I managed to slip into the outside lane and get past it. If I could get to the junction at the Rufford Arms, I could get out of the traffic jam and make a run for it. Maybe slip through a narrow gap somewhere that the Cherokee couldn't get through.

Something slammed into me from behind. I looked back. The Cherokee filled my rear-view mirror. As I pulled away, Kelly put her foot down and slammed into me again. There was nowhere for me to go, I was surrounded by traffic and hemmed in by the crash-barrier. I cut into the left-hand lane without indicating, and earned myself a blast from someone else's horn. If I was lucky, I could get through the lights and leave Kelly breathing my fumes. She saw what I was up to and drove straight into the left-had lane. The BMW I had cut-up had to slam on his brakes. Kelly narrowly missed taking off the M3's front wing, which was a pity: it's always good to see a BMW gain battle scars.

The lights ahead changed to amber. I stamped on the accelerator, hoping the car in front of me wasn't driven by some old fart who still stopped on amber. Seeing me coming up behind him at speed, he kept going.

I glanced in the mirror. A red light wasn't going to stop Kelly. She kept coming. The Cherokee almost ended up with a Subaru embedded in the driver's door.

There was no way I could outrun a four-litre engine, even one as old as the Cherokee's. I pulled into the pub car park, figuring I was safer facing Kelly in front of a table full of smokers, than doing it alone at the side of the road somewhere. I got out of the Honda and leaned against the bonnet.

"All right, Kelly?" I asked, as she got out of the Cherokee and slammed the door.

"Why did you run?" She demanded.

"Late for a lunch date," I said, nodding towards the pub.

"Arse," she said. "Let's get a drink."

Kelly had a pint of mild, but I only had half a Guinness because I was driving. We sat outside so she could smoke. When she pulled out her e-cigarette, I couldn't help flinching: it looked like a cattle-prod. She blew out a cloud that was heavily scented with vanilla.

"Still tastes like cack," she said. "Tried Johnnie's home-made cannabis juice, and can't get rid of the taste. It was like smoking cabbage stalks."

"Cheers," I said, raising my glass.

Kelly blew smoke at me. The smell made me think of cabbage ice-cream.

"Why'd you tell the police I was with Dick that afternoon?" she asked.

"I didn't need to tell them," I said, "they had the video."

"What video?"

"You and Dick doing the dirty behind the lino display," I said. "I think Dick liked to do it where he knew the cameras would catch it. He probably had quite a collection of CCTV porn."

"Pig," Kelly said. "He wasn't even that great. I've had a better time on my own with an aubergine." She clocked my grimace. "What? It's not like the fucking things are fit for eating."

That's me off moussaka for a good while.

"They think you killed him?" I asked.

"Who?"

"The Jehovah's Witnesses, who do you think I meant?"

"Oh, Plod and Plodder? No. Why would I kill him? Because he was a cheap bastard and lousy shag? If I killed every one of them I met, I'd be a top ten serial killer." She picked up her pint and drained it. "You any good at it?"

"Killing people?"

"At rolling a girl's eyes up to the back of her head. They reckon some of you skinny lads have a dick like a third leg."

"Yeah, but have you seen how thin my legs are?" I said.

Kelly laughed: it was the booming, wheezy laugh of a fat uncle. "You not up for a nooner then?" she asked.

To give myself credit, I managed not to shudder.

"Aren't you worried what your husband will do when he finds out you were having an affair?" I asked.

"Why would I be worried about that?"

Because they call him *Psycho*-Pete for a reason, I thought. But I didn't say it out loud.

Kelly stood and pocketed her e-cig. "You change your mind, come and find me," she said.

Then before I was aware what was happening, she leaned across the table and grabbed my jacket. She planted a kiss on my lips and managed to slip her tongue between my teeth before I pulled away. Vanilla, cabbage, and warm beer – not a combination you'll see any time soon on *Bake Off*.

Kelly staggered away on five-inch heels, guffawing like a trucker. The guys at the other tables were laughing too.

"Nice one, Kelly."

"Got a smacker for me too?"

I didn't know whether to spit, swallow, or puke.

As I climbed back into the Honda, I glanced across the car park to where a big red pick-up truck was parked half in shadow. I couldn't see the driver's face, but felt sure he had been watching me. A witness to my humiliation.

I pulled out of the car park and headed for Tesco's. I'd decided that only mouthwash was going to get rid of that taste. That or lighter fuel and a match.

* * *

I went downstairs to open the door. It was Shelly. Her greasy complexion shone in the twilight and there was dried egg-yolk down the front of her hoodie.

"You look nice," I said, "off out somewhere?"

"Don't be an arse."

So much for my seduction technique. I used to get her in the mood by suggesting we phone out for a pizza. But I didn't have money for pizza. Shelly pushed past me and stomped up the stairs. If she was hoping I'd restocked the fridge with lager, she was in for a disappointment: I'd just drunk the last one. I followed her up.

"This is twice in three days," I said. "Are we getting back together?"

Shelly dropped down onto the sofa, and I heard it gasp. "Do you think I'm *that* desperate?" she asked.

"I thought that since Big Dick had shuffled off to the shag-pile in the sky..."

"What makes you think I was humping him?"

"I saw the video," I lied.

"There's a video?" She seemed interested suddenly.

I nodded. "Saw it on YouTube," I said.

"You're such a knob."

We sat there and the silence grew awkward. Shelly scowled at me, and I shrugged in response, and it was just like old times.

"Why have you got those pictures of three pigs on the wall?" Shelly asked.

"They remind me of you," I said.

"Arse."

"We got them to hide the hole you punched in the wall, remember?"

We'd got them as a set from the discount store downstairs. It was either pigs with bow ties or the

Kardashians. We'd paid the extra and gone with the pigs.

"Oh, yeah. Why did I punch a hole in the wall?"

"You missed my head."

She nodded. "That sounds about right."

"Good times, eh?" I said.

Shelly frowned. Maybe she thought it was a trick question. Or maybe she was remembering how much fun it was to try and punch me in the head. I decided to distract her with a question, just in case. And there was something that had been preying on my mind for a while now.

"Can I ask you a question?" I said.

"If you must."

"Why did people call him 'Big Dick'? Was he really...?" I held my hands out, palms facing, about two feet apart.

Shelly closed her eyes and seemed to be conjuring up a mental picture. She smiled.

"It wasn't that long," she said, "probably not even as long as yours..."

Thank you, God!

"... but it was fat, you know, like a Coke can. You really knew that he'd been there, if you know what I mean."

The Lord giveth, and the Lord taketh away.

"I've got pictures on my phone, if you want to see them," Shelly said.

"You took pictures of his dangly bits?"

"No! He did. And sent them to me. And it wasn't dangling."

"Spare me the details," I said.

"You're the one started asking about his cock, closet case," she said. "Why the sudden interest in Dick Gorse, anyway?"

"Because he's dead," I said.

"You got a thing about dead guys?"
"That's sick."
"What then? Were you working for him?" she asked.
"If I was, I couldn't tell you."
"Does client confidentiality still count if he's dead?"
"He wasn't a client," I said.
"I don't know if I believe you."
"I don't care."
"If you weren't working for him, you must have been... following him! That's it, isn't it? Someone wanted to know who he was shagging."
"He was shagging everyone," I said.
"Were you following him on the night he was murdered? Did you see who did it?"
"I wasn't there," I said.
"What about before he was killed? Did you see what he was up to?"
"Apart from sticking his fat cock into someone else's wife, you mean?"
"He's been doing that for years and nobody killed him. Why now? There must be another reason he was stabbed. I bet it was some dodgy deal that backfired," Shelly said. "He never wanted to talk about what he'd been doing."
"Because it wasn't 'what' it was 'who.'"
"You've really got no idea what he was involved in? What sort of detective are you?"
"The sort who investigates things he's paid to investigate. I don't just poke my nose into things for the fun of it," I said.
"Don't I know it. Aren't you going to offer me a beer?"
"You drank it all last time," I said.
"You could go out and get some."
"I'm not thirsty."

She gave me the look people give a puppy that's just crapped on the carpet: sad and disappointed, with a hint of lip-curl.

"You used to be a lot more fun," she said.

"It used to be worth the effort."

"I thought you had your Spanish boyfriend for that now."

"Tiago's my brother-in-law."

"*Ex*-brother-in-law," she said. "He's not back with your sister, is he?"

"What do you think?"

"Where's he staying, then?" Shelly asked.

"I didn't ask him. Maybe his parole officer found him a flat. I don't really care. He and I are not friends."

"Then why was he here the other night?"

"I assumed he came over to break my jaw."

"Why didn't he?"

"He decided I wasn't worth the effort," I said.

"I know that feeling." She tried to heave herself up off the sofa. It took two attempts.

"It's getting late. I should let you get on with whatever you were planning to do," she said.

Like she thought I had anything to do.

"You sure you don't want to stay?" I asked.

"I have to get back."

As if I didn't know she had nothing to get back to.

"I'll see myself out." She got up and headed for the living room door.

"There's spare batteries in the drawer in the hall," I said, "if you need them."

"For what?"

"Captain Dildo," I said.

"You are such a fucking twat!"

She slammed the door behind her. A framed picture of a pig fell off the wall and crashed on the floor. One down, three to go.

Chapter Nine

Fat Duncan asked me if I would meet with 'a detective from another agency.' He was working on a case that might be linked to one of mine, and he wanted to 'compare notes over a coffee.' I assumed Duncan had agreed to the meeting because he wanted the other agency to owe us something in return, like access to online resources we couldn't afford a subscription to. We had access to *192*, and Wee Patsy's mum's password for Ancestry.com. If we wanted anything else, we relied on favours

The other detective was coming up from the city on the A60, and I was meeting him in one of the pubs on Nottingham Road. It was one of those places that tries to be a coffee bar in the morning and a gastro-pub in the afternoon. In the evening it would like to be a wine bar and serve cocktails, but Mansfield isn't quite ready for that. Bottled lager is about as sophisticated as we get. If we're trying to impress a date, we might go for Mexican lager with a lime wedge.

This time of day, the pub was home to a handful of guys with laptops, using the free wi-fi. Would-be entrepreneurs who didn't have their own offices, but could afford a bacon sandwich that cost more than I spent on food in a week. I don't object to paying to eat out, but I think six quid for a fishfinger sandwich is taking the piss, even if it's on a ciabatta instead of white bread.

Across the room, some poor sod was perched on top of a stool that was taller than he was, being interviewed for a job with an internet start-up. As far as I could make out, the CEO's grand scheme was to create a website that pretended to offer local news, but really sold advertising. I watched the other guy's eyes glaze over as the interviewer waffled on about his vision for his company's future. If the candidate had climbed down and walked away, I think the wannabe-mogul would have carried on talking and not noticed. Part of me wanted to go and rescue the poor victim. The other ninety percent of me was enjoying the fact that, right at that moment, someone else was having a shittier time than I was.

Urged on by his boss, a young guy with tattooed arms and a painfully trendy haircut came over to my table. It said 'trainee barrista' across the front of his t-shirt. Maybe they only spelled it correctly when you graduated to the next level. He asked me if I wanted a Danish pastry to go with my coffee. I told him I couldn't because I was diabetic. I don't think he believed me. He'd watched me drop half-a-dozen mini-meteors of brown sugar into my latte. I was trying to make it last as long as possible.

I'd arrived early so that the other detective wouldn't see me arrive in the rusty Honda Civic. But he was now twenty minutes late. I was about to call Fat Duncan to see if the meeting had been cancelled, when he came through the door. The other detective that is, not Fat Duncan. I could tell it was him, he looked like a private eye from an American cop show. Expensive haircut, brushed back and glossy. Black leather bomber jacket, also glossy, and glossy black brogues: the kind with leather soles that make you sound like a cart-horse. His navy trousers had sharp creases up the front, and he was wearing a shirt with no tie. He probably thought of this as 'smart casual,' but up here he was overdressed for a wedding. Or a funeral. He had a dimple in his chin that, for some reason, irritated me even more than the haircut. I watched him look around the room and frown, and wondered how Duncan had described me to him. He looked at me, then looked away, and then after a circuit of the other tables, looked back at me and moved towards my table.

"Joseph?" He asked.

"Joe," I said.

As he got closer I found myself enveloped in a mist of over-priced aftershave that hung about him like hill fog.

"Matt Lester. Good to meet you," he said, extending his hand. I stood and shook it. We sat. He looked me up and down.

"Are you undercover?" he asked.

"No, why?" I said.

"I just thought... never mind."

The misspelled coffee waiter scurried over.

"What can I get you?"

"Decaff caramel macchiato with a dusting of cinnamon," Matt Lester said.

"Anything else for you?" the waiter asked me.

I resisted the urge to say 'I'll have a coffee,' and just shook my head. The trainee barista skipped away to practice his pretentious coffee skills.

"How long have you worked for Donoghue's agency?" Lester asked.

"Four or five years," I said. "How long have you been with..." Whoever the hell it is you're with, I thought.

"Eighteen months," he said. "But most of that time has been training, obviously."

"Obviously," I said.

The only on-the-job training I'd received was how to bump-start the Honda Civic. Anything else I needed to know had come from YouTube.

"The best part was the defensive driving course," he said, "I loved throwing a car around the track. The self-defence was fun too. Of course, we didn't bother with weapons training."

"Oh, did you not?" I said, trying to imply that maybe we did.

"This is my first solo investigation," Lester said. "I only got my car this week. It's a Beamer, three series. You need something that says 'professional' without attracting attention, don't you?"

I nodded and bit the inside of my lip and said nothing.

"I have to ask: How did you get the..."

His finger drew a little circle in front of his face, mirroring my black eye.

"Someone I was following..."

"Got spotted, eh? That happens sometimes, I suppose."

The trendy haircut brought over Lester's coffee, blushed and then scurried away again.

"I think he likes you," I said.

"You think?" Lester frowned, unsure.

I guess some people go for that young Pierce Brosnan, hairy enough to be a werewolf look. It was only mid-morning, but already Lester's dimpled chin was showing a bluish shadow. And so was his neck. And there was a tuft of chest hair visible at his open collar. I'd shaved a couple of days ago, and still couldn't feel any stubble.

I watched him sip his coffee. It looked like a dessert that needed a cherry on top and a spoon to eat it.

"Duncan said you wanted to ask me about one of the cases I'm working on," I said.

"Yes, thanks for agreeing to talk to me."

I hadn't, but I let it pass.

"Always happy to help a fellow investigator," I said.

Duncan had told me I had to say that. He didn't say I had to sound sincere.

"I wanted to ask you about the Richard Gorse investigation," Lester said. "Obviously I'm not going to ask you to breach client confidentiality. But I understand that you had been following him for a while, before he was murdered?"

I nodded.

"We think Richard Gorse may be linked to something that we are investigating," Lester said.

"Oh, yes? What do you think he was mixed up in?" I asked.

"We're only speculating at the moment, and I can't really say anything until we have some proof," Lester said.

That sounded like something he'd been told to say. He'd clearly been told to make sure that the flow of information went only one way. Basically, he was acting like a Richard.

"The fact he was murdered suggests he was up to no good," I said.

"He could have been killed by a jealous husband," Lester said.

"You don't believe that," I said.

"No," he admitted. "We're not interested in the illicit liaisons. We think he took more than other people's wives. I can't tell you what I'm investigating, not without revealing my client's identity."

He paused to see if I accepted this. I accepted that 'protecting my client's identity' was what we said when we didn't want to share things we knew.

"Okay," I said, as non-committally as I could.

"I don't think Richard Gorse was acting alone: he couldn't have been. And now that he's dead, I need to find his accomplice."

Lester sipped his pseudo-coffee and let me think about that.

"You think this 'accomplice' could have killed Big Dick?" I asked.

"Maybe," he said. "But right now I'm more interested in something the two of them took."

"But you can't tell me what this thing is?" I said.

Lester shook his head. "Sorry. If I told you, you'd figure out who I'm working for."

"You want to know anyone he could have been in partnership with?" I said.

"Anyone he might have teamed up with from the carpet store. Or anyone he met up with away from there."

"It might have been one of his women," I said.

"It's possible, but I doubt it," Lester said. "It's certainly not his wife. I've already checked on her: she's a basket case."

I thought that was underestimating Charmaine.

"You're interested in who he met, places he might have gone, any shady characters turning up at his carpet store..."

"Yes," Lester said. "And anywhere that he might use for off-site storage: lock-ups or garages, shipping containers, old properties or warehouses..."

I stared over his right shoulder, pretending I was giving this serious thought. I wasn't, I was watching the interview victim shake the hand of his interrogator, grimacing and glancing towards the door, eager to make his escape.

"I probably shouldn't do this," I said, after the interviewee and gone. "But I've pulled together some bits and pieces from my surveillance notes. I've taken out anything confidential, but even so..."

This was another lie. I rarely make any notes. The folder I put on the table contained a few pages that Duncan had dictated to Wee Patsy. It included some of the stuff I'd reported to Duncan, and it included a fair amount that Duncan had made up. I kept my hand on the folder, pretending I was reluctant to give it up.

"I can assure you, we will treat it with the utmost discretion," Lester said.

I made him wait a moment longer, then slid the folder across the table towards him. He was eager to look inside, I knew, but he played it cool. He signalled to the waiter for the bill. I was going to let him pay.

"I really appreciate this, Joe," he said. "I'll look this over later."

"If you have any questions afterwards, please do give us a call," I said.

Again, Duncan hadn't said I must be sincere.

"I will, thanks. And if you think of anything else, however small, that might be relevant to our investigation, please let me know."

He took a business card out of his pocket. It was thick, with an embossed logo and printed in blue and gold. *Sherwood Investigations*. He put it on the table when I didn't reach out to take it. Wee Patsy printed my cards. The print was never quite level, and the edges weren't always straight. I didn't give one to Lester: he was a detective, he could figure out how to contact me.

Captain Coffee sent Barista Boy over with a little black folder containing the bill. He slid it onto our table, ignoring me and smiling at Lester, then turned and went away again. Without looking at the bill, Lester slipped a twenty pound note into the folder. Perhaps he thought I'd ordered breakfast.

"I'll put this on expenses," he said.

"Nice one," I said.

Lester stood up, clutching the thin folder I'd given him. "I will be in touch," he said.

Lester walked away, doing that catwalk strut thing blokes do when they think someone is watching. When he was gone, I was torn between ordering a sandwich and swapping the twenty for a ten. But I didn't have a ten. Then the waiter came over and picked up the folder, and I had to fight the urge to snatch it out of his hand.

"I'll bring your change," he said.

"Keep it," I said, "get your tee-shirt fixed."

He looked down at his shirt and his face flushed scarlet. "Brady said no one would notice."

"Brady's a dick," I said.

I waited until I saw Lester's grey 'Beamer' pull out of the car park, before I went out to the 'Honder.' I started it up and sat waiting for the blue cloud to thin enough for me to see to reverse out of my spot. As I moved towards the exit, I glanced in the rear-view mirror and saw that the red pick-up truck was parked at the back of the car park. I couldn't tell whether there was anyone inside.

Matt Lester thought he'd been smart and not revealed anything useful to me. But he was wrong. He'd used the old trick of including something significant in a list of insignificant things, watching me to see if it triggered any sort of reaction. But I'd been inwardly sneering so hard that no other expression stood a chance of showing.

He'd also given me a clue that ex-brother-in-law Tiago, aka the Spanish Twat, had been mixed up in whatever Big Dick had been mixed up in. It hadn't been a wasted morning after all. I'd also kept the receipt for the coffees, to put through on my expenses: if my luck held out, Duncan might even reimburse me.

Chapter Ten

"Why do you want to know?" Elise asked, suspicious.

I'd asked her where I would be able to find Tiago. In retrospect, I probably shouldn't have referred to him as 'that twat ex-husband of yours.' I think my sister had picked up on the fact that I might be slightly annoyed with him.

"I'm helping him," I said. "Because he's family, remember?"

"There's no need to snap at me, I haven't done anything," she said.

We were obviously still pretending that I didn't know she had engaged in coitus with him. I sighed and sought to regain my inner calm. Or at least an external pretence of inner calm.

"I know. I'm sorry," I said. "I'm just worried that he's got himself mixed-up in something dangerous. I want to help him, but he's not making it easy."

Elise looked at me, trying to decide whether to believe me. Our mother used to look at me in the same way – but she always knew when I was faking. I didn't think Elise had enough practice yet. I hoped not.

"He's got a job," she said, finally. "His parole officer set it up."

"Where's he working?"

"You can't go and ruin this for him, Joe. He needs this job."

"I'm trying to help him stay out of prison, believe me," I said. "I'm doing it because he's Jack's father."

And because you, for some crazy reason, still have feelings for him, I thought.

Elise opened the fridge door and poked her head inside.

"Dammit!" She said. "I've only got two eggs left."

"How many do you need?"

"At least a dozen."

"You planning to make omelettes for the whole street?" I sked.

"No, I'm planning to wait until it's dark, and then throw them at Mrs. Kepler's front windows."

Mrs. Kepler was Elise's next door neighbour, and she seemed to have a pathological dislike for my sister, simply because she was a crazy old bat. Mrs. Kepler, that is, not my sister.

"You want me to fetch some more eggs?" I asked.

"Of course not. I'm not going to waste fresh eggs on that old dragon."

"What did she do this time?"

"Why would you think she's done something?"

"You're planning a midnight raid with egg-grenades."

"Joe lost his football. The one Grandpa Max gave him. He wasn't sure where it went. This morning, it was lying in the middle of the back lawn – with holes in it."

"You think Mrs. Kepler stabbed Jack's football?" I asked.

"I think she sank her fangs into it!" Elise said.

"I'll bring Jack a new football," I said, "after I've spoken to Tiago."

This was her cue to tell me where Tiago was. She was still reluctant, but eventually she shrugged.

"He's driving a van for Samwells," she said, "delivering groceries."

Samwells Supermart was a local business with three stores that somehow still managed to survive, despite the competition of the major chains. In the spirit of its founder, Samuel Wells, the present management were too stubborn to submit to the might of Walmart and Tesco, and managed to sell their produce to customers who were too stubborn to shop elsewhere. Being a small chain with local suppliers, they could respond quickly to changes in customer preference, but for the most part I suspect they are still more Arkwright than Fearnley-Whittingstall.

"Please try not to upset him," Elise said.

* * *

Elise had told me what Tiago's delivery route was. I didn't ask how she knew, because then she'd have to lie to me about meeting up with him for lunch, or whatever it was the two of them did during his break. I estimated how far he would have travelled already that morning, and pointed the Honda towards where I predicted he'd be. Samwells livery was banana yellow with bright green trimming, so the van would be easy to spot. I passed a house that had a yellow and green plastic crate on the doorstep, so I knew I was on the right track.

Twenty minutes later, I spotted the van on the road ahead. We were on a quiet road in a housing estate made up of well-to-do homes. The kind with Marks & Spencer curtains and fake coach-lights either side of the door. Tiago was speeding, but he'd obviously not yet relaxed into that 'I have a delivery schedule so the rules of the road don't apply' way of driving that seasoned delivery-men adopt. I shoved my foot down on the accelerator, and the Honda's engine began to whine: it wasn't a turbo-charger, it was a warning of imminent destruction. Smoke billowed out behind me, causing trees to shed their leaves and sparrows to drop from the sky. Gradually the little car gained on the delivery van.

We hit a downhill slope and I pulled out to overtake the van. Blinded by the smokescreen, Tiago slowed and beeped his horn.

I slammed on the brakes and the Honda slid to a halt, slewing sideways and blocking the road. As the smoke from the exhaust and the tyres swirled, I heard the screeching of brakes as the delivery van bore down on the yellow hatchback.

The smoke drifted away and Tiago threw open his door and leapt out.

"¿Qué chingados?" he yelled, marching towards the Honda. *"¡Piche penjedo! Te voy a matar!"*

I wasn't sure what he was saying, but I could make an educated guess.

"Get out of the car," Tiago said. He stuck his head in through the open window of the Honda. *"No me jodas."*

"Who are you yelling at?" I asked.

I was standing behind him on the pavement.

Tiago whirled, eyes blazing.

"You idiot, you could have been killed!" He said.

"Only if I'd stayed in the car."

"Your car could have been destroyed."

"I was hoping," I said.

Tiago's jeans were skin-tight, and his plaid shirt was unbuttoned halfway down, showing off copper-coloured skin and curly black chest hairs. His fists were clenched, and seeing the look in his eyes, I could easily believe that he was capable of killing someone. Someone like Dick Gorse.

The delivery van was almost nose to door with the Honda, looming over it. The van's bright yellow paintwork looked almost luminous next to the dull custard-colour of the hatchback.

With conscious effort, Tiago controlled his breathing, and his eyes lost their red glow.

"You are crazy," he said. "I wreck this van, I could lose my job. You know what happens if I screw this up?"

"They send you back to jail?" I said, brightly.

"You would love that, eh, *capullo?*"

"I wouldn't cry about it."

"If I go back inside, the Rathbanians will have someone kill me. For them, it is easy. Again, you may not cry, but perhaps my son would, eh?" He was pacing and waving his arms about. His hands were rigid half-claws, as if he was still thinking about grabbing me by the throat.

"Okay, it was a stupid thing to do," I said. "I'm sorry."

"Why did you do this thing?"

"Because I'm pissed off at you."

"You are always pissed off at me. Get over it. The past is the past," he said.

"I have a new reason to be pissed at you," I said.

Tiago sighed loudly, letting his hands drop to his sides. "Why now?" he asked.

"You lied to me."

"I did?"

"About the missing shipping container."

"It really *is* missing," he said.

"You didn't tell me it belonged to Dick Gorse," I said.

Tiago glared at me, and for a moment the red glow appeared behind his eyes again. Then it was gone. He shrugged. "Okay. When first I asked you for help, I did not think it was important. Then after what happened to him, I did not think I should tell you."

"Are you crazy? Why not?" I asked.

"I thought if I told you that I did this job for Dick Gorse, you would think that I could have killed him," Tiago said.

He stared at me, and I felt my cheeks getting hot.

"Tell me you did not think that when you found out the container was his," he said.

"I wondered if you *might* have done it," I said. "But that was partly because you hadn't been honest with me."

"That was a mistake. I am sorry. But you know that Dick was involved in illegal things. He is the kind of person I must not associate with. If I do, I go back to prison."

The way he said 'athothiate' made me smile.

A car came up behind us and found its way blocked by the Honda. Thinking that we might have been involved in an accident, the old man behind the wheel took great pains not to look us in the eyes as he mounted the pavement and eased past the obstruction.

"If I'm going to help you, you have to be honest with me," I said.

"We have to be honest with each other," Tiago said.

I nodded.

"Tell me what was in the container," I said.

"I don't know." He held up his hand to ward off my protest. "I do not know *exactly*. Dick said it was something that someone was prepared to pay a lot of money for. I think he received the money before he asked me to move the container."

"But you don't know what it was?"

Tiago shook his head, emphatically. "He did not tell me, and I never looked. Why did I care?" He shrugged. "But," he said, "Dick did once use a word that I thought was strange. He said the shipping container was *evidenth*."

"Evidence?"

"He said that, I am sure."

"That *is* strange," I said.

"Are we through here?" Tiago asked. "I have groceries to deliver. And some of the rich ladies like to give a big tip to the sexy Spanish delivery man. If he is on time."

He wiggled his hips in a sexy Spanish way. That explained the lumberjack-stripper outfit.

"Vete a freir espárragos," I said, waving him away.

Tiago grinned. "Where did you hear such a thing?"

"Jack says it," I said. "That and: *Tu eres más feo que el culo de un mono.*"

Tiago laughed out loud at that. "My boy is bi-lingual!" He said proudly.

"Jack also says you call me *Paolo de Escoba*. Who is that?" I asked.

"Palo de escoba," he corrected. "Is not a person, it means..." He struggled to find the words, making gestures with his hands. Something long and thin. I guessed what it meant. But it turned out I was wrong.

"The stick of a broom," Tiago said, finally, and pointed at me.

"I have been called worse," I said. "See you around, Zorro."

"Catch you later, Broomstick."

I folded myself back into the little yellow Honda and fired up the engine. I wrenched the wheel round and round to get the car to face the right way. Tiago put on the delivery van's headlights as he pulled off through the poisonous blue cloud.

I now knew that Dick's death and the missing container were linked. And that both were in some way connected to the Rathbanian gang who had moved in on Tiago's turf. Unfortunately, what I wasn't sure of was how knowing this brought me any closer to solving either mystery.

If Tiago was right, and the container held 'evidence' of some kind, what did that mean? Evidence of what? And why was someone, presumably the Rathbanians, prepared to pay so much money for it?

I could spend hours mulling over what I had learned. Or I could go and get a burger from the fake KFC – 'Southern Fried Chicken' was fooling no one – on Outram Street. My stomach rumble loudly and the decision was made.

Chapter Eleven

My phone rang and when I answered it sounded like someone trying to sing underwater. At first I thought it was the bargain-basement handset playing up. I'd received my new SIM card and put it in the phone, and suspected it had gingerly touched the cheap hardware and thought: 'You've got to be kidding me!' But then I realised it was someone crying on the other end. I squinted down at the name on the tiny plastic screen.

"Charmaine?" I said.

The sobbing and snuffling continued at the other end, and I thought she was trying to say that Dick had just phoned her, but that couldn't be right. I asked her if she was at home, and she said yes. I said to stay where she was, and that I'd be with her in a few minutes.

When I got there, Charmaine's face was puffy and her eyes were red, but she'd calmed down apart from an occasional wet sniffle. She let me in herself, and I looked around cautiously as I followed her into the sitting room.

"My mother's not here," she said.

I instantly felt more relaxed. I saw that her phone was sitting in the middle of the dining table, and that she gave it as wide a berth as possible as she went over to her chair. She didn't even look at it.

"May I?" I asked, pointing at the phone.

Charmaine nodded, still not looking at it. "5891," she said.

I keyed in the number to unlock it. She must have been born the year before me.

I looked at the call log first. Incoming and outgoing calls were mostly 'Mum' and someone called 'Suze,' who was probably Susan Sanders. She had been in the same year as us, and Charmaine's best friend at school, and occasionally her arch-enemy. You know how girls are at school.

Then I looked at the text messages, and a tiny shiver ran through me. I could imagine how it had affected Charmaine, seeing it with no warning. There was a text from 'Dick' – it had been sent at 11.05am that day.

Tell Joe L to meet me at Four Seasons 4pm today

Charmaine was watching me as I looked at it. She seemed satisfied that I was suitably shaken by it.

"It's not from Dick," I said.

"Well, *duh!*" She said. "Someone's got his phone."

"Yes, they have," I said.

"Do you think it's the killer?" Charmaine asked.

"There's a good chance," I said.

"Do you think I'm in danger?"

"Probably not," I said. But I could be, I thought. Whoever had Dick's phone wanted me not her, and that wasn't a comforting thought.

"Are you going to go?" Charmaine asked.

That would be a crazy thing to do, I thought.

"Yes," I said.

"Should we tell the police?"

In an ideal world, we would tell the police and they would discreetly surround the shopping centre, and close in on the murderer when he showed. I would be there to lure the killer into showing himself, but I would never be in any danger, and nor would any of the other shoppers.

But I knew that if I told detectives Bob and Dennis, they would think they could handle the whole thing on their own, and the outcome would be a full-scale clown-cop clusterfuck. And I'd be on the receiving end.

"If they even suspect the police are there, whoever this is will just disappear, and we may never know why Dick was killed," I said. "I think they sent the text because they want to talk. And they've picked a public place. I won't be in any danger."

I hoped Charmaine was more convinced by that than I was.

"You won't go there on your own, will you?" she asked.

"Of course not," I lied.

* * *

The Four Seasons was Mansfield's central shopping mall. Outside it was concrete that looked like it had rock chippings blasted into it by a shotgun. Inside there was a single level of shops, some of which were vacant. Down the middle was a row of stand-alone stalls that sold phone cases, brightly painted false nails, or wigs and hair extensions. At the top end, up by Boots the Chemists, there was a coffee bar in the middle. The noise from passing shoppers was deafening, and I could never understand why anyone would want to sit there and have a coffee. It wasn't as if you could have a conversation with the person opposite you. Though thinking about it, that might have been its appeal.

It was late afternoon on a weekday, so the place wasn't exactly buzzing. I wandered up and down, trying not to look like I was nervously waiting for someone who was possibly a murderer. The only person who looked more uncomfortable than me was a young bloke dressed up in a duck outfit who was handing out flyers for pawnbrokers at the north end of Westgate. I couldn't help thinking 'Why a duck?' and my brain ended up making some tenuous Marx Brothers connection with Mansfield's dominant railway bridge. A simpler answer was probably that they'd got the duck suit cheap. Every so often someone would go up to him and say, 'Ey up, me duck!' and he'd have to smile and pretend he hadn't heard it three hundred times since lunch.

A bloke who looked like he spent half his time at the gym, and the other half applying spray-tan, tried to sell me a subscription to cable television and broadband. I told him I didn't have a TV or computer, and he backed away from me like I was a crazy person. Even if I had money, I'd never buy anything from a man who plucks his eyebrows. I wandered further along the row of stalls, and a young Asian guy with great hair asked me if I was looking for a new phone case. I showed him my sad little phone, and he laughed and said, 'No worries, mate.'

I turned around and found myself face to beak with the duck. He held a flyer out towards me, and I started to push it away.

"A big guy up there asked me to give this to you," the duck said. He tilted the flyer, and I could see that something had been written on the back.

"Thanks, duck," I said, taking it from him.

He waddled away, and could hear him grinding his teeth.

I looked down at the message scrawled on the back of the flyer in block letters: *OLD MEETING HOUSE*. This meeting was in danger of turning into a wild goose chase. The Old Meeting House was a Unitarian chapel somewhere at the back of what used to be the Tesco building and what used to be the bus station. It was a much more isolated location than the mall, and that made me nervous. There was an adjoining parsonage that had its front on Stockwell Gate, which was less isolated, and I decided to head there first.

The parsonage was now private offices. It was an old stone building, set back from the main row of shops, so you tended to forget it was there. There was a bench and a tree, and then half-a-dozen steps leading up to it. I was hoping there might have been someone waiting on the bench, but there was just a massive seagull perched on the back of the bench, giving me the evil eye. Or maybe it was looking for stray chips.

"*Joe!*"

A loud whisper. It took me a moment to locate the whisperer. There was a paved alley between the parsonage and the ex-Tesco building, and it led back to the Old Meeting House. A large, shadowy figure was leaning against the parsonage wall, beckoning me to join him. There were still a few shoppers about, but I didn't have any great hopes of any of them rushing to my aid if they heard me screaming. I edged closer, and as my eyes adjusted to the shadows I could see the man who was huddled in a padded jacket, with a scarf wrapped around the bottom part of his face. A Mansfield Town FC baseball cap topped off his disguise. He looked me in the eye, and I recognised him immediately. It was Kelly Kenway's husband, Psycho-Pete. Who was currently wanted by the police for questioning in relation to the murder of Dick Gorse.

"I need your help," he said. *"Please."*

There was something in his eyes, desperation maybe, that made me believe him.

I stepped towards him, and he surprised me by stepping out of the shadows. I'd expected him to walk up the alley towards the chapel; instead, he crossed Stockwell

Gate and walked up the pedestrian ramp beside the jewellers. I followed.

"Thanks for coming," he said, as we emerged into the daylight at the other end.

"You gave Charmaine quite a scare," I said.

"I did? Oh, the phone. Tell her I'm sorry about that. Here."

Pete handed me a phone. It was turned off.

"4891," he said, "if you want to have a look what's on it."

"How do you know his PIN?"

"Dick was fucking useless with phones, I set it up for him. Told him to change the PIN number when I'd done, but I knew he wouldn't."

"Where did you get it?" I asked.

"He left it in the van, it was plugged into the dash charging."

I looked down at the phone. Pete's explanation seemed plausible enough. I put Big Dick's phone in my jacket pocket.

We seemed to be wandering aimlessly, but then I realised that Pete was leading me around Mansfield's one-way system, and making sure our backs were always to the oncoming traffic.

"I didn't kill him," Pete said.

"Okay," I said.

"I know it looks bad, that's why I can't give myself up to the police. Not yet. I have to prove it wasn't me."

"And you want me to help you?" I asked.

"Yeah. I'll pay you, of course, whatever it is you charge for investigating. I can't pay you now, because if I draw out money, they'll know where I am."

"Let me think about it," I said.

"There's no one else I can ask," he said.

We walked on some more while I thought about what he'd said. If he was innocent, then I wanted to help him. The problem was, I wasn't sure that he was innocent. Everything seemed to be pointing to the Rathbanians being responsible for Dick's death, but there was still no solid evidence. And Pete *did* have a motive of his own, as well as access to the murder weapon.

Pete pulled some keys out of his pocket. We'd walked around the block, and were now walking past a row of houses not far from the football ground. They all looked deserted, grey net curtains at the windows, and their exteriors were either peeling paint or blistered pebble-dash. Pete stopped in front of one of the doors and unlocked it. I followed him in.

"A friend is letting me crash here," Pete said. "He used to rent it out, but it's been empty for a while."

He pulled off the cap and scarf, shrugged out of his coat. It turned out not to be a padded jacket after all: the bulges were his muscles. He had a massive V-shaped body, and his biceps were as big around as my waist.

For a moment I was overcome with that childhood feeling of not wanting to take my jacket off, in case people saw how thin I was under it. Then I made myself take it off and hang it on the hook next to Pete's.

The front door had opened straight into the sitting room. It was dark and smelt damp. There was some dark lumpy furniture and a low table in one corner where a television had once sat. The fireplace had been boarded up, and the board was stained and starting to bow outwards. I'd seen some grim places before – I lived in one – but this had to be the worst I'd seen.

"Do want a cuppa?" Pete asked.

I followed him into the tiny kitchen. He just about filled it.

"There's water, but no gas or electric," he said.

The wallpaper was peeling from the walls, and the wall-cabinet was hanging at a drunken angle. There was a yellowish net curtain over a window that looked out on a tiny, rubbish-filled yard. A large box of groceries sat on the little counter on one side of the sink. On the other side was one of those camping stoves that runs on canisters of gas. Pete lit the ring and put the kettle over the flame.

"I've got bottled water: I'm not drinking the stuff out of the tap. I'm trying to think of this as an adventure. You know, like one of the survival challenges I had to do in the army."

If I didn't say something soon, he was just going to keep on talking. His whole situation was a nightmare, and he was trying pretend that it wasn't. But it was obvious he was struggling. Looking around this dump, I had to swallow a lump in my throat.

"If I'm going to help you..." I said.

"Aw, thanks mate!"

"I said 'if.' If I'm going to help you, then you have got to be honest with me. No secrets, no half-truths. I need to know everything. If I ask you a question, you have to answer it. Even if you don't want to."

"I've got nothing to hide," he said. "I just need a chance to prove it."

"How are we going to do that?" I asked.

"I have no fucking idea," he said, "that's why I need your help."

This was going to be a challenge, I had to accept that. I would start with the obvious stuff.

"Are you able to prove that you were somewhere else on the night that Dick was murdered?" I asked.

He thought about this. "No, I was at home. There was no one else there. We'd sort of had an argument."

"That isn't good. You have a motive and no alibi," I said.

"Motive? What reason do I have for wanting Big Dick dead?" Pete asked.

"Apart from the fact he was shagging your wife, you mean?"

"I wouldn't kill him for that."

"Why not?"

"Because Kelly can shag whoever the hell she likes. And so can I."

"You have an open relationship?"

Pete looked at me as though I was the one saying crazy things. "You haven't figured it out, have you?" A smile tugged at the corner of his mouth. "Does being a detective interfere with your gaydar?"

"What?"

Pete pulled his wallet out of his back pocket. Opened it and took out a picture, and passed it to me.

The picture had been taken somewhere dark. A party or a nightclub judging by the shadowy crowd in the background. It showed Pete with his arm around another guy's shoulders. His friend had blue eyes, pale skin, and a crewcut: there was a tattoo on his neck that I couldn't quite make out. The two of them were grinning like kids at Christmas, and their pupils were dilated. Maybe it was the dark, maybe it was something else. I passed the picture back to Pete, who stared down at it.

"Me and Jerzy," he said, making it sound somewhere between Georgie or Gigi: Polish, I guessed, or maybe Rathbanian. "We've been together for six months."

"Longer than most marriages," I said.

"Yeah, but I'm still married," he said, frowning.

"Does Kelly know about Jerzy?" I asked.

"Yeah, but I don't know if she likes him. We had a barbecue a couple of weeks back, but it was a bit of a damp squib. The weather didn't help."

"Was Dick there too?"

Pete shook his head.

"Dick didn't do the whole relationship thing. Only the sex. But there's more to life than sex. I'm starting to discover that. Just being with Jerzy, going places, it's fun, you know?"

"I think I remember," I said.

"Now Big Dick is gone, I hope Kelly will find someone else. She needs someone better than him. Someone who will treat her better."

"You didn't come out until after you were married?" I asked.

"I've known since I was twelve."

"Then how come you and Kelly ended up married?"

"Long story," he said.

The kettle was boiling and the gas ring made a little popping sound when he turned it off. He dropped teabags into two mugs and poured water on them. He splashed milk in, then pressed the teabags against the sides of the mugs with a spoon before fishing them out.

"Sugar?"

I shook my head. I took the mug from him.

"Kelly needed to get away from home," Pete said. "I was in the army, and thought having a wife would keep people from finding out I was gay. Maybe not such a long story."

"You left the army?"

"Got thrown out. Because me and one of the sergeants ended up, you know..."

"In a fight?"

"No, in a sleeping bag. Some bastard got video of the two of us at it." He shook his head at the memory of it.

"It was Kelly's idea to tell people I got thrown out because of the violence. 'Psycho-Pete' was her invention. That's not who I am. She didn't want people to think she'd turned me gay, or that she was too stupid to know she'd married a gay bloke, or whatever."

"And no one here ever twigged?"

"A few people know. It's not such a big deal these days. I only kept up the pretence because of Kelly. Having a psycho boyfriend suited her image of herself. And it was kind of fun. You really didn't know?"

I shook my head.

Pete was looking at me and smiling.

"I need to ask you something," I said, "about Dick Morse..."

"I only ever saw him in the men's room. And I'd have to say that I've see longer cocks, but in terms of girth, I'd give him four stars. Maybe be five if I'd ever seen it hard."

"That wasn't the question."

"But you wanted to know, right? What all the girls saw in him?"

"You've told me more than I ever wanted to know," I said.

"Some folk like their men a bit rough. The smell of sweat on them. But Big Dick never really did it for me."

"Again, more than I needed."

"Sorry. It's just nice to have another guy to talk to about this stuff," Pete said.

"You used to drive for Big Dick didn't you?" I asked.

"The van, yeah."

"Ever drive anything bigger? Like a truck?"

"In the army. An eighteen-tonner. Almost turned it over when I backed it into a ditch. The sergeant threatened to give me a trashing for that, but he never did." Pete sighed wistfully.

"That the last time you drove a truck?" I asked.

"First and last. Haven't driven anything bigger than a Transit since. You got a thing for truck drivers?"

"No, I don't," I said. I sipped my tea, trying to think of some way to get the conversation back on track.

Pete had set down his mug and was watching me. "The worst part about all of this," he said, glancing around the Third World kitchen, "is missing Jerzy. We had an argument, then this thing with Big Dick blew up, and I've been in hiding ever since. I can't go anywhere near him, can't even talk to him, because the police will be watching him. I can't use my phone in case they're tracking it, so I can't even surf for internet porn. And I'm starting to get that itch, you know?"

He smiled at me again.

Call me naïve, but I really didn't know he was coming on to me. My sex drive had been turned off for so long that it wasn't until he put his arm around my waist and pulled me towards him that my starter-motor coughed into life and warned me. His lips were on mine before I could say anything.

I can honestly say that Psycho-Pete Kenway kissed me in a way that I had never been kissed before. I could say that I've never been kissed by anyone with stubble before, but Shelly has this thing where if she doesn't wax her upper lip regularly... but she never did with her tongue what Pete was doing at that moment. I wondered if that was the sort of thing Shelly had expected from me. Pete slid his huge hand down my back, I could feel the warmth through my shirt, and grabbed my bum. He pulled us together, his groin grinding against mine.

"It's true what they say about you skinny boys, then," he said, his voice hot and moist in my ear.

I tried to get my arm between us to push him away, and found my hand covering his bulging pectoral. I felt it twitch under my palm.

"What about Jerzy?" I squeaked.

Pete's arms relaxed and he stepped back. He looked guilty. "You're right, I wasn't thinking. I'm in a relationship now."

"Yes, you are," I said. I wiped the back of my hand across my mouth.

"I'm sorry, Joe. I really am attracted to you, but I can't do this. I'm with Jerzy."

"I understand," I said.

"Friends?" he asked, holding out his huge meaty hand.

I hesitated. Then held out my bony, veiny hand, hoping he wouldn't crush it. His handshake was surprisingly gentle.

"Friends," I said.

I left Pete heating up a can of soup for his evening meal.

"It's the chunky kind: a meal in a can," he'd said cheerfully, and I had to swallow that lump in my throat again.

I wanted to help him. But I didn't know how. His best chance might lie with me figuring out who really did kill Dick Gorse. I felt almost certain now that Pete hadn't done it. He was either innocent, or a bloody good actor.

As I was leaving, Pete had pressed an envelope into my hand.

"Will you find a way to get this to Jerzy? I don't want him to think I'm still angry, or that I don't want to see him."

"I'm sure he knows why you have to lie low," I said. "I'll make sure he gets it."

I looked down at the envelope.

"And please don't tell him about the kiss," Pete said.
"What kiss?" I asked.

The sad thing was, it was the best kiss I'd had in ages. No, the sad thing was, it was the *only* kiss I'd had in ages.

Chapter Twelve

I got an early morning call from Wee Patsy to say that someone wanted to talk to me. He'd been given her number because Uncle Benny didn't have mine.

"He said it was to do with *the job*," Patsy said.

I could hear the italics when she said it. I hadn't told her or Duncan that I was investigating the missing container, or about the possible link between it and Big Dick's murder. In theory, I should share everything with my employer, and I'm sure I would, if my so-called employer regularly paid me for the work I did. If Fat Duncan was going to withhold payment, I felt perfectly entitled to withhold information. That's why Patsy felt the need to resort to italics, to try and get me to share. If I wasn't careful, she'd be wheeling out the word 'disappointed' to shame me into spilling the beans. Let her try: my can opener would remain at the pawn shop until I got paid, so no beans.

"What did he say his name was?" I asked.

"Chapman," Patsy said.

I didn't know anyone called Chapman.

"Oh, he's the bloke who's doing my sister's downstairs loo," I said. "I must have given him my temporary phone number. I'm back on the proper one. I'm sorry he bothered you with this."

I could hear Patsy thinking on the other end of the phone. It's not as easy to lie to her as it is to Duncan: her brain's not ninety percent lard. She sighed. That meant she knew I wasn't telling the truth, but she couldn't be bothered to quiz me about it. She gave me Chapman's number and hung up.

I called the number, and a gruff voice answered.

"Mr. Chapman?" I said.

"Who is this?" He sounded suspicious.

"Joe Lucke. I got a message that you were trying to reach me."

"A message from who?" He sounded even more suspicious.

"Uncle Benny gave you Wee Patsy's number," I said.

It felt like some sort of test from a John Le Carré novel. Apparently, I passed.

"Not on the phone," he said. "Meet me at the Portland Retail Park, in front of the pet store. Midday."

I agreed and hung up. All very cloak and dagger.

Psycho-Pete's boyfriend, Jerzy, cut hair for a living. He rented a chair in a barber's shop just up from the bingo hall. The place was empty when I went in, apart from a slim young man sitting in one of the barber chairs reading that month's *Cosmopolitan*.

"Jerzy?" I asked.

He looked me up and down, evaluating me, and then nodded. He had dark hair that went upwards in unfeasibly tall spikes, pale flawless skin, and green eyes. I wasn't sure if he was wearing eyeliner, or if it was just the long eyelashes accentuating the outline of his eyelids. His lips were pink and smooth, and they weren't smiling. Maybe he was just having a rough day.

"Take the hat off," he said.

Without thinking, I reached up and pulled off the knitted hat. I smoothed my hair down as best I could.

From his sneer, I suspected that Jerzy wasn't a fan of my previous barber's work.

"What do you want me to do?" He asked. His tone said: I can't do miracles.

"I'm a friend of Pete's," I said.

Jerzy rolled his eyes. "Not another one. Just because he snogged you behind some pub doesn't mean I have to give you a discount," he said.

"He didn't snog me," I said, wanting to believe it. "He told me he couldn't because he was with someone now."

"He said that?" Jerzy smiled for the first time. Just call me cupid.

"Sit in the chair, then, let me see what I can do for you." He flapped the little nylon cape like a bullfighter.

"I didn't come for a haircut," I said, "just to deliver a message."

"In the chair. You can't stand in here with hair like that, you'll frighten off the punters. The first trim is on me: introductory offer."

I took off my jacket to hang it up, and slid Pete's envelope out of the inside pocket.

"What did Pete tell you to say?" Jerzy asked.

I held out the envelope. He looked at it like it was a snake.

"What is that? It's not a 'Dear John' letter, is it?"

"I don't think so," I said.

He took the envelope from me and slit it open with the tail of his comb. With a deep breath, he unfolded the piece of notepaper. I couldn't see what was written on it, but I stood and watched Jerzy read it from top to bottom, and then read it again. His eyes became shiny.

"Not bad news?" I asked.

Jerzy shook his head. "It's the sweetest thing anyone has ever written. I need a minute. Sit in the chair, I'll be right back."

He disappeared into the back room. Feeling at a bit of a loss, I sat down in the chair. Jerzy returned a few minutes later, dry eyed, and with a smile brightening his face.

"Right then, let's see what we can do with you. This Justin Bieber thing just isn't working. You look like a refugee from Woodstock. The sideburns I can live with, but we need to uncover your ears."

His scissors went *snip, snip, snip,* buzzing around my head like a metal insect. Little clumps of hair rained down around the chair.

"Do you know where he is?" Jerzy asked. "Pete, I mean."

"He's somewhere safe. For the moment," I said.

"Will you take him a message from me?"

His scissors were flashing about my ears, I wasn't about to say 'no' was I? But I'd done this message carrying before. In school, Trevor Loomis got all dewy-eyed about Lisa Scott, and asked me to take a note to her. He gave me a bag of sweets for doing it. But it didn't end well.

"Will you give Trevor something from me?" Lisa asked, after she had read his declaration of love.

"Okay," I said, in the hope of receiving another bag of sweets.

Lisa Scott hit me up the side of the head with a chemistry book.

"Give him that!" She said, gleefully.

She screwed up his note and threw it at me.

That was the first time I ever saw those little flying sparks you get when you're almost belted unconscious.

I decided to sugar the pill when I went back to Trevor. He was bigger than I was.

"She's just not that into you," I said.

"Fuck her, then. She's probably a lezzer anyway," Trevor said.

I learned two things that day. Never act as the go-between for two lovers. And, if you're going to write someone a love note, avoid using the word 'knockers.'

I felt safe in the assumption that Pete hadn't said how much he admired Jerzy's knockers.

"I'd be happy to take him a message," I lied.

The scissors stopped for a moment, as Jerzy thought about it. "I don't know what to say to him," he said. "What would you say to him?"

Keep your tongue to yourself, I thought.

"Well," I said, "he's hiding out somewhere that's a bit grim. He doesn't have any nice things. Perhaps you could send him a little care package?"

"That's such a *romantic* idea!" Jerzy said, his scissors flying once more. "What should I put in it?"

I thought it better not to say that Pete wanted some porn. I suggested some nice snacks and Pete's favourite tipple instead.

"And when this is all over, you should think about taking him away for a romantic weekend," I said. "He'll be ready for it, if you catch my meaning."

"That's it! You can tell him I'm planning a really dirty weekend for him when he comes home!"

"Lovely," I said. "But keep the details to yourself. Let it be a surprise."

"I will. There what do you think?"

He removed the cape with a flourish.

I looked in the mirror. I had a lot less hair, and it looked a lot neater.

"I like it," I said.

"I'd do you," Jerzy said, "if I wasn't already spoken for."

"Thanks," I said.

"If ever you want someone to go clothes shopping with you, give me a call," he said.

"What's wrong with my clothes?" I asked.

"Nothing," he said quickly. "But they're work clothes. You'll need something a bit more stylish if you're going away for a dirty weekend of your own."

"That won't be happening anytime soon," I said.

"Don't put yourself down. You have beautiful eyes – and great cheekbones."

"My girlfriend said I looked like a skeleton wrapped in cling-film."

"You just need a new look. And possibly a new girlfriend. I wasn't kidding about the clothes. That's what I do: fashion. Cutting hair pays the bills. I've got a show coming up. At the hall on Allandale Road, 7pm on the fifteenth. You should come."

Jerzy scribbled his mobile number on a corner torn from the magazine and handed it to me. I thanked him for the haircut, and told him I'd try and make the show if I was free that evening.

I left the barber shop with my hat still in my hand, the breeze around my ears feeling strange as I walked back towards the car. I was going to have to hurry if I wanted to be on time for my rendezvous with the mysterious Mr. Chapman. I wasn't really concentrating on the meeting, or the investigation. I was wondering whether to blow my remaining cash on a Whopper. There was a Burger King at the retail park, and I knew it would try to lure me in by wafting grilled beef smells towards me. I didn't think I was strong enough to resist.

I was on a little street, about five minutes from the retail park when a vehicle heading towards me flashed its headlights. It was the shiny red pick-up truck, and it was approaching fast. I slammed on the brakes, and the Honda slid to a stop. There was a bit of smoke from the front tyres, and just a whiff of burning rubber.

I'd seen the movies, I knew what a J-turn was, But I'd never attempted one before. I jammed the gear lever into reverse and accelerated away from the approaching pick-up. The trick, according to the stunt driver in the DVD extras, was to gain as much speed as you can backwards before beginning the turn. Grab the steering wheel at about nine o'clock with your right hand, and turn the wheel sharply; then break hard to lock the front wheels, dip the clutch, select second gear, and accelerate away. No handbrake necessary at any point.

It sounds easy enough and, in slow-motion on screen, looks perfectly do-able. But you have to do all of those things in the right way, in the right order, and within fractions of a second of each other. If you're going to try it, don't do it in a narrow street, and if you can, avoid having a monster truck bearing down on you. Remain calm, and hopefully your y-fronts will remain unsoiled. And it's probably best if your tyres aren't bald. Oh, and you're supposed to turn off your traction control, if you have a car that was built in this century.

Rally drivers, bootleggers and secret agents all like the J-turn, because it allows you to turn a car through a hundred-and-eighty degrees in the narrowest possible space. None of that three-point-turn nonsense. Professional drivers can do it in a space not much wider than the length of their cars. I had a space more than twice the length of the Honda. Easy.

Turn, break, clutch in – that part went okay, I didn't stall the engine. But the car slewed sideways and the rear wheel smacked into the kerb so hard the car shook. I thought it was going to end up on its side. Though perhaps it was only the kerb that stopped my J-turn becoming a three-hundred-and-sixty degree O-my-god turn.

With the pick-up truck now only inches from my rear bumper, I managed to find a forward gear and stamped down on the accelerator. The Honda did that wobbly, fish-taily thing that makes you feel like you're on a fairground ride, and the front tyres screamed in protest.

When it was new, the Honda Civic had a claimed nought-to-sixty time of something like sixteen seconds with the wind behind it. Its top speed is a claimed ninety-nine miles per hour, but I think you'd only achieve that if you dropped it vertically from a great height. I had to hope that the driver of the pick-up truck would be disoriented by the smokescreen the Honda blew out as I raced towards the dizzying speed of not-very-fast.

A kid on a fully-laden butcher's bike with no gears would be able to catch me, and I was pretty sure the red pick-up was sporting a two-point-something litre diesel engine, and probably had multiple turbos. I've never understood what turbos are, but I always imagined them being like the gas flame that shot out of the Batmobile on TV. I remember at school Gaz drooling over a picture of some shiny supercar with a 'V6 turbo' and saying it would fly like 'shit off a stick.' Unfortunately, the Honda didn't have a stick to launch it.

All of these mental distractions and life-before-your-eyes memories were an attempt to avoid the fact that if I was going to survive this encounter, I couldn't out-pace the pick-up: I was going to have to out-drive it. The only problem was, the J-turn was the only trick driving skill I could remember.

As the smoke behind me drifted away, I glanced in the rear-view mirror and saw the fog-lights of the pick-up truck bearing down on me. I was starting to feel like poor old Dennis Weaver in *Duel*. This cherry-red pick-up with chrome teeth had been haunting me for a week, and now it seemed to be closing in for the kill.

Judging by the spotless glossy paintwork and gleaming chrome, the driver of this all-wheel-drive Christine took a great deal of pride in it. That gave me just a glimmer of hope: he probably wouldn't be too keen on damaging it. He'd paid something like thirty-thousand pounds for it, whereas the Honda was worth the price of a fish supper. I could afford to take a few chances. But I also had to remember that his vehicle was fully-equipped with anti-lock brakes, crumple zones, and air-bags. While the chief safety feature of the Honda was thin metal that's easy for the firemen to cut you out of.

His chrome grill was almost in my back seat: too close for me to try any sudden left or right turns, so no opportunity for losing him, or disappearing into hiding before he could follow me.

If ever you find yourself being followed, the best advice is to drive to a well-lit place where there are lots of people, or to the nearest police station. I was being chased in broad daylight, and I was trapped in Mansfield's one-way system, and couldn't figure out how to get to the police station from where I was. And besides, what sort of private detective goes running to the police when he gets into a spot of bother? A smart one, probably.

I didn't want to put anyone else at risk by running a red light at a junction. That always looks great in movies, but all the other cars that get crunched are driven by stuntmen, so real people don't get hurt.

A quick glance in the wing-mirror showed me that the driver of the pick-up was waving his arm out of the window, trying to get me to pull over. As if that was going to happen. But I slowed down, hoping he'd think I was stopping. I even put my indicator on, so it looked like I was pulling in to the kerb. I almost came to a stop, and he pulled in behind me.

Just ahead on the left was a narrow street with 'No Entry' signs, meaning that I shouldn't try to turn in and drive down there.

As soon as I saw the pick-up truck's door start to open, I shot forwards, past the turn-off, and then stopped. I put the car in reverse and backed into the one-way street. Technically, I was driving the wrong way, but my car was pointing the right way. And, as the old joke had it, I was only going one way.

There was no other traffic on the little road, and no pedestrians on the pavements. I carried on backwards. I saw the nose of the pick-up truck edge into view. Then it pulled away, making no attempt to follow me. But I knew he could easily get to the other end of the one-way street and block it, or drive down towards me.

The road curved to the right, so I couldn't see what was coming down it. The pick-up could appear without warning. Right on the bend was a ramp for pedestrians that went up to a metal bridge, leading across to the new bus station. Beneath the bridge was a narrow tunnel for pedestrians. It was only twenty or thirty feet long, the path through it leading to a grassy recreation area beyond. They call it a recreation area: what they really mean is 'dog toilet.'

The Honda Civic was a small hatchback. I thought it should be perfectly possible to drive it through the pedestrian tunnel. Backwards. At speed.

As I mounted the pavement, I caught a glimpse of the red pick-up truck coming around the bend. He was just in time to see me disappear into the tunnel, like a rat into a drainpipe.

I wasn't too worried about hitting anyone. The underpass was only really used at night when people were drunk and desperate for a piss. And besides, even if someone did walk into the tunnel, there was room for me to pass them safely. Probably. Though there was every chance they'd be gassed by the carbon monoxide from the exhaust.

The street end of the tunnel went dark as the pick-up truck stopped across it. I saw the shadowy driver glance my way, but there was no way that he could follow. And to get around to the recreation area by road would mean a fairly long detour, and I'd be long gone before he got there. I hoped.

I emerged from the tunnel and slowed, turning the car so I was facing forwards again. Then I had to stop and consider my options. The entrance to the recreation area was blocked by galvanised barriers designed to allow pedestrians and cyclists in, but to prevent cars from being able to enter. Or, in my case, leave. I briefly considered going out the way I'd come in, but I thought that might be pushing my luck. There was every chance that someone had already reported seeing a car drive through the underpass.

There was a gap in the hedge a little way to the right of the blocked entrance. I drove towards it slowly, trying to see if there was any barbed wire stretched across it. It looked clear. The gap was just about wide enough to drive the Honda through – if I didn't mind a few scrapes to the paintwork. I edged forward, hoping there wasn't a hidden ditch on either side of the hedge.

I tried to shut my ears to the screeching and scraping as the car passed through the hedge. It sounded like someone rubbing chunks of polystyrene together. But that was as bad as it got. The front wheels spun briefly on the wet grass on the other side of the hedge, and that was it. I was through. I paused, with the car sitting on the grass verge at right-angles to the road, and looked left and right. There was no sign of the red pick-up truck.

I drove forwards, across the pavement, and bounced down the kerb onto the road. There was a *clunk* underneath the car, and then a metallic scraping noise. The noise didn't go away as I drove up the road. I looked in the rear-view mirror and saw that the Honda was leaving a trail of bright orange sparks as well as the usual cloud of smoke behind it: it looked like the exhaust of a *Flash Gordon* spaceship.

I wondered what I should do, but then there was a clattering sound, and I didn't need to worry about it anymore, as the silencer made a bid for freedom, commando rolling across the tarmac into the gutter. The sawn-off exhaust didn't seem to make the poison cloud behind me any worse than usual, and the absence of a silencer made the Honda sound mean, rather than breathless. I just wouldn't be able to sneak up on anyone. If I'd had a radio, I would have turned it up.

My phone buzzed in my pocket like a sarcastic wasp. I pulled in at the side of the road and answered. It was Chapman.

"Sorry I missed you," I said, "there was something else I needed to take care of."

"Are you taking the piss?" he asked. He didn't sound happy that I'd stood him up.

"No, no, I'll meet you. Now. Tell me where."

He was quiet for a moment, probably deciding whether or not to tell me to fuck off.

"You know Morton's Haulage?" he asked.

"I've seen their trucks," I said.

"Meet me in their yard. Its off the A38."

He hung up.

Head out of Mansfield on the A38, past the King's Mill Hospital and the reservoir, and keep going, and you eventually cross the border into Derbyshire. Before you get there, you come to the 'Designer Outlet,' which is a slightly more upmarket retail park. Between there and Mansfield is a long stretch of road with turn-offs for a few farms, one of those big second-hand car chains, a pub, and a handful of big industrial sites. I remembered seeing the sign for Morton's Haulage on the side of the road. The site wasn't one of their distribution warehouses, it was more like a big carpark for HGV trailers and containers. They also had a workshop there for repairing trucks.

I turned onto the road that led up to Morton's, and then right through a gate into their yard. Sitting in the car park in front of the main building was the red pickup truck.

How had he got there before me?

Chapter Thirteen

I drove to the other end of the car park and chose a spot where I could see the pick-up truck. There didn't seem to be anyone in it. The car park held half-a-dozen other cars, but there was no sign of movement anywhere. I stayed in the Honda, looking around. Tall metal posts were dotted about the site with CCTV cameras on top. No way to tell whether they were monitored by security staff on-site, or remotely by staff in a control room in another part of the country.

I got out of the car. The site was eerily quiet. It was the middle of the working day, and this was a big site. But nothing moved. Cautiously, I walked towards the pick-up truck. When I got close enough I stopped and fumbled in my jacket pocket for a pen. I wrote the pick-up's registration number on the back of my hand. Maybe I'd ask Duncan to check it out later. It was a Nissan Navara with a double cab; the sort of thing footballers drove for a while, until Bentley tempted them away. It wasn't a truck a tradesman would use. There were no scratches on the floor of the load area. I guessed the driver might easily be dressed up like a country and western singer. I was wrong about that. But not by much.

I looked around for something that I could use as a weapon, in case I needed to defend myself. The only thing I could see was a rusty shovel leaning against a bin of rock salt. It looked like it had been there since last winter. I picked it up and put it over my shoulder. I could swing it easily if I needed to.

As I turned back towards the pick-up truck, I saw the vinyl lettering that had been applied to the side of it. The owner's name. I wouldn't need Duncan's help after all.

The sign on the pick-up said 'Chapman.'

I'd spent the morning trying to escape from the man I wanted to meet. Was that irony, or idiocy? An engine rumbled to life, startling me. The sound seemed to be coming from behind the main building, so I made my way towards it.

I rounded the corner and was in time to see an articulated lorry reverse over a line of traffic cones, flattening them all. At the side of it, a short woman in jeans and a red and black plaid jacket was shouting up at the driver in what sounded like Polish. I watched as the driver stopped the truck and set the brake. The driver leaned out of the cab, nodding his head as the woman continued to yell at him. The poor man looked terrified.

"He'll be fine as long as he doesn't try and argue with her," a voice said at the side of me. "I know that from experience."

I spun to face the speaker. The man looked like an extra from *Pirates of the Caribbean*. Long white hair in a ponytail, with a red bandana tied over it. A thick gold earring, and at least one gold tooth. He was wearing oily-looking black jeans, a battered leather jacket, and square-toed biker books. They'd hire him if Brian Keith and Willie Nelson weren't available. He was also the sort of man who called a spade a spade, and asked me what I was doing with it.

"Might need it to dig myself out of a hole," I said.

He seemed to think that was worth unveiling his gold teeth for. I set the shovel aside, and he extended his hand to shake mine. His left hand was bound up with sticking plaster and what looked like aluminium splints.

"Len Chapman," he said, "but most people call me Gingerbread."

"They do? Why?" I asked.

"Because of my red hair, of course," he said, as if this was blindingly obvious.

His hair was white, with odd flecks of grey. No red. A question about carpets not matching drapes ran through my head, but it was not something I wanted to think about.

"Gingerbread used to be my handle," he said. "You know what that means?"

"CB radios," I said. I'd seen *Convoy*.

He nodded approval. In these days of mobile phones, not many people had heard of citizen band radio.

"I heard you wanted me," he said.

"Who said that?" My turn for a bit of the George Smiley.

"Uncle Benny said you were interested."

"Ah," I said.

"Ah?"

"A flamboyantly dressed older man sent by Uncle Benny? You'll understand if I'm suspicious," I said.

"Flamboyant, really?" He looked down at his clothes, then shrugged. "That why you brought the spade? You thought I might have a dungeon waiting for you?"

I shrugged and he grinned.

"He said you were interested in truck drivers," Gingerbread said.

Again, I was worried about the context of the conversation he'd had with Uncle Benny.

"Okay," I said.

"Regarding a missing container?"

And now I could relax.

"I wanted to ask you some questions," I said.

"You're not planning to slam my fingers in a car door, are you?" he asked.

"No, why?"

He held up his splinted and bandaged hand. "You're not the only one interested in the shipping container."

"Who did that to you?" I asked.

"Let's go and talk in private," he said.

He turned towards the woman, who was now instructing the driver in English, telling him to pull the truck forwards and have another go at reversing it between the two lines of squashed cones.

"Maggie!" He yelled. "Me and the kid are going to get some coffee!"

The woman waved her okay, and turned back to her trainee.

"That's my wife, Margaret," he said. "Been together forty years this year."

"She's Polish?" I asked.

"No, but he is. Maggie learned how to swear in Polish: it gets their attention. A lot of the blokes we get for training now are Polish. I don't have a problem with that: my daddy was Polish. Or so my mother said." He grinned and winked.

We walked towards a workshop behind the main building. It had a huge, hangar-like door that allowed trucks to be driven inside to be worked on. Inside, we stopped to look up at a Mercedes truck painted in Morton's Haulage colours. Gingerbread had that nostalgic look in his eyes.

"You miss it?" I asked.

"I miss being young enough to enjoy it," he said. "It's not the same since the big logistics companies moved in. I liked being my own boss. I've shifted biscuits and rock bands in my time. But now..."

"Now you train the next generation?"

He nodded. "I still do a bit of local work, now and then, to earn a little pocket money. I couldn't stay away completely. What would I do?"

"Spend time with your wife?" I said.

"She's worse than I am. Her father drove fairground trucks, and she was driving lorries before she ever drove a car. She wants to rent one of those big RVs and tour the States."

"But you don't?"

He looked down at his damaged hand.

"Maybe it's time," he said. "It just sounds like something old folks would do."

He led me towards a refrigerator at the back of the workshop. Opening it, he took out two chilled Budweisers.

"Coffee?" he asked.

I took the bottles, twisted the caps off and handed one back to him.

"Who broke your fingers?" I asked.

"He wasn't Polish," he said.

"Rathbanian?"

He shrugged.

"Did Dick Gorse hire you to move the container?" I asked.

"I got a call from someone I sort of knew. Said he needed a driver because someone had let him down. Cash in hand, no paperwork, no questions asked."

"You think Dick stole it from the Rathbanians?"

"No. But there was something in it they wanted."

"Did they say what?"

"Their guy was asking, not telling."

"And you didn't see what was in the container?"

"I had no reason to look. I went there, hitched up the trailer, drove it to a car park, and unhooked it," he said.

"Where did you collect the trailer from?"

"There's an empty warehouse off Hermitage Lane; it was parked in the yard behind that. The gate was open. I drove in. There was nobody there, just the trailer."

"And you took it to...?"

"You know the industrial area where the Kodak Factory used to be? Just off Junction 27?"

I nodded.

"A staff car park in front of one of the units," he said. "There was a big 'To Let' sign in the window, so I'm guessing there was no one in there."

"And none of this struck you as odd?" I asked.

"Of course it was odd. But I've done stranger things. I once had to winch a dead hippo onto the back of a truck and drive it across London in rush hour during a heat wave: I thought it was going to explode."

I tried not to let myself get distracted by that image.

"It sounds as though someone wanted the container moved in stages, so no one driver knew where it came from and where it ended up," I said. "That's a lot of trouble to go to."

"The bloke who did this wanted to know who else was involved," Gingerbread said, holding up his injured hand. "They already knew about Big Dick."

"Do you know anyone else who was involved?" I asked.

"Someone must have picked up the trailer after I dropped it off," he said.

"Someone?"

He looked away, so I wouldn't see him grimace. He wasn't quick enough. "Tiago," he said, still not looking at me.

"How do you know he was the other driver?" I asked.

Gingerbread finished his beer before answering me. "Because I thought it was odd, like you said. I drove off and stashed my truck, and then walked back to see what happened to the trailer. I was half-expecting to see a dozen illegal migrants climb out of the back of it. But there was just another truck backing up to the trailer."

"And you recognised the driver?"

"I knew Tiago when he used to drive trucks up from Spain. We both used to do the Amsterdam-Newcastle ferry, because it was easier to smuggle stuff in that way. Or it was before all this immigrant nonsense locked the place down.

"That's why I wanted to talk to you. You need to warn him, about the Rathbanians. Tell him I'm sorry, but..." He held up his bandaged hand. "He said he'd do the same to Maggie."

"I'd have given him the name if it was me," I said. "I'll speak to Tiago tonight."

"You want another beer?" he asked.

"I should go," I said.

Gingerbread walked with me back to my car. He looked at the Honda and shook his head.

"Most folks today want a car that'll drive itself," He said. "They can't reverse a Fiesta into a parking bay without video cameras and radar. At least you know how to drive that thing. Nice moves this morning."

"I thought you were the Rathbanians," I said. "Wanted to get away."

"You made a pretty good job of it."

"I was a bit worried about scratching the paintwork," I said, "I just had it waxed."

He looked at the rusty Honda and laughed out loud.

"Waxing is for pussies," he said, and winked.

Chapter Fourteen

I'm not one of those people who eats fast food and then tosses the wrapper over his shoulder into the back of the car. No, I screw the paper up into the smallest ball possible and jam it into the glovebox. I've gone almost a year without needing to empty it. Obviously, I don't keep the paper cups hanging around; especially when I've reused them. Today I had treated myself to a budget menu cheeseburger and a chocolate shake: sometimes you just have to push the boat out because, as the advert says, you're worth it. I hadn't had to refill the paper cup, because I wasn't on a stake-out.

I was just slamming the over-stuffed glovebox shut when I caught something out of the corner of my eye. Someone approaching the car. Ever since school I've had superhuman peripheral vision. It was a defence mechanism. Everyone wanted to sneak up on the skinny kid and drop cockroaches down his shirt or fill his blazer pockets with custard. But the rapidly approaching figure wasn't bearing gifts of insects or dessert sauce.

I recognised the shiny hair, the gleaming black jacket, and the buffed shoes. It was ace detective Glossy Matt Lester. He seemed to have acquired a limp since the last time I'd seen him. He wrenched open the passenger door and poked his head in.

"I'd like a word, if I may?" he said.

"Step into my office," I said.

He looked down at the passenger seat, and his lip curled just a little bit before he could stop it. He squared his shoulders manfully and folded himself so he could slide into the little car. His jacket creaked against the ancient vinyl, sounding a lot like my sofa. Farty.

"I was wondering when you'd show up," I said, pretending his arrival hadn't surprised me.

"You were?"

He didn't look comfortable. I liked that.

"Is this your surveillance vehicle?" he asked.

"This is Mansfield," I said, "can't have anything that stands out."

"Undercover in a yellow car, who'd have thought," he said, slamming the door shut.

I'm used to the car. But the smell is probably a bit overwhelming when you're new to it. The vinyl had that ancient cigarette smell all old cars used to have, and on top of that there's the lingering scent of fast-food. And probably piss as well, if I'm honest.

Lester went to open the passenger-side window, and seemed shocked and embarrassed when the winder came off in his hand.

"Don't worry, it always does that," I said.

He managed to slot it back in place and get the glass down about an inch or so.

"Are you surveilling someone?" he asked, peering out through the slightly misty windscreen.

Surveilling?

"No one you care about," I said.

"Not watching Tiago, then?" He asked, not at all casually.

"Why would I be?"

I tried to pretend his question hadn't caught me off-guard. I don't think I fooled him.

"He moved the container for Dick Gorse," Lester said. "But I suspect you know that already."

"I suspected he might have been involved," I said.

That answered his question without actually being a lie.

"Any other suspects you haven't told me about?" Lester asked.

"Psycho-Pete, maybe," I said.

Pete was safely in hiding, so I didn't feel it was too much of a betrayal to point Matt Lester in his direction.

"I've already spoken to him," Lester said. "Pete Kenway doesn't strike me as being the type."

There was a hint of a smile as he said that.

"He didn't try to kiss you, did he?" I asked.

"I didn't get close enough for him to try. Did you?"

Lester laughed when I blushed.

"How did you find him?" I asked.

"The boyfriend, Jerzy Bednarczyk. He managed to lose his police tail, but he didn't know I was following him."

That seemed plausible. I was glad to know Lester hadn't followed me to Pete. Pete must have contacted Jerzy and suggested he deliver the care package in person.

"You don't think Pete Kenway killed Dick Gorse, do you?" Lester asked.

"No," I said. "But I don't think Tiago did either."

"I can understand why you'd want to protect him. He is your brother-in-law."

"*Ex*-brother-in-law," I said.

"From what I've seen, he and your sister are having a trial reconciliation."

"You've been following them?"

Lester nodded.

"But you haven't spoken to him?" I asked.

"I tried," Lester said. "He wasn't very keen on stopping for a chat."

"No?"

"Have you ever been pushed down a flight of stairs?"

"More than once," I said.

"It was my first time. Thought my knee was broken."

I bit my lip so that I didn't laugh. For some reason, I felt I owed Tiago a drink.

"What makes you think Tiago is involved in – whatever it is you're investigating?" I asked.

Lester stared at me. I guessed that he was wondering how much he ought to tell me.

"If you don't want to share information…" I said, twisting the knife.

If he wasn't going to tell me anything, how could he expect me to give him what I had?

He sighed. "I have to protect my client."

I nodded and waited for him to continue.

"But in order to help you understand how urgent this is, she's agreed to let me share some of the details with you. I won't tell you who she is, but I can tell you about her problem. I need you to understand: someone's life is at stake here."

I thought that was a bit melodramatic: he'd been watching too many detective shows.

"Whatever you tell me will be treated in the strictest confidence," I said.

I felt like I was reading the small print for a radio commercial. Terms and conditions apply, errors and omission excepted, void where prohibited by law. I favoured him with my most serious expression. This seemed to satisfy him.

Lester reached into his creaky jacket pocket and pulled out a plain white envelope. He handed it to me. It was ordinary, cheap stationery with a little strip of waxy paper still protecting the sticky bit that you used to seal it shut. I turned it over: there was nothing written on it. I lifted the flap and carefully took out the folded paper that was inside. It was a standard sheet of photocopier paper.

"That's not the original," Lester said.

It was a copy of a ransom note. The original had been put together by gluing down mis-matched letters cut from magazines. Either that, or someone had spent a lot of time in Photoshop making it look like pasted letters had been used. Some parts of the note had been blacked out with a Sharpie, presumably by Lester, before it had been copied.

Mrs. [Blank]

If you want to see your husband alife again, deliver £[blank] to 453449, 361721 at 6pm on Thursday.

Do not tell the police, or he dies.

When money is received, we will text cordinates for husband.

"The kidnapper wasn't an English graduate," I said.

Lester looked at me the way my English teacher used to.

"The co-ordinates are for where?" I asked.

"The money was to be taken to a gym on the north side of town. There was a locker key with the original note," Lester said.

"The ransom was paid?"

He nodded.

"And you got the location for picking up the missing husband?" I asked.

"Yes. It was a lay-by near the golf course."

I thought about that, trying to keep my expression neutral. "But when you got there, no husband?"

"No husband."

"The money was collected from the gym?"

"What do you think?"

"Was it a lot of money?" I asked.

"It was a lot of money," he confirmed.

I wondered how many zeroes were involved.

"What makes you think a shipping container was used?" I asked.

"The text we received said 'Container at' and then co-ordinates."

"That would be a clue," I said.

"We think two drivers were employed," Lester said. "The container was moved in at least two stages. They didn't want us to be able to track where it came from."

"That would make sense. Assuming there *was* a container, and that it *was* moved," I said. "If all you've got is a text from the kidnappers saying…"

"We know the container was used. And we know it was moved. I've spoken to one of the drivers," Lester said.

The one that wasn't Tiago. You know that feeling when things fall into place in your mind, like Tetris pieces? That happened to me at that moment. And you know the scary feeling you get when your stomach drops like when you're in a lift? That happened too.

Either Matt Lester, or someone he was associated with, had discovered that Tiago had driven one of the trucks that moved the container. And Lester had just revealed that he'd spoken to Len 'Gingerbread' Chapman. Was it much of a leap to think that Lester had been the one to break Gingerbread's fingers to get him to talk? I didn't think so.

"Something wrong?" Lester asked.

"I'm trying to figure out how all of this is connected to Dick Gorse's death," I said.

"I would have thought that was obvious."

"There's an obvious explanation," I said, "but I don't like it."

Lester smiled his glossy smile. I wanted to push him down some stairs.

"You're saying that Dick Gorse kidnapped your client's husband and held him for ransom," I said.

"Am I?"

"And that Dick had an accomplice. That accomplice murdered Dick, presumably so he could keep all of the money himself," I said.

"No honour among thieves," Lester said.

"You also think this accomplice decided not to deliver the husband after the ransom was paid? But why? Especially if the container with the husband in it was already in transit?" I asked.

"My guess, and it is only a guess at this point, is that Mr... the husband is dead. The accomplice had to kill him because he was afraid the husband had seen his face and could identify him to the police."

Lester watched me as I thought this over. I still thought he watched too many cop shows.

"Accepting your guess, for the moment," I said, "you are suggesting that this accomplice, the man who murdered Dick *and* your client's husband, is Tiago Zambora."

"As a theory, it explains all the facts," Lester said.

"You said your investigation was urgent. That someone's life depended on it. But you think the husband is already dead?" I said.

"I'd be willing to put money on it. But my client wants to believe he may still be alive, so I must appear to be acting with all haste in trying to find him."

Everything he was saying made sense, in a warped kind of way. But I didn't like any of it. And I didn't like the way I was nodding in agreement with him.

"We need to find the container," I said.

"Tiago will lead us to that, I am sure of it," Lester said.

I nodded again. I wanted to stop doing that, but I couldn't.

"Bring me Tiago," he said. "Or at least arrange a meeting so I can talk to him."

"A meeting," I said. "But you and I will both be there. I'm not handing him over to you until I have some proof that he was involved. All I've seen so far is a photocopy of a ransom note."

"I accept that. But you're not exactly an impartial observer here, are you?"

"I helped put Tiago behind bars once," I said. "I'll do it again if I need to. If what you say is true, I don't want him anywhere near my sister and her son."

Lester was staring at me. I'd obviously summoned enough determination to satisfy him. He nodded and reached for the door handle.

"Make it happen quickly," he said.

He left me holding the copy of the ransom note.

After he'd gone, I opened all the windows. The scent of his aftershave had overwhelmed everything, and I found myself longing for the smell of old grease, cigarettes, and pee.

Chapter Fifteen

"I need to speak to Tiago," I said.

"What makes you think he's here?" Elise asked, avoiding looking at me.

"The fact that it's three in the afternoon and you're in your dressing gown," I said. "Or are you making tea for your *other* fancy man?"

"What's up, Joe?"

Tiago stood in the kitchen doorway in just his boxers, looking like the guy on the cover of a trashy romance.

"Aren't you supposed to be out with your limp vegetables?" I asked.

"My vegetable's not limp," he said, "and I've earned a day off."

"We need to talk," I said.

"Then talk."

"Put some clothes on. We need to talk in private," I said.

Elise glanced from Tiago to me and back.

"It's nothing," Tiago said. "Joe's just helping me out with something. I'll be back down in a minute."

He disappeared upstairs.

"What's this about, Joe?" Elise asked.

"It's what he said. I'm helping him out with something."

"What?"

"He'll tell you if he wants you to know," I said.

"*Joe!*" She learned that tone of voice from our mother.

"Before he went into prison, he was involved in – some things," I said.

"I know, I was there."

"Now he's out, there are some loose ends that need tidying up," I said.

"You two aren't involved in anything illegal, are you?" Elise asked.

"I'm on the side of law and order, remember?"

"You are when it suits you," she said.

"Trust me," I said, "we'll soon have this stuff sorted out, and he can concentrate on his new life. He seems to have decided what he wants that to be."

Elise blushed a little. Ah, the subtle art of flattery as misdirection.

"Where's Jack?" I asked.

"He's going to Nathan's straight from school," Elise said.

We both looked round as Tiago's footsteps thundered down the stairs.

"He didn't mess about," I said. "He's not that quick at everything, is he?"

Elise slapped my arm. "No, he's not. We were at it for hours."

Now she was trying to make me blush. Nice try, sis, but nothing shocks me: I've seen the inside of Uncle Benny's dungeon.

"I hope you kept the noise down," I said, "we don't want Mrs. Kepler complaining to the council again."

"Pour the tea. I'm going up to get dressed."

"Hardly seems worth it: it's almost bedtime," I said.

"You're an arse, Joe, have I ever told you that?"

Elise passed Tiago in the hall, and gave him a look I wasn't supposed to see. He bent to kiss her, but she dodged him.

I was spooning instant coffee into a mug when Tiago came into the kitchen.

"What about the tea?" he asked.

"You hate tea," I said.

"Elise is trying to 'civilise' me."

"Yeah, well, she always was a dreamer," I said. "Let's take this outside, see how the back garden is doing."

I handed him the mug of coffee.

We stood in Elise's back garden with our steaming mugs of coffee.

"You helped Elise fix this place up really nice," he said. "Thank you for doing this."

"Grandpa Max did the garden," I said.

"How is he?"

"He forgets some stuff, but mostly he's okay."

"I like him, he is a character."

"He's stopped referring to you as 'that Dago bastard.' Though I suspect he might start up again soon."

I glanced towards the upstairs window, where Elise was looking down at us.

"Do not give Elise a hard time about this, please," Tiago said. "It is not her fault."

"Not her fault that she can't resist your Spanish charm?" I said. "She's a grown-up, she's responsible for her own choices."

"You think I am a bad choice?"

"Based on past experience?" I said.

"I hoped you and I could be friends this time. A fresh start," he said.

"I'm just worried about how Jack will take it, when he finds out. He's already lost his father once."

"Elise and I are going to talk to him when he comes home tonight. No more sneaking around behind his back. He's not going to lose me again."

"Isn't he?" I asked.

"No, this I promise."

He looked sincere. And if he and my sister had got to the stage where they were going to talk to Jack about being a family again, maybe he really did want this to be true. But I couldn't afford to accept it at face value. I didn't want Elise and Jack to have to watch as he was led off to prison again.

"What did you do with the money, Tiago?" I asked.

"Money?" He frowned.

"For the shipping container."

"I have it," he said.

He put down his mug and reached into the back pocket of his jeans, pulling out a worn leather wallet. He opened it and took out some folded bank notes, held them towards me. I didn't take them.

"I haven't spent any of it. One hundred pounds."

He gestured for me to take it. I didn't.

"That's all there is?" I asked.

"How much do you think there should be? It was one night's work. Cash in hand. Here, take it. For your – what is the word? *Retainer.* Twenty dollars a day, plus expenses, yes?"

He was absolutely earnest. And there were no alarm bells ringing in the back of my head. But maybe Glossy Matt was right, maybe I was too close to this.

"Keep it," I said, "I don't charge family. Use it to take Elise and Jack somewhere nice. No pizza."

Tiago refolded the twenty-pound notes and put them back in his wallet.

I took the white envelope out of my jacket pocket and pulled the ransom note out of it. I passed it to Tiago and watched him as he unfolded it. His forehead creased into a frown.

"What is this?" he asked. "A case you are working on?"

There had been no hint of recognition in his face, and the paper in his hands hadn't shaken in the slightest. He was either the coolest customer I had ever come across, or he was telling the truth.

"Yes, it's a case," I said.

"Kidnap?"

I nodded.

"Who?" He asked.

"I don't know," I said. "Another detective is investigating it. He thinks the missing man was in the container you moved. And that he was probably dead."

I saw the colour drain from Tiago's face, and in a weird way, it made me glad. You can't fake something like that. And there was a faint tremor when he passed the paper back to me. I didn't say anything, because I wasn't sure what to say. I'd just pissed on whatever dreams he'd had for a new life with his son and ex-wife. I'd told him there was every chance that he could go back to prison. For a long time. And for a crime he hadn't had any real involvement in. He seemed stunned, and for a second I thought he was struggling to breathe. I think it was just a long, shuddering sigh.

"What should I do?" He asked.

"Stay out of sight," I said. "Call in sick tomorrow. Do you have a doctor?"

He shook his head. He really did look sick.

"I know a doctor," I said, "he'll give you a note that'll keep your boss and your probation officer happy. Tell them you have a stomach bug, they won't want you anywhere near food with that."

Tiago nodded. "What about Elise?" he asked. "What about Jack?"

"I don't know," I said, "you have to make that decision."

He took a moment to think about that.

"I will not see Jack today," he said. "I will ask Elise to tell him that I am no longer in prison. And that I would like to see him at the weekend. On Sunday. She must see what is reaction is before we rush into a big reunion."

He nodded, satisfied with his plan, but not happy with it.

"And Elise?" I asked.

"I will tell her that you and I had the heart-to-heart, and that you told me I must not rush into things," Tiago said. "You said it was not reasonable for me to come back into their lives and expect to be welcomed back with open arms, after what I did. We must all get to know one another again. For Jack's sake."

That sounded like the sort of over-protective bullshit I might come out with. And if Elise could blame me, then her relationship with Tiago might not be affected too badly. I couldn't ask him to take a bullet to protect the family if I wasn't prepared to do the same, so I nodded agreement.

"We will not tell Elise about this. Not yet," he said. "But if you and I decide that Sunday with Jack should not happen, I will tell her everything."

Today was Tuesday. I had until Sunday to come up with something that would stop my nephew and my sister losing Tiago again. And in the meantime, we had to make sure that the police, Glossy Matt, and the Rathbanians didn't get their hands on Tiago.

"Why the Rathbanians?" I asked.

"What?" Tiago said.

"When you first asked me to find the container, you said the Rathbanians wanted it. What is their connection to it?"

"Something Big Dick said to me: Do not let the Rathbanians get their hands on it. I thought perhaps he had stolen whatever was in the container from them."

"Do not let the Rathbanians get their hands on it," I repeated. "Maybe that's what happened to it. Maybe they have it."

"Is possible, I guess. But why would they want a container with a dead husband in it?" Tiago asked.

"We won't know that until we find out who the dead man is," I said.

"How do we do that?"

"I have to trick someone into telling me," I said. "But first, we need to get you someplace safe."

I knew someone who'd be happy to help him. And who had somewhere secure for him to stay. I smiled.

"You have a place in mind?" Tiago asked.

"I do," I said. "I think it's time you met Uncle Benny."

Chapter Sixteen

Mansfield after dark can be intimidating if you're not used to it, especially on a Friday night, when it's almost, but not quite, as scary as Blackpool. But midweek it's generally quiet, with only a handful of hard cases hanging about on the street comparing scars and tattoos. And a few tough-looking men as well. I was used to it, and didn't let it put me off heading out in search of a late-night snack. But I did drive. And keep the car doors locked.

The chip shop nearest my flat didn't do great chips; they were usually a bit soggy and never seemed quite hot enough. When I fancy chips, I usually drive a couple of miles down the road to *Dave's Fish Bar*. Dave's chips are fifty-pence dearer, and there's always a queue, but they're worth it. Golden and crispy. And so hot you have to blow them before you eat them. A tray of chips, salt and vinegar, what more do you need? On my budget, nothing.

I couldn't park in front of the shop; the street in front is always jammed with cars and scooters. I'd pulled into the one-way street up the road. There was a public phone box on the corner, and I ducked inside and dialled Uncle Benny's number.

"Did you get Tiago all settled in?" I asked.

I expected him to start gushing madly about his gorgeous Spanish houseguest.

"He never showed up," Uncle Benny said. He sounded like he'd been pouting for hours.

Tiago had said he would pick up a few belongings from home, and then make his way to Uncle Benny's house. I should probably have known better than to believe him.

"I was making paella," Uncle Benny said.

Perhaps Tiago had been right to do a runner, what with Uncle Benny's cooking and the after-dinner tour of his 'special room.'

"I'm sorry we put you out," I said, "something else must have come up."

"I was only doing it as a favour to you," Uncle Benny said. "Give me your number and I'll give you a ring if he turns up."

Not going to happen, I thought.

"I'll check with you again in a couple of hours," I said, and hung up.

I headed back to the Honda, blowing on my chips. The fumes from the vinegar made my eyes run.

Sometimes you'll get a cheeky kid come up to you and say, 'Gis a chip, mate,' and if his hands look clean, I'm usually happy to offer him one. What you don't usually get is some bloke in a leather bomber jacket falling into step beside you, his elbow rubbing yours.

"All right, chief?" I said.

He just carried on walking, staring straight ahead. Then another one appeared on the other side of me, dressed the same: black leather jacket, black jeans, boots, military haircut. Same stony expression. They both had that broad shoulders and no neck thing going, and while their knuckles weren't dragging on the floor, I'm pretty sure these apes could scratch their ankles without bending. Neither of them spoke or even looked at me.

"Chip?" I asked, extending the tray towards one, and then the other.

No response.

I didn't like the feeling that they were some sort of escort, leading me off somewhere, so I stopped suddenly, to see if they'd carry on without me. But all that happened was that a third ape, who had obviously been following, bumped into the back of me. Before I could turn, he shoved me with both hands, sending me stumbling and my chips flying, scattering them all over the pavement. I whirled round, angry now, and found myself face-to-face with another blank-faced thug.

"What?" I said.

"Move," he said, inclining his head slightly.

"What's going on?" I asked.

"Get on the bus." He had an Eastern European accent, Rathbanian I guessed.

There was an orange single-decker bus waiting at the side of the road, its engine idling, smoke rising from its exhaust into the night air. It was the regular service to Nottingham, and it seemed to be waiting for us.

"Thanks, but my car is round the corner," I said.

He took a step forward and shoved me again. I glared at him. If I'd thought he would have noticed, I'd have pushed him back.

"Bus," he said.

"I hope you've got a Mango Card," I said, "because I just spent all my cash on chips."

Surrounded by the three Big Gorillas, I approached the open door of the bus. As we got there, a young couple tried to board, but the first BG, let's call him Barry, stepped forward to block their way.

"This one is out of service," Barry said.

The young man looked like he was going to challenge this, but he glanced at the other two, Robin and Maurice, and thought better of it.

We climbed aboard and the doors folded shut behind us.

"Drive," Barry said.

The bus pulled away, the driver looking straight ahead, determined not to see anything that was about to happen.

This wasn't one of the smart new buses with wi-fi and air-conditioning: it was the night service, with ancient, mis-matched seats, and vinyl floor they could swill down to get rid of the spilled curry sauce and vomit. Normally at this time, it would have been at least half-filled with young folks who couldn't afford to stay out and get any drunker. But the bus had been emptied. There was just one person standing at the back of the bus. He was older and heavier, but he was obviously another BG. I'd run out of band members, so I'll call the fourth ape Sergei. I'll spell it that way, but in my head it's more like Saggy. Someone behind me pushed me in his direction.

The neon lights inside the bus had that slightly bluish glow that make you feel like you're in a fish-tank. Everything seems too bright and too sharp, even when you haven't had a drink.

Sergei sat down on one of the seats, and indicated that I should sit on the opposite side of the aisle to him.

"Thank you for joining us," he said, as if I had been given a choice in the matter.

"I'd offer you a chip, but..."

I held out the tray, which now only contained a few hard remnants of broken chip. Sergei snatched the tray from me and tossed it onto the back seat.

"I'd done with it anyway," I said.

Who Killed Big Dick?

Bullies are only happy when you show them fear. I try not to give them that satisfaction.

"You are the detective, yes?" Sergei asked.

"Joe," I said, "Joe Lucke, with an 'e.'"

"Okey dokey, Joe Lucky. Let us see if you live up to your name, shall we? We will play a game."

"You're not going to break my fingers, are you?" I asked.

"No!" He seemed genuinely shocked by the suggestion. "Why would you ask that?"

"I thought that's what you did."

"Never! I break a man's legs – but that was only once."

"I was misinformed," I said.

Sergei reached into his pocket and pulled out a handgun. It was a short-barrelled revolver of some kind. I'd only ever seen them on American cop shows. He held it out so that I could see it clearly in his hands. It was a sort of gunmetal grey, unsurprisingly, and looked a lot heavier than the pistols you get with a PlayStation. He snapped open the cylinder and spun it, showing me that it was unloaded. Then he took a shiny brass bullet from his pocket, showed that to me, then slotted it into one of the six empty chambers. It was like watching table-top magic for Mafiosi.

"You have heard of Russian roulette, yes?" Sergei said. "They put one bullet in the gun, close it up and spin the cylinder. And then they pull the trigger. Does the gun shoot the bullet or not? Are you lucky or are you dead?"

He looked down at the gun, and then reached into his pocket and took out a second bullet. He slid it into one of the empty chambers. He closed the cylinder and gave it a spin. It made a sound like a metal rattlesnake.

"The game we will play is similar, but it is Rathbanian roulette. We put *two* bullets in the gun.

Twice the fun, eh? And a much quicker game. Like your T20, eh?"

"Like what?" I asked.

"T20. Cricket!" He said. "Are you not English?"

"We don't all like cricket," I said.

"Good, then we will not play cricket. Here is our game. I will ask you a question. You will answer. If you give me the wrong answer, I will spin the cylinder, and I will fire the gun at your head."

Sergei smiled and pointed the revolver at the middle of my forehead. I felt cold sweat trickle down my neck into my shirt.

"These questions, they're not popular music, are they? Because I'm rubbish on boy bands."

His eyes bulged and he looked for a moment as if he was going to explode. And then he did. His laugh was a great big guffaw that turned his face red.

"I like you, Joe Lucky. Humour in the face of death!"

"I'm going to die, then, am I?"

"That is not up to me, is it?" Sergei spun the cylinder of the gun. "Are you ready, Mr. Lucky?"

"Fire away," I said. Then: "No, wait! I meant ask your first question."

"He is amusing, this one," Sergei said to Robin.

Robin grunted non-committally.

Outside, the streets were just passing smears of light. I had no idea where we were, but it seemed that the bus driver was following his normal route, heading for Sutton bus station.

"Where is Tiago Zambora?" Sergei asked.

"He's gone into hiding," I said.

Sergei sprang forward and pressed the muzzle of the gun against my cheek.

"Tell me something I do not know," he said.

He stared into my eyes, and I stared back. His finger tightened on the trigger, and the hammer began to move. I didn't breathe, wondering whether I would hear the dry click of the hammer finding an empty chamber, or an explosion of heat and light and pain that would mean that my luck had run out. I didn't flinch, I didn't blink. I felt my eyeballs drying out in that eternity of a heartbeat, but I was determined to die with my eyes open, staring into the eyes of my killer. I owed myself that much.

Sergei's finger eased off the trigger.

"Tiago doesn't know where the container is," I said.

Sergei lowered the gun and moved back to his seat. "What do you know about the container?" he asked.

"Only that Tiago was paid to move it. He doesn't know what was in it. And he doesn't know what happened to it after he left it in the lay-by."

"He said this to you?"

"Yes."

"And you believe him."

"He has no reason to lie to me. I'm trying to help him," I said.

"Hmm. He is your brother-in-law, perhaps he does not lie to you."

Perhaps Sergei didn't have a brother-in-law. Mine lied to everyone, including himself.

"Do you know where he is?" Sergei asked.

I shook my head. "Tiago was supposed to go and stay with Uncle Benny, but he ran away."

"Who is this Uncle Benny?" Sergei asked.

"He's an older guy who has a dungeon under his house," Maurice, the youngest of Sergei's apes, said. Before he'd finished speaking, you could see that he was regretting having said this.

"And you know this how?" Sergei asked.

The younger man had luminous patches of red on his cheeks as he stuttered out his reply.

"I-I've heard people t-talk about him."

Sergei shook his head and turned back to me.

"Tiago has disappeared. How do we find him?" he asked.

"Why do you want to?" I asked. "If you find him, he will only tell you what I have already said."

"I think we should have a little talk with him anyway."

"Do you want Tiago, or do you want the container?" I asked.

"You know where it is?"

"No, but I think I can find it. That's what Tiago asked me to do. If I hand the container over to you, will you leave Tiago alone?"

"I think about it. We may have to hurt him a little bit; show him that it is a bad idea to cross us. But nothing that will leave a scar."

I wondered if I should try and negotiate a better deal for Tiago. But I was also keen to get away without being hurt a little bit myself.

"You will find the container," Sergei said. "You will tell us where it is. You don't look inside."

I nodded, accepting these terms.

"Very well. I will give you forty-eight hours. If you do not find the container by then, we will find you. And the next time we speak, I will put *five* bullets in the gun, and we will have a very short conversation."

He leaned over and pressed the button to ring the bell. The 'Bus Stopping' sign lit up, and the bus slowed.

As the bus stopped, two cars appeared: one pulled up in front of the bus, the other behind it. Sergei, Barry and Robin left the bus and got into the car in front. Sergei told Maurice to take me back to my car. The two of us got into the rear of the second car, and Maurice said something to the driver in Rathbanian. The car u-turned and headed back towards Mansfield.

Maurice tried the silent, staring ahead thing, but I could tell his heart wasn't really in it.

"What's your name?" I asked.

"Evgeny," he said, not looking at me.

"I'll tell Uncle Benny you said hello, shall I?"

I saw the driver's shoulders shaking in silent laughter.

Evgeny's face was flushed scarlet again, and the heat kept us warm all the way back to the chip shop.

Chapter Seventeen

Indigestion kept me awake, so I hardly slept. I don't think it was the chips: I'd only managed to eat a handful before the Rathbanian ape-man had knocked them out of my hands. Perhaps it was performance anxiety. Last night's magical mystery tour with the monkey troupe hadn't changed the focus of my investigation: I still needed to find the shipping container. But my new Eastern European friends had put added pressure on me to find it quickly. I had two days, after which I'd be playing my first, and last, game of Rathbanian roulette.

Lying awake in the dark, I'd gone over everything I'd discovered so far, and tried to come up with some possible next moves. I needed new information or some clue that would lead me to the container's hiding place. If Matt Lester was right, Dick Gorse had an accomplice; someone who helped him carry out the kidnapping. I didn't want to believe that Tiago was the one involved, because this co-conspirator was also the most likely person to be Big Dick's murderer. But guilty or not, I needed to talk to Tiago again. If I could find him.

Assuming Tiago wasn't Big Dick's partner in crime, I needed to know who was. Maybe not-so-psycho-Pete would have some idea who Dick had chosen to work with. And failing that, Dick's wife Charmaine might be able to tell me who her husband's drinking buddies were. Assuming he had time for drinking in between the time he spent working and the time he spent shagging.

Exhaustion must have overcome me as dawn was starting to lighten the sky, because I remember hearing the first twittering of the birds outside, and then nothing until I rolled over and saw that the clock said 10am.

I pulled on some clothes and walked down to the corner shop. I thought milk would help to settle my stomach. I drank from the carton as I walked back towards the flat. The late spring sun was shining brightly, and a couple of small brown birds in a tree were being unnecessarily chirpy. I decided not to go back upstairs. Instead, I turned towards the Honda. I'd head over to the house where Pete was holed-up and see if he knew who Big Dick's partner in crime was.

There was no answer when I knocked. This was annoying, but not really surprising. Matt Lester had said that he'd tracked Pete down and questioned him, so this hideout was no longer hidden.

I pulled out my phone, intending to text Jerzy to see if he knew where Pete was now hiding, but it rang in my hand before I'd managed to call up the minuscule menu and select the 'message' option on the little screen.

"Joe? It's Charmaine, I need your help. I don't know what to do!"

There was a note of panic in her voice.

"What's happened?" I asked, keeping my voice calm.

"I just got home. From Tesco," she said. "Someone has been in the house. A burglar!"

"I'll be there in a few minutes," I said. "I want you to leave the house now and go to a neighbour's. Stay on the phone until you're inside with them."

There was a chance that the burglar was still in the house, and I didn't want her to risk confronting them alone. Once she had assured me that she was safe in her neighbour's kitchen, I went back to the car and drove straight over to Charmaine's house.

I found Charmaine inside waiting for me. Her neighbour's husband had come back with her, and he'd checked every room. He was armed with a *Game of Thrones* replica sword, and was just leaving as I got there.

"Winter's coming," I said, as he left.

"You nor nothin', Jor Lucke," he said, grinning.

He knew me, but I didn't recognise him. To be honest, all the dick-heads that had flushed my school books tended to look the same. More like Hodor than Jon Snow.

As I went in the house, I could see that the front door hadn't been damaged.

"I'm sorry to bother you with this, but with Dick gone I didn't know who else to call," Charmaine said.

"It's no problem," I said, "security is one of the things we do."

Many private detective agencies provide security advice, and we liked to pretend that we were just like a proper agency.

"How did they get in?" I asked.

"Back door," Charmaine said.

She showed me through to the kitchen. The bottom section of the back door had been kicked in, and the hole was easily big enough for an adult to climb through.

"We never replaced it when we had the double-glazing done," Charmaine said. "They got into the garage and the shed as well. Cut the locks."

Whoever broke in had come prepared. Opportunist thieves don't carry bolt-cutters in their back pockets: they're the size of hedge-cutters and weigh a lot more.

"Darren is going to come back and nail a board over it for me," Charmaine said.

Presumably Darren was the swordsman.

"What was taken?" I asked.

"That's the odd thing. As far as I can tell, they didn't steal anything."

I looked around. There was a TV that would have filled one wall of my flat, with a Sky box, a Blu-ray player and a PlayStation underneath: they hadn't been touched. There was also a decent-looking hi-fi with a turntable. From what I could see, every cupboard and every drawer had been opened. Papers and small items were strewn everywhere. But nothing was broken: this wasn't an act of vandalism. Whoever had done it was obviously searching for something. My guess was that they were looking for something that would lead them to the location of the container and the missing husband.

"Perhaps they were disturbed before they'd finished?" Charmaine said.

"Perhaps," I said. "Did Dick keep any paperwork at home; work-related stuff?"

Charmaine shook her head. "He never brought work home."

"What about money? Do you have a safe?"

"There's a floor safe," she said. She didn't seem keen to reveal its location, and I didn't really need to know.

"Any papers in it?"

"Just cash and my jewellery. The deeds for the house and our wills are at the bank."

I walked around the house. The front door and all the windows looked new. The back door had been the weak point. That happens quite often: people replace the stuff neighbours can see, and leave themselves vulnerable in out-of-the-way corners.

"Do you have a burglar alarm?" I asked.

I'd seen a box on the front of the house, but that didn't mean there was a working system.

Charmaine nodded.

"We set it at night," she said, "downstairs. I don't always set it when I go out. I don't like it when they go off and upset the neighbours."

I wasn't going to argue with the logic of that. I would write a brief security review for her later, and I'd mention it then. I'd also spotted a couple of places where she should put in additional sensors to beef up the protection from the alarm. And I'd suggest she clean the fingerprints from the floor where the safe was hidden. From a certain angle, in a certain light, they were a dead giveaway.

"We always advise that you set the alarm whenever you leave the house," I said.

"I should," Charmaine said. That didn't mean that she would.

"Apart from the carpet store, did Dick have any other business premises?" I asked.

"No, we only had the one place," she said.

"No houses or flats that he rented out to tenants?"

"Nothing like that. We sold carpets and beds. And did some carpet-cleaning, and that was it."

I would ask Duncan to run a few searches to double-check that, though I suspected they wouldn't turn up anything useful. It was unlikely that Big Dick would have left a paper-trail leading directly to his criminal side-lines.

"Do you think this is related to Dick's death?" Charmaine asked, indicating the chaos all around her.

I didn't want to frighten her unnecessarily. But lying to her might mean she didn't take all the precautions she ought to.

"I think it's possible," I said. "And I think whoever did this, may not have found what they were looking for.

They will probably want to search Dick's car, and the carpet store, if they haven't already."

Charmaine thought about this, and then nodded. It made sense.

"It's unlikely that they'll come back here," I said. "But you should be careful, just in case."

"I'm going to make sure it's all locked up, and that the alarm is on," she said.

She probably would, for a few days, before all this faded from memory.

"Do you want a hand tidying all this up?" I asked.

Charmaine shook her head. "Mum's coming over."

"Oh good."

"I'll be fine," she said. I don't think she said it to convince me.

"Apart from the carpet-cleaning, did Dick have any other side-lines?" I asked.

"Not that I know of," Charmaine said. "He did a few jobs off the books, but other than that..." She shrugged.

"But you didn't want to call the police about the break-in," I said.

She looked away, guiltily. "Dick never liked the police."

"Has anyone else been here asking questions about Dick?" I asked.

"No," Charmaine said. "Apart from that reporter from the *Post*. Said he was going to write a short piece about Dick's death."

"Tall bloke, shiny hair and a dimple in his chin?" I asked. Not exactly a stab in the dark.

"Yes. You know him?"

"He asked me some questions too," I said.

"He asked me who would continue Dick's business now that he's..." Charmaine's eyes filled up with tears.

"That's not something you need to think about right now," I said. "The guys who worked for Dick will keep things ticking over."

Charmaine nodded. The store was closed for now, but Big Dick's crew were around to receive and deliver anything that been ordered before his death.

"Thanks, Joe," she said, "for everything."

"If you need anything, or you just want someone else to talk to, give me a ring," I said.

She nodded again. She looked like she needed a hug, but I didn't know her well enough to provide one. Though I suspected her mother wasn't big on hugs, so maybe I ought to step up? In the end, Charmaine saved me from having to make the decision. She wrapped her arms around me and squeezed. I was just getting giddy from lack of oxygen when the front door opened and Charmaine's mother breezed in.

"You didn't waste any time getting your feet under the table, did you?" she said, with a stare that a sphinx would have been proud of.

"Mother!" Charmaine said, releasing me. "Joe just came round to review my security."

"Is that what he calls it? Checking your bra was securely fastened, was he?"

"Mother!"

"In my day, we allowed an appropriate period of mourning before we went around embracing other men."

"The only reason you didn't go around embracing other men is that none of them would touch you," Charmaine said. "And besides, Joe's not like that."

"I'm not gay," I said.

"You just be careful, that's all I'm saying," Charmaine's mother said. "Some of them only act gay."

With that she swept past us and disappeared into the kitchen.

"I should go," I said. "When you're tidying up, if you discover anything is missing, let me know; then I can put the word out."

Charmaine nodded. "I will. Thanks again."

The neighbour, Darren the Barbarian, was returning with a stout piece of plywood and a toolbox as I left.

"Hold the door," he said, grinning again.

"What you talkin' about, Willis?" I asked.

He just frowned at me.

As I drove away, I thought about what Charmaine had said. Glossy Matt Lester had been to see her, posing as a reporter for the local paper. That wasn't necessarily suspicious in itself. But the fact that her house had been broken into soon afterwards did seem too much of a coincidence. Matt Lester wasn't quite the rookie detective he had made himself out to be. And it was possible that burglary wasn't the only thing he was prepared to do to get what he wanted.

I went back to the flat and put two slices of stale bread under the grill. There were a couple of jars in the cupboard that held enough jam between them to cover two slices. Or so I thought. One of them turned out to be an old jar of Branston pickle that was now the colour and consistency of tar. Lunch ended up being one dry slice of toast, and one thinly smeared with strawberry jam.

I thought about using the black pickle to fill a crack in the bathroom wall under the sink, but it smelled funny so I threw the jar in the bin.

I turned on the laptop and searched for the detective agency Matt Lester worked for. They had a smart modern website, using a slightly lighter blue than the police used for theirs, but suggesting a similar dedication to crime investigation and safety. I found the 'contact' page and dialled the number given.

"Good afternoon, Sherwood Investigations, how may I help you?" The receptionist's voice was bright and professional.

"Good afternoon, I'm trying to reach one of your investigators: he gave me his card, but I'm afraid I misplaced it," I said.

"That's not a problem. What was the name of the agent you spoke with?"

"It was Matt Lester."

The pause at the other end lasted for a beat too long, and when the receptionist spoke again, her tone was subtly altered.

"Please hold the line a moment, I'll see if he's in the office."

She put me on hold and the music sounded like someone playing *Greensleeves* on a kazoo. But that might just have been my crappy phone. If I had a detective agency, the hold music would be the theme from *Magnum P.I.* or *The Rockford Files*.

There was a click and the music stopped.

"Hello? I understand you were trying to reach Matt Lester?" A male voice, not Lester's.

"Yes, it's in relation to the kidnapping case," I said.

I thought I'd say that, in the vain hope that he might let slip the name of the kidnap victim.

"I'm afraid that's not something I can help you with," the man said.

"Could you let me have his number, so that I can call him directly?" I asked.

"I'm afraid Matt Lester is no longer with the agency, and hasn't been for some time."

"Oh," I said.

"Can I ask who's calling?"

I thought about hanging up, but didn't.

"I work for Donoghue Investigations," I said.

"You must be Joe Lucke."

He didn't need to be Sherlock Holmes to figure that out: I was the only person who worked for Fat Duncan.

"That's me," I said.

"James Croft," he said, "it's good to finally talk to you. Duncan speaks very highly of you."

"I should ask for a raise," I said.

James Croft forced a laugh. "When did you meet Matt Lester?" he asked.

"Last week," I said. "He told me he was with your agency."

"That's a bit naughty," Croft said.

"Did he leave to set up on his own?" I asked.

"Er – I'm not sure."

The way he said it made me think Matt Lester hadn't chosen to leave Sherwood Investigations.

"I heard that he can be a bit heavy-handed interviewing witnesses," I said.

"I can't really comment on that," Croft said, "but he didn't really fit in here. We like to do things in a certain way."

"No breaking people's fingers, eh?" I said.

"Sorry, what was that?"

"Nothing important," I said. "Thanks for taking my call."

I hung up and stared at my phone. Something in the way James Croft had evaded my questions had made me suspicious, and that had set my mind whirling even as I was speaking to him.

I called Gingerbread's number and got his voicemail. I left a message, asking him to give me a ring when he could. I felt sure Matt Lester had been the one who broke Gingerbread's fingers when he 'questioned' him, but I needed to be absolutely sure. Evidence was beginning to point to Lester being tangled up in the conspiracy surrounding Dick Gorse's death, but it was all circumstantial so far. Gingerbread was the only potential witness.

Chapter Eighteen

As I sat pondering my next move, the phone rang in my hand. It wasn't Gingerbread, it was my sister.

"Hey," I said. "Any word from Tiago?"

"I was 'phoning to ask you that," Elise said.

I thought it was more likely Tiago would call her than me.

"He's probably just worried that our phones are being monitored," I said.

"You think that's all it is?" She didn't sound convinced.

"He'll let us know where he is, when he's sure it's safe," I said. "It's probably better that we don't know."

"Why? I wouldn't tell anyone. Would you?"

I thought about Gingerbread's fingers being slammed in a car door, and wondered if I would give Tiago up if someone did that to me. I decided not to ask Elise what she'd do.

"Of course not," I said, "he's family."

Even if he is a pain in the arse and doesn't trust me to help him, I thought.

"You don't think anything's happened to him, do you?" Elise asked.

"Tiago can look after himself," I said.

"But what if there was more than one of them?"

I wondered if Tiago had mentioned the Rathbanians to her. It seemed unlikely. But Elise wasn't stupid, she could figure out who he was likely to be in trouble with locally.

"Isn't there anything we can do?" she asked.

The best thing I could do for Tiago was find that blasted shipping container and try and bring this whole sorry mess to some sort of conclusion. But I couldn't tell Elise that without explaining a whole lot of backstory, which would include admitting to her that both Tiago and I had been lying to her about his involvement in a kidnapping and, possibly, a murder.

"I'll stop by his place later and see if he left any clue to where he's gone," I said.

"Thanks Joe. Let me know as soon as you find something."

"He'll be home soon," I said.

After Elise hung up, I stared at my phone. I hated it when family were caught up in the cases I was working on. It seemed to happen too often. And El Zorro always seemed to be to blame.

Gingerbread called me mid-afternoon and asked me if I wanted to go and get a 'coffee.' I told him I was in need of several coffees. We decided to meet at the new pub that had been built near the hospital. It was at the northern end of a new housing development, and looked like it had been built from Lego.

Gingerbread was sitting at one of the tables outside when I got there, an empty pint glass in front of him. I went inside and fetched two more pints.

"How's your hand?" I asked, setting the drinks down.

Gingerbread had his hands on the rough wooden table and had been staring at the bandaged hand when I came out.

"Hurts like hell, and it's extremely frustrating," he said. "I put on boots this morning and couldn't tie the laces. You never realise how many things you need a left hand for."

"You'll soon be back playing the piano," I said.

"That'll be good, because I couldn't before." He picked up his drink and downed about half of it.

"What can you tell me about the bloke who did it?" I asked.

"He was a cunt."

"Did he tell you his name?"

"Yes, he said: Good evening, my name's Raymond, I'll be your torturer tonight."

"You've no idea who he was?" I asked.

"Never seen him before."

"Was he about my height, straight dark hair, shiny, blue eyes, and a dimple in his chin?"

Gingerbread nodded, narrowing his eyes. "Who is he?"

"He told me his name was Matt Lester. When I met him, he was pretending to be a private detective."

"Who is he working for?"

"I don't know. Maybe nobody. He was fired by his last employer. They didn't approve of his methods."

"Can't say I'm a big fan," Gingerbread said. "Did he kill Big Dick?"

"It's possible. But I don't have any evidence that proves he did," I said.

"What would it take to prove it? I'd like to see that bastard put away forever."

"I need to find the shipping container," I said. "I have no idea what is inside it. It's like that suitcase in *Pulp Fiction*. I think if I find it, I'll have all the answers I need. I can put an end to this thing. But I have no idea where to look for it."

I told Gingerbread about my encounter with the Rathbanians, and my deadline which was now almost half gone. We drained our glasses, and he went to fetch another round, coming back with two glasses balanced on a round plastic tray.

"You need to look for it in a more obvious place," Gingerbread said, sitting down.

"What?"

"Where did they hide the purloined letter?" he asked.

"The what letter?"

"Purloined. Stolen."

"No idea," I said.

"Edgar Allan Poe," he prompted. "Inventor of the mystery story?"

"I thought he wrote those Vincent Price movies?" I said.

"Those as well. In 'The Purloined Letter,' the thief hid the stolen item in plain view, where no one would think to look for it."

"Where did he put it?"

"Are you sure you're a detective? Use your analytical skills."

"I mostly follow blokes who are cheating on their wives or watch employees to see if they forget to pay for the things they sneak out down their trouser-legs."

"Where's the most obvious place to hide a letter?" Gingerbread asked.

"Written or French?" I asked.

He gave me what my mum used to call a 'Paddington Bear stare.'

"The missing letter was hidden in a letter rack," Gingerbread said. "Many people *saw* it there, but nobody actually *found* it."

That sounded like one of those puzzles that sounds too clever to be true. But what he'd said did make some sense.

"If you wanted to hide a container, you'd put it among other containers, so it wouldn't look out of place," I said.

Gingerbread pointed at me and tapped the side of his nose.

"The trouble with containers is that you see them all over the place," I said. "On trucks; in lay-bys; used as tool stores in yards; lined up and hired out for storage... they don't look out of place anywhere."

"True. But if you can narrow down the search area, there's only a finite number of possible hiding places," he said.

"How do we narrow the search area? A container on a truck can be driven anywhere. It could be in Europe by now."

"But it isn't," Gingerbread said. "Think about it. Whoever has it intends to either use it or destroy it. They're going to keep it close to them, where they can keep an eye on it. They stole it, so they'll worry about it being stolen."

"Okay," I said.

"The last-known position of the container was that lay-by where Tiago left it. We take that as the centre of our search zone."

I nodded: that made sense.

"I moved the truck less than ten miles," he said. "Tiago moved it less than ten miles. Let's begin by assuming that whoever took it, moved it a similar distance. We draw a circle with a radius of ten miles around our starting point, and look inside that for potential hiding places."

"Why ten miles?" I asked.

"Why not? You have to start somewhere. If there's nothing within that first circle, you move out another five or ten miles, expanding the search area."

"You're talking about searching an area twenty miles across and twenty miles from top to bottom. It would take forever. Unless you have a helicopter?"

"Or Google Maps," Gingerbread said. "Aerial photos."

"Those pictures will have been taken months ago. They won't show the container."

"No, but they may help us spot potential hiding places for it."

I could see some merit in what he was suggesting. But it still sounded like looking for the potential location of a needle that hadn't yet been hidden in the haystack. Especially when you didn't know what you were really looking for.

"If you were going to hide a truck with a container on it, where would *you* put it?" I asked.

"I don't know. A lorry park. A lay-by. A building site. A factory yard. The side of a railway. There would have to be a road nearby that an HGV could get down…"

"You know what to look for," I said, "why don't you have a look at the maps and the aerial views?"

"I'm sorry, did I say I wanted to volunteer to do your job for you?"

"No, but you said you wanted to see the bloke who broke your hand behind bars," I said.

"I'd like to see him hit by a train," Gingerbread said.

"The container will lead us to him, I'm sure of it. Help me find it."

"If we find him, can we throw him under a train?"

"I don't promise," I said.

Gingerbread had asked if I thought Matt Lester could have killed Dick Gorse. Lester hadn't originally been on my list of suspects, but in the last couple of days, he seemed to have climbed his way to the top of it. He'd lied to me about working for the detective agency. And while he'd told me that he had spoken to one of the truck drivers who moved the shipping container, he'd neglected to mention that he'd broken a man's fingers in order to get him to talk.

Matt Lester had said he was working for a client, but I had no way of knowing whether that was true or not. Lester might even have been Big Dick's partner-in-crime. They may have been in on the kidnap plot together. Perhaps Big Dick tried to double-cross Lester, and ended up dead as a result. There were still too many possibilities to be sure of anything. The only person with the answers I needed was Matt Lester, and I didn't think he would be forthcoming with them. The only way I was going to get to the bottom of this was to find the container before he did.

The ransom money had been paid, I felt sure of that. And the container holding the kidnapped husband hadn't been handed over in exchange. If he was telling the truth, Lester had then been paid to recover the missing shipping container. He'd broken into Big Dick and Charmaine's house hoping to find a clue to the container's whereabouts, and perhaps also a fat envelope of ransom money

There was also the question of what interest the Rathbanians had in all of this. Was the kidnapped husband Rathbanian? Could Big Dick really have been stupid enough to kidnap a gang member and hold them for ransom? It seemed unlikely he'd have taken that sort of risk, but who knows how people think when greed takes hold of them? Smarter men than Dick Gorse had died because they thought they'd dreamed up the perfect get-rich-quick scheme.

On top of this, I had the matter of Tiago's disappearance to worry about. I'd assumed Tiago had gone into hiding. But there was a possibility that Matt Lester had taken him. Perhaps Tiago was being held somewhere. And if he was, he was probably being tortured, because his captor thought he knew where the container was. Where would someone like Lester hold a person prisoner? It would need to be somewhere where no one would hear the screaming. Perhaps I should ask Uncle Benny's advice?

I'd used up the first of my two days, and wasn't any nearer to finding the container. As I drove back to the flat, the car started to fill with exhaust fumes. I opened the window, but the carbon dioxide combined with the booming of the damaged exhaust pipe to give me a pounding headache. By the time I got back home, I was thoroughly pissed off. I stomped up the stairs and threw open the door.

"You look like crap," Shelly said.

She was lying on my sofa with the crocheted blanket over her. I really must change that lock. She looked a little bleary-eyed, as if she'd fallen asleep waiting for me.

"Rough day," I said. I felt dead on my feet.

"Your lips are blue."

"Carbon monoxide poisoning," I said. "I'm going for a shower."

"Is that an invitation?" Shelly asked.

"What?"

"Shower sex?"

"You?" I asked.

She didn't use the shower after sex, never mind during. Besides, skinny as I was, there wasn't room for her and me in the shower cubicle.

"I could wash your back," she said.

"I'll manage."

"You want me to phone for a pizza?"

"Only if you have money," I said.

"Why don't you get a new job?" she asked, digging out her purse.

"Why don't you get a new boyfriend?" I asked, wandering through to the bedroom.

Shelly was calling the pizza place when I walked back through to the shower. She didn't ask me what I wanted. She never did.

I shampooed my hair and scrubbed my body with a loofah to try and get some life back into it. Then I stood under the shower until it started to run cold. The cool water on my face helped ease the headache.

I towelled myself dry, then pulled on a t-shirt and jogging bottoms and went back into the living room.

Shelly looked at me, tilting her head to one side, and smiled.

"What?" I said.

"I like your hair like that."

"Wet?"

"Short. It looked like a lampshade before."

"Thanks."

"You wearing anything under those joggers?" she asked.

"You'll have to find out, won't you?" I was feeling slightly less walking dead after the shower.

"You're not wearing those baggy y-fronts, are you? Because that would be a real turn-off."

"I'm not wearing y-fronts," I said.

"Commando – sexy!"

"You order the pizza?"

"It'll be twenty minutes," she said.

Often twenty minutes was enough, but tonight I was hoping we might at least double our previous best.

"I ordered pepperoni," she said.

Pepperoni was my favourite. Usually we ended up with one that had anaemic pink ham on, and I had to pick sweetcorn and pineapple off it.

"Thanks," I said.

"Sit down, I'll get you a beer," she said.

It wasn't my birthday, that was in September. But she'd brought beers with her, and she was paying for the pizza. And, hopefully, that was just for starters.

We sat together on the sofa, sipping our lagers, and it was nice.

"I miss this," Shelly said.

"Me too."

"You're not like other blokes."

"Aren't I?"

"You're sweet."

I think Shelly may have had a couple of beers before I got home.

"I really did think you were gay, you know," she said, leaning her head on my shoulder. "I think that's why I liked you."

"Eh?"

"You're not full of all that macho bullshit. And you're interested in doing things other than sex."

"I am interested in sex," I said, "I'm hoping to do it again, one day. Before I forget how."

"And you definitely wouldn't want to do it with another guy?"

"Why, would you want to watch?" I asked.

"Eww!" She said. Then: "But it might be sexy to see you kissing another guy."

That made me laugh, but I wouldn't tell her why when she asked.

Shelly put her hand on my thigh and began to stroke it.

"When was the last time I gave you a blow job?" she asked. Her lips were warm and moist close to my ear.

"Never," I said.

"No, I mean seriously."

"Seriously never," I said, "I would have remembered."

"Looks like I get the meat feast tonight then," she said, as I began to respond to her touch.

The doorbell rang.

Shelly's fingers continued to massage me through the fabric of my trousers. I groaned.

"Pizza," I said.

"I'm happy to stick with the sausage," she said.

The doorbell rang again.

Shelly sighed. "I'll go down," she said.

"Better fetch the pizza first," I said.

"Arse," she said.

Shelly got up and went down to the street door. I was glad of a moment's breather. If she'd kept going, I don't think I could have contained myself. I stood up and shoved a hand down the front of my trousers to adjust Little Joe. I was mid-adjustment when Shelly came back in. She didn't have pizza. And she wasn't alone.

"I'm sorry, are we interrupting something?" Detective Dennis Dockgreen asked.

Detective Bob Keystone stood beside him, and they both looked a bit uncomfortable. I wanted to yell at them. Tell them yes, they were interrupting: I had just been about to receive my first blow-job ever! But I couldn't yell that at them. I didn't want to see their pitying looks.

I pulled my hand out of my trousers.

"Jeez, it's true what they say about you skinny guys," Bob said, unable to look away.

The fabric of the trousers was quite thin, and I wasn't wearing underwear. Little Joe slowly went into retreat.

"I'm glad my wife's not here to see that," Dennis said.

"Did you just come to ruin date night, or was there something you wanted?" I asked.

"We just got a report in," Dennis said, "Big Dick's carpet place is on fire. We thought you'd want to know."

Chapter Nineteen

"What have you done to this fucking car?" Shelly shouted over the din.

"Exhaust fell off!" I said.

The fumes were making us both cough, so we were driving with the windows open, and that only made the noise worse.

After Dennis and Bob had gone, Shelly and I decided we'd go down to see what was going off down at *Big Dick's Floors 'n' Beds*. I pulled on clean clothes while Shelly went down and paid the pizza delivery guy. We took the pizza with us in the car.

I could say that I wanted to go down to the scene to get a look at whoever was out watching the fire, on the grounds that arsonists tend to think of themselves as performance artists, and like to see their creations appreciated by an audience. But if I'm honest, I went there for the same reason as everyone else out there that night. Who doesn't love watching a big fire? The attraction of the light and warmth in the dark, it's a primitive instinct. And it gives you something to post about on Facebook.

It was already a fully-fledged 'incident' by the time we got there. The crossroads near the store had been closed, police cars blocking all four roads. We pulled into the supermarket car park, and drove into a space that overlooked the scene. We had a decent view down on what was going on. We weren't the only ones. Other cars had taken up similar spots, people sitting on the bonnets watching, their faces washed by the blue lights of the emergency vehicles and the orange of the flames.

There were three fire tenders parked around the store. Two had hoses already attached, and firefighters were spraying water onto the back of the store, and also dousing nearby buildings to reduce the risk of them catching light. Hoses were being unrolled from the third engine, ready to be connected to a fire hydrant in the pavement nearby,

"I didn't know their hoses were flat," Shelly said.

I was going to ask if she wanted to see my hose, but decided that crudity might ruin the moment. Leaning on the bonnet of the Honda, sharing a pizza with Shelly, and watching a building burn: it wasn't as good as a blow-job, but as date-nights go, I'd had worse.

Flames seemed to be coming from the back of the carpet store, but it was clear that they were spreading quickly. Through the windows, you could see that most of the sales area was already filled with orange fire.

The sky was dark, so you couldn't really see the smoke, it was black on black. A change of wind direction sent the smoke into the faces of one crowd of onlookers down at street level, and they staggered back coughing and eyes streaming.

We watched as the police led a family out of the house next door to the carpet store: their home must have been in danger from the flames. Not far away the detectives, Bob and Dennis, were conferring with one of their uniformed colleagues.

I remember when I was a kid we had a new carpet fitted, and the smell of it reminded me of crushed geranium leaves. I've associated the two ever since. But all we could smell tonight was that stink you get when you burn polystyrene and rubber. Two firemen wearing breathing apparatus approached the building, but quickly retreated. I imagine that there were concerns about some of the things that might be kept in the carpet store: adhesives, solvents, and possibly even gas canisters.

Along the front of the store, plastic softened and sagged, and then the heat was melting the corrugated aluminium that ran around the top of the building above the windows. It began to bulge and droop. The masked firemen made another attempt to get close, and then backed away again as the roof fell inwards and the walls began to collapse.

The building folding in on itself was the dramatic climax, and people began to drift away after that.

"Shall we go back?" I asked.

I guess after watching a bunch of hunky firemen at work, the thought of spending a couple of hours between the sheets with me didn't hold quite the same appeal it had earlier.

Shelly looked back at the Honda, and said that she'd sooner walk home. I should probably have abandoned the car and walked home too. But I was afraid if I left it, the supermarket would have it towed away and crushed.

"Thanks for the pizza," I called after her, as she walked away.

She turned back and winked. And that wink said that this was just a rain-check: a blow-job was still on the cards. At least, I hope that's what it said. Shelly waggled her impressive hips as she walked away, and that was enough to wake Little Joe again.

There were daylight images of the scene of the fire on the morning news on television. Just the twisted, blackened framework sticking out of charred and still-smoking debris. Police and one fire crew were still at the scene, but the roads had been reopened. The police were treating the blaze as 'suspicious.'

I'd left the clothes I'd worn last evening in the sitting room. They reeked of smoke, and it smelled like I'd held a barbecue in there. I scooped them up and put them in a bin bag with the rest of my laundry. I was down to my last pair of jeans and a *Magnum P.I.* t-shirt my sister had bought me as a joke when I started working for Fat Duncan.

* * *

Tiago's flat was somewhere you wouldn't want to live if you had a family: it was on the top floor in an old building with a tiny back yard, and the street door opened directly onto a main road. He'd got it with the help of his probation officer. Not everyone likes to rent to an ex-con who might suddenly disappear back behind bars if he doesn't do as he's told.

I have a nice set of lock-picks that I bought from a seller in Germany: he advertises them on Amazon. I learned how to use them from YouTube videos. Big locks and expensive locks, I can't open. But most average locks will yield to my picks, given long enough. I'd also bought one of those little gun-shaped things you see in TV shows, that are supposed to bounce the pins in a lock so you can open it: I'd never got it to open anything.

The street door on Tiago's building had an old, worn Yale lock. I had a skeleton key for those. Though, to be honest, I could probably have used the key from the Honda to open it. The lock of Tiago's door was a better one, and it took me the best part of ten minutes to tease it open. I should practice with the lock-picks a lot more than I do; but this was only the second time I'd picked a lock in the course of my work.

The flat had a sitting room and a bedroom. The kitchen was a little alcove that you could close a door on, and off the bedroom there was a combined toilet and shower room that was smaller than anything you'd find in a hotel. The front window looked out on the road, and the bedroom window out onto the grey slate roof of the building next door. It wasn't much, but it had a door you could lock and unlock yourself, so I suppose it was better than a prison cell. It was decorated throughout with paint from the Magnolia to Beige colour chart, and the carpet was brown and nylon. The furniture was the kind of stuff you had to put together yourself. There were no ornaments and no pictures on the walls. It was bare and characterless. Maybe Tiago was hoping he wouldn't have to stay there long.

The bed was neatly made. I wondered if that was something he learned in prison. The top drawer in the bedside cabinet held underwear and socks; the other two drawers were empty. Three t-shirts and a pair of new jeans were folded up on the shelf in the wardrobe. A worn pair of brown boots and an old khaki canvas holdall lay in the bottom. There was nothing else.

Soap, toothbrush, toothpaste, a disposable razor and a can of shaving foam sat on the shelf above the tiny washbasin.

As far as I could see, Tiago could have packed his whole life into the holdall, but he had taken none of it with him. Perhaps he'd been afraid to come back here before he ran away and went into hiding. It wasn't as though he'd left behind anything of sentimental value. But it did make it look as if he had simply vanished off the face of the earth.

At first glance, then, nothing seemed amiss. It looked as if Tiago had just walked out and left it. But somehow, it didn't feel right. Everything was too orderly. I'd seen the flat Tiago and my sister used to share: Tiago didn't live like this. Unless he had acquired a housekeeper.

There were no food scraps in the kitchen bin, and it had been lined with a clean white plastic bag. There wasn't even a used coffee cup in the sink. And the bathroom too looked as if the maid had come in and cleaned away all signs of habitation. Like a hotel room.

I didn't want to think that something could have happened to Tiago. I tried to shrug it off. But as I walked back into the sitting room, I spotted something on the floor. The light coming in from the window spread across the brown carpet beside the sofa, and I could just make out the shadows of four small indentations, making a square about eighteen inches on a side. A piece of furniture had stood there, probably a small side-table. I got down on hands and knees and looked more closely, like a proper Sherlock Holmes.

Caught in the loops of the nylon carpet were a few pale flecks. Tiny splinters of wood that a vacuum cleaner hadn't been able to pick up. The kind of splinters you might get if a piece of particle-board furniture was broken. None of this proved anything. Some homes, unlike mine, got cleaned. Furniture got broken and was thrown out. But still, I couldn't shake the uneasy feeling.

I pulled Tiago's door shut behind me, checking that it had locked. I made my way downstairs, listening as I went. There were no sounds from the first floor or ground floor flats.

At the bottom of the stairs, a dark little corridor led to the back of the house. There was a back door out onto the tiny yard, where two large dumpsters had been provided for rubbish from the three flats. The one for recyclable waste was empty. The one for general waste was filled almost to the brim with black plastic bags.

This wasn't the first time I'd poked around in someone's rubbish, but experience doesn't make the smell any easier to deal with. That vomity whiff of spoiled milk mixed with the fish-like reek of rotten meat. I ran my hands over the outside of the black bags at the top of the dumpster, trying to feel what was inside. Nothing that felt like broken furniture. I pulled the bags out, dropping them on the ground, and tested the next layer of bin bags. Nothing but things that felt like rubbish. I heaved them out of the way. When I got to the point where I couldn't reach down far enough to fondle the last couple of layers of bags, I climbed up and lowered myself into the dumpster. This was always my favourite part. My foot slid over something that felt like it could be a leg. Furniture not human. I knelt and tore open the bag. It was the pieces of broken table I had half-expected to find.

At that moment, I heard something that could have been the latch on the yard gate. But I was sure the gate could only be opened from the inside, to allow the dumpster to be pushed to the kerb on collection day. I listened, but heard nothing else.

I pulled out the bits of wood and broken particle board, to see what else had been stashed in the black sack. Crouched in the bottom of the dumpster, I couldn't see much in the gloom, so I relied on touch to explore the contents. It held all of the things that had been cleared from Tiago's flat: a half-empty two-pint carton of milk; a few slices of bread in a bag; some apples: all of the perishable stuff from the kitchen. There was also something pale, fabric that felt like a towel. I stood up, holding the remains of the bin bag, and climbed out of the dumpster. I lowered myself carefully to the ground, seeking out firm footing among the piles of bin bags I'd tossed out into the yard.

I opened the torn bag, wanting to get a better look at the towel and whatever else was in there. Then I heard a growling sound behind me.

I turned slowly, catching a whiff of cigarette smoke as I did. Standing by the gate was a short, wrinkled woman in a shapeless flowered dress. She wore hiking boots. A translucent nylon headscarf covered a head full of curlers. A hand-rolled cigarette dangled from her lip. It hadn't been her that growled.

One the ground beside her sat a lumpy-looking dog that looked to be part pit-bull and part velociraptor. The old woman held it on a short leash. Strings of drool hung from black lips – the dog's, not hers, and the growl rumbled in its chest again.

Chapter Twenty

"Fuck you doin'?" The old woman was a bit growly too.

"Er – my friend," I said, "he accidentally threw out some washing with the trash."

As proof of this unlikely story, I pulled the towel out of the bag.

"Friend just got his period, did he?" she growled.

I looked at the towel I was holding up. It was a bath towel and there was a dark red-brown stain in the middle of it.

I grinned weakly.

The pit-raptor grinned back. Its grin wasn't at all weak.

"Want to try me with another story?" The old woman asked. The cigarette bobbed up and down as she spoke, sprinkling ash onto her mid-body bosom.

"I'm a detective, investigating Tiago Zambora's disappearance," I said.

There was a flicker of recognition in her face when she heard the name.

"Makes you think he's missing?"

"Hasn't been to work," I said, falling into her speech pattern. "Hasn't called his ex-wife."

"He want with her?" she asked.

"Sex, I think," I said.

I wondered if the old witch remembered what sex was. Then I was afraid she'd read my mind, because her scowl suddenly deepened.

"Going to open the gate," she said. "Two minutes, then I send Brutus out after you."

I looked down. Brutus was grinning again. Nice doggy.

The old woman backed towards the gate and reached for the bolt.

If you worked for a proper detective agency, you'd probably get training in 'what to do when confronted by a dangerous dog.' I got nothing. Everything I knew, I'd learned when I had a temporary job as a postman after I left school. As a postman, I'd never been attacked by a dog. People yes, but never a dog. Thankfully, I could still remember some of what the trainer taught us.

First, never turn your back on an angry dog, and never run. A dog's instinct is to chase its prey, and you're never going to outrun it.

The second piece of advice was: Don't scare the dog. This got a laugh when the trainer said it. It's a bad idea to make the dog think you are challenging or threatening it. Do not make eye contact. Do not smile: baring your teeth is a sign of aggression in a dog. Do not try and make yourself look bigger: that only works with bears. And don't make any sudden movements. You're supposed to turn sideways, keeping the dog in your peripheral vision; that way you seem less of a threat, and you also present less of a target.

"Two minutes?" I said, trying to turn sideways as slowly as I could.

"If you're lucky," she said.

Then her mouth twitched, and her grin was scarier than the hellhound's.

Don't let the dog see that you're afraid. That got a laugh too. People say animals can sense fear, and that's sort of true. They can also smell it if you shit yourself. Dogs want you to be afraid of them. If they see that you're not, it may make them think twice about attacking you. Remain calm, and speak assertively to the dog: tell it to 'go home' or 'fuck off' in a confident voice. Make it think you are prepared to defend your turf, but that you are not threatening him for his. If Brutus wanted my turf, he was welcome to it, all I wanted to defend was my own limbs.

All of this went through my head as I stood there, trying not to make eye contact with the Hound of the Baskervilles. And her dog. Maybe it was another one of those life flashing before your eyes moments.

The old woman unlatched the gate and pulled it open.

If I ran, I was breaking the first commandment. I stood among the black bin bags and didn't move. You're supposed to try and keep something between you and the dog if you can, but there was nothing for me to hide behind.

The old woman looked at me, and then looked down at her watch.

"Two minutes, starting... *now!*" She said.

I had the option of running or not. Either way she was going to release the beast.

I leaped over the bags, towards the gate. The dog snapped its jaws at me as I passed, but I was just out of reach.

Then I was out in the street. And running.

When you're waiting in a supermarket queue, two minutes seems like forever. When you're running for your life, not so much. Behind me I heard a sound like marbles clattering on the pavement: the veloci-bull's claws finding purchase on the flagstones as it launched itself through the gate.

During my postman training, we'd covered 'five signs of aggression,' that tell you Fido doesn't want his tummy scratched, and then we'd had a break for coffee. The second part of the morning covered what to do if you're actually attacked by a dog. I felt sure I was about to put what I had learned into practice for the first time.

If a dog attacks, try and trick it into biting something that isn't really part of you. The empty sleeve of your jacket; your bag; even a shoe. Let the dog grab it, then let go of it yourself and back away. You want the dog to think it's bitten off a chunk of you, that you are wounded and no longer a threat to him.

Failing that, you have to defend yourself. Hit or kick the dog in the throat, nose, or back of the head. Hit it hard and try to stun it, so that you can get away. If you've got a stick, use it. But don't whack the dog on top of its head, because they have thick skulls.

If you fall, or if you are brought down by the dog, try and use your weight to your advantage: dogs are good at biting, but they're not so hot at one-on-one wrestling. Keep your hands away from its jaws, and use your knees and elbows. Hit it in the throat or the ribs. Do it hard and do it fast.

And if all of that fails, tuck your knees and arms in, roll so you are face down, and protect your stomach and throat. When Brutus hit me, I was thinking of making this my first move.

"What's the best place to get bitten?" Our instructor had asked. Apparently the correct answer is not 'outside a hospital.' It is best to avoid being bitten in the face or hands, as these are bits of yourself that you really don't want to lose. And a bite in the thigh or the throat can cause fatal bleeding. The 'best' place to be bitten is the shin or the forearm. As the instructor put it: Whatever the dog is doing to your arm, it's not doing to your bollocks.

His final piece of advice was: if you are bitten, don't try and break free. You could end up tearing your flesh and doing more damage. Let the dog hold on: one bite is better than half-a-dozen.

This was all running through my head on fast-forward, as I pounded along the pavement, hearing the clicking of the monster's claws getting closer and closer behind me. At any moment, I expected it would leap, its weight crashing into my back, sending me tumbling forwards as its jaws clamped shut on the back of my neck.

I felt something grab at the back of my trousers, behind the knee. I stumbled and tried to keep myself from falling, arms flailing. I'd almost regained my balance when there was another tug at the bottom of my trouser leg. This had to be the closest you could come to a shark attack on dry land. I fell, face forwards. I tried to roll as I hit the ground, tucking my elbows in and balling my hands into fists.

Here's a fun fact about dangerous dogs: the story about them being able to 'lock' their jaws closed after they have bitten you is a myth. There is no mechanism in any dog's skull to lock the jaws, it is only the strength of their muscles that does it. This is good news, because it means you can insert something strong and flat between the dog's gums, behind its teeth, and twist it to pry open the jaws. I tell you this so you know what to do if you ever come upon a hapless detective trapped in the jaws of a monstrous mutt with blazing eyes.

I lay on my back, gasping for breath. And then Brutus leapt onto my stomach, and the air just whooshed out of me. It was like being hit by a car. I didn't have time to get my arms up to protect my face. His grinning face loomed over me. Our eyes met, and in that moment, something passed between us – hunter and prey.

Then his head dipped towards me. And Brutus began licking my face. I couldn't believe it. Here I was, for the third time in a week, being kissed against my will. It tasted horrible. As if this wasn't humiliation enough, the dog's feet dug into me as it shifted its weight, making sure I was properly pinned down. Then Brutus started humping my right thigh.

I closed my eyes, and thought of England. And all I could hear was the dog's heavy breathing, and the old woman down the road, cackling like a hen.

* * *

I was dirty, and tired, and bruised, and embarrassed. And my trousers were sticky with dog semen. The racket from the exhaust and the fumes seeping up through the floor didn't do anything to improve my mood. When I pulled up opposite the flat, my head was thumping and my vision was blurred. I marched upstairs and threw open the front door. Maybe if Shelly had been there to deliver on that offer of a blow job, things might have turned out differently. I was in no fit state to make rational decisions, which probably explains why I did what I did. Instead of climbing into a hot shower and changing into clean clothes, I turned around and went out again, slamming the door behind me and stomping down the stairs, back out to the Honda.

The drive over to Tucksfield should have cooled my head, and made me realise what a dangerous and stupid thing I was doing. But the droning exhaust and fumes just topped up my anger, making me even more determined to take action. They also made me decide that tomorrow, if I survived that long, I would book the car in at KwikFit. Duncan wouldn't be happy about this, because a proper fitter would draw my attention to the illegal tread-depth of the tyres, and I'd have to have them replaced too. Duncan usually made me go to an independent trader who was an old friend of his. But his garage had been closed down after the Department for Transport had prosecuted him for issuing MOT certificates to death-trap cars. Technically, the Honda's MOT was currently invalid, but no one had caught up with us about it yet, because the car was still registered to the former owner, who had died during the Black Death.

That was for tomorrow. This evening I was going to confront the Rathbanians on their home turf.

Chapter Twenty-One

If we've learned anything from the movies, it's that criminal gangs always have a favourite restaurant. The owner is always a respectable businessman who ends up owing money to the gangsters, who then take a stake in his business. And then they move in and make the restaurant their unofficial headquarters. It's a tradition the Mob started in Chicago and, like McDonalds and Coca-Cola, it has gone international.

Whether Kamal Bharani was ever a respectable businessman is open to question. He owned a couple of restaurants and had a controlling interest in several other eateries, including a takeaway that had been shut down twice by Environmental Health. As far as anyone could prove, he was a legitimate businessman with a perfectly normal contempt for the taxman. As well as the restaurants, he had a wholesale business run out of a warehouse near Loughborough that supplied market traders and dodgy fast-food outlets in three counties. I'd heard a few people refer to Mr. Bharani as the 'Indian Chief,' making him sound like the head of a mid-level criminal empire, but that reputation could well have been of his own making.

Bharani was one of those late-middle-aged Indian men with a moustache and haircut out of the seventies; a covering of fat that he was convinced was muscle, and thick black body hair that he thought was testament to his virility. He didn't really strike me as a 'Godfather' figure, even a low level one, but presumably a successful crime boss doesn't actually look like a crime boss.

The Raj Lion in Tucksfield was the jewel in Mr. Bharani's self-made crown. It had been a country pub, and he bought it in the nineties when property prices slumped and cheap supermarket booze killed off hundreds of local watering holes. He turned it into a restaurant that became popular with the kind of people who drove shiny Range Rovers and Jaguars. Knobs and crooks.

I'm guessing that the Indian Chief got out of his depth somewhere along the line, and attracted the interest of the Rathbanians. How he came to owe them money, I don't know, but The Raj became the favourite hang-out of the Rathbanians a couple of years ago. At one time you could hire the top room in the restaurant for parties, but now it was permanently booked by just the one private party. The menu is still Indian, but I'd heard that the chef could also provide Rathbanian dishes on request.

I didn't know if Sergei would be at The Raj, but there would be someone upstairs who knew him. And if I caused enough trouble, they'd send for him.

It was midweek, so the parking lot was only half-full. I pulled the Honda up next to a gleaming Mercedes the size of an ocean liner. I'm sure it curled its grill and leaned away as I got out.

Outside, the restaurant was styled after a traditional coach inn, sandy coloured stone and diamond leaded windows. Inside it was a mish-mash of traditional English oak beams and furniture, and Indian kitsch. The red flock wallpaper and the warm golden lights gave it a cosy feeling, and the aroma of curry made my mouth water as I walked in. I'd never been able to afford to eat here.

"I'm sorry, sir, you can't come in dressed like that," the Maitre d' said, heading me off as I crossed the lobby. He was dressed like an English waiter, but with a paisley cummerbund.

I looked down at my stained and dishevelled outfit. "What, you don't like my tie?" I asked.

"Please don't make a scene, or we will have you ejected."

"You're going to throw me out, are you?" I favoured him with my best tough-guy sneer.

"No sir, they will."

He made a fey hand gesture that took in two men who had appeared from nowhere. They both looked like Oddjob from the Bond movie. Only Indian. And without the bowler hat.

I moved closer to the dining area, and the Oddjobs moved to block my way.

"I'm here to see Sergei," I said loudly, trying to peer round them to see if he was in the dining room. "Is he here?"

I had attracted the attention of some of the diners at the tables nearest the entrance, and I could see their disdainful looks.

"Is he drunk?" someone asked.

"His lips look blue."

"Perhaps he's a zombie."

"Don't be stupid, Kenny."

Attracted by the buzz, Mr. Bharani himself appeared. "What is going on?" he asked.

"This gentleman was just leaving," the Maitre d' said.

"No I wasn't," I said. "I came to see Sergei."

"There is no one of that name here," Mr. Bharani said.

Then I remembered that 'Saggy' wasn't actually the man's name, I'd made that up. I had no idea what his real name was.

"He's one of the Rathbanians," I said. "The one in charge. I bet he's upstairs."

I made a move towards the stairs, and one of the Oddjobs moved to block my way. It was like one of those games of chess they play on a big board with people for pieces.

"Take him outside," Mr. Bharani said to the Oddjobs. "Make sure he can't crawl back in."

"You think you're the big man, ordering people around," I mocked, "why don't you come outside and hit me yourself?"

"One doesn't have a dog and bark oneself," Mr. Bharani said.

Mentioning dogs in my presence wasn't a wise move.

"They might be dogs, but you're a chicken," I said. I started making chicken noises. Then I flapped my elbows like wings.

In the dining room, almost everyone had stopped eating, and some of the diners were standing to get a better view of what was happening in the lobby.

I strutted around making pecking motions and clucking.

Someone in the restaurant sniggered.

Mr. Bharani's colour had slowly risen. His face and neck were now brick-red, and beads of sweat stood out on his forehead.

"Chick, chick, chick, chick, *chicken!*" I sang.

Mr. Bharani roared and leaped towards me.

"Kamal!"

A commanding voice stopped Bharani in his tracks, his arms still outstretched towards my throat.

Everyone turned. Sergei was standing on the little landing near the bottom of the stairs.

"What is the meaning of this?" he asked, looking at me.

"Where's Tiago?" I asked.

"Mr. Lucke, please..."

"What have you done with him?" I asked, loudly.

Sergei's eyes flicked nervously towards the dining room. He stepped down into the lobby and took me by the elbow.

"This way," he said.

He led me towards a little office beside the reception desk. Mr. Bharani started to follow us in, but Sergei closed the door in his face.

I turned on Sergei immediately, knowing I needed to try and keep the upper hand.

"We had a deal," I said. "I bring you the container, you leave Tiago alone!"

"Have you brought me the container?" Sergei asked, keeping his voice calm. He probably had experience dealing with crazy people.

"I don't have it. Yet."

"Then you should get on with your search, instead of wasting time on theatrics," he said.

"I'm not going until you free Tiago," I said.

"Why do you assume that we have him?"

"Who else would want to hurt him?"

"Perhaps the same person who broke your friend's fingers?" Sergei said.

This was a reasonable suggestion, but Sergei might just have said it to direct my attention elsewhere.

"Why should I believe you?"

"I have no reason to lie," Sergei said. "If you wish to look around, search for Tiago, then do so. My men will not prevent you."

"I can look upstairs?"

"Look anywhere you like. But, please, do not disturb the diners. We have our reputation to think of."

His smile involved a lot of teeth, and I was reminded of that shark in the cartoon.

If the Rathbanians did have Tiago, it was unlikely they would be keeping him here, so searching the place would be a waste of time. But on the other hand, Tiago might be here, and Sergei could be bluffing, hoping I wouldn't search the place; in which case, I should call his bluff.

"I will go upstairs," I said.

Sergei rose and opened the office door. "After you," he said.

I crossed the lobby carpet, heading towards the stairs, and expecting with every step that someone would pounce on me. But all I felt was their eyes on me.

I walked slowly up the stairs. Into the villains' lair.

As I went, I took the little phone out of my pocket and scrolled through the contacts to find Tiago's number.

If anything had been going off in the upstairs room before I arrived, the Rathbanians had plenty of time to hide all evidence of it before I went up there. When I stepped into the room, there were three islands of tables, all of them empty except one. Sergei's three apes were sitting at this table, tucking into a meal that I didn't recognise. The only one who even acknowledged my presence was the youngest, Evgeny, and he just blushed. There was a fourth place at the table, Sergei's presumably.

"Would you care to join us in some bat'leth," Sergei asked, coming in behind me. At least that's what it sounded like.

"Thank you, but I dined earlier this evening," I said, as graciously as I could.

Keeping the phone my pocket, I thumbed the dial button. If they didn't have Tiago here, I thought that someone might have his phone in their pocket, or in a drawer nearby. I listened, but heard nothing.

I turned and went back out into the little corridor at the top of the stairs. I ducked my head into the toilets, and then into the little room that held the dumb-waiter to carry food up from the kitchen. I dialled Tiago's number again. Still nothing.

"Is there anything else you would like to see?" Sergei asked.

"I'm finished up here," I said.

I headed down the stairs, and Sergei followed. There was only one Oddjob standing by the entrance to the dining room, presumably to make sure I didn't try and duck in there and eat anyone's brains. There was no sign of Chicken Bharani.

"I'm going to head out to my car," I said.

Sergei seemed pleased by this.

I started towards the exit, and then changed course. "I'll go out the back way," I said.

A flicker of annoyance crossed his face, then Sergei smiled again. "But of course," he said.

I headed down the corridor towards the kitchen.

"You don't mind if I speak to the staff?" I asked.

"Not at all."

As we moved deeper into the building, I kept calling Tiago's number and listening for faint sounds of ringing. Still nothing.

The kitchen, as you might expect, was hot and steamy. There was a hot oily smell over everything, but the undertones of spice were incredible.

"This is *Mrs.* Bharani's domain," Sergei said, "we're not normally allowed in here."

There was no sign of the owner's wife. Two young Indian men were scurrying around, under the watchful eye of an older man who was obviously the chef.

"Mr. Lucke would like to wander around before he sees himself out," Sergei said. "Please show him anything he wishes to see, and answer any questions he has."

The chef smiled and nodded. Sergei smiled his shark smile at me, and wandered away.

"The secret of our food is the spice pastes to which Mrs. Bharani attends herself," the chef said. "Do not touch that red one, that's for any idiot who asks for the super-hot vindaloo. It'll take the skin off your finger. We use it for scouring the pans."

I smiled and nodded in appreciation of his joke.

"What was it that you wished to see here?" he asked. "I am happy to show you everything. Nothing to hide. We run a very clean establishment. No rat droppings anywhere."

"I'm not looking for anything like that," I said. "I was looking for a friend of mine. Tall, black curly hair, neat little beard. He's Spanish."

There was no flicker of recognition from the chef, or the two kitchen-hands.

"Ah, no, the only thing Spanish here is the onions," the chef said.

"May I see the cellar?" I asked.

"Yes please, this way."

He led me to the door and turned on the light. A little wooden staircase led down into the stone cellar.

"No rats," he said, shaking his head fiercely.

"Anybody down there?" I asked.

"No bodies," he said, waving his index finger from side to side.

I walked down the little stairs into the cool, dry space below. Cases of lager and soft drinks lined one side. Racks and crates of wine lined the other. I pulled out my phone: it showed one bar of signal. I dialled Tiago's number, and heard nothing.

"No bodies," I said, as I went back up to the kitchen. "May I speak to the others?"

I indicated the kitchen hands. The chef shrugged, and indicated that I was free to do as I wished.

"Good evening," I said to the first one. "I wondered if you'd seen my friend, Tiago. Tall Spanish bloke, tattoos?"

"Apni gaand mein muthi daal," the youth said, and smiled.

The other one sniggered. I looked to the chef for a translation. He looked mildly shocked.

"He is disrespectful," the chef said, "but he says he cannot help you. You must look for him yourself."

"And you have not seen him?" I asked the second one.

"Mera hovarakraapht sarpameenon se bhara hai," he said.

The chef frowned. "He is telling you that he is a big fan of *Monty Python*, I think," he said.

"That word sounded like hovercraft," I said.

"That is not a coincidence," the chef said.

"Thank you all for your help," I said.

"Bhaand me jaao!" The two kitchen hands said in unison, smiling and waving as I headed for the back door.

"Back to work!" The chef snapped at them.

I stepped out into the cool night air. The smell of grease and Indian spices clung to my clothes. It was an improvement on the scent of dog spunk. I looked around, but there wasn't much to see at the back of the restaurant. A garden stretched back into the darkness, trees beyond. No outbuildings. As I walked back round the car park, I dialled Tiago's number one final time. Nothing.

Sergei was standing outside when I got back to my car. "We did not take Tiago, I give you my word," he said.

"I went to his flat, there were signs of a struggle, and blood," I said.

"And you thought of me?" He seemed genuinely offended.

"I'm sorry," I said.

Sergei shrugged. "You must investigate as you see fit," he said. "I could say to you that I will give you extra time to deliver the container. But time is running out, I think, if you wish to find Tiago alive."

I nodded, then turned to go.

"Mr. Lucke," Sergei said.

I turned back.

"Do not come here again," he said. He reached into his pocket and pulled out a phone. He tossed it towards me and I caught it. "When you find the container, call me; the number is in the phone."

I nodded. He went back inside.

I sat in the Honda, wishing I'd asked the chef to put together some food for me to take away. I looked down at the phone Sergei had given me. It was a neat little Sony smartphone. Not an expensive one, but a damn sight better than the toy one I'd been using. There was one number in the contacts list. No messages or call history. I resisted the urge to swap my SIM card into it, and tucked it into my jacket pocket.

Chapter Twenty-Two

I drove the Honda to the KwikFit in Sutton, because there was a laundromat within walking distance. I lugged the bag of smoke scented and semen-stained clothing away, while the fitters performed major surgery on the car.

I was pulling my tangled washing out of the dryer when my phone rang. It was Detective Dennis Dockgreen. He didn't make any reference to my hand-in-trousers embarrassment of the other evening, so I knew it was something serious.

"Where are you?" he asked.

"Laundrette."

Again, no sarcastic comment about it being my birthday or something.

"Can you meet us? Say half-an-hour? At the station."

I wondered for a moment if I was in trouble, but they would have come for me if that was the case. I said I would be with them as soon as the Honda was out of intensive care.

I neatly folded my clothes and placed them in a fresh bin bag. I was just tying it shut when I got a call to say the Honda had not died on the table. It now had four legal tyres and a new exhaust. The KwikFit guy told me how much 'the damage' was: about double what the Honda was worth. But I was paying it on my credit card, so it wasn't real money.

*

"The fire investigator has given us some preliminary findings," Dennis said. "An accelerant was used. That means that..."

"I know what it means. The fire was started deliberately," I said.

We were sitting in a bare office in the police station on Central Road. It was about the size of a broom cupboard.

"We also got the CCTV footage from the cameras across the road from the carpet store," Bob said. "We've still got people going through the footage, but they've pulled a few images off the video."

He handed me two A4 sheets of photo-paper: each had two images printed on it. They were pixilated blow-ups from video, dirty blacks fringed with peacock blue, but you could make out the figure in the images well enough. Four frames showing a man apparently going into the back of Big Dick's carpet store.

Most people would have looked at the pictures and said, 'It could be anyone.' Johnny Depp maybe. But I looked at them, and I knew why detectives Bob and Dennis had called me in.

"It's him, isn't it?" Dennis asked.

I nodded.

It was Tiago.

"You suspect him of starting the fire?" I asked.

They exchanged that look again, the one that said they knew something I didn't. But there was no gloating involved this time. I wished there had been.

"Tiago Zambora being an arsonist is one line of enquiry we will be following," Dennis said. "But I should also tell you that, when the wreckage was examined – we found a man's body."

"Tiago?" My voice was croaky.

"We don't know. It's going to take a while for it to be identified," Bob said. "The body was..."

"Burned," I said.

They both nodded.

"It may not be him," Dennis said.

"You will let me know – as soon as you find out?" I asked.

Dennis nodded.

"I don't want Elise to know about this," I said. "Not until we're sure."

They looked at each other, and then they nodded again.

"You want some tea?" Bob asked.

"No, thanks."

I'd had the cop-shop tea before: it was dreadful.

"Chief's opened those biscuits, if you want one?"

"No, I'm fine."

Dennis looked at me, and I could tell he wanted to say something fatherly. I didn't want him to.

"For the record," I said, "I haven't been investigating Dick Gorse's death."

"And off the record?" Bob asked.

"There's someone I think you should check out. He's involved in this somehow, but I'm not sure how. All I have are suspicions, no evidence."

"Give us a name," Dennis said.

"Matthew Lester. He used to work for the Sherwood Investigations detective agency. He was fired, but I don't know why. I do know that he can be dangerous. I think he may have attacked Tiago in his flat."

I gave them the address, and told them about the broken furniture and the towel I had found there, and left at the scene. I didn't tell them I'd been humped by the landlady's dog.

"We'll look into it," Bob said.

"You don't need me to tell you that this is dangerous, Joe. Two people are dead now. And I know this won't do any good, but I have to warn you to stay out of it. Me and Bob don't want to turn up somewhere and find you being zipped into a body-bag."

"I know, thanks," I said. "I'll be careful."

They looked at each other and decided that they'd done the best they could with me.

"If you find out anything else, tell us, please?" Dennis said.

"I will."

"And if you need help, call us," Bob said. "Do you need a ride home?"

"I've got the Honda outside."

"Is that thing still running?" Dennis asked.

"I've had it fixed, and it is now totally road legal."

Apart from the MOT, I thought, but they didn't need to know that.

* * *

"Joseph Lucke? A friend gave me your number."

The voice on the phone sounded young and refined. No hint of a Mansfield accent. It said *Number Withheld* on my phone, in very small writing.

"And you are?"

"Lila Frayne," she said.

"I don't think I..."

"I am Matt Lester's client," she said. No nonsense.

"Ah," I said.

"May I speak with you?"

"Of course."

"I don't want to do this on the phone. Can we meet?"

"I'll come to you," I said. "What address?"

She was silent for a moment.

"Franderground Hall," she said. "Shall we say two-thirty?"

"Two-thirty," I confirmed

She hung up.

Franderground Hall and Spa sat in the middle of an area of sandy heathland that had once been surrounded by forest. Now it was mostly surrounded by roads that led to more interesting places. According to their brochure, the hall had been a health spa since Victorian times, but this wasn't strictly speaking the whole truth. Its isolated location was a clue to its original use: it had been tuberculosis sanatorium. That explained why it looked more like a red-brick hospital than a country house. It had been updated in the eighties, when a uPVC conservatory was tacked on one side. The front portico was painted white in an attempt to make it more welcoming, but that had obviously been done some time ago. Rather than somewhere for relaxing and pampering, it looked the ideal place to stage a murder-mystery.

The brochure featured fresh-faced young women with washboard stomachs in crop-tops and leggings. The reality was that the place seemed to be filled with dumpy middle-aged women in fluffy towelling robes and turban-hats that were meant to look like artfully wrapped towels. Everything was meant to be blinding white cotton, like a soap-powder commercial, but it looked as though a black sock had got in with the wash.

A bored-looking receptionist in heavy Cleopatra make-up took my name and asked me to wait in the visitor's lounge while Ms. Frayne was informed of my arrival. I wasn't sure whether the receptionist bestowed her sneer upon all male visitors, or just me.

The 'visitor's lounge' was half-a-dozen faded brown chairs in a little alcove by the main door. A tubby man in a pale blue cable-knit sweater and tan slacks was sitting on one of the chairs. He looked even more uncomfortable than I did.

"Just here to pick up the wife," he said, his mouth twitching briefly into the shape of a smile.

I'd never understood why some men referred to their wives in the same way they did the lawnmower, the car, and the dog. But I'd never owned any of those things, so perhaps I wasn't in a position to judge.

There was a deafening clicking noise and a whine of feedback, then a woman with a sing-song voice made an announcement over the tannoy.

"Good afternoon, ladies. Would anyone who is attending this afternoon's session with Ramone kindly note that, due to an unfortunate incident with a bucket of avocado and peach-pit skin scrub, yogalates will now take place in the Idleass Lounge. That's yogalates now in the Idleass Lounge. Thank you!"

"Hi-de-hi!" Cable-knit sweater said, his mouth twitching again.

"I think she meant Edelweiss," I said.

"Isn't that what she said?" He looked confused. "Ah, here's my petal now."

Perhaps years of saying 'yes, dear' meant he could no longer remember her name.

"She's positively glowing, isn't she?" he asked me, as he stood up to greet her.

Parts of her certainly were. There was an angry red smear between her top lip and nose where her moustache had been waxed and forcibly removed. Her mouth twitched, either the beginning of an angry retort or a smile, but it was obviously too painful for her to complete it. Her hair had been scraped back under an Alice band and her eyebrows had been plucked to the thinnest of lines. This, combined with the shininess of her skin, made her looked like a blotchy, over-inflated balloon.

"Come on, let's get you home," Cable-knit said. "The neighbours will think I've traded you in for a younger model!"

He was obviously making the most of his freedom of speech: as soon as her face deflated enough, he wouldn't be able to get a word in edgewise. I could see his wife trying to frown, but her forehead remained crease-free, courtesy of the Botox that had been pumped into it.

"Mr. Lucke?"

The receptionist had come over to show me her sneer again.

"Ms. Frayne would like you to join her on the terrace. This way."

I followed her down a corridor towards the back of the building. In her dark stockings and flat shoes, she probably wasn't that far removed from the nurses that used to sneer at people within these walls. Rather than the relaxing scents of frangipani and ylang-ylang massage oil, the whole place smelled like the chlorine footbath in a school swimming pool.

There was a large garden behind the hall, mostly lawn and dark bushes. It looked like something the local council would take care of. Even in the early afternoon sunlight, it looked slightly ominous.

There were half-a-dozen wrought-iron tables on the terrace, painted in the spa's signature grey-white. They were all empty except one. Everyone must have gone in for a session with Ramone. Or perhaps they'd been injured in the unfortunate avocado skin scrub incident.

A woman sat alone at the only occupied table. She had her back to me, and wasn't wearing the bathrobe and turban of an inmate. Instead she sported a white linen trouser suit and a patterned silk blouse the colour of peacock feathers. She looked like a rich woman disguised as a housewife. The headscarf was overdoing it a bit. I walked towards her. A tray of tea things and a two-tier plate of store-bought scones and biscuits were on the table in front of her.

"Miss Frayne?" I said.

"Mr. Lucke."

She held out her hand: I wasn't sure if I was supposed to shake it, or bend and kiss it. I went with shaking: this wasn't exactly Downton Abbey.

"Please sit down," she said. "I've ordered tea, I hope that's all right. There's a menu if you'd like to order lunch?"

"I'm fine, thank you," I said.

"A wise choice, I think," she said. "It's a dreadful place, isn't it? I wanted to meet somewhere that I wouldn't be recognised. Nobody I know would be seen dead here."

"The whole place reminds me of a Victoria Wood sketch," I said, smiling.

"It does?"

She was obviously not a fan.

Lila Frayne reached up and unfastened her headscarf. The hair she shook free was an unnatural shade somewhere between blonde and platinum, and the styling looked expensive. She had dark blue eyes, almost lost because her eye make-up was too dark. Her skin was flawless, but there were eyes on either side of her mouth. Thin lips were painted a pale glossy pink that reminded me of a medicine I'd had to take as a child. It had tasted of almond. I idly wondered what her lips might taste like. Bitter, I supposed. Her whole demeanour suggested tiredness and disappointment with life.

"Is something wrong?" she asked.

"You wanted to speak to me," I reminded her.

She pressed the pink lips together and looked at my face.

"Anything I tell you is in complete confidence, isn't it? Like in confession?"

As Bogart might have said, she didn't look like the kind of woman who went to confession.

"If you become a client of our agency, then we treat everything you say in the strictest confidence," I said.

"How do I become a client?"

"If you pay us a retainer, then we are working for you," I said.

"A retainer, of course. Matt Lester said he wanted a thousand pounds to begin with, would that be all right for you?"

"That would be an excellent way to begin," I said.

She opened her handbag, which wasn't much bigger than a child's pencil case, and drew out an envelope. She handed it to me.

Until that moment, I had never handled a fifty-pound note. Now I had twenty of them.

"Cash is okay, isn't it?" she asked.

"Very much so. Miss Frayne, welcome to the Donoghue Investigations client roster," I said.

I rose and shook her hand, in an attempt to provide some sort of formal recognition of our agreement. The contents of the envelope seemed to demand it.

"Thank you," she said.

I sat down again.

"I'm not sure how much Matt Lester has told you," she said.

Chapter Twenty-Three

"He told me that your husband was kidnapped," I said.

Lila Frayne took one of the scones and cut it in half on her plate.

"It doesn't feel quite real, even now," she said. "It seems like something I saw in a film."

She began cutting the scone into smaller and smaller pieces with the knife. When she noticed me watching her, she pushed the plate away and set down the knife.

"My husband is a businessman. Sometimes I have to play the dutiful wife. I attend functions and pretend to be nice to people. I go to parties and pretend to be interested in things people say. I eat terrible food and tell our hosts how wonderful it is. I tell a lot of lies," she said.

"We all tell white lies to get along in life," I said.

She was perhaps five years older than me, but gave the impression of having lived a lot longer.

"It's all so fake. There are times when I don't even know I'm doing it. I lie even when I don't need to."

"It would be better if you didn't lie to me," I said.

She looked at me across the table and smiled her sad little smile. "I think you'd know if I was lying to you," she said.

"Tell me what happened on the night your husband was taken," I said.

She sighed, and stared out at the garden. "We'd gone to one of those dreadful parties. People I didn't know.

Chad had met the husband – somewhere, I don't even remember."

"Chad is your husband?"

She nodded.

"They had this mock Tudor farm house way out in the country. Hideous place. I've seen garish décor in my time, but this was – well, you'd think a footballer lived there. I'm sorry, I sound like a frightful snob, I know."

"Money can't buy good taste," I said.

She pressed her pink lips together and the corner of her mouth turned up a little. "You're not impressed by material wealth, are you, Mr. Lucke?"

"I'm interested in what a person chooses to do, not what they can afford to buy," I said.

"People should be judged by their actions," she said, nodding. "We were on our way home. We really were in the middle of nowhere, driving along a pitch-black country road. It was cloudy, no moon, so only the headlights to show us a little patch of the world coming towards us.

"I was telling Chad I thought our hostess, Jinny or Jeannie or whatever her name was, had had caterers in to prepare the meal she'd claimed to have cooked: no one slices vegetables like that in their own kitchen. Chad laughed, and said I was a bitch."

She reached for her plate and began crumbling the pieces of scone between her fingers.

"And then another car came up behind us. Its headlights were very bright. It pulled out to overtake us. I thought Chad would put his foot down to outpace them, he did that sometimes; but he just let them pass. They cut back in front of us much closer than they should have. Chad swore and flashed his lights at them. And that's when they braked. Suddenly.

"Chad had had a few drinks at dinner, but even if he hadn't, I don't think he could have reacted quickly enough."

"You hit the back of the other car?" I asked,

She nodded. "It all happened so very quickly. The airbags exploded in our faces, and the car was filled with mist. I remember my ears popping, like when you fly. Chad was swearing, saying the driver of the other car was a maniac, and an insurance scammer. I didn't know what he was talking about."

"People cause accidents like that, and then claim they have whiplash injuries," I said. "Your insurance company can end up paying thousands."

"I've heard of that," she said. "Chad got out of the car. He told me to stay where I was, and he closed the door. Locked it with the key fob.

"Two men got out of the other car. They were dressed in black, wearing hoodies, I think: I couldn't see their faces. Chad said something to them. Probably calling the driver a fucking idiot, knowing him. Then the other man, not the driver, hit Chad. They must have hit him hard, because he doubled over, holding his stomach.

"I was fumbling for my phone, wanting to call for help. And I could see them bundling Chad into the back of their car."

She had reduced the scone to what looked like a pile of breadcrumbs on the plate. She brushed crumbs from her fingers.

"I tried to get out of the car, but the door was locked. I had to use the release button. I got out and went up to their car, grabbed the door handle, but it was locked, of course. I could see Chad curled up on the back seat, still holding his stomach. I banged on the driver's window. They drove away at speed."

"Did you try and follow them?" I asked.

Lila Frayne shook her head slowly. "Our car was damaged. The headlights were smashed and the front bumper was hanging off. If I'd had the keys I might have chanced it, but Chad had taken them. I called for someone to come and pick me up. A taxi."

"You went home?" I asked.

"I didn't know what else to do. When I got home, I was going to call someone. But there was a note taped to the front door."

She reached into her bag again and pulled out another of the white envelopes. She pushed it across the table towards me. I didn't pick it up.

"Matt Lester showed me the ransom note," I said.

"I phoned Matt as soon as I got inside," she said.

"Why him?"

"He was someone my husband knew. I needed someone to help me. To tell me what I should do. I thought that if we did exactly what the kidnappers said, everything would be all right. That they would let Chad come home."

"You delivered the ransom money to a gym locker, the next day?" I said.

"There was a key in the envelope with that note," she said. "Matt told me the numbers in the note were co-ordinates. We looked them up, and saw it was the gym. And then he said the key was for a locker."

"After the money had been delivered, you received more co-ordinates; telling you where your husband could be found?"

"I received a text giving the details. Matt drove over there. It was a lay-by near the golf course," she said.

"There was supposed to be a shipping container there, and Chad was meant to be inside. But it wasn't there. There was no sign of my husband."

If she'd cried at this point, I would have suspected she was lying: women like her didn't cry. Not in front of other people.

"You received no other messages from the kidnappers?" I asked.

Lila shook her head. "I've tried calling the number, the one the text came from, but no one answers."

"They will have ditched the phone, so that no one can trace it."

"That's what Matt said."

"Matt Lester has been searching for your husband ever since?"

"He said he'd do everything he could to find Chad and bring him home," she said. "He hasn't had much success so far."

"Is that why you wanted to hire me?" I asked.

"I want to do whatever I possibly can to get my husband back, Mr. Lucke."

She stared me in the eye as she said this. What she had said matched what Matt Lester had told me, but you'd expect that it would. I had a nagging suspicion that both of them had left out something important.

"Matt Lester thinks Dick Gorse was one of the kidnappers: why is that?" I asked.

"I'm not sure. Matt said he'd found something, a clue, that led him to Dick Gorse. I don't think he said what it was. You can ask him."

"Big Dick was murdered two days after your husband was taken; possibly by the second kidnapper, his accomplice," I said.

"Matt said he thought that's what happened."

"Did Matt also say that he thinks your husband is already dead?" I asked.

"Yes, yes he did. That's another reason why I wanted to hire someone else. I can't give up hope. Not yet."

"You paid the ransom, but your husband wasn't returned. Did you think that Dick Gorse had double-crossed you?" I asked.

"Of course we did."

"Did you ask Matt Lester to confront him about it?"

"I didn't need to ask," she said.

"Did you ask Matt Lester to kill Big Dick?"

"No! I wouldn't do anything that would put Chad at risk. And Matt would never do anything like that."

She had more faith in Matt Lester than I did. But she was right about one thing: it would be a mistake to kill Big Dick until they knew what had happened to her husband. Lester would have had no qualms about torturing Dick Gorse, but he almost certainly wouldn't have killed him unless he'd revealed the location of the shipping container. And Matt Lester was still searching for the container, which meant he probably wasn't Big Dick's killer.

But there was every chance that Matt Lester *had* lured Tiago to Big Dick's store and tortured him to learn the location of the container. Then killed him and left the body in the store, and torched the place.

"Are you all right, Mr. Lucke?" Lila Frayne asked.

"Just trying to piece things together," I said. "I need to know where it happened. The spot your husband was taken from."

"Why?"

"I want to look at a map, see where they might have taken him. It had to be somewhere where there was a shipping container; perhaps more than one."

Lila was nodding, accepting the logic of what I was saying.

"Which road was it?" I asked.

"I have no idea," she said.

"How can you not know?"

"I wasn't driving, Chad was."

There had to be some way to find out where they had been.

"When you called for the taxi, how did you tell them where you were?" I asked.

"I got it from the satnav in the car. We'd used it to find our way to the dinner party, and then used 'take me home' to show us the way back."

"Do you know which taxi firm you called?" I asked.

"I Googled, rang the nearest one on the list."

"Is the number still in your phone?"

"I don't know." She dug in her little handbag and pulled out one of those rose-gold iPhones. The screen looked bigger than my TV. She unlocked it.

"It'll be in your call history for that night," I said.

Lila looked down at her phone and frowned. Then she held it out to me.

"You do it."

I took the phone and pulled up the call log. I scrolled back through it.

"Can you remember what date it was..?"

"The seventh, 2:07am," she said.

I raised an eyebrow.

"It's one of those events you're unlikely to forget," she said.

There was one call listed for that time, and another ten minutes later; neither had names against them. I wrote them down on the back of the envelope she'd put on the table. Her call log had a fair number of calls to and from Matt Lester. And a good few to someone called Edgar. But that really wasn't any of my business. I wrote Edgar's number down anyway.

"Is the text from the kidnapper still on here?" I asked.

"I never delete anything," she said.

"Okay if I look?"

"I've nothing to hide from you, Mr. Lucke."

The text was just as Matt Lester had described it: co-ordinates and the word 'container.' I copied down the number it had been sent from. I knew the phone wouldn't lead us to the kidnappers; but we might be able to see what other calls had be made from it, or received by it.

I swiped back to the home screen and handed the phone back to Lila.

"If I'm going to help you, I need you to tell me everything," I said.

"I have."

"There's something you're not telling me, Mrs. Frayne," I said.

"Miss," she said.

"Miss Frayne?"

That was what she wasn't telling me. I reached for the envelope and took out the ransom note. This copy hadn't been censored by Matt Lester. It wasn't the size of the ransom that drew my eye, even though the sum was a couple of hundred times more than the envelope of twenties she'd given me. No, it was her name at the top of the note that made me gasp. The thud I heard at that moment was the other she dropping.

"Mrs. Kazimir?" I said.

She smiled. "I often use my other name – when I don't want to advertise my connection to Chad's family."

"Your husband is Charles Kazimir? Youngest son of Rathbanian crime boss Tobias Kazimir?"

"He prefers import and logistics director," she said.

"The son of Tobias Kazimir has been kidnapped," I said, trying to make myself believe it. "I can't do this."

"We have a contract," she said.

If I could have given the thousand pounds back and walked away from this, I would have done. But I'd made a deal with the pink-lipped she-devil, and now I was cursed.

"Help me. Please?" Lila Kazimir-nee-Frayne said.

Tiago had asked me to find the shipping container, and I owed it to him to do that. And if he *was* dead, I wanted to know who killed him. Dick Gorse's killer had to be brought to justice too, whether or not Big Dick was a kidnapper. I would take the money, and I would investigate this case. Not for this awful woman and her husband, but for Charmaine, for my sister and my nephew.

"If I do this, I do it my way," I said. "If I discover that Matt Lester is guilty of murder or torture or anything else, he will have to pay for it."

Lila shrugged. "I don't owe him anything."

I assumed she'd abandon me to my fate just as easily. I stood and pocketed the second envelope.

"I'll be in touch."

As I walked towards reception, a tall blond man in short-shorts and a tight t-shirt was coming towards me. He grinned; I don't think I'd ever seen teeth that white.

"If you fancy a massage, I have a room free," he said.

I don't have enough flesh to massage, he'd get splinters.

"Maybe another time," I said.

"Ask for Matty," he said, and fired up the grin again.

As I walked past him, he slapped me on the bum. I walked on, not daring to look back.

Chapter Twenty-Four

The moment I pulled up outside my sister's house, Mrs. Kepler appeared at the side of the car. From nowhere. I sniffed the air, expecting to smell sulphur. The old woman was wearing a shapeless dress the colour of dead leaves, and her iron-grey hair was pulled back into a tight bun. She scowled at me over glasses that must have come from SpecSavers Dame Edna collection.

"That nephew of yours has been banging his balls against the garage door all afternoon. Please make him stop."

I knew what she meant, but I still had to hide my smirk. "I will ask him to put them away," I said.

"Hnph" she said, or something like that, and turned and sluthered away in her trodden-down carpet slippers.

I still wasn't sure if it was sulphur or mothballs that I could smell.

I headed up the drive, to where Jack was bouncing two tennis balls against the metal garage door with a steady rhythm.

"Jack, Mrs. Kepler says you are making too much noise with your balls," I said.

Jack didn't try to hide his smirk. He caught the tennis balls and turned, thrusting his groin towards me and waggling it.

"Too noisy?" he asked.

He was definitely spending too much time with Nathan's older brother.

"Throw them against the side of the garage, it makes less noise," I said.

"You want me to bang my balls against a *brick wall?*" He asked.

"I thought you were supposed to be throwing them in the air?"

Jack had been trying to juggle for the last couple of weeks, but hadn't managed to master the required hand-eye co-ordination.

"Where are you going?" I asked.

Jack was walking towards the gate. "If Mrs. Kepler is so interested in my balls, I thought she might like to see them."

"Don't you *dare!*"

"I meant *these,*" he said, holding out the tennis balls, his face a mask of innocence. "What were *you* thinking?"

"Is your mum inside?" I asked.

"No, she's abandoned me again. She's off cavorting with her fancy man."

"Jack!" Elise's voice boomed from inside the house.

"She must have just got back," Jack said. Then he whispered, "How did she *hear* that?"

"Women have ears like bats," I said. "That's something to bear in mind as you get older."

Jack looked like he was giving this serious thought.

Inside, Elise was ironing furiously. This wasn't a good sign. It's another thing she inherited from our mother.

"You okay?" I asked.

She glared at me.

"You haven't heard from Tiago?" I asked.

"Not one word." Elise slammed the iron down on a pair of Tiago's boxers.

"What did you *say* to him?" she asked.

"I told him that bad people were looking for him, and that he needed to be careful," I said.

There was a cold lump in my stomach that I had been trying to ignore. It had been there since I spoke with Dennis and Bob. I hadn't seen the charred body the police had pulled out of the wreckage of Big Dick's store, but images of it kept popping into my head when I least expected them. The images were never detailed enough for me to tell whether the blackened corpse had Tiago's face. But that meant the fear was always there. The not knowing. At the moment, I felt suspended in a place where Tiago was both alive and dead. Like Schrödinger and his cat. For now, I had to behave as though he was alive. Because that's what I *wanted* to believe. And it's what Elise needed to believe.

"He's really in trouble?" she asked, seeing something in my face.

"I'm trying to get him out of it," I said. "Can you smell burning?"

Elise looked down at the ironing board. "Shit!" She said.

"*I heard that!*" Jack's voice floated in from outside.

Elise held up the boxers. There was a big brown iron-shaped mark over the crotch.

"Ouch," I said. "Mrs. Kepler knows Tiago's been staying over, does she?"

"Why would you think that?" Elise said. Her innocent expression was no more convincing than Jack's.

"You're letting Jack bang tennis balls against the garage door, and he just used the phrase 'cavorting with her fancy man.'"

"Hey, maybe you are a detective after all!"

"What happened?"

"Nothing."

I didn't say anything. I knew she'd tell me. She'd been bottling it up all day.

"That bitch next door came round to complain because I hadn't fetched our wheelie bin in. I said I was sorry, I'd forgotten about it. And she said, *Perhaps if you hadn't been cavorting with your fancy man, the bin wouldn't have slipped your mind.*"

"Bitch, definitely," I said.

"Why are you smiling? That cow is making life a misery for us."

"I come bearing gifts," I said.

"Oh yes?" Elise looked at my empty hands.

"Gossip."

"About Mrs. Kepler?"

"Yes. Or rather, no," I said.

"Eh?"

"She's not really Mrs. Kepler."

"Is this some stupid made-up story about her being an undercover nun?" Elise demanded.

"No," I said, hurt. "That's Mrs. White at number 83. What would you say if I told you that your neighbour was never actually married to the late Mr. Kepler?"

"Really?!"

"The two of them lived in sin for 57 years," I said. "They couldn't get hitched because he was already married to a woman called Gretchen: she wouldn't give him a divorce."

"How do you know this?"

"Hey, maybe I really am a detective after all."

"You're *sure* about this?"

I nodded. "You should casually ask her, 'What happened to the first Mrs. Kepler? Gretchen was her name?' and see what reaction you get."

"She'll spontaneously combust!"

"Mrs. Kepler's real name is Daphne Squitz," I said.

"*Daphne?*" Elise asked, snorting.

"*That's* the part you find funny?" I asked. "You should tell her that Tiago wants to move in with you, but that you couldn't possibly live with a man that you're not married to!"

"You are such a *bitch,* Joe. Are you sure you're not gay?"

"Positive," I said, too quickly.

Memories of my first same-sex snog were too fresh in my mind. I'd been using mouthwash for days, and my tongue still didn't feel right. Elise obviously saw some hint of this in my expression.

"Is there something you're not telling me?" She asked.

"You know that song, *I Kissed a Boy and I Liked It?*" I said.

"Yes," she said, drawing out the word.

"Well, I didn't like it."

I told her about my encounter with Psycho-Pete.

"Then you're not gay," Elise said. "At least you know now."

"I've *always* known," I said.

"Of course you have. We all have. We never thought so for a minute," Elise said.

"Thought what?" Jack asked, coming in from outside.

Blood tricked from his left nostril. He reached for a box of tissues.

"Uncle Joe is not gay," Elise said.

"He's not?" Jack looked at me, clearly not convinced.

"What happened to your nose?" I asked.

"I threw the ball at the wall quite hard. It bounced back and hit me in the face quite hard," he said.

"Maybe you should go back to throwing them at the garage door," I said.

"No," Elise said, "we mustn't upset Mrs. Kepler."

"We mustn't?" Jack looked from his mother to me and back, confused at this change in attitude.

"Not until the moment is right," Elise said.

"You didn't let her have gin, did you?" Jack asked, screwing up the tissue and poking it up his nose. "She makes no sense when she's had gin. And she tries to give you kisses all the time."

I laughed.

"Uncle Joe's had quite enough kisses for a while," Elise said.

"Someone kissed Uncle Joe?" Jack looked at me as if to say 'Who would do such a thing?'

"You staying for tea?" Elise asked.

"Does it involve green vegetables?" Jack and I asked simultaneously.

Elise shook her head in exasperation.

"That was a *no*," Jack said.

"That's true," I said. "No backsies."

"What, are you both seven years old?" Elise asked.

"Can we have spaghetti Bolognese?" Jack asked.

"But not from a tin," I said.

Elise glared at us, and Jack and I favoured her with angelic smiles.

"Fine!" She said. "Jack, why don't you put the TV on? And ask Uncle Joe who kissed him."

She unplugged the iron and disappeared into the kitchen.

"Was she fit?" Jack asked. "Uncle Joe, why are you banging your head on the wall?"

Chapter Twenty-Five

When Fat Duncan phoned, I could tell he wasn't very happy. I didn't know if it was because I'd sent him the bill for repairs on the Honda, or because he'd found out I'd been investigating Dick's death, and had now taken on a client without consulting him. Or maybe he'd just run out of shortbread.

"You need to go and find Stacey," he said.

"Not again," I said.

Stacey Pearce was fifteen years old, and had been a missing person case I'd investigated a couple of years ago. She'd run away from home because or mother had said she couldn't have a unicorn tattoo, or something. She hadn't been hard to find. Stacey had obviously enjoyed the attention her little escapade gained her, and now we got three or four calls a year from her mother. This time she'd only been AWOL for three hours.

"Where is she?" I asked.

"Gosforth Street," Duncan said.

"Okay, I'm on my way. I'll need to get petrol sometime soon."

"Get a receipt," Duncan said, and hung up.

Gosforth Street. That meant Stacey was at the chip shop. Probably with her emo boyfriend.

Stacey was sitting on the railings outside the bingo hall when I pulled up. She was evidently still going through her Goth phase.

"About bloody time," she said, "I've been sat her so long my bum's numb."

"You were waiting for me?" I asked.

"I didn't think it would be the fat bastard, did I? I know he put something on my phone to track me. And I needed a lift home."

"You told your mother you were hitch-hiking to get the ferry to Calais!" I said.

"She pissed me off earlier."

She climbed down off the railings and massaged her butt cheeks.

"You're still driving this, then?" she said, looking down at the Honda.

"If you'd sooner walk?" I said.

"Don't get arsey. It's not like I'm slagging off your bird." She got into the car and slammed the door shut. Then slouched down in the seat so no one would see her. "Who drives a *yellow* car?" She asked.

"You told your mother you were running away, just so you could get a free lift home?"

"Genius, eh?" She grinned. "Spent all my cash in the chip shop. Daz's broke again, so I had to pay for him an' all."

"You deserve better than that, Stacey. It's time you found a bloke who can pay for his own chips. And yours."

"Yeah, but Daz's cute, in't he? If he knocks me up, at least the kid won't look like Quasimodo."

"Do you love him?" I asked.

"Nah, not really. But when we're doing it, he's not just in it for himself, you know what I mean? Most blokes only want to kiss above the waist."

"Too much information, Stacey."

"You're still not getting any, then?" she said.

"What would your mum think?" I asked.

"She'd be dead jealous, I reckon. She ant been with a man for so long hers has probably healed shut."

"Stacey!"

"I'm just saying. Can we stop at the corner and get some cans of cider?"

"I thought you'd run out of money?"

"Your treat, then, eh? I'll blow you for it, if you like."

"I'm not swapping you a blow job for a can of Strongbow," I said.

"Not one can, a four-pack. How cheap do you think I am?"

I gave her a tenner. It was preferable to answering her question. As we pulled up, I saw Daz sitting opposite the off-licence; further proof of how carefully this sting operation had been set-up.

"I'll phone your mother and tell her you're not going to Calais," I said.

"To where? Oh, yeah. But don't tell her the other stuff I said. She doesn't even know I'm on the pill."

I was sure that Mrs. Pearce would have been relieved to hear this, but I promised not to breathe a word.

"Don't even tell her I suck his knob. She'll just get embarrassed when he comes round for tea on Saturday."

Stacey kissed me on the cheek as she got out, and I couldn't help wondering where her lips had been this afternoon.

Daz was a pale, scrawny kid with a pierced lip. He had black hair with ginger roots, and a couple of nasty-looking patches of acne on his cheeks. But he was getting more sex than I was. He raised his black-gloved hand and gave me the finger as I drove off. I was so tempted to tell Mrs. Pearce about the knob-sucking.

All that talk about eating had made me hungry, so I headed back to the chip shop. I ordered a portion of chips with a meat pie and gravy. I couldn't face the sausage. I sat parked on a double-yellow line and tucked in. There were no traffic wardens in Mansfield, and you wouldn't see a traffic cop even if you handed out free doughnuts. And yet somehow the town hadn't descended into anarchy.

I was just drinking the last of the gravy out of the bottom of the tray when a car pulled up behind me. Blue lights flashed briefly, identifying it as a police car. I wound down my window.

"Excuse me, sir, would you mind stepping out of your vehicle," a voice said.

"What do you want?" I asked.

"Do you know that you're parked on a double-yellow line?"

"If I move my car now, I might accidentally reverse it into that shiny new Volvo back there," I said.

"You wouldn't?" Bob said.

"I might, if I got all flustered from being harassed by a police officer," I said.

"Just get out of the car, Joe. We're not getting in there, it stinks of chips," Dennis said.

"Did you save us one?" Bob asked.

I held out the empty tray. "Sorry," I said.

I got out of the Honda and stuffed the tray and papers into the bin on the corner. Bob and Dennis were leaning against their car when I turned back. They probably thought they looked like something out of *The Sweeney*. They looked more like something to go into Mrs. Lovett's pies. Try a little police.

The two detectives seemed to have fallen back into their bright-cop-thick-cop routine, which I took to be a good sign. And they also had that 'we know something he doesn't know' thing going again. It was too soon for them to have DNA test results back on the body from the fire, so I wondered what confidential information they couldn't wait to reveal.

"I'm not keeping you from anything important, am I?" I asked. "No criminals to arrest or anything?"

"This from a man we saw standing around with his dick in his hand," Bob said.

"But we did admire you that night," Dennis said.

"We did?" Bob looked a little worried.

"We always admire a man who can take care of himself," Dennis said.

"Good one!" Bob said.

"I wasn't alone that night," I reminded them.

"That's true. We didn't interrupt anything, did we?" Bob asked.

I expect my squint made me look a lot like Popeye.

"I'm sorry, mate," Dennis said. "We didn't know it was your birthday."

"Better luck next year," Bob said.

"Finished?" I said.

Bob looked at Dennis for guidance.

Dennis nodded: they'd run out of gags.

My turn. "What do you call a detective with an IQ of 12?" I asked.

"Gifted!" Bob said triumphantly. He'd heard that one before.

"I rest my case," I said.

"What?" Bob asked.

Dennis was scowling at him.

"How many detectives does it take to change a light bulb?" I asked.

"Enough!" Dennis said. "We didn't come here to trade insults."

"We didn't?" Bob said.

Dennis shook his head, and Bob mirrored him.

"Why *did* we come here?" Bob asked.

It looked like Dennis was winding up to punch him on the nose.

"Tell me your news," I said quickly.

Dennis turned his attention back to me, relaxing his shoulders.

"We went to Tiago Zambora's flat," he said, "that towel with the blood on it? It wasn't his."

"Wasn't his towel or wasn't his blood?" I asked.

"Wasn't his blood. Wrong type. We got his medical records from the prison."

"Dental records too," Bob said.

"The body from the fire?" Dennis said. "Also not his."

"Tiago's not dead," I said.

"Not as far as we know," Bob said.

"Then who was it died in the fire?" I asked.

"We don't know for sure yet, but we think he may have been dead before the fire started," Dennis said.

"Do you know who it was?" I asked.

"We wouldn't know, if it hadn't been for you," Bob said.

"What did I do?"

"You asked us to check out Matthew Lester," Dennis said.

"He had a health care plan from his previous employer. Do you get one of those from Fat Duncan?" Bob asked.

"I get a box of band aids."

"They got us his dental records. And they matched," Dennis said.

"Matt Lester was the dead man from the fire?" I asked.

Bob nodded. "And possibly also the blood on the towel. Types match. We're waiting for DNA."

They both looked at me. I didn't know what to say.

"He doesn't look happy to know his brother-in-law isn't dead," Bob said.

Dennis didn't say anything. He knew what I was thinking.

It was great news that Tiago wasn't dead. But he had been at the scene of the fire, and that was terrible news. Even though Bob and Dennis hadn't said as much, I knew they now regarded Tiago as a suspect. He was suspected of arson. He was suspected of murdering Matt Lester. And he was a possible suspect in the murder of Dick Gorse.

"If you see Tiago Zambora, will you tell him we'd like to speak to him?" Dennis asked.

"I will," I said.

I wanted to speak to him myself. I opened the car door.

"Wait!" Bob said. "How many does it take?"

"What?" I said.

"The lightbulbs."

"Three," I said.

"But... why?"

"You're the detective, figure it out."

Chapter Twenty-Six

"Joseph, how lovely to see you again." Uncle Benny's face lit up with a smile that might have been genuine affection, but probably had more to do with him imagining me naked and restrained. He looked like a fat baby that has just spotted puréed apricot dessert. We began our slow-motion bookshop *paso doble* as he came around the counter and began stalking me, and I attempted to keep some piece of furniture between us at all times.

"Looking for something exciting to take to bed?" he asked.

"Still making my way through *Lord of the Rings*," I said. I'd been reading it since I was twelve and still hadn't got past half-way.

"I have the DVDs, if you'd like to watch them," he said, "we could make a night of it."

I'd watched the special editions over Christmas, and it had taken me almost a week to get through all the discs. And I was sure Uncle Benny's idea of 'extras' would involve more than a documentary about how the frocks were made. In a hole in the ground lived a pervert; it wasn't a dirty, smelly hole, but it did house a selection of latex appliances...

"I need some information," I said, stepping behind a glass case of crumbly leather-bound books.

"Ask away, dear boy," he said, feinting to the left and then coming straight towards me.

"What do you know about Chad Kazimir?" I asked.

"He's Tobias Kazimir's youngest son. Nice looking, but a bit of a brat. Always gets what he wants. Unlike us normal folk."

Uncle Benny's definition of 'normal' was more flexible than a Chinese contortionist.

"Tell me what you know about him," I said, moving a folding stepladder to block his advance.

Uncle Benny peered at me through the wooden framework of the ladder and sighed.

"You only ever come here when you *want* something," he complained. "And it's never the same thing I want."

"Perhaps we're just not compatible," I said.

"I'm sure we could adapt. A relationship's all about give and take."

"But I don't want to take what you're thinking of giving," I said.

"I'm sure I don't know what you mean," he said.

Pouting, he headed back to his stool behind the counter.

I relaxed a little, but knew better than to let down my guard completely. There might still be traps hidden around the shop.

"Tell me about his wife," I said.

"Lila? Another spoiled bitch. They've only been married for eighteen months, and by all accounts it has been pretty stormy. I've heard accounts of spousal abuse."

"Chad's a wife-beater?"

Uncle Benny shook his head. "She hit him. With a foot spa. He probably deserved it. Chad has a mistress, and he isn't very discreet about it."

"I think Lila has a lover too," I said.

"I didn't know that."

"Perhaps she *is* discreet about it."

"Who is he?" Uncle Benny asked.

"She's my client," I said, "I can't tell you. I need to talk to Chad's mistress."

Uncle Benny smiled. "Dolores Melrose," he said.

He had a far-away look in his eyes, and for some irrational reason I felt a twinge of jealousy. 'Dolores Melrose' wasn't the name Uncle Benny gave me, but I promised not to reveal her real name. And every story should have a Dolores.

* * *

Cornflower Crescent was in one of those characterless new-build estates that are springing up all over the place. The houses on the estate were mostly big family homes, two-storey, three and four bedrooms, tiny front and back gardens. There were also a couple of rows of three-storey, one-and-a-half bedroom 'townhouses,' in a nod towards affordable housing.

Number seven was just like all the others on the crescent: white uPVC window frames and a brown wooden door. The car in the driveway was a light blue Volkswagen, one of the ones with a folding metal roof. It was pulled up close to the garage door, leaving room behind it on the drive for another car. Just waiting for the husband, an estate agent perhaps, to come back from work. Except there was no husband. I parked on the street a couple of houses up, and walked back.

There was a woman kneeling in the front garden, digging out weeds with a stainless-steel trowel. She was wearing a light green dress with a pattern of small white daisies. A wide-brimmed sunhat hid her face from me. She wasn't at all what I had been expecting. I checked the little brass number on the door. Seven.

"Miss Melrose?" I asked.

She turned and looked up at me, shielding her eyes from the sun. She looked to be in her mid-fifties.

"Dolores," she said.

I stared at her without meaning to. On a good day, I might weigh as much as nine stone. I guessed that she was more than double that. A lot of effort had gone into her make-up to give the appearance that she wasn't wearing any. That's a rare skill. Her eyes were a very pale blue, and she had a slight overbite that meant she tried to hide her teeth when she smiled. Dolores tilted her head on one side, watching me look at her.

"I'm sorry, I was expecting..." My voice trailed off.

"... someone taller?" she asked, gently mocking.

If I had offended her, she hid it well.

"I don't know what I was expecting," I said.

With a little effort, she got to her feet. "Not your typical mistress, am I, Mr. Lucke?"

"You know who...?"

"Alfie said you'd drop by," she said.

"Alfie?" I frowned.

"Uncle Benny," she said. "Didn't you know his real name?"

"I try to know as little about him as possible," I said.

She laughed. "He's an odd little man. But harmless, I think."

"You're only saying that because you're not a skinny white boy," I said.

"I'm not a skinny anything," she said. "Let's talk inside."

I followed her in. She took off the sunhat, dropping it on the hall table. She cast a quick look in the mirror, adjusting a stray strand of hair. She caught me watching her, and smiled. "Come through," she said.

The house was pleasantly furnished. The three-piece was plump and flowery, the carpet a plain wool twist.

There was an arrangement of dried and artificial flowers in the empty fireplace. A bowl of potpourri on the side-table scented the air with oranges and spice. It was like being in your aunt's house.

"Would you like some tea?" Dolores asked. "I have fruitcake. Or biscuits."

I politely declined, unsure whether she was just being polite, or thought that I needed fattening up. That thought brought to mind the witch from Hansel and Gretel, so I decided to stay well away from the oven.

"You're not afraid of me, are you?" she asked, smiling at my discomfort. "I don't gobble up young men for breakfast."

"I didn't think you did," I said.

If she'd worn glasses, she would have looked over them at me: she could tell I was lying.

I had a bit of a crush on Kathleen Turner when I was younger, and Dolores reminded me of that. There was a hint of Jessica Rabbit in her voice. Playful and sexy, with a hint of vulnerability. It was like revisiting that moment when you look at your friend's mum and wonder what she looks like when she's taking a shower. One of those moments that feels exciting and yet wrong, all at the same time.

"Shall we sit?" Dolores said. She clasped her hands in front of her in a way that looked like she was trying to shake hands with herself, and I realised that she was nervous too. Like someone anticipating bad news.

I sat on the sofa, and she lowered herself into an armchair. I tried to think of some way to break the ice.

"You're wondering what a thirty-year-old man is doing keeping me, when he has a pretty blonde wife at home," she said.

"I wasn't... actually, I was. But I'm not judging," I said.

That was a lie too, of course. I was thinking what everyone else must have thought. What's Chad doing with a woman who's old enough to be his mother? Old guys with young women, we seem to accept. If we're generous we'll refer to them as May-December romances. If we're not, we refer to him as a randy old goat. But either way, we accept it. But with older women, we haven't progressed much in the fifty years since *The Graduate*.

"I met him when he was nineteen, and I was forty-three," she said. "If you're thinking that I seduced him, took advantage of a teenage boy desperate for a first sexual experience, it wasn't like that. There had been girls before he met me. I think he was bored with them. He wanted someone who had..."

"... more experience?" I asked.

"Yes. But not in the way you think."

I supposed she'd had a lot of time to think about what other people might be thinking.

"It wasn't just sex. Though god knows, there was plenty of that! But he wanted more out of life than that. Travel, and dancing, and – and laughing. We were always laughing!"

"Sounds romantic," I said.

"It was. It really was. I think he could just – relax when he was with me. Away from his family."

"He told you about his family?" I asked.

"I knew what he did, Mr. Lucke. He bought me a car, and this house, and I have money in the bank. I didn't think he worked on a market stall or dug ditches. But we didn't talk about any of it. That was the whole point. I was his escape."

"Was?" I asked.

She'd been referring to Chad in the past tense since I got there.

"It's over, isn't it?" she said. "That's why you're here."

"When was the last time you saw him?" I asked.

She wasn't smiling now. And it was as if the years had all piled up on her suddenly.

"A fortnight ago," she said. "It's the longest he's ever gone without calling me or sending me a message. The last time he was here, he wanted to have a barbecue in the back garden. I don't think he'd ever cooked anything in his life. You've never see so much smoke. None of it was edible. And we just..."

"... laughed?" I said.

"Yes, we laughed. I didn't know then that he was saying goodbye."

"I'm not sure he knew either," I said.

"I'd seen less of him since he got married. I expected that. But that made the times we did have even better. I appreciated them. Didn't take them for granted. He's not coming back is he?"

"I don't know," I said. Then I felt bad about lying to her. "I don't think so."

"Has something happened to him? Something bad?"

I didn't want to answer, but I suppose she could tell from my face. She got up and looked down at me.

"Please tell me," she said.

"I'm trying to find out what has happened," I said. "I was told he had been kidnapped, shown a ransom note."

"He's dead, isn't he?"

"I can't be..."

"I have to know. Don't make me have to sit here not knowing. No one will come and tell me. They don't care how the mistress feels. Our grief doesn't count."

"I don't have any proof, but... yes, I think he was killed," I said.

"Thank you," she whispered.

For a moment, she just stood there. A picture of dignity in the face of tragedy. Then her knees buckled and she staggered backwards, dropping into the armchair. Her face was expressionless.

"I'm sorry," I said.

She didn't look at me.

"Is there anything I can do?" I asked. "Someone I can call?"

"There's no one." Her voice was a hoarse whisper.

I stood and went through to the kitchen, filled the kettle. I put teabags into the little red teapot, and went to the fridge for milk.

"Please, don't..." Dolores stood in the doorway, leaning against the frame.

"I don't want to just drop a bombshell and then leave," I said.

She smiled sadly. "You're sweet, Joe. But I need to be alone."

"Are you sure?"

She crossed the kitchen and turned off the kettle.

I looked at her, not knowing what to say. I took out my wallet and found one of the home-made business cards. I placed it on the counter.

"If you need anything, call me," I said.

She nodded.

"If I hear anything, about what happened, I'll let you know," I said.

"Thank you, Mr. Lucke."

Chapter Twenty-Seven

I was in Aldi car park, loading groceries into the boot of the Honda. I'd decided to splurge using some of Lila Frayne's cash. I had given Fat Duncan a hundred quid and told him that's what she'd given me as a retainer. He didn't query it: we didn't usually get even that much. I was returning my trolley to the bay when a phone rang in my pocket. This confused me. It wasn't my phone that was ringing. It was the one Sergei had given me.

"Hello?" I said.

"My employer wishes to speak to you." Sergei's voice.

"All right. When and where?" I said.

He hung up. How rude.

A grey limousine slid to a stop in front of me. When you're a crime boss, you have to know how to make an entrance. It's not every day you see a limo in Aldi car park. Posh folks usually send their servants to do the weekly shop and pick up the Thursday specials. It was one of the big Jaguars, the kind the Prime Minister uses. I suppose BMWs and Range Rovers are too passé for crime bosses these days. It was so clean and shiny that it didn't look real. Someone had Photoshopped it into an ordinary car park scene.

Sergei climbed out from behind the wheel, walked around the back of the car and opened the rear door. When no one got out, I figured he must be waiting for me to get in. I slid into the back seat.

Sitting in the back on the cream leather, Mr. Kazimir also looked computer-generated. His dark suit was just too crisp; shirt too white; skin too smooth; and his pale grey hair cut too evenly. He was Steven Berkoff playing Hannibal Lecter. Only scarier. If he'd smiled and revealed fangs, I wouldn't have been surprised. He didn't smile.

Inside the Jaguar was cleaner than my Aunt Sadie's bungalow, and she has that obsessive cleaning disorder. Baths the cat twice a day, and has the scratches on her arms to prove it. It smelled of leather and expensive cologne. Kazimir's car, not my aunt's cat. That smelled of Johnson's baby shampoo and tuna fish.

"Mr. Kazimir," I said, to break the ice. My voice wasn't as strong as I'd hoped it would be.

"Mr. Lucke," he said.

Quiet and confident. Hint of an accent. I think he'd spent a lot of time in Newcastle. He sounded like a Geordie Orson Welles. Probably the scariest voice in the world, pet.

"No thugs today?" I asked.

"Do you think I need any?"

He turned towards me, and I noticed a scar on his upper lip on the left side. He probably had scars on his knuckles too. He didn't need a back-up team.

Sergei got back behind the wheel, and the car moved away. It was very quiet inside. I could hear my own heart beating.

"What do you want?" I asked.

"I want to apologise," he said. "I thought I ought to do it personally."

"Apologise?"

"The other evening, when my boys came to speak with you – there was a misunderstanding, I think."

"Was there? I think I understood what they were saying. Give us the shipping container *or else*."

"I did not intend that they should threaten you," he said. "Dominic will be reprimanded."

I glanced towards the front seat. Was Sergei's real name Dominic? He looked straight ahead.

"He will swim with the fishes?" I asked.

"He will work at the car wash. Learn some customer service skills," Mr. Kazimir said.

"I should take my car over there," I said.

"I wouldn't advise that," Mr. Kazimir said. "I think only the dirt is holding it together."

He was probably right. I glanced out of the window: we'd just turned off Nottingham Road and seemed to be heading towards Berry Hill. There were trees here, and the houses were built from orange stone, not brick. It was a different world.

"Now that we have cleared up that misunderstanding, perhaps we may have a little chat. As friends."

"Steady on," I said.

"Would it make things easier if I offered you money?" he asked.

I was tempted to say, 'How much?' – but it wouldn't have mattered. Probably.

"No," I said.

"I thought not. What *do* you want, Mr. Lucke?"

"I want to see whoever murdered Dick Gorse brought to justice," I said. "I don't care who killed him, they have to answer for it."

"Do you think it could have been me that killed him?" he asked.

"I'm sure you didn't do it personally," I said.

"What reason would I have to kill him?"

"You think he kidnapped your son," I said.

"What do you know about that?"

"I've seen the ransom note," I said, "I know the money was paid."

"Then you also know that my son was not returned by the kidnappers."

"The container with him inside was not delivered," I said. "Or perhaps it was, and was then taken by someone else, I'm not sure about that yet."

"Lila has asked you to find the container?" he asked.

"I was looking for it anyway. Tiago asked me to find it: he feels responsible for losing it. Especially since your 'boys' threatened his life."

"Did they do that?" Mr. Kazimir asked.

"I think it highly likely," I said, "based on my own experience."

"You think your brother-in-law is innocent, that he played no part in my son's kidnapping?"

"I know he moved the container," I said. "I don't think he knows where it is, or who took it. Beyond that, I don't know what his involvement is."

"And if it turns out that he is the killer of Dick Gorse, or of Lila's other detective?"

"Then he must face the consequences of his actions," I said.

Mr. Kazimir stared into my face. Perhaps he was trying to determine my resolve.

"Where is my daughter-in-law, Mr. Lucke?"

"Lila's at home, as far as I know," I said.

Mr. Kazimir turned and looked out of the window, and I guessed that meant she wasn't.

Mr. Kazimir turned back and looked into my eyes. I think he was trying that vampire hypnotism thing.

"Tell me where she is," he said.

"If I knew, I wouldn't tell you," I said.

"I think you would," he said, "eventually."

And we were back to threats again.

"The problem with torture is that the victim either tells you nothing, or exactly what they think you want to hear. They rarely tell you the truth. It's all a lot of wasted effort and unnecessary suffering."

"The thing about pain," Mr. Lucke, "is that it isn't always about obtaining information. Sometimes it is about establishing a relationship. Demonstrating a place in the hierarchy."

"Just because someone is afraid of you doesn't mean they respect you," I said.

"If they fear me, I do not need their respect."

"Frightened people are more dangerous," I said. "They'll do anything to protect themselves.

"Are you afraid of me, Mr. Lucke?"

"Should I be?"

"Yes, I think you should."

"Lila is my client. My duty is to protect her."

"You are a man of honour."

I wasn't sure if that was something he approved of.

"I take my job seriously," I said. "If you want me to take a message to Lila, I will."

"What I want, Mr. Lucke, is to get my son back. Do not misunderstand me, I am not some ridiculous optimist: I know he is dead. If he was not dead before the ransom was delivered, he is dead now. His body is in the shipping container, and I will have it back. And if the people who killed him are still alive – I will deal with them. You may tell Lila that."

"She wants the same thing you do," I said. "Though I think she would prefer it if Chad wasn't found dead."

"She is a woman," he said. "When you find the container, you will tell me where it is. Use the phone Dominic gave you."

"Dominic?"

Mr. Kazimir nodded towards our driver. He meant Sergei. He would always be 'Saggy' to me.

The car drew to a stop, and I could see that we were on the road not far from the entrance to Aldi. I hoped my frozen food hadn't defrosted.

"I will have my son and his killer, Mr. Lucke. Stand in my way, and you will know what it is to be afraid."

Sergei got out and opened the door for me. My audience was over.

"Good luck with the car wash," I said, as I walked away.

Chapter Twenty-Eight

Nad's Cabs was run out of a little shop on Church Street, just down from the viaduct. The window and door were completely covered by blue and yellow signs with the phone number in three-foot letters. The same number I'd gotten from Lila Frayne's phone.

I opened the door and stepped inside. There was an odd sort of blue and yellow twilight within. The air was smoky and filled with the aroma of incense. Or something. Behind the counter were two young Indian men. Identical twins.

"I'd like to speak to the manager, please?" I said.

"That would be Nad," said one of the young men.

"An audience with Nad cannot be had," said the second.

"We are not Nad," said the first.

"Nad is our dad," said the second.

"We are Nad's lads," they said in unison.

I felt like I'd stepped into a Dr. Seuss story. I wasn't sure if they were treating me to a well-rehearsed routine. Or if they were just stoned.

"When will Nad be back?" I asked.

"No time soon. Nad's back is bad."

"I was hoping to get some information," I said.

The telephone rang, and the first youth held up a hand, while the second answered it.

"Nad's cabs – if you need a ride, you've dialled okay. If you need a kebab, your call's gone astray. Asif speaking, how may I help you?... What address, please?... How many persons?... And what name?... Thank you, a driver will be with you in ten minutes..."

He hung up.

"... and if you're lucky, he'll have a car with him."

Manning the phones at a taxi company must be mind-numbingly dull.

"You wanted information about Nad's?" the first youth asked.

"I want to ask about a fare you picked up on the seventh – around 2 am."

"What, they still haven't arrived? Probably delayed by roadworks."

"Don't be an idiot," I said.

"Don't you tell my brother not to be an idiot," the other one said, "that's asking the impossible!"

His brother nodded in agreement. "Our mother dropped one of us on the head when we were young, and since that day we don't know which of us is which, right Asif?"

"Absolutely not wrong, Asif."

"The seventh?" Asif asked. He turned to his brother. "Were you driving that day?"

"Yes, you were," Asif replied.

"Then it was you that picked up the pretty blonde lady from the side of the road?"

"Indeed you did. And let me tell you, she had never in her life been so pleased to see Nad's coming towards her in the dark."

His brother giggled at this.

"You drive a taxi?" I asked, looking from one stoned brother to the other.

They both nodded and smiled.

Then Asif looked at Asif.

"Do we?"

Then they both nodded again. Then in a heartbeat, their expressions changed to ones of suspicion.

"Why do you want to know?"

"If you're from the tax office, let me say that I completed the form to the best of my limited abilities," Asif said.

"But sometimes I become confused between imperial and metric measures. Especially when it comes to money," Asif added.

"I'm not from the tax office," I said.

They didn't look convinced.

"I'm a private detective," I said.

Both faces brightened into smiles.

"Ah, you are like Lew Archer. Asif and I are both big fans, are we not, brother?"

"Indeed, we have borrowed them all from the public lending library. And some of them we actually read."

"Private detective, eh? A life of good food and fast women, eh?"

I didn't like to tell him mine was a life of fast food and no women. And sometimes no food. I'm sure I'm not typical of the industry, and I don't want to tarnish the image for others.

"What crime are you investigating?" Asif asked.

"I'm not at liberty to say," I said.

They both nodded at this.

"Do you have a gun?" Asif asked.

"Have you ever killed anyone?" his brother asked.

I shook my head.

"Only in videogames," I said.

"I too have never killed anyone," Asif said. "Except for the man I hit with my car. But I think he was already dead. He was lying in the road when I got there. This happened in India, near the village of my father's family."

"People lie in the street all the time," his brother said. "Have you seen *Slumdog Millionaire?*"

I nodded.

"Where we grew up, it was very much like that. Do you know Bulwell at all? It is without doubt the arsehole of Nottinghamshire. Our parents moved us to Hucknall as soon as they could. The air is much fresher. No dead dogs in the street.

The atmosphere in the shop was beginning to make me feel woozy.

"What crime did you say you were investigating?" Asif asked.

"I didn't," I said.

"You should," he said. "If you want us to be your prime witness who must be protected."

"I'm investigating the theft of a shipping container – off the back of a truck," I said.

"You are looking for something off the back of a lorry? That is what my cousin Rajesh does. He makes way more money than a taxi driver," Asif said.

"His father used to beat him for stealing," the other Asif said, "but now he drives around in a Mercedes Rajesh got for him and asks no questions."

The Asian doobie-brothers looked at each other and shrugged, as if to say 'What can you do?'

"Tell me about the fare you picked up on the seventh," I said.

"It wasn't me," Asif said, "it was Asif. Wasn't it Asif?"

"I'm sure it was. I think. I drive a lot. I drive into Nottingham sometimes. Sometimes to the airport. I am often having famous people in the back of my cab. Oh yes. Once I had the man who plays the villain in the spray cream commercial."

"I've seen that one," I said.

"*I have all the cans, and now you shall have scones without cream! Bwahaha!*" He misquoted. "Unfortunately he had no free samples, which was a big disappointment to my brother and I. He and I very much enjoy spray cream. We put it on all of our things."

"It has many uses," I said.

Asif and Asif nodded.

"My brother squirts it up his nose and then snorts it down and swallows it," Asif said, "but that is because he is uncouth."

"Young people today, eh?" I shook my head. "Let me take you back to the night of the seventh..."

"You wish me to play a part in your investigation?" Asif asked.

"I do," I said. "I would like you to tell me about the woman you picked up early that morning."

"What character do you think I should play?" Asif asked his brother.

"You cannot sing or dance. You must be the comedy Indian character," his brother said.

"Do you think I could carry that off?" Asif asked me.

"I thought you already were," I said.

"I will be the comedy Indian, oh yes, indeed. It will be very much the wheezing of the wizard, will it not?"

If Apu in *The Simpsons* makes you cringe, Asif's fake Indian accent would have had you doubled-over and running for the hills. I felt too dizzy to run.

"It was being a dark and stormy night," Asif began, staring into the middle distance and making a sweeping theatrical motion with his hands.

"It was dry and starry," his brother corrected.

"It was? Perhaps this was another night."

"Stay with the seventh," I urged.

"The call came in a little after two, a damsel in distress," Asif said. Now he was Asian Humphrey Bogart.

"Do you have a record of the call?" I asked.

"An LP?"

"Do you note down the details of the location for the pick-up?" I asked.

"Of course we do, I have to tell him like a million times before he gets there. He never remembers. I think it comes from being dropped on his head as a child."

"That or the weed," his brother said.

"Weed? Have you been smoking again? You promised father you wouldn't."

"No, I promised him you wouldn't."

"Could you tell me the location where you picked up the blonde lady from the side of the road? Please, just look it up."

I was worried that I might spend the rest of my life in this smoky little room having this conversation. I was sure I'd already missed two birthdays.

"Location," Left Asif said. An instruction to his brother.

Right Asif rattled off a series of numbers. Fifty-three point something. GPS co-ordinates? If they were, how could he have remembered them?

"He's like Rainman," his brother said. "I'm the handsome one, he's the genius."

"He thinks *he* looks like Tom Cruise," his brother scoffed.

I asked Asif to repeat the numbers, so I could write them down. Writing was more difficult than I usually found it, but things improved when I got the cap off the pen.

"You've been very helpful, thank you," I said.

"We have?" Asif asked. "How did that happen?"

His brother shrugged.

I moved towards the door.

"You must come back and tell us when you have apprehended the dastardly do-badders, yes?" Asif said, in his cartoon accent.

"I shall," I said, backing away.

"Perhaps you will even come to dinner with my brother and myself. You could have spray cream on your spotted dick."

I exited, leaving them giggling to themselves.

Outside I took several deep breaths and waited for the pavement to stop swaying.

As I made my way back along the street towards the Honda, a smartly-dressed woman stopped me.

"Excuse me, can you tell me where I can find Nad's?"

I just looked at her and giggled.

* * *

I had a couple of Mars Bars for lunch, and then had a bit of a lie down on the sofa. I woke up just after three in the afternoon with a slight headache.

I drank a pint of cold tap water while I waited for the laptop to boot up. Once I'd dismissed the pop-ups telling me my anti-virus subscription has expired, I fed the co-ordinates from the Brothers Asif into Google, and peered at the aerial photograph of the location.

It was a narrow country road in the middle of nowhere, with trees on one side, and a field on the other. The Honda didn't have sat-nav, so I printed out a step-by step route that would take me from the door of my flat to the spot where Lila Frayne's husband had been abducted. I grabbed a six-pack of sausage rolls from the fridge: I was starving again.

It wasn't just a narrow country road. It was a deserted narrow country road. Even at the time of day, when parents are usually causing two-mile traffic jams as they drive the two miles to pick up their children, there was nothing on this road. It was like a road from a time before cars existed. It was creepy: *Twilight Zone* stories could take place on roads like this.

The GPS co-ordinates were only a general location; they didn't pinpoint an actual spot. I drove along slowly, looking for any indication of vehicular wrongdoing. The weather had been dry for the past month, so I was hopeful that any signs at the scene would still be there. At one point, a woman on a big, dark-coloured horse with white feet waved in thanks at my snail-pace, horse-friendly driving. I waved back. I hadn't seen her approach. If she'd been on my side of the road, I would probably have run into the back of her horse.

A few minutes later, I saw an area where the grass had been disturbed on the other side of the road, near the trees. It looked like a car had driven off the road onto the grass. I drove on a few more yards, then executed a text-book three-point turn, and pulled off the road a short distance from the potential crime-scene. I got out of the Honda and approached the spot.

If I hadn't heard Lila Frayne's account, I couldn't have made anything from the marks at the side of the road. Except for the fact that a car had pulled off the tarmac there. There was a small skid mark, hardly more than scuffed gravel, and further along, you could just about make out tyre marks on the road where brakes had been applied sharply to halt a car. Other than that, nothing.

There were no obvious signs of an impact. No pieces of broken plastic bumper, no fragments of glass. Someone had done a good job of the clear-up. There were a couple of patches of reddish sand sprinkled in the middle of the road. They didn't look like anything significant. I brushed aside the dry top layer with the toe of my shoe. The sand underneath had a darker tint to it. It had been put down to soak something up. Maybe oil from the damaged car engine. Maybe blood from the damaged husband.

I could have scooped up a sample and taken it home. There are tests that can be done to determine whether blood is present. But I'd seen enough evidence to suggest that Lila Frayne's story was probably true. I couldn't tell whether there had been a truck at the scene, but something had taken the damaged car away.

I sat in the Honda looking out at the empty road, trying to imagine the scene as the kidnapping took place. Something about the whole set-up didn't feel right, but I couldn't decide what. Two men had staged an accident and whisked Chad Kazimir away. It sounded like the opening scene of a cop show. One of the men had been Dick Gorse, and the other had yet to be identified. It may have been Matt Lester. Or it may have been Tiago Zambora. Or it may have been someone else. I needed to do some more of the gumshoe thing.

I took out my nasty little phone and sent a text to Jerzy: *Where's Pete?* I got a reply almost immediately: young people always have their phones to hand, and rarely delay their responses: you have to move quickly if you're going to keep up with the constant stream of trivia that floods in. Thinking of Jerzy as 'young people' made me feel old suddenly. His message looked like some sort of code: *Allandale hall C U soon*.

Chapter Twenty-Nine

The old hall was on Allandale Road. I thought Pete was there because it was out-of-the-way and seldom visited. I was wrong. When I got there, it was buzzing like a drop-kicked hornets' nest.

The red bricks of the hall's façade were stained and faded, and the cornerstones had been painted cream at some point, but they were flaking now. Weathered stone steps led up to battered double doors, and one side the steps had been clumsily adapted to make a ramp for wheelchairs. It had originally been a theatre and dance hall, back in the days when everyone smoked and all men wore hats. The stage and the parquet floor were still in place, but the entertainment it hosted had changed over the years. It had been a discotheque in my mum's day. Then a bingo hall, until one of the big chains moved into town. Then I think it briefly re-opened as a roller-skating rink. Now it was just a run-down space that you could rent to hold your yoga class or your 'indoor car boot sale.' Or your local fashion show.

Inside, it looked like a free-for-all, where Goths, hippies, and punks were battling it out to see who had the wildest hair. Down both sides of the hall, local makers and students were setting up stalls. Home-brewed cosmetics; pre-painted false fingernails; wigs and hair extensions; and eye-lashes that looked too big for human eyelids, were all mixed among displays of tie-dyed, retro, and unclassifiable displays of clothing. Jerzy had told me about this show when he'd cut my hair, but I'd forgotten to mark the date in my calendar.

The middle of the hall was dominated by a catwalk, about waist high, that extended outwards from the stage. It seemed to have been constructed from scaffolding and plastic pallets. I spotted Jerzy trying to organise a handful of people who were attempting to fix a little curtain of fabric all along the sides of the catwalk to hide its construction. He was dressed in tight black jeans and a black turtle-neck, and his hair had been teased up to even greater gravity-defying heights. As I got closer, I could see that he was also sporting immaculate eye make-up – as good as any I could see in a fashion magazine, if I'd ever looked at one. He saw me and gave a little finger wave.

Big black speakers had been set up on either side of the stage, and music suddenly blared from them. People were either startled by it, or winced and frowned.

"Turn the fucking music down!" Jerzy yelled, but no one heard. I only know what he said because I was standing next to him and could see his lips move.

"Where's Pete hiding?" I shouted.

"What?" Jerzy yelled back.

"I need to see Pete!"

"What?"

I put my lips close to his ear and yelled at the top of my lungs. *"Where's Pete?"*

Of course, the music cut out at that moment, and everyone heard me yelling in the silence.

"I'm not deaf," Jerzy said, and that got him a laugh.

"Where is he?" I asked.

"Probably taking his shirt off again," Jerzy said. "He can't get enough of people admiring his body."

Jerzy turned to one of the students who was trying to staple the valance to the catwalk. "Leslie, darling, I said make it look like curtains, not a hospital bed," he said. "Pleats, please love, it's not a shroud."

"Sorry," Leslie mouthed, and pulled at the fabric. Twisted staples came flying my way, and I ducked.

"I'm liking the hair," Jerzy said, "that bed-hair look is cute on you."

It wasn't a 'look.'

"I wasn't sure if it was worth the effort," I said.

No effort had been involved.

"It totally is," Jerzy said, "goes with that whole waif-like thing you've got going."

If he didn't lay off with the compliments, he'd make me blush.

"Where is Pete?" I asked.

"Up there," Jerzy said, waving a hand vaguely.

I looked around the room, but couldn't see him.

Music came from the speakers again, at a slightly less ear-splitting volume.

"Where?" I asked.

"Catwalk, sweetie," Jerzy said.

I looked up.

George Michael's *I'm Your Man* was blaring from the speakers, and Pete was strutting down the catwalk in time with the beat. He was wearing black lycra leggings with fluorescent yellow stripes up the side of each leg. His trainers were the same radioactive lemon. He wasn't wearing anything else. His bulging upper body seemed to have been given a coat of fake tan, and a topcoat of something shiny with glitter in it.

People were clapping and cheering and wolf-whistling as Pete walked up and down like the Hulk doing Mick Jagger.

"That's my boyfriend up there!" Jerzy yelled, grinning proudly.

"Very impressive!" I shouted.

"He's going to model my designs! Can you think of a better body to show them off?"

"I thought he was keeping a low profile?" I shouted.

"He's a gay man, love, how long did you think that would last?" Jerzy said.

Pete spotted me, pointed, and waved both hands above his head, hips swaying in counterpoint.

The music cut out again, and Pete leaped down off the catwalk and came over to us.

"What do you think?" he asked.

I wasn't sure if he meant the fashion event or him, but it probably didn't matter: in his head, they were the same.

"Terrific!" I said.

"You two have ten minutes, then I need *you*," Jerzy pointed at Pete, "out of those leggings and into the first outfit for the rehearsal. Ten minutes."

Jerzy held up ten fingers, in case we'd forgotten what ten looked like. Or perhaps he was just showing off his manicure. He strode away to supervise some other aspect of the set-up.

"He's had me in and out of my clothes constantly for the last two days!" Pete said. He did that thing that made his pecs jump up and down like excited water-balloons.

"I thought you were hiding?" I said.

"I was."

"What happened?"

"I needed a shag. Really, really badly. So I gave myself up to the police."

"And they gave you one?" I asked.

"Naughty!" Pete said. "Though there were a couple of them I think would have been up for it. And you've got to love a man in uniform. But no, there was no strip search, and no getting banged while I was banged up. Do you have prison fantasies too?"

"Mostly I have escape fantasies," I said.

"You should let yourself get caught: it's much more fun!"

"What happened?"

"Me and Jerzy spent nearly a whole day in bed, and we got through a whole jar of peanut butter!"

"Peanut butter?"

"It's all we had. You should try it." He made obscene licking movements with his tongue.

"I've always found crushed nuts a bit of a turn-off," I said. "What happened with the police?"

"Jerzy and I talked it over, and we figured that they couldn't have enough evidence to actually charge me with Big Dick's murder: because I didn't do it. The worst they could do was lock me up for a couple of nights while they questioned me."

"And a cell would be better than that house," I said.

Pete grinned again. He and Jerzy seemed to be doing a lot of that. I didn't like it. It made me jealous, and I didn't want to be.

"In the end, I was out of there in a couple of hours. They already knew about me and Jer, and they said they didn't think I had a motive for killing Dick. They just had to question me because they had to dot all the tees, or whatever."

"That sounds like the police all right," I said.

Pete was still grinning.

My phone vibrated in my pocket. It was Gingerbread. I'd left him a message, asking him to call me.

"Give me a second," I said to Pete.

"Hello!" I said, loudly because of the music.

"Where *are* you?" Gingerbread asked.

"Fashion show," I said.

"*You?*" he asked.

Why did everyone assume I had no interest in fashion?

"I'm at the old hall on Allandale," I said.

"I'm not that far away," Gingerbread said, "I'll see you in a few minutes."

As I put my phone away, a young woman tapped me on the shoulder.

"There's a stall with more retro clothing over there," she said, pointing. "Nineties stuff is going to be big now."

"Look at you, leading a trend," Pete said, smiling. He put his huge arm across my shoulders in a rough hug, and a few people cast jealous looks my way; and they didn't even know I'd snogged him.

"I'm staying with Jerzy," Pete said, "but his flat is too small. We're going to get a place together."

"Kelly is okay with that?" I asked.

"She's going to help us move."

I guess that meant she was also okay with her husband publicly flaunting his sexuality. On a catwalk.

"You're a free man," I said.

Pete nodded. "Feels good," he said.

"What about work?" I asked.

With Dick gone, the carpet store had been closed for over a week now, a hand-lettered sign taped inside the door saying it was due to a family bereavement.

Pete shrugged. "No one knows. That'll be up to Charmaine, I suppose. She may just stick with selling beds, that was her side of it. She may let the carpet side of it go; or let someone else run that department."

"You don't fancy taking it over?" I asked.

"No way am I organised enough to run a business," Pete said. "I just turn up and do the grunt work. I'm happy if someone's telling me what to do."

He grinned at me, wanting me to acknowledge the innuendo: he wasn't just talking about laying carpet. I tried not to think about the peanut butter.

"I used to do some carpet-laying for other stores," Pete said, "but I never told Dick about it. I'm going to be okay: there's always someone looking for muscle!"

He flexed his arm and his bicep pumped up like Popeye's. He kissed it, and looked at me to see if I wanted to do the same.

"Did you ever do anything for Dick other than carpet laying?" I asked.

"Nah, he only did women."

"I meant work-wise."

"I know, I just like seeing you blush. He got me to do the carpet cleaning a couple of times, but it wasn't really my favourite job: the van with that thing in the back, and the huge pipe you had to drag upstairs. And the smell of the cleaning solution clings to your clothes."

"Nothing else?"

"I got called in once to help him on one of his off-the-books clean-up jobs," Pete said. "He usually did them on his own, but he needed someone to help shift furniture around. People used to call him in if there had been a party and a place had been trashed: he tidied it all up and made sure no evidence was left behind. If it was really bad, he used to bring in a decorator as well. Dick sorted out the floor, Lenny did the walls."

"Lenny?" I asked.

"Lenny Graves. You know him?"

I shook my head.

"He doesn't do houses, says you don't make enough tarting up semis. More money in shops and hotels, that sort of thing. But he's going to do our place when me and Jer find one."

"He sounds like a nice bloke," I said.

"He is. Swings both ways, if you fancy a hook-up? His number's listed. Just be careful if his wife answers."

Gingerbread entered the hall, looking much as he had when I'd last seen him. He seemed less out of place in this crowd than I did. He saw me and raised his good hand.

"Who's the attractive older man?" Pete asked, raising an eyebrow.

"That's Gingerbread," I said.

"Of course it is," Pete said. "I'll get off, don't want to cramp your style."

Pete winked at me and sidled away.

"What's his problem?" Gingerbread asked.

"He thinks you're my boyfriend," I said.

"In your dreams. This really *is* a fashion show," he said, looking around.

"You didn't believe me?"

"It seemed unlikely."

"Why would you think that?"

He looked me up and down, and didn't say a word.

A willowy Goth girl in what looked like a black lace wedding dress and patent leather Doc Martens touched Gingerbread on the arm.

"I love your look," she said, in a husky voice, and then she swept away.

"I get that a lot," Gingerbread said.

"Let's talk outside," I said.

"You sure you don't want to pick up a few more things from the nineties stall before you leave?" he asked, eyes twinkling.

"I can see why people slam car doors on your hand," I said.

As we were going out, someone else stopped Gingerbread to compliment him on his look. They obviously didn't know that nineties fashions were about to be big again.

"Who was the hunk in spandex?" Gingerbread asked, as the hall doors swung shut behind us.

"Pete," I said. "He laid carpet for Dick Gorse."

"That's *Psycho*-Pete?"

"I think he's planning to change his name," I said.

"Did he kill Dick Gorse?" Gingerbread asked.

"Big Dick was shagging Pete's wife. But I don't think Pete cared," I said.

"Guess he wouldn't," Gingerbread said. "Who's Pete shagging?"

"A fashion designer. Jerzy something. He did my hair," I said.

"I hope you didn't pay him," he said. "I'm kidding. He's not a bad kid."

"Pete?"

"Jerzy. He's Mrs. Bednarczyk's youngest. Nice-looking boy, if you fancy a man who looks like Audrey Hepburn."

"I don't."

"What do you want your man to look like?"

"A woman."

"I know a couple of those," Gingerbread said, grinning.

"That's not what I meant!"

We were standing on the stone steps in front of the hall, leaning on the chipped railings.

"Why are we here?" Gingerbread asked.

"I have some news," I said.

"You found the shipping container?"

I shook my head. "Not yet. But I got some information from the police. About the fire at Big Dick's. They found a body, in the wreckage."

"Did they say whose body?" Gingerbread asked. I think he guessed where I was going with this.

"Matt Lester," I said.

He was silent for a moment, looking down at his bandaged hand. "Do they know who did it? *I* didn't kill him."

I couldn't tell whether he was relieved or disappointed.

"They think Tiago might have done it," I said. "They have CCTV footage of him at the scene before the fire started."

"You think he did it?" he asked.

"I hope not."

"Whoever killed that bastard did the world a favour," Gingerbread said.

"Yeah, I know. But still..."

"What's done is done," he said, slapping me on the arm with his good hand and trying to brighten the mood. "I've identified a couple of sites where the shipping container might have been stashed: Maggie and me are going to check them out. You want to come?"

"There's someone else I need to speak to," I said. "He might know where the container is."

"Let me know if you find out," he said.

I nodded.

Inside the hall, the music started pounding again, rattling the dusty windows.

"Sounds like the show's starting," Gingerbread said. "Do you want to go back inside?"

"No, I think I missed my turn on the catwalk," I said.

"You're skinny enough to be a supermodel, you know."

"I can't walk in heels," I said.

"Tell me how you *know* that?"

Chapter Thirty

The van was white, one of those little boxy Fords. It said 'Lenny Graves – Painter & Decorator' on the sides in vinyl letters. In smaller writing it said '20 Years Experiance' – presumably not in spelling. Even without the clue of signage, you could tell it was a decorator's van. The rear bumper was splashed with paint, like an abstract impressionist painting of one of those shit-covered rocks you see in sea-bird documentaries. The van was parked outside an empty shop on Nottingham Road.

The shopfront had 'Vin's Vinyl' over the window, and the paintwork was in suitably retro shades of red, white, and blue. Inside, the counter was painted in the same shades. There was a strong smell of gloss paint and turpentine. Lenny was putting the finishing touches to the walls with a roller on a long stick. The white walls looked a bit clinical, and the emulsion didn't do much to hide the moon crater quality of the underlying plaster, but I assumed they'd soon be covered with LP covers and old posters.

'Vin' was probably another entrepreneur who had made a few quid at car boots and on eBay, and thought it was time to open a shop. His dream would die after three months, and then he'd hang on for another three, to see out his lease, before leaving the shop available for the next Richard Branson wannabe. Lenny Graves had probably repainted the same shop half-a-dozen times.

Lenny himself wasn't tall. He was wearing dungarees that used to be white, but had been given a Jackson Pollock make-over. The trouser legs were too long and bunched up over paint-splattered work boots that looked like they belonged to a much bigger man. They made him look like one of those *Camberwick Green* figures. You could imagine him coming up out of the music box. He had the face for it too: that wide-eyed, slightly stunned look that toddlers have. As if he couldn't quite understand what he was seeing. His almost bald head and soft, round features only added to the vulnerable child look. The smudge of white paint on his chin could easily have been din-dins.

"Lenny Graves?" I said, standing in the shop doorway.

He turned and blinked his big blue eyes at me, making me wonder if anyone was at home. I resisted the urge to ask if I could talk to his mummy.

"Yes?"

"I'm Joe Lucke, I called you earlier?"

"Yes?"

"I wanted to talk to you about Dick Gorse," I said.

He swallowed, then nodded his head. "Close the door, the paint's dry."

I pushed the door shut.

Lenny seemed nervous. Maybe he was always like that.

"You're investigating Dick's murder?" he asked.

I nodded. "I've been working for Charmaine."

"How is she? I should have gone round to see her, but I didn't know what to say."

"She's coping," I said. "She'd like it if you went to Dick's funeral."

"Do you know when it is?" he asked.

"Not yet. The police still have Dick's body."

His Adam's apple bobbed up and down again, and he stared as his paint-stained hands.

"I need to ask you about some of the work that you and Big Dick did," I said.

He looked up quickly, a startled rabbit. "What about it?"

"Did he do something that made someone want to kill him?" I asked.

Lenny looked down at his hands again. He rubbed at a patch of dried emulsion. When it didn't budge, he picked up a damp rag and started rubbing his skin with that. If I'd been a psychologist, I could have had a field day. I did my not saying anything routine. It always worked.

"I told him he was insane to even think about something like that," Lenny said, still concentrating on his hands. "They're people you shouldn't mess with. You do what they want, you take their money, and you don't look back."

He looked at me, and I nodded as if I understood what he was talking about.

"But Dick thought he could move up to the premier league," Lenny said. "And look where it got him."

"Do you know who killed him?" I asked.

"I never dealt with anyone directly. Didn't want to. Dick handled everything. He'd just phone me and say, 'I've got another clean-up job.' He'd give me the location, and I'd go and do whatever needed doing. I'd help him with the carpet if he needed it, but mostly I just painted walls. Wallpapered sometimes. He'd hand over the cash, and that was it for me."

"When you say a 'clean-up job,' you mean...?"

"Blood on the walls, blood on the carpet, that sort of thing," Lenny said.

"Crime scenes?"

Lenny nodded. "The first couple we did were hotels. They like to keep things quiet if something like that happens – suicides or whatever. It puts customers off. Or it attracts the morbid emo-types. No one wants to become known as the suicides' preferred hotel."

"Not much repeat business," I said.

Lenny frowned. "Dick got a couple of referrals from the police, I think. Word got around that we were reliable and discreet. And then Dick stopped telling me where the jobs came from. I think the criminals started coming to him directly."

"When they needed a crime scene cleaning up?" I asked.

"I didn't ask any questions. I did my work, took my money..."

"And never looked back," I said.

"I never hurt anyone."

"Not directly," I said.

Lenny looked down and did the scrubbing thing with the cloth again. He'd obviously lain awake at night, thinking about the moral questions. If you take 'dirty' money, how far removed are you from the actual crimes? Can you honestly say that your hands are stain free, when what you are doing is destroying evidence?

"When did Dick decide to try his hand at kidnapping?" I asked.

Lenny stopped cleaning his hands and stared at me. "What?"

"When did Dick decide to kidnap someone and hold them for ransom?" I asked.

Lenny's frown deepened. "He didn't."

"You said Big Dick wanted to join the premier league."

"Yeah, he thought he could make good money if he tried to blackmail them."

"Blackmail?"

"I thought that's what you were asking me about," Lenny said. "He did a clean-up job on a crime scene. One of the ones he did solo, didn't need a decorator. And instead of getting rid of all the evidence, he kept some of it."

"And threatened to hand it over to the police if they didn't pay up," I said.

"I told you he was crazy. You don't do things like that. Not with people like that," he said.

"The Rathbanians?"

"Maybe. I'm not sure. I told Dick I didn't want to know anything. It was too dangerous. Crazy."

Lenny seemed genuinely upset about the whole thing. As he should have been. If anyone else made the connection between him and Dick Gorse, then Lenny could well end up dead in a skip.

"You don't know who Big Dick was blackmailing?" I asked.

"No," Lenny said. "As soon as he told me what he was planning, I told him I was through. I didn't want any part of it. I didn't see him again after that."

"And you don't know what evidence it was that Dick kept?"

Lenny shook his head again. His eyes were shiny and wet, and I had to stop myself going over and hugging him and saying that everything would be okay.

Whatever piece of evidence Dick used to blackmail his killer would fit comfortably in a container, I felt sure of that. But that still left a lot of scope. You could fit anything in there, from a blood-stained carpet to a freezer with a body in it. And if you connected the container to a power supply, you could even keep the corpse chilled.

"Can you think of anywhere that Dick might have stashed a container, off a lorry?" I asked.

"Only the carpet store," Lenny said. "I don't think he had anywhere else."

"Did you ever go and do a clean-up at an old warehouse or a factory?" I asked.

Lenny thought about it.

"Nothing like that. Hotels, a couple of private houses, an office complex, a Chinese restaurant, that was about all."

"Okay. If you think of anywhere else, let me know. It's important."

"I'm in danger, aren't I?" he asked.

I wasn't going to lie to him. Lenny Graves was stupid and selfish, but he wasn't really a bad person. Relatively speaking.

"If I were you, I'd go away for a couple of weeks," I said. "Somewhere no one knows you. Take your wife. Wait for this to blow over."

"When will that be?"

"Hopefully as soon as I find the container," I said.

He looked at me, then nodded and began packing up his stuff.

"Did Dick ever bring other people in to work on the clean-up jobs?" I asked.

"I don't think so. I know he did some on his own. He may have brought people in, if he needed help with heavy-lifting. But I don't think he worked with anyone else regularly."

I stepped aside as Lenny knelt to roll up the old blankets he'd spread on the floor.

"Did you ever meet someone called Matt Lester?" I asked. "Dark hair, smart, dimple in his chin?"

Lenny looked up from his crawling position. "Doesn't sound like anyone I ever met. Did he work with Dick?"

"I don't know yet," I said, "but he's involved somehow."

"You think he killed Dick?"

"I have no idea who killed Dick," I said, "but he's definitely a suspect."

"Am *I* a suspect?" he asked.

"Until I know who did it, everyone's a suspect."

"I hope you find who did it," Lenny said, getting to his feet with the rolled blanket under his arm. "Dick was a twat, but he didn't deserve to die. Not like that."

"You know how he was killed?" I asked.

As far as I knew, the details of Dick's injuries still hadn't been made public.

"I know they found him in a skip," Lenny said. "No one wants to end up like that. Tossed out like garbage."

Lenny gave me his number, and I put it in my phone. I could have taken it off the side of his van, but it might have been spelt wrong.

"Let me know when you get the date for the funeral," Lenny said.

"I will. And I'll give you a call as soon as this thing is over."

"Thanks, Joe."

Afterwards, I sat in the car watching as Lenny loaded up his van and locked the shop. I wasn't sure if I was waiting to see if he did anything suspicious, or if I was waiting to make sure he got away safely. The van pulled away, and I watched it disappear up the road.

Chapter Thirty-One

Elise asked me to meet her in the marketplace, 'near that stone monument thing.' Everyone called it that stone monument thing, because nobody knew what it was or why it was there. It was a memorial to some wealthy Victorian landowner's son, whose family once had a coal pit named after them. Or something like that. People met there because it was easy to find: the pointed bit sticks up above the market stalls. It was also close to the 'food court' section of the market, so I grabbed a burger while I waited.

There has been a market in Mansfield for seven-hundred years. I think a couple of the stallholders have been there since the beginning. My burger had probably only been on the grill since the 1600s. Elise arrived in time to see me shove the last of it in my mouth, and turned up her nose.

"How can you eat those things?" she asked, shaking her head.

My mouth was too full to reply. I know what she meant, we used to call them camel-burgers when we were kids. I managed to swallow it and licked my fingers.

"You want anything?" I asked, sweeping an arm to take in all the food stalls. "I'm buying."

"Had a win on the slot machines?" she asked.

"Wealthy client," I said. "Paid cash."

"For what?"

"My professional detective services," I said, as if that should have been obvious.

"Then don't spend it all, in case she wants a refund," Elise said.

"You sure you don't want a burger? Or some mushy peas? You know you get grumpy when you're hungry."

"I'm not hungry."

"Then you're grumpy for another reason?"

Elise looked at me, and for a moment I thought she was going to give me both barrels. But she just sighed.

"I *hate* this, Joe. I don't know what to do. I don't feel comfortable in my own home."

"I told you, the police haven't bugged your house or your phone."

"Then I'm just being paranoid?" she asked. "Because I thought someone was watching the house earlier, from a car across the street."

Technically that was possible: the police might be staking out her house to try and catch Tiago sneaking in for a nooner. But I wasn't going to tell her that.

"Why would they watch your house?" I asked.

Answering her question with a question meant I didn't have to lie to her.

"The police are still trying to find Tiago," she said. "Those two detectives came round this morning."

"What did they want?"

"They wanted to know if I've seen him or heard from him. They seemed to think he's involved with drugs again."

"They're just trying to rattle you," I said. "They want you to doubt him. It makes their job easier if you turn against Tiago and help them trap him."

"But what if they're right?"

"Those two are never right. They're a comedy double-act: good for a laugh, but not much else."

"Really?"

I think she wanted to believe me. That helped.

"Tiago is not dealing drugs again," I said. "For one thing, he's learned his lesson. Prison didn't agree with him. And for another, someone else has taken over his old turf."

"They also think he may have killed someone," Elise said. "They didn't say that, but I'm sure that's what they were getting at."

"Tiago was seen near Dick's place before it was torched. And a body was found in the wreckage. That's all they know."

"If that's all it is, why is Tiago hiding?" Elise asked.

"He's afraid they will try and pin the murder on him. If it *was* murder. He has even less faith in those two detectives than I do. I'm trying to help Tiago by finding out who really was responsible for the fire. And the dead body."

"How can you do that, on your own, if the whole of the police force can't do it?"

"Because I am a detective, and I'm worth a dozen of them," I said.

This was bollocks, of course, but Elise needed to believe it. She may have seen through my little ruse.

"Thanks, Joe," she said.

"I'll talk to Bob and Dennis, see what they know. But if they really had any evidence connecting Tiago to a murder, they'd be making more of an effort to find him than they are."

I hoped that sounded like it could be true.

"You honestly don't think Tiago's guilty?"

"He's not a drug dealer," I said.

If Elise noticed that I hadn't said I thought he was innocent of murder, she didn't show it.

"Now, do you want a camel-burger or not?" I asked.

"Only if I can have it on cancer-bread," she said.

Our mother had been convinced that sliced white bread gave you bowel cancer, and she tried to make Elise and me eat wholemeal. We always tried to avoid it, asking in a wheedling voice: Can I have mine on cancer-bread, please mum? Then she tried to feed us that mutant-hybrid stuff that was supposed to be as good for you as wholemeal, but we were never fooled by those greyish slices: Mum, why does this bread look dirty? In the end, she gave up. But she would never have allowed us to eat burgers from the van in the marketplace, because 'you don't know what's in them.' They became outlaw food to kids like us, and we'd secretly buy them whenever we escaped parental supervision, because, who knew, maybe we really were eating camel. Or hippopotamus.

I was heading off, leaving Elise to enjoy her burger in peace, when I had a *Columbo* moment. I turned back.

"Elise, do you know which gym Tiago goes to?" I asked.

"The one up near Tesco," she said, "the membership's cheaper there, I think. You thinking of joining?"

"You think this physique could be improved upon?" I asked, turning a full circle to give her a better view.

Elise laughed. I'm not sure why.

* * *

Bob and Dennis's Volvo was parked outside Burger King. It was easy to find: I just followed all the kids that were running with keys in their hands.

"What happened to your car?" I asked, sitting down at their table.

"Nothing happened to it, why?" Bob said.

"There's a big white scratch down one side," I said.

"Not another one," Dennis said.

"Fuckin' kids," Bob spluttered around a mouthful of Whopper.

I hadn't actually seen a scratch, it was just fun to wind them up.

"How did you know we were here?" Bob asked.

"Detective work," I said, "you must have heard of it?"

"He's upset because we talked to his sister," Dennis said to his partner.

"I'm upset because you told Elise her husband was a murderer," I said.

"*Ex*-husband," Bob corrected.

"We did not say he was a murderer. We said he was someone we needed to interview in connection with two murders," Dennis said.

"Now you're suggesting he's a multiple murderer, and a drug dealer?" I asked.

"We said we were afraid he *might* start dealing again," Bob said, "we phrased it very carefully."

"You've got nothing except CCTV footage that places him at the scene of the second murder," I said.

"Is that all we've got, Dennis?" Bob asked.

"You know, I don't believe it is, Bob. Haven't we also got fresh evidence that links Tiago Zambora with the murder of Dick Gorse?"

"Oh, yes, Dennis, I'd almost forgotten about that."

If *Acorn Antiques* had been a cop show, these two would have been the stars.

"What fresh evidence?" I asked.

If they did their patented 'we know something he doesn't know' routine, I was fully prepared to demonstrate my 'assaulting a police officer with a plastic tray' routine.

"We had uniform officers go door-to-door questioning Dick Gorse's neighbours. Bob and I went through the notes," Dennis said.

"We have a witness who saw Tiago visiting Dick the night before he was murdered," Bob said.

"Big Dick and Tiago knew each other, so what?" I said.

"Do you know *how* they became acquainted?" Dennis asked.

"A line-dancing class at the YMCA?" I said.

"Tiago was Big Dick's dealer. Dick used to buy small amounts of cannabis for recreational use. It was recorded on Dick's file when the police were investigating your ex-brother-in-law, just before Tiago's arrest."

"Tiago had hundreds of customers buying pot for personal use," I said.

In this job, you have to keep in mind the idea of six degrees of separation. Take two people, and look hard enough, and you can almost always find some link between them. Beyond first- and second-degree, the links start to get tenuous and can't be regarded as significant.

"But Big Dick is the only one that was murdered," Dennis said.

"That we know of," Bob added.

"Tiago's also the only one that was heard arguing with Big Dick the day before he was killed," Dennis said.

"Someone saw that?" I asked.

"We have two separate witnesses. I cannot name them, of course, but their stories corroborate each other," Dennis said.

They were trying the same tactic they'd used on Elise, trying to make me doubt Tiago so I'd help them track him down.

"Charmaine heard someone arguing with Big Dick, downstairs, the night before he was killed," I said. "She was in bed and didn't go down. She didn't know who it was."

Dennis nodded. "That's one witness. The second was a neighbour who looked out of the window and saw a vehicle parked outside Dick and Charmaine's at about the same time."

"A vehicle?" I asked.

"A particular kind of vehicle," Bob said.

"A Samwells delivery van," I said.

Bob seemed disappointed that I'd figured it out.

"The neighbour remembered it, because she thought it was odd for anyone to have groceries delivered that late at night," Dennis said.

"Two witnesses. Put their stories together, and the whole is bigger than the sum of the parts," Bob said, "does that sound like detective work to you?"

"A neighbour saw a van that might have been Tiago's, and Charmaine heard Big Dick arguing with someone about something. That's a whole lot of not very much," I said.

"Big Dick and Tiago were arguing about money," Dennis said. "Charmaine heard that much. When Tiago opened the downstairs door to leave, she heard him say 'I want that money, Dick. I need it.'"

"And you instantly assumed they were talking about money for drugs?" I asked. "Do dealers make house-calls now, like the Avon lady?"

"I don't think Big Dick was buying," Dennis said. "I think Tiago was trying to get Dick to invest, so he could start up his business again."

"The franchise has already passed into new hands," I said.

"Maybe Tiago was planning to open a branch somewhere different," Bob said.

"There's no unoccupied turf," I said. "Deadman's shoes: you only get an area if someone goes inside or goes into the ground. You plods put anyone away recently?"

Dennis looked at Bob, who shrugged.

The other thing we have to remind ourselves of is the problem-solving principle of Occam's Razor. It basically says that if you see a shaving implement lying around, it most likely means someone wants to remove their beard. The simplest explanation, the one that uses the fewest assumptions, is preferable. Bob and Dennis's theory relied on too many assumptions for my liking. There had to be a simpler explanation. In the interests of full-disclosure, I will also say that I didn't want them to be right.

"There's no evidence Big Dick was killed because he and Tiago were involved in drugs," I said. "For all you know, the two of them were arguing about a tenner they'd won on a scratch-card. It just sounds like wishful thinking to me, not detective work."

"How about DNA tests, would that come under your heading of detective work?" Dennis asked.

"Of course. As long as you two didn't do them yourselves."

"We got the results back on that blood-stained towel you found," Dennis said.

"It was Matt Lester's," I said.

Dennis nodded. "That provides a direct link between Tiago and the second murder. The fact that Matt Lester's body was found in Big Dick's store provides a probable link between the two murders."

"That's all the reason we need to question Tiago Zambora about *two* murders," Bob said. "If you see him, you'll ask him to give us a call, won't you?"

"I will," I said. "Let me know if you trip over any more clues."

Technically, I'd handed them the clue of the bloody towel. Or at least dropped it at the scene when I was chased by the randy pit-bull. If anyone had tripped-up, it was me.

* * *

I leaned against the bonnet of the Honda and stared at the front of an empty retail unit. With the evidence against him mounting, things were starting to look bad for Tiago. The links between Big Dick and Tiago that the defective detectives had unearthed were tenuous, but there was more that they would uncover before too much longer. Big Dick had hired Tiago to drive a truck and move a shipping container. My guess, at this point, would be that Dick had refused to pay Tiago when the container went missing.

Presumably, Big Dick did ultimately pay up, because Tiago had given me the hundred quid from Dick. At least, that's where Tiago had told me it came from.

Tiago had said his only involvement that evening had been driving the truck. And that he didn't know what was in the container. Perhaps it was only a coincidence that the gym that had been chosen as the drop-off point for the ransom was the same gym Tiago went to.

I didn't like coincidences, they made my scalp itch. I hoped it was that. And not my hair now being home to randy-dog fleas.

Had Tiago been hired for a one-off contract job? Or had he been Big Dick's partner in a kidnapping conspiracy? If they had been partners, that would give Tiago a plausible reason for falling out with Big Dick. And a falling out was a possible motive for murder.

How ever you looked at it, it seemed more and more likely that Tiago was guilty. In a movie, the more the evidence stacks up against someone, the more likely they are to be exonerated at the end. But real life doesn't work like the movies. If this was the movies, I'd be Ryan Gosling and Shelly would be Michelle Rodriguez, and we'd tumble into bed in the final reel, having successfully saved the people we cared about. Spoiler alert: that ain't going to happen.

I dialled Fat Duncan's home number and got no reply, so called him on his mobile. When he answered, it didn't sound like he was out; he'd probably got his arse wedged in a chair and couldn't get up and reach the house phone. If you are wondering, the answer is no, you're never going to see him. You wouldn't want to. It's better for all concerned that he is just a voice on the end of a phone. He is Charlie and I am his only Angel. And if that image doesn't disturb you, I'll have to try harder.

"Joe," Duncan said.

I think someone once told him you pay for mobile phone calls by the word.

"Duncan," I said.

"What do you want?" He was up to five-pence already.

"I need you to check out a phone number for me: all calls to and from."

"Number?"

I gave him the number I'd taken from Lila's phone; the one the kidnapper, who may or may not have been Dick Gorse, had used to text her the details of the drop-off point.

"Name?"

"I don't know. It it's registered, the account is probably fake."

"Burner?"

I wanted to say 'No, only scorched her slightly,' but given the current investigation, jokes about fire were probably in poor taste. Fat Duncan loves jargon. He probably got that off *C.S.I.* Burner phones were used by drug dealers. They're supposed to be untraceable but, strictly speaking, they're not. They can be tracked, and their calls are logged just like any other phone. The only difference is that the phone isn't actually registered to a particular user. They're cheap phones, bought over the counter with a SIM installed, and £10 of call credit. Crooks bin them, or pass them on, changing phones regularly. I think 'burner' is Cold War spy jargon. Or maybe it's from one of those curries that passes through you very quickly.

"I should have something for you after three," Duncan said.

That was more than a dozen words in total. Almost the price of a whole biscuit.

I was hoping Duncan would come back with a list of numbers that was both short, and contained no numbers I recognised, other than Lila's. If Tiago's number was there, I wanted it to be listed only a couple of times: once a day or so before he moved the container, and once on the night itself. If we found a series of calls between Dick's burner phone and Tiago's number, over a number of days, it would strongly suggest that Tiago and Dick were partners in the kidnapping of Chad Kazimir. This would not be a good thing. Of course, if Tiago's number wasn't there at all, it might mean that Tiago had a burner phone of his own.

I was about to hang up, when Duncan said he had something else for me. I expected it to be another taxi run for knob-sucker Stacey, but it wasn't.

"The client, Lila Kazimir," Duncan said, "she told you her maiden name was Frayne?"

"It's the name she first gave me, I assumed it was her maiden name."

"It wasn't. It's an alias. Her maiden name was Fuxhall."

"I wonder why she doesn't use that?" I said.

"Who knows," Duncan said, lightning fast as ever. "Just thought you should know."

"See if Lila Fuxhall has any history," I said, "especially any enemies she might have, or ex-boyfriends."

"Will do. Lila Fuxhall boyfriends and enemies," he said, obviously writing it down. Then he snorted.

"You just got it, didn't you?" I said.

"Yeah, good one. I'll let you know what I find."

Chapter Thirty-Two

Fat Duncan was checking out the kidnapper's phone calls. That left one last number that I hadn't investigated: the mysterious 'Edgar' who had appeared multiple times in Lila's call history. Too often to be a hairdresser or a therapist; often enough to be a lover. It wasn't a premium rate number, so that ruled out a daily reading of the tarot cards or the stars.

I'd put Edgar's number into my phone along with the others, unsure whether I would ever call it. Investigating a client's lover is one of those things that falls into the grey area that I try not to cross into. Unless I have to.

The police had almost formally named Tiago Zambora as a suspect in the murders of Dick Gorse and Matt Lester. The only reason they hadn't included the name of Chad Kazimir on the list was that they didn't know he'd been kidnapped and (probably) murdered. Yet.

If I wanted to help Tiago, and I did, I was going to have to come up with a more convincing murder suspect. Preferably one who wouldn't turn up dead only hours after I'd identified him. That's why I was staring at 'Edgar' in the contacts list on my phone, and wondering whether to step over into the Grey Area.

I stabbed the green 'call' button.

"Hello, Edgar? Is Lila there?" I asked. "She's not answering her phone and I need to talk to her."

"Who is this?"

"My name's Joe Lucke, I'm working for Lila. Helping her deal with her little problem."

"You're the detective?"

"Yes."

"She's not here," he said.

"And you don't know where she might be? I need to speak with her urgently."

"I have no idea where she is. I don't manage my sister's diary. Send her a text, she'll get back to you."

"I already have. If you hear from her, will you ask her to call me?"

"All right."

"Sorry to have bothered you," I said, and ended the call.

Edgar was her brother. Not her lover, then. Unless they were a particularly close family.

Lila called me about an hour later. She said she'd got my message from her brother. I couldn't tell from her voice whether she was annoyed with me for having called him. She must have guessed that I'd taken his number from her phone. And that I'd called him to check out who he was. She said she didn't want to talk to me on the phone, and asked me to meet her at the railway station.

Mansfield railway station isn't one of those quaint Victorian places, with its name spelt out in white pebbles in the flower bed, and a romantic little tea room on the platform. There are railway tracks, a car park, and a ticket office in a blocky building made from that buff-coloured stone all our old buildings are made from. It's functional, but they won't be filming the Hollywood remake of *Brief Encounter* there.

Trains went south to Nottingham, via a handful of nondescript little ex-mining towns, or north, where the line crossed the border into Derbyshire and stopped at Cresswell, which has some crags, before heading back into Nottinghamshire and terminating at Worksop, which is cragless. Cresswell Crags were nominated by the BBC as one of the Seven Natural Wonders of the Midlands. I've never seen them. But then, I've lived in Mansfield for thirty-odd years, and never seen the river that supposedly gives the town its name. I just don't get out much. You don't stay skinny and pallid by exercising outdoors.

As I walked from the car park towards the station building, a dumpy woman wearing a man's raincoat and one of those polythene rain-bonnets stopped in front of me. There wasn't a cloud in the sky.

"Are you looking for the hospital, love?" she asked.

"Er, no, why?"

"Oh, you poor dear," she said, and waddled away, dragging her tartan shopping bag on wheels behind her.

I'd felt perfectly fine until that moment.

Lila was standing outside the station waiting for me. I don't know whether she'd gotten off the train, or just wanted me to think she had. She didn't smile when she greeted me, but in Mansfield we don't do that anyway, so it didn't strike me as odd.

"Do I look ill to you?" I asked.

"Of course not," Lila said quickly.

I didn't like the way she looked over my left shoulder when she said it.

"Let's walk," Lila said.

We walked down Station Road to the dual-carriageway. Left, and we could go to St. Peters and have a mooch round the pound shop; right and we could head for the old bus station, and the discount store where some things cost more than a pound. Lila led us off to the right: she was an upmarket girl. We walked on in silence.

"You can just say it," I said. "I handle rejection well. Years of practice."

"Say what?" she asked, but she was kidding no one.

"You're fired."

"Is it that obvious?" she asked.

"Like I said, years of practice."

We turned right onto the pedestrianised section of Stockwell Gate.

"I heard the police are looking for your brother-in-law," Lila said.

That was as good as reason as any for her to fire me.

"You think I have a conflict of interests?" I asked.

"Don't you?"

"I still want to help you," I said.

"Are you going to arrest your sister's husband?"

"If he's guilty, I will."

"If?"

"He may be innocent," I said.

"Tiago Zambora killed my husband. He helped Dick Gorse kidnap him, and then the two of them had a falling out. Tiago killed Dick. I hired a private detective to find my husband's murderer, and he was killed as well. It all fits, doesn't it?"

"It's a workable theory," I admitted. "It would need some evidence to back it up."

"But you don't want to look for it, because you don't want it to be true. I can understand that. He's family. That's why I don't think you can help me."

"What about the shipping container?" I asked.

"You know where it is?"

"Not yet."

"Then you've got nothing for me, have you?"

We had stopped and were staring at the used furniture in a charity shop window.

"If Tiago Zambora didn't kill Dick Gorse and my husband, who did?" she asked.

This was a good question. Matt Lester had been my prime suspect, but that theory had gone up in smoke. So to speak. Edgar, the 'jealous lover,' had been a stab in the dark, and he'd turned out to be neither jealous nor a lover. Who else was there?

"I'm grateful for what you've done, I want you to know that," Lila said.

She dipped a hand into her shoulder bag and pulled out another one of those white envelopes. It was thicker than the one she'd given me before. One part of my brain wanted to refuse it, but it was quickly drowned out by the part that shouted: *Don't be an idiot! Take it!*

I pushed the envelope into my inside jacket pocket without opening it.

"Thank you," I said. "Do you want me to send you a receipt?"

"I don't need one," she said.

A couple of grand was probably pocket change to her. Also, I don't think she wanted me to know where she was living.

"Goodbye, Joe."

"Good luck," I said.

She gave me a weak smile and headed off down towards the market.

I could understand why she wanted rid of me. Even without the family connection to Tiago, I probably wasn't much use to her. I'd been looking for the shipping container even before she'd hired me, and I was still no closer to locating it.

I turned back to the window of the second-hand furniture store, wondering if I had space for a grey knitted pouffe that looked like a giant sea urchin.

The phone buzzed in my pocket. It was Fat Duncan.

"Got the information you wanted," he said.

I could have explained to him that mobile phone calls weren't like telegrams, but I didn't want to encourage him to talk to me any more than he did.

"Not much traffic," he said. "Two calls to our client, Lila Kazimir nee Fuxhall. And half-a-dozen calls to, and three from, an unregistered pay-as-you-go phone that was activated six weeks ago."

"It belongs to Tiago," I said.

"What makes you think that?"

"It's been that sort of day," I said. "Lila Kazimir nee Fuxhall nee Frayne just terminated our contract."

"You need to send her a bill," Duncan said quickly.

"How much should I charge her?"

"I don't know – three hundred quid? And include the last tank of petrol you bought," he said.

"I'll do that," I said.

"Pity she fired you," Duncan said, "I dug up some information on her."

"You did?"

"I made some discreet enquiries," he said.

That meant he'd phoned someone with access to the police database. Probably Dennis of Dockgreen.

"Turn up anything interesting?"

"Fuxhall was her mother's maiden name. Lila's father is Dirty Harry Clapham. That's interesting, huh?"

Dirty Harry was a mid-level crime boss in Doncaster. He didn't get his nickname because he looked like Clint Eastwood. He had a face like a dead rat. And the resemblance hadn't led some Cagney wannabe to call him a 'Dirty Rat.' No, they called him 'Dirty' because he once stood on a box and tried to fuck a filly. And ended up covered in horseshit. Allegedly.

"Why do you think she didn't take her father's name?" Duncan asked.

"Who knows," I said.

"Rumour is she married Chad Kazimir to cement ties between the two families."

"An arranged marriage?" I said. "People still do that?"

"Immigrants and the Royal family," Duncan said.

And criminal royalty too, apparently.

"Anything else?" I asked.

"She was charged with assault, years ago. Bloke at a party tried to get a little hands-on with her. She stabbed him."

"Glad I kept my hands to myself," I said.

"She stabbed him with a kitchen knife," Duncan said. "Guess where?"

"In the kitchen?"

"In the groin," Duncan said. "That's possibly significant."

No shit, Sherlock, I thought.

"What happened?" I asked.

"She pleaded self-defence, said the bloke tried to force himself on her. She got away with it. Guess it helps to have an expensive lawyer."

Only people who watch too many cop shows call them lawyers.

"What happened to the bloke?" I asked.

"He didn't die. She missed the artery. But he did lose the end off his best friend, if you know what I mean?"

I thought of asking him to explain what he meant, out of spite, but I didn't have the energy to listen.

"A potential enemy, then?" I said. "Harbouring a grudge? Seeking revenge."

"Possibly," Duncan said. "He's now a priest. On Orkney."

Fat Duncan didn't really say Orkney, but he may as well have done, and it wouldn't be right to reveal the padre's home town. I know all priests aren't saints – hell, not all saints were saints – but I doubted he would have come back south to kidnap and murder Lila's husband. A man of the cloth wasn't likely to go off half-cocked, was he?

"Nothing else?" I asked. "No jealous lovers or other potential enemies?"

"Nope. Despite her name, Lila doesn't seem to have been much of a one for the boys," Duncan said.

"Despite her name?" I asked. I couldn't help myself.

"Fuxhall?" Duncan said.

"Right," I said, not laughing.

"I've heard that she doesn't even let her husband touch her," Duncan said.

"Maybe he doesn't want to," I said, "he has a mistress."

"He does? I hadn't heard that."

"Aside from a demi-castrato priest, we've no new suspects," I said.

"We haven't?" Duncan asked.

"Not unless you've saved the best for last," I said.

"I haven't. Is there anything else you want me to ask Den – my source?" he asked.

"Not right now," I said.

Duncan hung up.

I should have felt happy: I'd just cheated Fat Duncan out of a lump of cash. But I didn't. Maybe I didn't handle rejection as well as I thought. Still, I had cash in my pocket, and I could cheer myself up with a giant sea urchin.

"Dammit!" I muttered.

A young couple were leaning into the window and had their hands on my pouffe.

"It's very good of you to think of others," a voice said at my elbow. The little woman in the plastic rain-bonnet.

"It is?"

"Selfless," she said. "Brings a lump to my eye, it does. Donating your furniture to others when – when you're gone."

She sniffed loudly and coughed, a tear in her throat perhaps, then turned and hurried away.

"I'm not dying!" I called after her.

She looked back.

"That's right, love, there's always hope," she said. "So brave."

She waddled away, shaking her head and muttering to herself. As I watched, a little Yorkshire Terrier popped up from under the tartan lid of the shopping basket: it looked at me and shrugged apologetically.

Chapter Thirty-Three

Charmaine led me through into the front room. There was no sign of her mother, which was a relief.

"Thanks for coming," she said.

She offered me tea and biscuits, which I turned down, and then we sat.

"How are you doing?" I asked.

"Okay," she said. "Mum came round yesterday and helped me clear out Dick's things. I feel I can move back into the front bedroom now."

"Your mum's a real... trooper," I said. Put on the spot, it was the best I could come up with.

"She's a battle-axe," Charmaine said, "but I couldn't have done it without her."

"I think you're handling it incredibly well," I said. "A lot of people would have gone to pieces."

"Getting emotional doesn't get the cat fed." She sounded spookily like her mother when she said it.

"There's some truth in that," I said.

"We still haven't sorted out the funeral. The police haven't said when we'll be able to have his body."

In cases of murder, the delay in releasing the body can be months. If someone was charged with Dick's murder, they, or the defending barrister, could request a second post-mortem. The body couldn't be buried before then.

"I'm sure it won't be too much longer," I said.

"I just wish we could, you know, get it all over with. Is that a terrible thing to say?"

"Not at all. A funeral is an important part of the process. It's hard to let someone go until, you know..."

"He's in the ground or up the chimney?" Charmaine said.

"I wouldn't put it like that."

"I know, I'm sorry. Half the time I want to hide under the duvet and cry. But sometimes I feel like going out and just having a drink and a laugh."

"That happens to everyone," I said. "Dick would want you to mourn his loss, but he'd also want you to go on and live your own life."

"You're right, I know that. I'm sorry to pour all this out on you. But you said I could call."

"I meant it," I said. "If you need anything..."

"That's sort of why I called. I wanted to ask you something."

"Yes?" I was hoping this didn't suddenly become awkward, and tried to prepare myself in case it did.

"Do you know any truckers?" Charmaine asked.

This was a question I hadn't prepared for. Was she ready to start dating already? Why did she think I might know truckers?

"I know Dick had van drivers," she said, "but I'm looking for someone who can drive an HGV."

"I might know someone," I said. "What do you need them to do?"

"There's a trailer, it needs to be moved. I need a driver who has his own truck."

"I can arrange that," I said. "Is there – is there anything on this trailer?"

I was trying not to get my hopes up, but I couldn't help holding my breath until she answered. Did she know the location of the elusive shipping container?

"I haven't actually looked at it," she said. "It's in a field at the side of the road. It's the one with the big sign on it, for Dick's – for the carpet store."

I knew the sign she meant. It was up on a slope above the A38, where passing traffic could see it as they headed down the dual-carriageway. It had been there for years. Putting a sign on a trailer in a field used to be a sneaky way of avoiding the need for planning permission for a permanent billboard. Local councils got most of them removed a few years ago, but I guessed that Dick had managed to find an administrative dead-spot on the border of two counties. Or he'd bribed a councillor.

"Are you in a hurry to get it moved?" I think I managed to keep the disappointment out of my voice.

"It's not urgent," Charmaine said. "I got a call from the farmer earlier. Dick had just paid him for another six months, and he offered me the money back. I'm not bothered about the money, but I thought we should take the sign down, seeing as..."

Her voice trailed off.

"Seeing as the store is no longer there," I said.

"Yeah. I don't want to go out there. I think if I see that sign, I'll just start blubbing again."

"I'll go and check it out," I said. "And then I'll get it moved. I have a friend with a truck."

"Thanks, Joe, I appreciate it," she said.

The sun was going down by the time I got chance to drive up to the A38 and check out the sign. In the twilight, it looked bigger than I remembered: huge white letters standing out starkly on a dark background.

BIG DICK'S FLOORS 'N' BEDS

It was one of those big vinyl banners with metal eyelets around the edge that allow you to tie them up with rope. It looked new, so maybe Dick had renewed the sign when he made the latest payment to the farmer. Seeing it out there on the hillside, I could understand why Charmaine hadn't wanted to see it. A sad reminder of the store and its owner.

I turned into the side road, heading for the farmhouse. I'd make arrangements to get the trailer moved out of the field later in the week.

* * *

I parked the Honda in my usual spot, and headed across the road to the flat. I was trying to decide whether to go and fetch a curry, or stay in and make something healthier. Normally the curry would have been an easy choice, but the old biddy in the rain-bonnet had rattled me. I was still debating as I slid the key into the lock of the street door.

"Fuck it, I'm having a curry!" I said, pushing open the door.

I hadn't even taken a step inside when a body appeared, flying out from the top of the stairs, hitting the steps about halfway down, and then tumbling to lie on the floor at my feet. The man didn't move, but I could see his eyelids flickering and he still seemed to be breathing. He was young and well-muscled, wearing black jeans and black police-style boots. There was a logo embroidered on the chest of his polo shirt, but I couldn't make it out properly. I think it said *Rent-a-Thug*. His mousy brown hair was spiky short on top, and almost shaved away at the sides.

As I straightened up, I smelled a familiar scent in the air. Aftershave.

"*Tiago!*" I yelled.

"Up here, Joe!" He called back cheerfully.

I stepped over the unconscious man and walked up the stairs.

There was a man sitting in my armchair. Blood trickled from a small cut in his lower lip. He looked like a clone of the man downstairs, except that his hair was slightly less shaved at the sides, and he had a blond moustache that was almost as pale as his skin. He had a mole on his left cheek, and another one on his neck. His eyes were dark blue, and the whites showed all around. He was perspiring and looking nervously up at Tiago.

Tiago stood over the man, holding a carving knife and a matching meat fork. Elise had bought them for me, so I could do a proper Sunday roast. I'd had them years. They'd never been out of the box until now.

Tiago was wearing jeans blotched with reddish mud and a vest that had once been white. The same red mud stained his Converse high-tops. His dark curly hair was missing its usual oily sheen, and looked wild and unwashed. But somehow, he still looked like he'd stepped off the cover of a magazine.

"All right, Joe?" he asked.

"I'm not sure," I said.

"No?"

"Do I look ill to you?"

Tiago leaned forward, peering at my face. Then he shrugged. "No more than usual," he said.

I found that oddly reassuring.

"You're back late tonight," Tiago said. "I was about to start without you."

"Out investigating," I said. "I think I have found the you-know-what."

Tiago frowned, and then broke into a broad grin, nodding. "The I-know-what!"

"What are you doing here?" I asked, nodding towards his captive.

"Saving you," Tiago said.

"Do I need saving?"

"You would have done. These two were waiting to ambush you. They've been following you all day."

"How do you know that?"

"I was following them."

I wanted to ask how they had all managed to get here ahead of me if the three of them had been following me. But I felt there were more important things to ask.

"Did you throw that man down the stairs?" I asked.

I edged over to the top of the stairs. The other one still lay on the floor by the open door.

"But of course," Tiago said, "we only need one of them alive."

"Why's that?"

"This one will tell us everything. Do you have neighbours?" Tiago nodded his head towards the adjoining wall.

"No, it's a shop. No one there now."

"Good, no one will hear the screams," Tiago said.

The young man in the chair was looking from one of us to the other, like a spectator at Wimbledon. His expression was struggling to accommodate the mix of emotions he was obviously feeling.

Tiago looked at me, and I knew what he expected.

"You think he'll scream?" I asked.

"They always do. Eventually."

Tiago raised the torture implements.

The second intruder leaped from the chair and threw himself down the stairs in his eagerness to get away. As he picked himself up, he didn't even slow down to help his friend up. He was limping heavily as he ran out into the street.

"You let him go," I said.

"You said you already knew where the container was," Tiago said.

"I do. I think."

"Let's go and get it." He started towards the stairs.

I shook my head.

"What?" he said. "You don't trust me?"

"It's not that," I said. Actually, it was.

"Then what?"

"We need a truck to hook up to the trailer to move it."

"I'll get one. Come on."

"We can't move it until morning. It's locked up in a lorry park."

I could tell he didn't believe me.

"We'll go first thing in the morning," he said.

Tiago dropped down onto the sofa, which let out a loud farting sound. He didn't seem to notice. He clearly intended to stay with me until morning.

"Tiago, I'm not taking you with me. Gingerbread has a truck, he's taking me."

"Gingerbread?"

I nodded.

"I know him. He is still driving?"

"Semi-retired," I said.

"Why not me?"

"The police are looking for you, and the Rathbanians are looking for you. I don't want anyone to see the trailer until I've had a chance to look what's in it."

"No one's following me," Tiago said.

"You can't know that for sure. And if that container is going to prove you innocent, it can't be you that retrieves it. No one will believe that you didn't tamper with the evidence. You have to stay away from it."

"*If* it proves me innocent?" Tiago said. "You think it won't?"

"I have no idea what's in it. I have to find out. And then decide what to do with it."

I could see he was getting angry. I picked up the carving knife and meat fork, and held them out towards him.

"Do you want to try and torture it out of me?" I asked.

Tiago slapped them out of my hands, sending them skittering across the floor. Then he folded his arms and sat glaring at me.

"Do you want a curry?" I asked.

"Yes. I am starving." His arms were still folded.

I went and peeped over the top of the stairs. The second man was gone, and he'd pulled the door shut behind him.

"Come on, the coast's clear," I said. "We'll get a bottle of wine as well."

"Two bottles. And I am still angry with you," he said. But his arms were uncrossed now.

"Where's your jacket?" I asked.

"What are you, my mother? I have no jacket." He got to his feet. "Come on, before they run out of pilau rice. And you're paying."

He thundered down the stairs, and I followed.

"Tell me about the argument you and Dick had the night before he died," I said.

I'd waited until we were well into our food, and most of the way down the first bottle of rioja. We were sitting cross-legged on the floor in the flat, eating out of the polystyrene trays and sharing a massive garlic naan bread.

"What argument?" he asked.

I watched him shovelling rice into his face.

"What?" he said.

"I can see where Jack gets it from," I said.

Tiago grinned, and there were yellow rice grains stuck to his teeth. "Haven't eaten for two days. What argument?"

"Charmaine heard the two of you arguing about money," I said.

"She was there? I did not know. I should have kept my voice quiet. Dick would not pay me for driving the truck, because the container had gone missing. I told him he was a lousy bastard, and I left."

I liked the way he said louse-ee.

"Then what?"

"Then he paid me the next day. I suppose he slept on it and realised it wasn't my fault that the container went missing."

"It didn't go missing," I said. "Dick knew where it was all along. He just wanted you to *think* he was angry because you lost it."

"I do not understand."

"Dick took the container and hid it somewhere else. I think I know where."

"But you don't trust me enough to tell me where."

"Tiago, if you're innocent, I will do everything I can to prove it," I said.

"And if I am not?" He looked up at me from under the curly fringe of his hair.

"I'll do whatever I need to do to protect Elise and Jack," I said.

Tiago stared at me. Then started eating again.

"Be careful tomorrow," he said, "I won't be there to save you."

Chapter Thirty-Four

I've always had a thing about seventies movies; *Smokey and the Bandit* and *Convoy*, things like that. Anything where the car stunts were done with actual cars and not computers. I love those American supercars with engines that growl like a bear, and those massive eighteen-wheel trucks with their airhorns and gleaming chrome. Today I felt like I'd stepped into one of those movies. For the first time in my life, I was sitting in the cab of one of those trucks. Or the European equivalent, at least.

The dashboard looked like something out of a starship, and in the co-driver's seat I had more legroom than in a limousine. There was a bed in the back of the cab, but I was too excited to sleep. Though I may have bounced on it to test the mattress. The cab had that new car smell, and I felt like I was sitting on the top of a double-decker looking down on the world. Yes, the truck had an airhorn, and yes, Gingerbread had to slap my hand when I kept sounding it.

We were currently only a tractor, but even without a trailer, Gingerbread reckoned the truck weighed twenty tonnes. It was one of the big Mercedes-Benz ones, and the engine was something like four-hundred horsepower: more than eight times the power of the Honda Civic.

"How fast will it go?" I asked.

Gingerbread looked at me and shook his head, but I think he was enjoying playing with this borrowed toy too. The metal splints were gone from his fingers, but his hand was still bound up with tape. He looked like a boxer without a glove.

"They're limited to fifty-five miles an hour," he said, "on the road."

"What if they're not on the road?" I asked.

"When I gave up driving, I thought I might have a go at truck racing," he said. "I'd seen it at Donnington a couple of times, and it looked like fun. I took one of these things out on the track, just to try it."

He shook his head.

"What happened?" I asked.

"On my own on the track, it was the most fun I'd had behind the wheel. But the thought of sharing the track with a bunch of other guys? No thank you. They limit them to a hundred miles an hour for racing, but even so... It's a young man's sport. Those guys reckon they can out-accelerate a Porsche 911."

"I have to go and see a truck race," I said.

I'd given Gingerbread our destination, and he'd programmed it into the sat-nav. I'm pretty sure he could have pressed the 'go' button, and the truck would have driven itself.

"You were right about the container being hidden in plain sight," I said.

"I didn't think it would have a sign on the side of it!" He said. "I've driven past that thing a thousand times, and I'd never have thought of using it as a hiding place."

On paved roads, riding in the truck was like being in a top of the range saloon car. When we turned off onto the road up to the farm, it was still quiet and smooth, but being so high up meant there was a certain amount of rocking as the wheels bounced over potholes. It was like being on a gentle fairground ride.

"You're grinning like a kid at Christmas," Gingerbread said.

It looked like the grin was contagious.

As we approached the farmhouse, the farmer appeared to greet us. He waved us through the yard, and opened the gate for us so we could drive through into the field where the trailer stood.

"He seemed pleased to see us," Gingerbread said.

"I think he's glad we're taking this thing away," I said. "Not everyone enjoys being associated with a local murder."

We bounced across the grass, and in front of us we could see where another truck had crossed the field recently. There were muddy wounds in the grass that had not yet healed over.

The trailer had been turned, so that its longest side was presented to the traffic on the dual-carriageway that ran a few hundred feet from the bottom of the field. The sign itself was dark blue vinyl with huge white letters, and it ran the length of the trailer, so that none of the shipping container was visible from the road.

"This is what everyone's been searching for?" Gingerbread asked.

He stopped the truck some yards short, so he'd have room to turn it around and reverse it up to the trailer.

"I checked the markings last night," I said.

"Did you look inside?"

"No, it was too dark to start untying the ropes."

"You want to get yourself a good knife," he said.

The knife he was brandishing looked big enough to be a sword, and made him look even more pirate-like.

"Let's get that bloody sign down," he said.

We jumped down from the cab and walked towards the container.

"Take this." Gingerbread handed me the knife.

I walked around the container, sawing through all the bits of nylon rope I could reach, pulling them free. The knife was razor-like, and I tried to keep my fingers well clear of the blade.

As the vinyl sign began to sag, Gingerbread pulled down on it with his good hand. We managed to get all of it down except the top left corner, where the rope snagged on the container. I pulled myself up and clung to the back of the container, climbing like a skinny white monkey, and began cutting through the snagged rope.

"Do you want to open it up?" Gingerbread asked.

"I know what's in it," I said.

"What?"

"A wrecked BMW, with a dead body in the boot."

"You're not kidding, are you?"

"Nope."

"How do you know if you didn't look?" he asked.

"Deduction. You can check, if you want."

"That's something I don't want to see. Let's just get it away from here."

The sign finally fell away completely, and I was just about to drop to the ground myself when a flash of light caught my eye. I glanced over to the road, where traffic was moving in a steady stream. A rusty white pick-up truck had pulled up at the side of the road, and the sun had been reflected of the side window as the door opened.

"What is it?" Gingerbread asked, trying to see what I was looking at.

"I think someone's watching us," I said.

The man who had climbed out of the pick-up truck vaulted up into the back of his vehicle and then bent over. It seemed an odd thing to do. But probably no more odd than clambering on the back of a shipping container wielding a large knife.

"Get down," Gingerbread said, his voice suddenly serious. "Now!"

He was still looking towards the road, where the man in the pick-up truck seemed to be raising something up onto his shoulder.

"Run!" Gingerbread yelled.

I jumped down onto the grass, rolled, and began to run. Gingerbread was just ahead of me.

"Why are we running?"

"RPG!" He yelled.

From the speed he was moving, I don't think he meant role-playing game.

There was a sound behind us like a massive shot-gun blast, and it was followed by an explosion up on the hill behind us.

We threw ourselves down on the ground as fragments of shipping container metal flew through the air above us.

"What is this, Beirut?" I asked, gasping.

"Mansfield, mate," Gingerbread said.

I rolled over and looked back towards the container. As the smoke cleared, I could see that the metal box was gone, leaving only the flat bed of the trailer. The car that had been inside, presumably Chad Kazimir's BMW, was nose down towards the ground, its back wheels still up on the trailer. As I watched, there was a second blast. The grenade slammed into the tail end of the car, lifting it up and exploding it in the air.

It wasn't like the movies. There was no whooshing sound, no trail of white smoke. Just *Bang! Bang!* Devastation. Through the smoke, I saw the mangled remains of the car land on its roof. It was burning like a bonfire, thick black smoke from the tyres rising into the sky.

"Stay down," Gingerbread warned.

The air was filled with smoke, and the smells of fireworks and burning rubber.

The clouds gradually thinned, and I saw the white pick-up truck bounce down off the grass verge and then accelerate away along the dual carriageway.

"Dammit!" Gingerbread said. He was standing up, looking over at the truck we'd arrived in.

There was a piece of twisted metal embedded in the windscreen on the co-driver's side. Apart from that, it was unscathed.

"What the hell was that?" A voice over to our left.

The farmer was marching through the gate. He did not look happy.

"I thought you were going to tow it away," he said, "not blow the fucking thing up!"

"That wasn't us," Gingerbread said, "we were the targets."

I pulled out my phone and dialled Tiago's number.

"We found the container," I told him. "I think you should come and take a look at it. Oh, and bring your landlady's dog."

I hung up.

"Why the dog?" Gingerbread asked.

"We need to know if there's any burned meat among that debris. I don't want to go looking, do you?"

Gingerbread turned towards the burning wreckage, his face pale.

"The dog is a smart move," he said.

Chapter Thirty-Five

I pulled up outside my sister's house. I still wasn't used to the fact that I no longer had to wait for a cloud of poison smoke to clear before I got out of the car. As I slammed the door shut, I saw Elise's neighbour, the so-called Mrs. Kepler, look up from her gardening. I waved.

"Afternoon, Miss Squitz," I said, cheerfully, "those foxgloves look lovely."

She gave me the evil eye.

The front door was open, and I walked in. I resisted the urge to shout *yoohoo!* We never did that in my family. The fact that I'd even thought about it, was probably the first sign that I thought something was wrong. The house seemed unnaturally quiet, and I knew, just standing on the threshold, that there was no one there. I shouted anyway.

"Elise? Jack!"

Silence.

I glanced up the stairs, and shivered. I felt like I'd wandered into one of those supernatural TV shows. The sun was on the back of the back of the house, and the kitchen looked brighter and more inviting than the gloomy staircase. I headed that way.

On the breakfast bar was a mug of tea and a glass of milk. Both looked untouched. I brushed my fingers on the side of the mug; it was barely warm. A little Batman action-figure lay beside the glass of milk. Jack had given me the matching Joker figure when I said he was my favourite villain. Hardly aware that I was doing it, I picked Batman up and put him in my jacket pocket.

The back door was propped open with one of the kitchen chairs. I looked out into the empty garden. A partly deflated football sat in the middle of the grass, and an orange and blue water canon lay off to one side. I was standing in direct sunlight, and I still found myself shivering again. I went back inside.

The stairs creaked as I walked up. Do stairs ever not creak? Normally you aren't allowed upstairs in outdoor shoes, but I thought Elise would forgive me this once.

I went from room to room, knowing I'd find nothing, but needing to look anyway. I wanted them both to leap out at me and shout *boo!* I wanted them to laugh at my discomfort, in that way families were supposed to do. But there was nothing. An empty bedroom at the front of the house that smelled of whatever Elise used after she'd showered. And an empty bedroom at the back of the house that smelled of Jack's trainers and that weird plastic smell toys give off.

I felt a cold, sinking feeling, and my chest tightened. Breathing became almost impossible as panic overwhelmed me. Suffocating. No, no, no. My eyes burned, my lungs burned, and my head throbbed. Someone had taken Elise and Jack. And it was my fault.

I made my way downstairs. I closed and locked the front door, because you were supposed to do that after the horse had bolted. I went back into the kitchen. I tipped the cold tea and milk down the sink, rinsed the mug and glass, and put them on the draining board. I switched on the kettle so I could make myself a drink, but when it boiled I didn't feel like it.

My phone sat on the breakfast bar, and I perched on a stool staring down at it. There was no one I could call to get me out of this mess. No one who could take away these feelings. Anger and impotence. And above all, fear. I was supposed to protect my sister and my nephew, and I'd failed.

All I could do now was wait for the phone to ring. For whoever had taken Elise and Jack to tell me what they wanted.

A shadow passed the kitchen window, and I shivered again.

"Hello, Joe."

I looked up.

Lila Frayne, or whatever her true name was, stood outside the back door. She seemed taller, and there was a poisonous green aura boiling around her. Or maybe I imagined that. If I didn't invite her in, she couldn't cross the threshold.

"Where are they?" I asked.

"Not here," Lila said.

"What do you want?"

"I think you know that," she said.

I had a good idea of what she wanted. But I didn't want to say it out loud.

"I'm not going to pretend I know how someone like you thinks," I said.

"Don't be like that. You make me sound like some sort of monster."

"The sort of monster that would abduct a mother and her child?" I said.

"No harm will come to them."

"As long as I give you what you want?"

Lila smiled. "All I want is the man who kidnapped and murdered my husband," she said. "I want Tiago Zambora."

"I don't think Tiago killed your husband," I said.

"The police think he did. So do the Rathbanians. Everyone does. Even you're not sure."

"And when Tiago is dead, no one will ask any questions, and you will live happily ever after?"

"I'll do my best," she said.

"That's your deal? Tiago's life for Elise and Jack's?"

She smiled again. "Take it or leave it."

"Tiago didn't kill your husband." I was sure now.

"Does that really matter? We're not talking about Chad's death. We're deciding whether your sister and nephew get to live. Your choice."

She stood leaning in the doorway, the sun behind her. A witch must have made her a daylight ring.

"Elise and Jack in exchange for Tiago," I said. "All right. How do you want to do it? Bearing in mind that I don't trust you, and you don't trust me?"

"The exchange will happen somewhere public," Lila said. "No ambush. No guns. Keep Dominic and his stooges out of this."

"At the wake," I said.

"The what?"

"Wake. For Chad. It's being held tomorrow at the Raj Lion. 3pm. Downstairs. No weapons, no soldiers. Just family and friends."

"You found Chad's body?" she asked.

"Not exactly," I said. "I found the container, and then lost it again. I think it was cursed."

"What?"

"The container was blown up. Tiny pieces. We never got to see what was inside. If your husband was in it, there isn't enough of him left to fill a matchbox, never mind a coffin."

"He's gone?"

"We brought in an expert: he couldn't find anything to get excited about. We had to leave when the police arrived, but I don't think they found anything either."

"Then the wake?"

"There'll be a coffin, but no body. There won't be a viewing before the funeral."

Lila was silent as she considered this.

"Mr. Kazimir will allow the exchange to take place?" she asked.

"Why would he object? He wants the same thing you do: Tiago Zambora dead. You'll just have to convince him that you won't botch the job."

"I won't mess this up," she said. "I want it over."

"We all do. I just want Elise and my nephew back. As long as they aren't harmed, I'll do whatever you want."

"The wake, then," she said. "But if I see even a hint of a double-cross, I will kill them. And the boy will go first."

I'd taken the action-figure out of my pocket and was looking down at it, turning it over in my hands.

"I'm not going to do anything that will put them at risk," I said.

I looked up, and Lila had disappeared. Turned back into a bat, I wouldn't wonder.

Chapter Thirty-Six

I took out the phone Saggy-Dominic had given me and called the number. He answered after a couple of rings.

"I found the shipping container," I said.

"Where is it?" Dominic asked.

"It was blown-up by someone with a grenade launcher."

There was a moment's silence.

"Are you all right?" Dominic asked.

It's not every henchman that would have asked.

"I'm okay. But I need your help," I said.

"What do you want?"

"I need you to organise a wake. Tomorrow at the Raj Lion. I've already given out invitations."

There was a longer silence.

"Please," I said. "Lila Frayne has taken my sister and my nephew, she's holding them hostage. She will exchange them for Tiago."

"And you want to make the exchange during a wake for her husband?"

"It was the first thing that came to mind," I said.

Another silence. Shorter this time.

"Come to the Lion. I will listen, but I promise nothing. Be here after six."

* * *

You never really know what sort of person you are, until you see what action you're prepared to take. I don't have a gun, and I hope I never end up in a situation where I'd need one. But I do have a cheap knock-off Taser that I bought online. I've never fired it. And I'm not sure I'd ever want to be somewhere that I'd have to rely on it. It's illegal to own them in the UK, but I work on the principle that it's only illegal to own a stun-gun that actually works. Mine probably doesn't. It usually lives in a locked box under my bed; but this evening it was down the side of the cushion of the armchair. I'd recharged it, and it was ready to go. Probably. I'd considered getting all macho and shoving it in the back of my waistband like a TV cop's gun. But knowing my luck, I'd Taser myself in the arse. I also had a little squeeze-bottle at the side of the chair, filled with home-made pepper spray. I'd Googled the recipe.

I was all set for a rendezvous with my brother-in-law.

Tiago came pounding up the stairs. I'd left the street door on the latch to save him having to pick the lock again.

"What happened?" he asked, not even breathless.

Tiago paced around as I told him what had happened at Elise's. I watched him go through the same emotions I had, though with him anger and desire to take action showed through more strongly.

I had stayed in my armchair throughout, my fingers never far from the stun-gun. I watched him closely as I told him about Lila's demand: his own life in exchange for the lives of Elise and Jack. He stopped pacing. He didn't even take time to think about his response.

"That's it then," he said, "she shall have me. How can we do this thing?"

"Do you trust me?" I asked.

Tiago looked at me. "I trust you to do whatever you have to in order to save Elise and Jack, and they are all that matters to me."

I felt able to stand up then and leave my chair. No need for the stun-gun. I wanted to hug him and tell him everything would turn out fine. That I had a plan that would ensure that everyone came through this unscathed. But I couldn't lie to him. He had just agreed to sacrifice himself for Elise and Jack: that made him the hero.

I only had half a plan so far, and I'd made that up on the hoof. The police, the Rathbanians, and Lila Frayne wanted Tiago, and much as I wanted to help him, I couldn't make him my first priority. The thing that made this harder was that he didn't expect me to give any thought to his safety.

"You can do this," Tiago said, "you can save them."

"I will," I said.

I told him to arrive at the Raj Lion before 3pm the following day, and that he should come through the kitchen and straight into the dining room.

"Don't let anyone stop you, don't let anyone take you anywhere else," I said.

He nodded.

"I have to go and make other preparations," I said.

"Where are you going?"

"Into the lion's den," I said.

"You want me to come along?"

"No. I need you to stay out of sight until the wake tomorrow," I said.

At which point, I was going to feed him to the lions.

* * *

"A wake?" Dominic said. "What are we supposed to put in the coffin?"

We were sitting in the upstairs room at the Raj Lion. The big gorillas were lounging about the room, and Mr. Bharani was standing by the window. They were all pretending not to listen to our conversation.

"Don't you have a body lying around here somewhere?" I asked.

"You are not funny, Mr. Lucke."

"You could just kill someone," I said. "Who's expendable?"

I looked around the room. The apes looked distinctly uncomfortable. Especially the one wearing the red shirt.

"We have some legs of lamb you could use instead," Mr. Bharani suggested, scurrying towards us.

I think he was trying to prove that he wasn't expendable.

Dominic nodded and waved him away.

"But why a wake?" Dominic asked.

"We need to draw people out," I said. "Who doesn't enjoy a good wake? And if we say that there is a corpse in the casket, that ought to get all the attention we need."

"Tiago Zambora has agreed to attend?" Dominic asked.

"He'll come," I said. "He'll do whatever it takes to save his wife and son."

"He knows that Lila intends to kill him, and he is willing to give his life?"

"It's the only way he can save them. She wants him dead because of what happened to her husband," I said.

"As do we all," Dominic said. "But why should she be the one who gets to kill him?"

"Does it matter who does it? If we let her kill him, my sister and nephew get to live. I vote Lila gets to pull the trigger."

"I think a wake is a terrible idea, but I can see how it might work," Dominic said.

"We have to make it a no guns event," I said. "There will be innocent people there."

I'd promised Lila there would be no guns. But I was more concerned about Elise and Jack, and me, being caught up in the middle of a gunfight.

"That might prove difficult," Dominic said.

"Put a metal-detector on the door," I said.

Dominic tried to picture this set-up downstairs. "It could be done," he said. "When do you want to do this?"

"Tomorrow," I said.

"Impossible!" Mr. Bharani exclaimed, throwing up his hands. "We have reservations."

"We hold it at 3pm," I said. "The dinner crowd will have gone, and we'll be done before the first diners arrive in the evening."

"It would be a challenge," Mr. Bharani said, "it must all run like clockwork."

"And you're just the man to do it," I said.

Mr. Bharani smiled and puffed out his chest. "I think so too. We will do it!"

"I don't like it," Dominic said.

"No, no, it is a *terrible* idea," Mr. Bharani said, scowling at me.

"I think there's something you're not telling me," Dominic said.

"There's a whole heap of things I'm not telling you," I said. "All the bits of the plan I haven't made up yet!"

"This is no way to run a railroad," Mr. Bharani said.

"But this wake will draw all of the interested parties together in one place," I said. "Who knows, we may even have one or two surprise guests."

"Those two detectives, Dim and Dimmer?" Dominic asked.

"Them as well," I said.

Dominic gave all of this serious consideration. The room was silent in anticipation of his next words.

"Go ahead and plan your wake," he said.

I didn't like the way he called it my wake.

"It is a *brilliant* idea, I said so from the start," Mr. Bharani said.

"I will talk to the boss," Dominic said, "He may take some convincing. We are, after all, talking about his son's murderer."

"Alleged murderer," I said. "Tomorrow, I hope to prove that Tiago is innocent."

"How are you going to do that?"

"That's one of the parts of the plan I haven't made up yet," I said.

Chapter Thirty-Seven

When I pulled into the Raj Lion car park, the last of the lunchtime diners were just leaving. I'd arrived half-an-hour early because there were a few details I needed to take care of. As I passed the main window, I could see a couple of members of staff in the main dining room, moving tables and arranging chairs ready for the wake. They were creating a long buffet table along one side. Chairs were being set in semi-circular rows, and a couple of trestles were set up near the front, presumably to hold the casket.

I walked around the back and in through the kitchen door. There was no sign of the chef, but the same two kitchen hands were hard at work, preparing plates of finger food. They looked up as I entered.

"*Namaste, lund khajoor,*" the first said, smiling and giving a little respectful bow.

"*Gaand chaat mera,*" I said, bowing back.

Mrs. Chaudary in the newsagent had taught me that. I'd heard her say it often, but had never known what it meant before.

For a moment, the young man just stared at me, and then he laughed out loud.

"Your accent is terrible, white boy," he said. His was pure Birmingham. "I'm Jalal and this is my friend Sandeep," he said, in his best Brummy Kenneth Williams voice.

"I'm not gay!" I said.

"Then how do you know what he's talking about, dude?" asked the one who was probably not Sandeep.

I was saved from further *Carry On Up the Curry House* dialogue by the entrance of Mr. Bharani. He looked flustered.

"Where are my bhaajis?" he asked. "People will be arriving shortly. And where is the lamb, we must get in in the casket."

Not-Jalal pointed to a row of trays on one side, where half-a-dozen legs of lamb were resting.

"You *cooked* them?" I asked.

"You said the corpse had been burned," Mr. Bharani said. "I thought the smell of cooked meat would be more authentic."

"Should have used pork," Not-Sandeep said.

"The long pig," Not-Jalal said, nodding.

"Hurry up with those samosas," Mr. Bharani said, clapping his hands briskly. "Come on, chop-chop."

I left them to it, and wandered along the corridor to the lobby. I'd been expecting to see more signs of life, but there was nobody. Presumably the Rathbanians were all upstairs talking team tactics.

"This your wake, mate?" someone asked, off to my left.

"I hope not," I said.

"Where do you want the cameras?"

He looked about twelve and had a haircut like a pastry-brush. I have no memory of what his face looked like, because all I could look at were the three rings in his left nostril.

"Where do you usually put them?" I asked, playing for time.

"I don't. Normally I do the disco," he said.

"At a wake?" I asked.

He shrugged. "Some dead people are cool."

"Put one where it will capture anyone who steps to the front to speak, and one in a corner where it will pick up the whole room, including the audience," I said.

"Gotcha."

He disappeared back into the dining room. He was wearing twenty-eight-hole oxblood Doc Martens and spray-on jeans that finished just above his knee. The combined effect made me worry I was turning into an old person.

"He's got a cute bum, hasn't he?" a voice behind me asked.

"What?" I turned.

Lila was coming in the front entrance, ushering Elise and Jack before her.

"Sorry, I thought that's what you were looking at," Lila said.

"I wasn't," I said firmly.

Elise and Jack both looked tired and pale, but otherwise unharmed.

"I brought Mummy and Baby. Where's Daddy Bear?" Lila asked.

"He'll be here," I said.

The Batman action-figure was still in my jacket pocket. I took it out and gave it to Jack. He took it from me, but didn't look at it.

I looked around the deserted lobby, casting a quick glance towards the stairs.

"If you're wondering where all your Rathbanian friends are, I sent them on a little errand," Lila said.

I frowned.

"You didn't think I would just walk into a room full of Mr. Kazimir's soldiers, did you?" she asked.

I'd hoped she might. The absence of the Rathbanians didn't affect my so-called plan, but it did make me feel a little less confident about its success.

"What did you do?" I asked.

"Dominic might have received an anonymous tip-off, telling him that Chad's body was stashed in a lock-up in Pinxton," Lila said.

"You found the container?" I asked.

"You know it wasn't in there," Lila said, "and you know what happened to the container."

"That was you?" I asked.

"Not me personally," she said.

"Your two thugs, Zig and Zag?" Tiago said, entering from the direction of the kitchen. "I just met them again outside. They had to leave suddenly."

Jack's face brightened when he saw his father. Elise managed a weak smile too.

"What did you do to them?" Lila asked. She obviously didn't like this sudden change in odds.

"All I did was smile at them," Tiago said. He smiled.

Perhaps he was telling the truth, and had grazed his knuckles trying to get the back door open.

"Since we're all here, why don't we do this?" Lila said.

"Clear the way, clear the way, food coming through!"

Mr. Bharani flapped his hands and ushered us out of the lobby into the dining area and away from the door. Behind him, the two kitchen hands were pushing metal serving trolleys laden with plates of appetisers and dishes of rice and sauces. It smelled wonderful, and reminded me that I had skipped lunch.

Not-Sandeep and not-Jalal began laying out the buffet, the hot food being placed over little spirit-burners to keep warm, along a table that looked long enough to land a 'plane on.

Mr. Bharani turned to survey the assembled crowd. All five of us. He looked from us to the food and back again.

"Where is everyone else?" he asked.

"We're going to start without them," Lila said.

Mr. Bharani shook his head and went away muttering.

Not-Sandeep looked at not-Jalal and rubbed his hands, smiling. "Left-overs!" Then he turned to me and whispered: "Distract the others while we slip the lamb into the coffin."

The lower level of his serving trolley was laden with cooked lamb legs, hidden under a white cloth. The coffin now sat on the trestles at the front of the room. Large flower arrangements had been placed at either end of it.

"Can we get a move on?" Lila said.

"Where do you want this setting up?"

It was pastry-brush boy, pulling a wheeled nylon holdall the size of three suitcases. It looked heavy.

"What is it?" I asked.

"Metal detector," he said.

"At the door over there," I said. "No one gets in unless they hand over their gun."

"Am I supposed to give them hat-check tickets?"

"Do you have hat-check tickets?"

"I've got raffle tickets," he said, "they're the same thing."

"Then give them a raffle ticket when you take their gun," I said.

"What if they refuse to hand over their guns?" He asked.

"Shoot them," I said.

"Cool!" He went away to set up the metal detector.

We all watched as he unzipped the huge bag and took out six square plastic lattices, like giant black potato waffles, and began slotting them together.

"It's like Lego," Jack said. "What is it?"

"It can tell if people are carrying knives or guns," Tiago said, "like the airport."

"Can we focus?" Lila said. "I'm going to walk out of here with Tiago and the boy. As soon as he is in the car," she nodded towards Tiago, "I'll send the boy back inside."

"You're not taking Jack," Elise said, pulling Jack towards her.

"My game, my rules," Lila said. "Piss me off, and I'll kill all of you, right here."

She pulled a bundle of plastic cable-ties out of her coat pocket and tossed them to me. I fumbled the catch and had to pick them up.

"Put one on him," Lila said.

"Jack?" I asked.

"His father, you idiot. And make sure you tighten it fully."

Tiago turned his back to me and presented his wrists. I wrapped the cable-tie around them and pulled it closed. Lila came forward and tightened it when I'd done.

"This is the weirdest part ever," Pastry-brush boy said, coming up behind us. "Someone want to test it?"

He meant the metal detector. It was now standing in the doorway, looking like a garden gazebo or a telephone box open on two sides. Anyone entering would have to pass under its arch.

As we looked, an old woman in a motorised wheelchair passed under the arch. The alarm shrieked loudly.

"Never mind, it's working," Pastry-brush boy said. He hurried back to his equipment and silenced the alarm. "Sorry, it was the wheelchair set it off."

"Do you want to frisk me, young man?" the old woman asked.

Face flushing red, he told her that wouldn't be necessary.

The old woman rolled towards us. She was dressed in a black funeral dress that looked Victorian, with a matching pill-box hat with a black mesh veil attached to it. A black and green tartan blanket covered her legs. Her face, what I could see of it, looked pale and lined. Her eyes were rimmed with red. It was impossible to guess her age.

"Have you all been scanned?" she asked, her voice wavering, but still forceful. She sounded like Maggie Smith with a cold.

"Er, no," Elise said, answering for us all.

"Come on, then, let's have you all out and back in under it," the old woman said.

"I don't think that's..." Lila began.

"Don't argue," the old woman snapped. "If we're to have security measures, there can be no exceptions. Otherwise there's no point."

I had nothing to hide. I went out through the black plastic arch and then came back into the dining room. The machine remained silent.

Elise went next, leading Jack behind her. Out and then back in one at a time. No alarm.

Tiago shrugged and made the same trip. No alarm.

"Lucky you didn't bring metal cuffs," I said.

Lila scowled.

"Your turn," the old woman said.

"Who *are* you?" Lila asked.

"Ruth," the old woman said. "Chad's great aunt."

Lila looked uncomfortable. She sighed loudly, then shrugged off her coat, tossed it over the back of a chair, and marched out through the plastic arch. In the lobby, she did an exaggerated turn, like a fashion model, and then strutted back into the dining room.

"Satisfied?" she asked the old woman.

"You should keep your back straight when you walk," Aunt Ruth said. She turned her wheelchair and surveyed the rest of us. "This is a poor turnout, isn't it?"

"It's not quite three yet," I said, "there's time."

"Where's Toby?" Aunt Ruth asked. "It comes to something when a father can't turn up for his own son's funeral."

She called Mr. Kazimir Toby?

"He's running an errand, he'll be here later," I said.

"Or not," Lila said.

"Who the hell are they?" Aunt Ruth asked, as three middle-aged women entered under the metal detector. They all seemed to be unarmed.

"Wake-crashers?" I said.

Lila shifted her weight from one foot to the other, clearly frustrated. I'm sure she could feel her grip on the situation slipping away. That's certainly what I was feeling.

Pete Kenway arrived, ducking to get under the metal detector. He'd never met Chad Kazimir, as far as I knew, but I'd asked him to attend. Jerzy and Kelly followed him in. They all seemed to be on friendly terms. Gingerbread came in next, followed by his wife Maggie; they gave us a little wave, and then went to find seats near the back.

"I know none of these people," Aunt Ruth said.

"I invited a few people," I said, "wanted to make sure there was a decent turn-out for your nephew."

"That's the problem when you put on a decent spread," Aunt Ruth said, "the riff-raff are attracted to it like flies."

Three men in dark suits arrived. The first tried to enter, and the detector shrieked angrily. The man took a hand-gun out of a shoulder holster and handed it over. Pastry-brush boy gave him a little pink ticket in exchange. I couldn't wait for the raffle draw later: *26 pink, for a .357 Magnum, anybody got 26 pink?* The other two men handed over their weapons. As the three of them came into the dining room, I saw they were the three gorillas I'd first met on the bus with Saggy-Dominic.

"Please tell me there's not going to be hymns and a priest," Aunt Ruth said.

"It's a wake, not a funeral," Lila snapped.

"Is there a bar?" the old woman asked.

"Speeches first, drinks afterwards," I said.

Three o'clock came and went, and more people arrived. Some had to hand over artillery, most didn't. There was a nice selection of weaponry on the table behind Pastry-boy when I went to speak to him, guns and knives, each with a little pink ticket attached to it with a rubber band. And so far, he hadn't had to shoot anyone. I wondered if he was disappointed.

"Get the rabble seated, let's get this thing started," Aunt Ruth said.

"Shouldn't we wait for Mr. Kazimir?" I asked.

"We'll be here all night. Toby won't turn up until the bar opens," she said.

I went to usher people into the rows of seats, and heard Lila draw a loud breath behind me.

Dolores entered. She was wearing an amazing black satin dress, and her hair and make-up were immaculate. She looked very much like a movie star. People turned to look at her.

"What are *you* doing here?" Lila snarled.

"I came to pay my respects," Dolores said.

"If you had any respect for my family, you wouldn't be here," Aunt Ruth said, obviously relishing her role as matriarch.

Dolores blushed. "I'm sorry for your loss," she said.

The old woman held up a gloved hand. "Stay away from me. In my day, a whore knew her place, and didn't show her face in public."

Lila was smiling smugly, enjoying Dolores' discomfort.

"You can wipe the smile off your face, girl. If you'd been a proper wife, Chad wouldn't have had to go looking for it somewhere else."

The room was almost silent, the seated mourners leaning forward to watch this venomous outburst.

Satisfied that she had everyone's attention, the old woman leaned back in her chair. "Now, who's going to tell me how my nephew died?"

"He was murdered!" Dolores said.

"I'm old, not senile," Aunt Ruth snapped. "I want to know *how* he came to be murdered."

"Lila, why don't you tell Aunt Ruth about the night your husband was taken?" I said.

Lila's glare was icy.

"Yes, child, tell us what happened," Aunt Ruth said, her eyes closing to dark slits.

Chapter Thirty-Eight

Lila found herself standing at the front of the room in front of thirty people, all of whom were staring at her and waiting for her to speak. She cleared her throat. I don't know what her plan had been for the afternoon, but I think it is safe to say that it hadn't included a show-and-tell.

"That night, Chad and I had gone to a party," she said, glancing towards the coffin, even though she knew Chad wasn't in it. "They were friends of his, I didn't know them. They had a big old farmhouse in the middle of nowhere.

"We drove back along a dark country road, and out of nowhere, another car overtook us. I remember Chad swearing as the car cut in front of us. And then that car slammed its brakes on. They were so close, Chad didn't have chance to miss them. We ploughed into the back of the other car. The airbags went off, and it was quite shocking."

Lila paused, reliving the shock of the moment for her audience.

"I was stunned by what had happened," she said. "At how quickly it had happened. But Chad was out of the car straight away.

"*Stay here,* he said. He slammed the door, and I think he must have locked it.

"Two men got out of the car in front. They were both dressed in dark colours. I couldn't really make out any details in the darkness. Couldn't see their faces."

Lila shook her head.

"What happened then?" Aunt Ruth asked, still watching Lila closely.

"I think Chad said something to them. And one of them swung a punch. It must have hurt him, because Chad doubled over. And then they bundled him into the back of their car."

"You didn't do anything to help my nephew?" Aunt Ruth asked.

"I tried to get out of the car," Lila said. "But it was locked, and it took me a minute to remember how to unlock it without the key. I got out and ran up to their car, tried to open the back door, but they drove away."

Lila seemed visibly shaken by this retelling.

"Did you go after them?" Aunt Ruth asked.

Lila shook her head.

"The car was too damaged to drive, and Chad had the keys. I called for someone to come and get me."

"What did you do then?" Aunt Ruth asked.

"I went home. I didn't know what to do. Who to call. The ransom demand was taped to the door when I got there."

"Did you pay it?" Aunt Ruth asked.

"Of course I did! I wanted Chad back. I hired someone, a private detective, to deliver the money for me."

"Did he?"

"Yes."

"And yet, Chad is not here," Aunt Ruth said.

Aunt Ruth was doing my job for me. And I think she was better at it. Maybe she thought she was Miss Marple.

"The kidnappers told me they would release him. That we'd find Chad locked in a shipping container on the back of a trailer, in a lay-by near the golf course. But the trailer wasn't there."

"You asked your private detective to search for Chad?" the old woman asked.

"I did. But there was no sign of him. No clues. And then – then the detective was killed."

"I see," Aunt Ruth said. "And Chad was never found?"

"No," Lila said.

Aunt Ruth shifted her weight in the chair.

"Lila, dear, do you know who kidnapped Chad?" she asked.

Lila nodded.

"Who was it?"

"I think... I think it was Dick Gorse," Lila said.

Whispering among the assembled mourners.

"And this Dick Gorse was also..."

"Murdered," Lila said, nodding. "I believe he was killed by his accomplice, the second kidnapper."

"And is that second kidnapper in this room today?" Aunt Ruth asked.

She'd moved on from Miss Marple to Perry Mason.

"Yes," Lila said.

"Point him out, dear."

Lila raised her arm, and pointed a finger towards Tiago. Her hand was shaking visibly.

"It was him, Tiago Zambora," she said.

Aunt Ruth looked from Lila to Tiago and back.

"If Chad's body was never recovered, what is in this coffin?" Aunt Ruth asked.

"I–I don't know," Lila said.

"Body double," I said.

Aunt Ruth turned her interrogation light on me.

"And what's your part in all of this?" she asked.

"I was hired to find the shipping container with Chad's body in it," I said.

"You're another half-wit who couldn't complete a simple task?"

"I didn't fail," I said. "I found the container. Chad's damaged car was in it; his body wasn't."

"You don't know that!" Lila objected. "The container was completely destroyed."

"We had the wreckage examined by experts. There was no evidence of a human body," I said.

I didn't think it was necessary to tell them that one of our 'experts' was a randy pit-bull called Brutus.

"You seem surprised to hear this, Lila dear," Aunt Ruth said.

"I just thought that – the kidnappers said that Chad was in the container."

"Perhaps he managed to get out," Aunt Ruth suggested. "He could have run away."

Lila shook her head.

"Lila thinks that is extremely unlikely," I said.

Lila threw me a warning glance, and then deliberately looked over at Jack.

Aunt Ruth must have recognised the look for what it was. A threat. She turned towards Jack.

"What's your name, boy?" she asked.

"Jack," he said, "Jack Zambora."

The old woman's eyes flicked towards Tiago.

"Come here, Jack," Aunt Ruth said.

Jack looked at his mother, who nodded that it was okay for him to go. He walked slowly towards the wheelchair, and stopped a few feet away.

Aunt Ruth smiled behind the veil. "I want you to go over to the buffet table and get me a samosa. Do you know what that is, Jack?"

Jack nodded. He moved towards the buffet table and reached for a plate.

"You are his mother?" Aunt Ruth asked.

"Yes," Elise said. "And Tiago is his father." She moved closer to Tiago.

"How did you know my nephew, Mr. Zambora?" Aunt Ruth asked.

"He was one of Chad's kidnappers!" Lila cried.

Aunt Ruth's face was expressionless as she turned to Lila. "You're not going to stick with that kidnapping story, are you?" she asked.

"It's *not* a story," Lila insisted.

"It's certainly not much of one," Aunt Ruth said.

Jack was standing beside the wheelchair, holding a samosa on a plate.

"Thank you, dear," Aunt Ruth said, taking the plate. "Why don't you take your mother and father over to the buffet and help them select something to eat. I don't think we need wait any longer for the others to arrive."

Elise and Tiago moved up behind Jack.

"Mrs. Zambora, you should find a knife to cut that thing from your husband's wrists. It looks terribly uncomfortable," Aunt Ruth said.

"I will," Elise said. "Thank you."

She, Jack, and Tiago moved off to the buffet table.

Aunt Ruth looked at the plate with the samosa on it, and then put it on top of the coffin. Then she manoeuvred her wheelchair until she had her back to the coffin. The whining of the chair's motors was the only sound in the room.

Aunt Ruth stared at Lila for a moment, and then turned to me. "Can you tell us a different story, young man?" she asked.

I glanced towards Lila. Jack and Elise were on the other side of the room, but I wasn't sure how much of a threat Lila still posed to them.

"Tell the story to *me*, Mr. Lucke," Aunt Ruth said.

I turned my attention back to her.

"Well?" she said.

"Chad wasn't kidnapped," I said.

I heard a small collective gasp from the audience. And I saw Aunt Ruth smile.

"Tell us what did happen," she said.

"I've worked some of it out," I said, "but only Lila knows all of it."

"You start, and then Lila can fill in any missing details."

I saw Lila's shoulders droop. Was she admitting defeat?

"There was no second car on the road that night," I said. "The only people there were Lila and Chad."

Chapter Thirty-Nine

"What Lila said about the party was true," I said, "they did drive out to somewhere in the middle of the countryside, and they did drive back along an isolated country road. I've seen it, and it was almost deserted in the day time. At night, no one would have seen them, and there was no other traffic.

"Driving along in the dark, I think they did stop for some reason. I'm not sure why."

"My dear husband suddenly decided he needed to pee," Lila said. "I told him to get his prostate checked, but you know what men are like."

"Chad stood at the side of the road," I said.

"With his cock in his hand, pissing like a bull," Lila said, rolling her eyes.

"And then what?" I asked. I knew what happened, but I didn't really have any idea why.

Lila sighed. "I was suddenly overcome by this desire..."

"To kill him?" I asked.

She nodded. "I slid across into the driver's seat, revved the engine, and backed the car up a bit. Then I drove at him."

"Chad just stood there and let it happen?" I asked.

"He turned round. I suppose he thought I was going to drive off and leave him there. He was still peeing. When he saw me coming straight at him, he tried to leap out of the way. I had to swerve, but I hit him. He went up in the air, over the car, I suppose, and landed on the road. Face down. I was going to back up and run over him, to make sure. But I looked in the mirror, and he wasn't moving. I thought he was dead."

"Was he?" I asked.

The whole audience was leaning forward expectantly. Aunt Ruth was watching Lila, her eyes glittering behind the veil.

Lila shook her head. "I pressed the button that popped the boot open, and went to get the picnic blanket. I was going to cover him up. Don't ask me why. Then, when I turned towards him, I saw him move. I knew if he got up, he'd kill me," she said.

"What did you do?"

"I stabbed him with a screwdriver," Lila said.

There was a gasp from the audience, and at least one person said 'No!' It was like being on the *My Lousy Cheating Husband Peed in the Street* episode of Jerry Springer.

"A screwdriver?" I said.

"It's all I had. In the car. I mean, there was a spanner and a hammer, and some other bits, in the tool roll. But the screwdriver seemed best."

"You ran over your husband with your car, and then you stabbed him with a screwdriver to make sure he was dead?" I asked.

Lila nodded, smiling. Not much by way of remorse that I could see.

"You were standing in the road, and your husband lay there with a screwdriver in his chest. What did you do next?" I asked.

"The car was a mess," Lila said. "The front was all bashed in where it had hit him, and there was blood on it. There was no way I could drive it home."

"Of course not," I said. "You called someone to come and clean up the mess?"

Now that I knew exactly what had happened that night, the rest of it slotted neatly into place.

Lila nodded.

"Did you know someone who did that sort of thing?" I asked.

"No," she said, "but my husband did."

"Your husband had used Dick Gorse's services before?" I had to ask.

"A couple of times, at least," Lila said. "I knew he was reliable. Or I thought he was."

"Dick Gorse turned up at the murder scene, and took away your damaged car and your dead husband?"

"He did."

"Were you there when he did it?"

"Good lord no, I wasn't sitting out there all night. I called a taxi and went home."

"You asked Dick to get rid of your car. Not get it fixed?" I asked.

"I could never have driven it again." Lila gave a little shudder. "I have reported it stolen. The insurance will pay up. Eventually."

"Dick Gorse came and cleared up your mess. You paid him. Then what?"

"And then nothing. That should have been it," she said.

"But it wasn't, was it?" I asked.

"No, it wasn't."

"Dick contacted you, and said he hadn't destroyed the evidence. He'd kept it."

Lila nodded.

"How much money did Dick Gorse want?" I asked.

"Half-a-million pounds," she said.

The same figure she'd given me as the ransom demand. It caused some muttering in the audience.

"You paid him the money?" I asked.

"Yes, Matt said I should."

"You hired him when?"

"As soon as I received the blackmail demand."

"Why Matt Lester?"

"He was someone my husband had used," she said.

"And you still thought that was a reliable endorsement?"

"I didn't have much choice," she snapped. "I'm a woman – I don't have those sorts of connections."

"Why did you have a fake ransom note?" I asked.

"That was Matt's idea. He said I should tell people my husband had been kidnapped, and then I could say that I needed the money to pay the kidnappers. The ransom note was to explain why I withdrew the money – if anyone asked later."

"Anyone like the police, you mean?"

"Them as well," she said. "If people thought my husband had been kidnapped, that explained his absence."

"And if the body was ever discovered, his death could be blamed on the non-existent kidnappers."

"It was a good plan, wasn't it?" Lila asked.

"It might have been, if it had worked," I said.

She scowled. "It should have worked. It's so unfair!"

The woman standing in front of me had just confessed to stabbing her husband. I had to be careful not to start thinking of her as a victim. No matter how hard she tried to convince me.

"Matt Lester took the money and put it in the locker at the gym?" I asked.

She shook her head.

"I took it myself. It had to go into a locker in the ladies' changing room," she said. "Matt was supposed to go and check that the container with the evidence in was delivered to the correct place."

"The lay-by off the crossroads on the A611," I said.

"Near the golf course," she said.

"But it never turned up?"

"Matt went there, and he waited. But there was no sign of the container," she said.

"Did you think that Dick Gorse had double-crossed you?"

"Yes, I did."

"Did you then kill Dick Gorse?"

"No!"

"Did you ask Matt Lester to kill him?"

"Why would I do that? Dick Gorse still had the evidence. If we killed him, the evidence could have ended up with the police. And I would have been in all kinds of trouble."

"Matt said he'd help you get the evidence back?" I asked.

"Yes. But he turned out to be useless," she said.

"Is that why you killed him as well?" I asked.

"I didn't kill Matt Lester," Lila said. "I'm not going to pretend I'm sorry he's dead, because I'm not. He was a sleaze, and... well, he wasn't much of a gentleman," she said. "I didn't kill Matt Lester, and I didn't kill Dick Gorse."

"But you did kill your own husband, who was the youngest son of a Rathbanian crime boss," I said. "Did it ever occur to you that might not be a good idea?"

"Of course I knew what it meant," she snapped. "Why do you think I've been desperate to cover it up since it happened? I know what the Rathbanians will do if they find out."

Did she think, at this late stage, there was any chance of Mr. Kazimir not finding out? At least three of his men were sitting in the audience, and they were already glancing at the little pile of weapons by the entrance. But that didn't worry me too much: I'd taken precautions. The idea that Lila thought there might still be some way out of this for her *did* worry me. She had intended for Tiago to take the blame for her husband's death, but that couldn't happen now. Did that mean she had a Plan B?

Aunt Ruth's chair motors whined as she backed up a little bit, closer to the coffin, and further away from Lila.

"Chad was killed by his own wife?" Aunt Ruth asked.

"No," I said. "No, he wasn't."

Both Lila and Aunt Ruth seemed stunned by this, and a murmur ran through the audience.

"No?" Aunt Ruth asked.

"What Lila has said is true. But it's not the whole truth, is it?"

I was looking at Aunt Ruth as I said it.

"What are you talking about?" Lila asked.

"He's a much better detective than that first idiot you hired," Aunt Ruth said.

"There's no way that..."

Lila fell silent as Aunt Ruth threw aside the tartan blanket that covered her legs. For the first time, we could see the plaster cast that covered her right shin. And the sawn-off shotgun that was resting in her lap.

The audience muttered loudly, and Mr. Kazimir's men got to their feet.

Aunt Ruth raised the shot-gun. "Sit down and shut up!" She said.

The Rathbanians sat, looking longingly towards their weapons. Everyone else concentrated on not making noise.

While Aunt Ruth had been distracted, Lila had lunged towards her outdoor coat. She pulled a gun from inside it. Plan B was a chrome-plated Uzi submachine gun. One of the smaller ones.

Mr. Bharani scurried forward from the back of the room, waving his hands. "No guns! No guns!" He wailed.

Then he hit the floor as Lila opened fire. Bullets raked along the side of the coffin.

At the same instant, Aunt Ruth raised herself up, half-standing, and fired off both barrels of the shotgun. The recoil sent her and her chair over backwards, knocking the coffin off its trestles.

The coffin hit the ground and the lid burst open. Charred meat rolled out, and someone screamed.

After that, it was pandemonium.

Chapter Forty

Aunt Ruth lay on the floor beside the upset coffin. Behind me, the audience was in uproar. Lila was still on her feet, holding the Uzi in front of her. There was plaster in her hair, brought down when the shot-gun blasts hit the ceiling. She started towards Aunt Ruth, knowing that the shotgun was empty, and safe in the knowledge that she could finish off the old woman without challenge.

She had to be stopped. I looked around for something heavy to throw. A chair would have been ideal, but I was too far away to make a move before she could turn the gun on me.

Tiago must have had a similar idea. He jumped up onto a table and threw himself at her.

Lila saw him and turned, raising the machine gun, but she wasn't quick enough. Tiago hit her, and bullets sprayed into the wall, shattering a mirror. Tiago wrenched the gun from her hand and threw it to the far side of the room. He dragged her to her feet, twisting her arm up behind her back.

One of the Rathbanians made a dash for the weapons table by the door. He grabbed a heavy black handgun and turned, a triumphant look on his face. He pointed the gun at Lila and fired. It made a dry clicking sound. I'd asked Pastry-brush boy to empty the bullets out of the guns, pressing one of Lila's fifty-pound notes into his hand as I said it. I'd been expecting something like this.

But not *quite* like this. The Rathbanian's expression changed from triumph to anger, and then to shock.

I didn't see who threw the curry at him. The Rathbanian opened his mouth to scream, but the sound never came. A dollop of bum-burner vindaloo hit him in the mouth, and he went down gagging. I saw him crawl towards the buffet, retching, desperate for the antidote: yoghurt with mint.

Another of the Rathbanians must have seen who had launched the curry attack: he sprang towards the food table, and soon chicken drumsticks were whistling through the air like grenades.

"Food fight!" Someone yelled, and the whole audience moved as one towards the buffet.

"Please, no shoving, there is plenty food for everyone!" Mr. Bharani shouted, misreading the situation.

I watched as someone staggered backwards. Reaching out to save themselves, their hand caught the edge of a large serving bowl, and it was like touching off an IED: a cloud of yellow rice exploded upwards.

A samosa whistled past my ear like a throwing star.

Someone opened a large black umbrella to protect themselves from a shower of Bombay potato: I couldn't see if it was John Steed or The Penguin.

It was starting with appetisers and side dishes, but I knew it would soon escalate to mains. This was how wars began: someone threw a curried prawn, and nations ended up at each other's throats for decades. I'm sure the Cold War began with a diplomatic spat over who threw the first canapé.

I ducked as a squadron of poppadoms whizzed by overhead like UFOs.

A man ran past me, a spreading red stain on the front of his shirt. Goa chicken, possibly.

Some people, Mr. Bharani among them, took up defensive positions, tipping tables on their side and hiding behind them.

I swear I heard cries of 'Medic!' and 'Man down!'

From behind one of the overturned tables, my nephew was bowling appetisers overarm, despite protests from his mother. Jack's aim was good, but he wasn't particularly discerning in his choice of target. An onion bhaji exploded on my left, showering me with spicy shrapnel.

"Sorry Uncle Joe!" Jack shouted.

I waved to show I was uninjured, and a whole garlic naan came in from another direction and hit me in the face. I tripped over backwards, trying to claw the doughy face-hugger off before I suffocated. Jack thought this was hilarious.

From my position on the floor, I saw one of the Rathbanians gut-shot with spinach saag: it wasn't pretty.

The carpet grew slick with chana dal, like the bottom of a battlefield trench. A young man slipped; he was hit in the chest by a barrage of loaded pani puri before he went down.

One of the Rathbanian gorillas advance menacingly on Lila. She hit him a knock-out blow with a leg of lamb.

The walls were splattered with jalfrezi and korma, and their mouth-watering aromas hung in the air. Above the sound of battle, I heard my stomach rumbling, and all I could think of was that war was such a terrible waste.

And then it was over. The buffet table was empty. The floor of the dining room was littered with groaning bodies. Small fragments of food occasionally fell from the ceiling, but hostilities had ceased.

A face appeared above one of the overturned table defensive positions, a white napkin tied to a serving spoon, waving gently in surrender. Mr. Bharani. He rose cautiously, surveying the war zone. The upturned and damaged furniture. The bullet-ravaged coffin and trampled legs of cooked lamb. The casualties smeared with curry and rice and things unrecognisable. He drew a deep breath, and clasped his hands in front of him.

"Would anyone like to see a dessert menu?" he asked.

Groans all round.

"Just a coffee for me," someone said.

Over by the fallen coffin, Aunt Ruth stirred. She managed to raise herself to a sitting position, and looked over towards the wheelchair, which lay on its side some distance away. Carefully, she dragged her good leg under her, and then paused to rest, looking like someone kneeling to make a proposal or receive a knighthood from their queen. Her hat and veil were slightly askew. Then she slowly, painfully, raised herself to a standing position, all her weight on the one good leg. She swayed slightly, but remained upright.

Dolores appeared from somewhere, and picked her way across the battlefield, stepping over fallen bodies, and making her way towards the old woman. Dolores seemed untouched by the war that had raged in the dining room: her hair and make-up were perfect, and her black dress was unblemished.

Aunt Ruth watched her approach, and smiled.

We all watched as they faced each other.

"You bastard!" Dolores spat.

She drew back her arm and swung at Aunt Ruth. The right-hook connected with the old woman's jaw with a surprisingly loud *smack!* The force of the blow spun Aunt Ruth around a full hundred-and-eighty degrees, and almost in slow motion, she toppled face-forwards onto the floor.

We did the collective gasp thing again. Dolores had just punched a defenceless old woman.

"What have you done?" Lila asked, getting to her feet and facing Dolores.

Dolores turned to me. "You'll have to explain it to her, and to anyone else who isn't smart enough to have worked it out for themselves."

I stood up.

"What is she talking about?" Lila asked.

"Dolores has worked out who killed Dick Gorse and Matt Lester," I said. "It wasn't Tiago."

"It wasn't me either," Lila said.

"No, you didn't kill anyone," I said.

"Except her husband," Elise reminded me.

"We only have Lila's word for that," I said.

"I'm not going to lie about something like that, am I?" Lila asked.

"Joe, she's not," Elise said.

"She's not lying," I said. "Lila genuinely believes she killed her husband. How could she not? She hit him with her car, and then stabbed him with a screwdriver."

"I do not understand," Tiago said.

People were all climbing to their feet now, and they looked like extras from a zombie apocalypse. Everyone was looking at me.

"I'll tell you what happened, as near as I can work it out," I said.

"No, you won't!" Aunt Ruth was on her unsteady feet again. And this time she held the chrome-plated Uzi. It was pointed at me, and the aim was unwavering. She'd apparently adopted Lila's Plan B.

"Clear the room!" Aunt Ruth said. "I want only the main cast left in here."

She turned the machine gun towards the crowd. They scrambled to their feet, and began heading towards the exit.

Gingerbread came over to me. "You find out who really killed that bastard who broke my hand, let me know: I'd like to buy them a drink."

I nodded. He patted me on the shoulder, and led Maggie to safety.

Eventually it was just the six of us left in the devastated dining room. Me, Tiago, Elise, Jack, Lila, and Aunt Ruth.

"Now you can finish your story," Aunt Ruth said.

"It's not really my story," I said.

"Indulge me," she said, pointing the Uzi at me again.

Tiago righted one of the undamaged chairs and set it down near Aunt Ruth. When he'd backed away, she lowered herself onto it. The gun was trained on me the whole time.

"Everything Lila told us was true," I said, "up to a point. She did drive away in a taxi, leaving Dick Gorse to dispose of the body and the car."

"Which the bastard didn't do!" Lila said.

"No, he didn't," I said, "but there was a good reason for that."

"He wanted to blackmail me," Lila said.

"Yes and no," I said. I held up my hand to cut off her protests.

"Let Joe tell us what happened," Elise said.

"Lila went off in a taxi," I said, "driven by a young Indian guy who was probably half-stoned. He didn't think it was in anyway odd to pick up as lone female at 2am and leave her wrecked car in the middle of nowhere.

"Dick Gorse arrived in a truck. I don't know whether he turned up in an HGV with a trailer, or whether he came with an ordinary tow truck and put the car in a shipping container later. It doesn't matter. He loaded up the car to take it away.

"He probably planned to stash the body in the boot of the damaged car. That's what I would have done. But when he went to pick up the body, he saw something strange..."

I paused for effect.

"The body had disappeared!" Jack said.

"No, but you're not far wrong," I said. "Dick found that Chad was still alive. Badly injured, but not dead. If you were Dick, what would you do?"

"Stab him again with the screwdriver!" Jack said.

"Jack!" Elise said, shocked. "No more video games for you."

"Aw, mum!"

"Jack's right, though," I said, risking one of Elise's mum looks. "Dick could have finished Chad off. Done the job for Lila and taken her money. End of story. But he didn't do that.

"We all knew Dick Gorse. If he saw an opportunity to make some money out of a situation, he'd do it. And he knew he was onto a winner here.

"Dick picked Chad up and carried him carefully, setting him in the cab of the truck. And he drove him to see a doctor. I'm not sure which one, there are a few who will help out in situations like that, with no questions asked. For a fee. It shouldn't be too hard to track down the one he used.

"Dick Gorse saved Chad Kazimir's life," I said.

"He's not dead?" Lila said. "Bastard!"

"I'm guessing you never stabbed a man before?" Tiago said.

"Not in the chest," Lila said.

"You missed Chad's vital organs," I said, "and you left the screwdriver in him, effectively plugging up the wound and stopping him bleeding to death."

"I won't make that mistake again!" Lila said.

"Lila and Chad's BMW was brand new, top spec," I said. "It had all the latest safety features. And that includes those for pedestrian impact. The reason the car looked such a mess was because it was designed to deform to absorb the shock of impact. The bonnet and grill collapse and cause as little damage to the pedestrian – or the husband – as possible.

"Chad is a strong, healthy man. He suffered a broken limb, and maybe even a concussion. But beyond that, he could almost get up and walk away. The impact occurred at thirty- or forty-miles-an-hour, I would think; though it must have seemed faster, for both Lila and Chad."

"I didn't kill him!" Lila said, still adjusting to the idea.

"But where is he?" Tiago asked.

"Right here," I said.

They all looked at me like I was the one with a concussion. All of them except Aunt Ruth.

She reached up and pulled off the pill-box hat, the veil, and the silver wig she had been wearing.

Chad did not make an attractive woman. I could see why he'd gone for the veil.

"You look a complete twat in that frock," Lila said.

Chad pointed the Uzi towards her.

Chapter Forty-One

"That is what happened that night. No kidnapping and no murder," I said. "Now we just have to figure out what happened after that. Unless you'd like to tell us?"

Aunt Chad shook his head. "You tell us. If you get it wrong, I'll shoot you."

If I'd known how many bullets a mini Uzi held, I could have counted the bullet holes and worked out whether he had any ammunition left in the clip. But I had no idea.

"Given all he'd suffered, Chad needed a few days to recover," I said. "Ideally he'd have been with someone who could take care of him. I thought at first that Dick had taken him to stay with..."

"His old lady!" Lila said.

"His mistress, Dolores," I said. "But when I went to her house, there was no evidence that she was harbouring an invalid. And she genuinely seemed to be mourning Chad's death."

"Bitch!" Lila said.

"I can only guess that Big Dick stashed Chad somewhere, and played nurse-maid himself. Once he was feeling a little better, Chad had to decide what his next move would be. His wife thought he was dead, because she was the one who killed him. You can understand why he didn't go home straight away.

"But Dick Gorse knew he was alive, and Chad knew Big Dick wouldn't keep his secret for too long. Unless he had money to keep Dick quiet, and to pay for the services already rendered. Chad came up with a little plan that would get him some spending money, and also allow him to get a little bit of revenge on his murderous wife."

"He got Dick to blackmail me," Lila said.

I nodded.

"Lila paid up, and Tiago was hired to move the container that held the damaged car. But Chad couldn't let Lila have it, because she would discover his body wasn't in it. He got Big Dick to move it again. And Big Dick hid it behind the billboard for his own store. Hiding the container in plain sight."

"Bastard!" Tiago said.

"Having taken care of the money and the container, there was just one more loose end to take care of..."

"Dick Gorse," Elise said.

"Chad killed Dick Gorse?" Tiago asked.

"It's the only explanation that fits all the facts," I said.

"Who killed Matt Lester?" Elise asked, deliberately not looking at Tiago.

"Lila hired Lester when she first got the blackmail demand," I said. "It was his idea to pretend that Chad had been kidnapped. He made the fake ransom note. That way Lila could withdraw the money she needed from the bank, and she'd have an explanation for doing so, if the police, or her father-in-law, ever asked for one."

"She paid the money to get the container because she believed the wrecked car and her husband's body were in it," Elise said. "If they both had been, what would she have done with them?"

Everyone looked at Lila, but she pretended not to notice.

"I imagine Matt Lester had also come up with a way of disposing of those inconvenient bits of evidence," I said.

"But who killed him?" Elise asked again. I understood why she needed to know.

"Someone wanted us to believe that Tiago did," I said. "There is CCTV footage of him going into the carpet store just before the fire started."

"I was there," Tiago said. "I got a call from someone who said his name was Dominic. He said he was working for Mr. Kazimir. This person said I should go straight away to the carpet store; go in the back way."

"Tell us why you would do something that dangerous and that stupid," I said.

The call had come from Chad, not Dominic: Tiago didn't know this, but going to the carpet store that night had still been a crazy thing to do.

Tiago glanced at me, then looked at Elise. "He said that he was holding Elise there. He would kill her if I did not go there and tell him where the container was."

"You went, even though you didn't know where the container was?" I asked.

"What else could I do? I thought if I gave myself to them, they would let Elise go."

Elise looked at Tiago as if he was some kind of hero. No one ever looked at me that way. I needed a new agent.

"When I got there, no one was there," Tiago said. "No Dominic, no Elise. Just a body on the floor. I did not know who he was. I turned him over, to see if I could do anything, but he was already dead. I knew I had been set-up. And then someone threw Molotov cocktails into the store."

"Matt Lester had been stabbed?" I asked.

Tiago nodded.

"In the groin?"

He nodded again.

"You got his blood on your hands," I said, "and you wiped it on a white towel when you got home."

"How do you know this?" Tiago asked.

"I'm a detective."

The broken table had almost certainly been Tiago's work: in his anger, he had smashed it into matchwood.

"How did you escape from the burning store, dad?" Jack asked.

Everyone was looking at Tiago, longing to hear more about his heroic exploits.

"I hid in a rubbish skip behind the store," Tiago said.

I almost laughed out loud.

"I sneaked away when the fire brigade arrived and things started to get busy. It was getting pretty hot in the skip by then, I can tell you."

Elise was staring up at Tiago in a way that said she'd be inviting him into her knickers the first chance she got.

Jack was looking at his dad like Tiago was some sort of superhero.

"Bastard!" I said. It was my turn.

Tiago turned to Chad. "You were behind all of this? Good going for a dead man," he said.

Chad smiled.

"And he'd have gotten away with it, if it hadn't been for us pesky kids," I said.

"Why did you come here dressed as Aunt Ruth?" Lila asked.

"I wanted to tie up a few loose ends," Chad said.

"Loose ends?" Lila asked,

"He means us," I said. "Look around. The five people in this room are the only ones who know what he's done. If he gets rid of us, he's free to go and do whatever he wants. He can go back home to his father, explain how he had to get rid of his murderous wife. Or he can just stay dead, and go off to a new life with Dolores."

"She punched him in the mouth," Lila said, smiling.

"That's true," I said. I turned to Chad. "You should probably have told her you weren't dead."

"We're all going to die?" Jack asked, moving closer to his mother.

"No, we're not," I said. "That was Chad's plan, but it wasn't a very good plan."

"Come now, Mr. Lucke, don't lie to your nephew. It's wrong to give him false hope," Chad said.

"You're going to shoot all of us?" Elise asked.

"No, he's not," I said.

"Excuse me, but who's the one with the gun, here?" Chad said. "And don't imagine that you're going to overpower me and get away from here. I have men surrounding this place."

"No, you don't," I said.

Chad got to his feet, his face reddening.

"I'm sorry, but I think you've been reading the wrong script," he said.

"I've been writing a new one," I said. "I handed it over to the director earlier."

"Director? What are you talking about?" Chad asked.

"In the new script, your next line is going to be: *Hello, father,*" I said.

Chad looked at me. And then he looked at the man who had just ducked in under the metal-detector arch.

"Hello, Chad," Mr. Kazimir said.

"Hello, father," Chad said. Defeated.

Jack gave me a thumbs-up and grinned. And I felt like a hero.

Mr. Kazimir walked over and took the Uzi from Chad.

The three big gorillas came in from the lobby. One of them pushed Dolores in ahead of him.

"You do look a complete twat in that dress," Mr. Kazimir said.

If you're going to bring in a director, you want one that sounds like Orson Welles. Even if it's a Geordie Orson Welles.

"There are cars outside to take you all home," Mr. Big said.

Lila turned to me. "That's why you were wittering on like Hercule Poirot, you were stalling to give them time to get back here?"

"They've been here all along," I said. I took out the phone that Dominic had given me and held it up. "I'd already told Mr. Kazimir that his son was alive, so he knew Chad wouldn't be found dead in Pinxton. Who would? I just wanted to make sure we got the whole story for the cameras."

"Why bother?" Lila asked. "He's not going to hand us over to the police. We'll be executed."

"What do you mean *we?*" Chad said.

"Be quiet, both of you. I will deal with you later," Mr. Kazimir said.

He turned away, and walked to where Dolores was standing.

"You will go home," he said to her. "Forget about my son. I will see that you remain comfortable without him."

Dolores stared at him, defiant. Then she glanced towards Chad, but he just kept staring at the stained carpet. Disappointed, Dolores looked into Mr. Kazimir's eyes, and nodded.

"Go," Mr. Big said.

Without a backward glance, Dolores turned and walked out into the lobby.

Lila started towards the exit as well.

"Not you," Mr. Big said, "you will stay for a family meeting."

I was still holding the phone. Mr. Kazimir held his hand out for it, but I didn't surrender it.

"I thought I might keep it," I said, "in case I ever need to call and ask you for a favour."

Mr. Kazimir stared at the phone, weighing what I had said. Then he nodded.

"What are you going to do with them?" I asked, meaning Chad and Lila.

"I will take care of family business," he said.

Seeing my expression, he laughed. "Do not worry, they will not have to sleep with the fishes. They are my son and daughter-in-law, I cannot harm them."

"Then what?" I asked.

"I will send them back to the old country, to learn what it is to be a proper man and wife," he said.

I might be wrong, but I think he was proud, rather than disappointed in Chad and Lila. Perhaps attempted murder, and actual murder, and faking a kidnap, or faking your own death, were things that gained you kudos in a family like theirs.

"The old country?" I said.

"Middlesbrough," he said.

"Harsh!" I said.

"Compared to Mansfield? You think?"

"Thanks for the phone," I said. I turned to go.

"Be careful who you share that recording with, Mr. Lucke," he said.

I turned back. Busted. "You knew?"

I had used the voice memo app to record everything that had been said in the dining room earlier.

"It is what I would have done," he said. "I would prefer that it did not find its way into the hands of the police."

I held the phone out to him, but he didn't take it.

"I said to keep it. Call it a demonstration of my trust."

"It's not going to self-destruct when I get outside, is it?" I asked, still holding the phone at arm's length.

"You watch too many movies, Mr. Lucke. A phone doesn't hold nearly enough explosive to kill someone. We put a bomb in your car instead."

He smiled then, and I was sure he was joking. Fairly sure.

Chapter Forty-Two

"You told us we'd find a body in the bottom of that old septic tank," Bob said. There was a slight whine in his voice when he said it.

"Yeah, I'm sorry about that, I was misinformed: he wasn't dead," I said, trying to look suitably contrite.

I'd needed something to keep the two detectives distracted while the wake was taking place at the Raj Lion.

"When they took the lid off, there was a crust on it six inches thick," Bob said, "you could stand on it."

"You didn't, did you?" I asked.

"*I* didn't," Dennis said. "Do I look like someone who is stupid enough to stand on the crust in a septic tank and hit it with a pick-axe?"

"You don't," I said.

I looked at Bob.

"I had to have three injections," Bob said.

"I told you not to swallow," Dennis said. "Spit it out, is what I said."

"It went up my nose and down the back of my throat," Bob said.

"You did the same thing with custard," Dennis said.

"Wait, you two were friends at school?" I asked.

"Who said anything about school? I'm talking about dinner yesterday," Dennis said.

"You lied to us," Bob said. He sounded hurt. And there was still a whiff of the septic tank about him.

"I *always* lie to you," I said.

"I know, but we usually *know* you're lying," Bob said.

"I'll try and be less convincing next time," I said.

"Tell us the whole story," Dennis said.

"I'll give you the outline," I said. "You'll have to colour it in yourself."

Bob scowled. He'd probably forgotten his crayons.

"Dick Gorse and Matt Lester were working together," I said. "They decided it would be a brilliant idea to kidnap someone and hold them for ransom. You should probably write this down."

Dennis looked at Bob, who made no move to take out his notebook.

"I forgot my pen," Bob said. "Besides, you have nicer handwriting."

Dennis sighed and pulled out a notebook. It had a picture of a Smurf on the front, so I'm guessing it wasn't his official notebook.

"Dick Gorse and Matt Lester planned to kidnap someone," Dennis said.

"They didn't plan to, they actually did it," I said.

I'd put a copy of the ransom note in one of those plastic pockets with the strip of holes down one side. I slid it across the table to them.

"And they were paid the ransom money. That's the point at which they had a falling out," I said.

"And Matt Lester killed Dick Gorse," Dennis said.

"Yes," I said.

"Then who killed Matt Lester?" Bob asked.

"The family of the kidnap victim," I said.

"And the name of this family?" Bob asked.

"Three guesses," I said.

Dennis looked up from his notebook. "You're *kidding!*" He said.

"Yeah, stop mucking about and just tell us," Bob said.

"He doesn't need to tell us, you plank, we already know," Dennis said.

"Do we?" Bob asked.

Dennis closed his Smurf notebook. "You're not telling us the whole story, are you?"

"I told you I wouldn't. I didn't lie about that," I said.

"I don't like this," Dennis said.

"Dick Gorse's murder is solved, and the murderer is dead. No more expensive investigation, no expensive court trial. And it looks good on your statistics. Matt Lester's death goes down as gang-related, the public assume he deserved to die, and no one worries about it. What's not to like?" I said.

"It's too neat," Dennis said.

"By the time you two have done filling it in, there'll be so much colouring outside the lines that no one will think it's neat at all," I said.

I smiled.

Dennis didn't.

Bob said nothing.

"You know the next time you need our help...?" Dennis said.

"They'll need ice skates in Hades," I said.

Bob frowned: "Where's Hades?"

Dennis stood up, and slapped Bob's arm with the back of his hand. "Come on," he said.

Bob stood up. "Is it near Greenland?" he asked. "Or is it somewhere warm, is that the joke?"

"No, Bob, you are," Dennis said.

They walked out of the flat and down the stairs. I followed.

"I still haven't worked out who killed that phony detective," Bob said. "Which family was it?"

"It was The Windsors, Bob," Dennis said.

"Not *Barbara* Windsor?"

"Carry on, constable," I said, and closed the door on them.

Who Killed Big Dick? 361

* * *

Mark Twain once referred to the last part of a story as marryin' and buryin'. I'm not sure if he meant it literally.

Pete and Jerzy got married, after Pete and Kelly got unmarried. I went to the civil ceremony. Three older men gave me their telephone numbers. One of them was Uncle Benny. None of them kissed me.

With his murderer officially dead, and no need for a trial, Big Dick's body was released and he got a proper burial. His wake was much less eventful than the last one I went to.

Pete, Kelly, and Charmaine formed a business partnership and re-opened the bed and carpet store in a new retail unit. I also heard that Pete and Lenny Graves did the clean-up job at the Raj Lion, so I guess that part of Big Dick's business lives on too; though I think they're steering clear of crime scenes. And Pete, Kelly, and Charmaine all got Cookie Monster tattoos in memory of Big Dick. All right, I made that bit up.

I never discovered what happened to the blackmail slash ransom money. I thought it might have been hidden in Aunt Ruth's motorised wheelchair, but that turned out not to be the case. I still haven't decided what to do with the wheelchair. Jack's been riding it up and down their street. He's almost run Mrs. Kepler (nee Squitz) down twice.

Elise and Tiago remarried, and this time Jack got to be part of the ceremony. He was at the first one, but he was too young to remember it. This time he had a suit that matched Tiago's, and they made a very attractive family. Especially in the photos that I'm not in. Tiago asked me to be best man, proving they have irony in Spain too. Gingerbread and Maggie catered the reception, because no-one fancied another party at the Raj

Lion. Now Tiago drives trucks locally for Morton's Haulage, thanks to a good word from Gingerbread.

And if you're wondering what happened with Shelly and me, well, we're still sharing beer and pizza. And not having sex.

Did You Enjoy This Book?

If you did, will you do something for me?

I'm an indie author, and publish my books without the backing of a major publisher. That means no six-figure advances and no advertising budget. This makes it difficult to promote my novels so new readers can find them. But you can help me.

Honest reviews and genuine 'word-of-mouth' make all the difference. You don't have to write one of those awful 'book reports' we did at school. All I'm asking is for you to leave a star rating and a couple of sentences on *Amazon* or *Goodreads*. Or a short review on your blog. Or tell your friends about it on *Facebook* or *Twitter*.

Let people know what you liked about this book, and why they might like it too. And if there was something you didn't like, you can say that too: constructive criticism helps me write a better book next time.

But please, *no spoilers!*

Thanks for reading,

Acknowledgments & Apologies

I'm a big fan of the novels of Carl Hiaasen and the Lew Archer series by Ross Macdonald. At some point, I thought: Wouldn't it be fun to write a book like that. Set in Mansfield. I couldn't really imagine Lew Archer walking through Mansfield market, so I ended up creating a detective hero who was pretty much the opposite of Macdonald's sexy, tough-guy with a taste for great food. I'm not sure how much of me shows up in Joe Lucke, but that whole low self-esteem thing feels kind of familiar... and he's tall and skinny and blond, which is what I want to be when I grow up.

This book was planned and written during a period of change in my life. I began plotting it while I was working as a civil servant. I wrote it after that contract had ended, and when I was – for the first time ever – pretending to be a full-time author. But its roots lie very much in that pre-'retirement' period, and so I must say thanks to the NE crowd, who made working in that office bearable: Graham Murray, Mandy Ruddy, Suzie Price, Wendy Steadman, and Susan Zappala. And 'Roadkill,' the origami frog. Also hello to Amanda, Debbie, Sean, Dean, Debbie, Emily, Louisa, Kathy, Chris, James (who escaped before I did), and everyone else in the Nottingham office: I miss the themed lunches! And hi as well to the Commercial Services 'management' – Alison, Andy, Nick and David.

Thanks to Michael Carroll, who was the first to read this one, and helped me fix typos and continuity errors before anyone else saw them. He knows that I'd sooner hack off my own leg than submit what I've written for constructive criticism, and manages to give me feedback in a way that means I don't want to stab him in the groin. We've been friends for 20 years, and he knows me well enough to realise the last part of that sentence was a lie.

And thank you to the usual suspects: Mum and Dad, who read everything; to my Grandad; to Ange, Mike, Isobel, and Edward, who remind me to enjoy the good things in life – especially red wine and Lego; and to Mark, Keri, Jake and Alex, who got me three-litres of author-inspiration-juice for Christmas – who knew they made Jack Daniels bottles that big? Additional thanks to my nephew Alex, who really did give me that advice about peeing against trees.

In writing about people from other countries or ethnic groups, there is always a danger of stereotyping. Originally, I intended that the criminal gang in this story would be people from an actual European country, but in the months immediately following the 'Brexit' vote, I didn't feel comfortable doing that. Instead I have used a fictitious country, named in honour of Basil Rathbone.

I *am* guilty of using the 'comedy Indian' stereotype, but I try to balance that by giving the Indian characters some of the best lines. Apologies to any Hindi speakers for the swearing, and I hope I got it right! If you don't speak Hindi, Google Translate should tell you what people are saying – but don't look the phrases up on a work or college computer. And hopefully, making my Spanish character incredibly handsome with a sexy accent, makes up for the fact that he was also a (minor) crook.

As ever, I have tried to include gay characters that are not victims or freaks – but obviously I'm doing that in the context of a comedy, where just about every character is somewhat freakish, so it's all relative.

It is a tradition in private eye novels that the hero makes fun of official detectives and the police. Writers have done this since at least the time of Sir Arthur Conan Doyle and Inspector Lestrade, and I do it here. The detectives in these pages are in no way based on people working in Mansfield or Nottinghamshire. In my own limited dealings with the local constabulary, I have found them to be professional and courteous. And I have never seen any of them eat donuts.

Apologies also to the residents of Bulwell, which really isn't the arsehole of Nottinghamshire: I just said that for a cheap laugh. And I'm sure Pinxton isn't that bad either. I've never been to Middlesbrough, so can't honestly say how it compares to Mansfield. But Blackpool after dark really did feel scarier.

If you're familiar with the geography of Mansfield, you may notice that I have described places in a way you don't recognize: this is due to a combination of poetic licence and incompetence. All locations are used fictitiously. Any resemblance to real people is accidental, and let's face it, it's unlikely that people and situations like this really exist. Isn't it?

Finally, thank you to everyone who buys my books, reads them, and leaves reviews on Amazon, GoodReads or wherever: you are helping me to do this 'being an author' thing, where I get to write crazy stuff for a living. If you want to drop by and say hello, you can reach me via the contact page on my website or on FaceBook:

www.paultomlinson.org

@paultomlinson.org

"... a gentle parody of the classic whodunit mystery novel and a note-perfect example of how it should be done. Highly recommended!"

A retired stage magician and a chauffeur with a shady past team-up to investigate when a King Arthur-themed party in a Victorian castle climaxes with a scream, a splash, and a body in the pond. Can they reveal whodunit, or will Excalibur again be drawn from a stone-cold corpse?

Available Now in Paperback and eBook

About the Author

Paul Tomlinson was born in Nottingham in 1966, and has lived in Nottinghamshire for most of his life. He doesn't live in Mansfield, but if he did, he probably wouldn't admit it. He is the author of the science fiction novel *Robot Wrecker,* the 1930s murder mystery novel *The Sword in the Stone-Dead* and the fantasy novel *Slayer of Dragons.* That's probably too many genres for one author, but all the books do have something in common: they're meant to be humorous, in a macabre sort of way. And none of them have won the Booker or the Pulitzer. Or any award of any kind.

Made in the USA
Monee, IL
20 May 2020

31393337R00215